I0675276

The Ballad of Tul'ran the Sword

Book the First

Dale Wm. Fedorchuk

Ethriel Publishing

AN ETHRIEL PUBLISHING BOOK

CALGARY

The Novels

Novels in the *Tul'ran* series by
Dale William Fedorchuk

The Ballad of Tul'ran the Sword
A Time, and Times, and Half a Time
Abandon Hope
Wolf's Den
When the Stars Fall
Escape and Evade
The Sacrifice
Ichor: The Origin of Evil

Other Works

When Wrong Shall Fail: A Christmas Novella
Nine Tango X-Ray: A Spy Novel
Splash Two: A Spy Novel (coming soon)

All available in paperback, hardcover, and Kindle e-book editions from Amazon worldwide. My novels are works of fiction not created from Artificial Intelligence programs. These words are mine. Please enjoy them.

The Copyright

Copyright © 2023 Dale Wm. Fedorchuk

This book is subject to the laws of copyright wherever found; particularly, and without restricting the generality of the foregoing, the copyright laws of Canada and the United States of America.

All rights reserved. You may not reproduce or use this book or any portion thereof in any manner without the express written permission of the author, except for the use of brief quotations in a book review.

This novel is a work of fiction loosely based, in part, on the Holy Bible and should not be construed as a strict interpretation of Scripture. Names, characters, businesses, organizations, places, events, or incidents either are the products of the author's imagination or are used fictitiously. Any resemblance to actual people, living or dead, events or locales is entirely coincidental, unless they have given permission for the use of their names and characteristics.

Cover Art by Ashley Grady of SKGraphic Designs, depicting Tul'ran (pronounced "Tool'ron") the Sword on the front cover with his warhorse, Darkshadow, and Erianne of Kabolon on the back, standing in a Mesopotamian desert.

ISBN 978-1-7380077-0-7

First Edition

The Acknowledgments

Dedicated, first and foremost, and always to El Shaddai, who inspired it. His was the story, and I was the scribe.

Second, to my beautiful, patient, loving, and kind wife, Anika. Her ideas and suggestions made this book much better than it was when I first wrote it. Anika reads and edits every chapter I pen before the rest of the focus group sees the finished manuscript. She has been invaluable in helping me create my novels.

Third, to my nieces, Micayla Krahn and Nadia Krahn, schoolteachers and historians. They challenged me to draft this novel based on a series of poems I wrote about Tul'ran the Sword in the 1980s, and I don't think any of us expected this.

Fourth, to my focus group, who read the drafts and provided helpful insight, encouragement, and proposals: Anika Fedorchuk, Heidi Fallnich, Mike Bennett, Payton Goller, Mark Kendall, and Mikayla Johnson.

Fifth, to my family and friends, immediate and extended, in-laws and outlaws, Dad, Mom, Arnie, Connie, Shayla, Jordan, nieces, nephews, uncles, aunts, and cousins. We are, all of us, one of a kind.

Last, but not least, to my warrior brother, LTC Michael Bennett, Special Forces, US Army (Retired). Mike read the manuscript and offered encouragement and advice that could only have come from his unique perspective. He also authored the Foreword, in which he was most kind. Thanks, Brother. Jeff would be proud.

Special kudos to Amanda Muratoff, who co-authored the *Pantracia Chronicles,* for her advice and helpful insights.

This is an origin story. May it be to your eyes as fine wine to your lips.

The Tales

The Foreword

It was both a surprise and an honor that Dale would ask me to write the Foreword for this book. I first met Dale when we were teaching at the United States Air Force Special Operations School. A few years later, I had him teach in a course on Irregular Warfare we were conducting for the United States Special Operations Command-Joint Special Operations University.

As part of his duties, Dale developed popular briefings for special operations personnel, including Navy SEALs and Army Special Forces, before they deployed to the Middle East to support operations in Afghanistan and Iraq.

After reading his draft of this book on Tul'ran the Sword, I realized he had brought much of what he experienced in this martial environment to his tale of Tul'ran, particularly how stress forges relationships. As I read deeper into the story, more of Dale's background and experiences come into the storyline. That's why his account of the warrior he created rings true.

You'll find his knowledge lends itself to providing an extremely believable environment. His attention to detail makes this a story you get drawn into.

I am looking forward to more adventures of Tul'ran the Sword.

Michael Bennett
LTC Special Forces, US Army (Retired).

WHERE IT BEGINS

It was insidious, malevolent, caring not for station or person. Malign in the way of things steeped in evil; it was the place between life and death where hope perishes, and love collapses into a barren puddle. It was temptation warring with self-control, relentless ambition wrestling with selflessness, the eternal struggle between good and evil.

And it was getting old.

Tul'ran az Nostrom was bored.

His thirty-one-year-old body, dotted with ribbons of scars from more battles than he cared to remember, was tired. The barren fruit of his decisions littered his life and his chosen paths. Death, destruction, lust, and greed birthed skeletal remains that continued to imprint their tread marks upon his soul. Where once there was passion, there now only was... dust.

The Sword Himself, they called him; Tul'ran the

Sword, they whispered in fear, as if no one else wielded a blade in the land. As with every other living legend, a spark of truth birthed the tales of his ability with his weapon and his willingness to use it. Storytellers who never took up steel blew the spark of reality into the flames of myth. The greater his fame, the larger became his riches and the number of women who found an interest in his bed. And all of it, for what?

He didn't enjoy self-reflection. His father raised him to present a mirrored face to the world so others would see only what they wished. All else was weakness and weakness a madness, his sire taught. He had hated his father.

When he first became a warrior, a Judge in this Age while still a young man, he savored the strength of his arms, the deadly cuts they made in the tissue of his enemies, and the souls he released from their fleshy confinement. He swam in pools of flesh presented to him by women willing to share his bed for the bragging rights. His Legend made him rich, and he bathed in excess.

But excess extracts a price unforeseen. What was it for? Did the stilled hearts of his adversaries carve a better path in the vast and convoluted roadways of destiny? Were the lives of the women with whom he slaked his lust enriched by his brief dalliance with them? The silver and gold he concealed in certain places would provide for his needs for many years. But what, now, were his needs?

So, he was bored.

Bored with breathless nights of loveless lovemaking. Bored with the song of Bloodwing, his Blade, as it keened over the lives cast into the abyss with a practiced stroke.

A boredom which, in its very essence, was dangerous. It lingered in the mind of a man for whom being stalked by peril was as significant as his next choice of food.

Thus, it was on a brilliant morning; the sun rising to kiss a red sky flaring out beyond its reach, his back pressed against a palm tree tall and wide at its girth, Tul'ran the Sword took stock of his life, and found it wanting.

And, as with most of written history, the beginning looks like the end, the end is forsaken by the beginning, and neither is cemented in the purity of absolute Truth.

CHAPTER THE FIRST:
THE SCREAM

The Ballad of Tul'ran the Sword

Tul'ran the Sword was mightily bored
On the morn he set Kabolon free,
Bloodwing, his Blade, sat still in the shade,
Its edges as sharp as a scream...

Mesopotamia, the first day of the eighth month, 2005 BC
The scream sliced through the air and carved its essence into Tul'ran's ears before his brain registered its meaning. He was on his feet in an instant, Bloodwing in hand, the Blade finding his arm seemingly of its own accord.

Tul'ran's dark eyes searched the desert, stretching out before him, and rested on a caravan. He shook his head. He hadn't heard the clatter of a cart approaching the oasis. How deeply had his musings enslaved him?

Again, the scream. It was a woman's scream, filled with outrage and... fear? No, not fear, he decided. Defiance. Interesting. Anything interesting was better than the boredom and incessant brooding lingering at the back of his mind like a foul stench.

Bloodwing rotated in his right hand as Tul'ran considered his next step. It was a magnificent sword, balanced to perfection, and forged by someone whose brilliance exceeded his place in time, whose understanding of metallurgy bordered on the mystical. Bloodwing was longer and lighter than other swords of this Age. It was double-edged and as sharp as the scream echoing through the oasis. The blade was as black as a starless, moonless night, but the edges always glimmered with a sliver of brilliant blue.

Legends sang that the ebony blade sucked the souls of Tul'ran's enemies into its bottomless depths if they stared at it for too long. This, of course, wasn't true. His enemies never lived long enough to stare at anything, much less his sword.

A third scream undulated through the dawn's thin air, raising the hairs on Tul'ran's massive arms. The scream cried with urgency, demanded immediacy, and promised the prospect of battle. It was time to make an inquiry.

He strode to his horse, Darkshadow, grazing near the water. Darkshadow was as magnificent a horse as Bloodwing was a sword. He was tall, as horses go, with enormous feet serving him well on all terrains. The warhorse was jet black, as was his long, thick mane and tail. He was strong, beautiful, and more than a little crazy.

Horses are flight animals. They'll bolt if startled, choosing to use their speed to escape from danger rather than confront it. Not so with this stallion. He had a bloodlust rivaling his master's. It was for this reason he wore a breastplate attached to the saddle; a shield made of sheepskin and double-folded leather. The breastplate covered the entire front of the horse's chest, up to the base of his neck, and Tul'ran embellished upon it metallic symbols and decoration. Many an archer or spearman tried to penetrate Darkshadow's armor. All died, their heads finding freedom from their bodies at Bloodwing the Blade's bidding.

The prospect of battle demanded thorough preparation. The seconds blazed by in the face of his maddening deliberation. Tul'ran checked Darkshadow's feet and legs to make sure the horse wouldn't lame during a fight. He tested the cinching straps once and again for tightness and comfort. The warrior secured his weapons and made them ready for quick access. He measured his actions precisely, for his tradecraft demanded it and his life depended on it.

He had a code of honor, making it necessary he come to the aid of the weak, the oppressed, the widow, and the orphan. Every other situation merited an inquiry. There may be a legitimate reason for those screams. The situation may be none of his business. He would raise a question, and the subject of the interrogation would answer it. He grinned, a feral scowl. Those he interrogated always answered his inquiries. He was Tul'ran the Sword.

It felt like forever to prepare himself and his

horse, but there was still one last task.

Tul'ran looked up into the red-streaked morning sky. In obedience to his will, his efforts slowed to a stop, and he turned all thoughts elsewhere. So focused was he that the birds seemed to cease their trilling, the ever-present wind whispered to a halt, and everything became still.

"El Shaddai," he prayed, his spirit a well-spring of his heart's desire, "You who have chosen me as Your servant, protect me from death and release the souls of my enemies into Your hands if I am once more to war."

Tul'ran leaped into the saddle. Darkshadow wheeled and charged towards the caravan. The warhorse was a thundering fury, driving like a sandstorm over the wasteland. Darkshadow was fast; faster than he ought to be, given his size. A crosswind whipped back Tul'ran's long black hair and wide cloak as the desert sped by underneath his feet.

The caravan loomed larger, more distinct; a long, two-wheeled cart towed by two donkeys. The caravan was unremarkable by itself, made of faded, pitted wood. It lacked a driver, which made it remarkable. Of equal note was the canvas of the cart thrown back to reveal a cage of rough construction. The cage was big enough to hold a human, judging by the screams from within.

Tul'ran's keen eyes found six men near the caravan, and his lips drew back in a snarl.

Gutians. Gutians were barbarians from the Zagros Mountains.

It was enough to know they were barbarians.

So much for the inquiry. He wouldn't investigate the source of the screams and the manner of their extraction. The barbarians' pleas for mercy would go unanswered. There would be no negotiation, no bartering of goods or shekels for life and limb. Their deaths would be as inevitable as the drop of the sun at the day's end. He drew his magnificent sword, freeing it for mayhem.

He heard oaths and exclamations as the men scrambled to organize against his charge, but they were already too late. Bloodwing bit through the chest of the first man, blood sweeping left to right, and ending the man's life as surely as if it were the neck and not the chest taking the worst of the blow.

Darkshadow wheeled in front of the two donkeys. To escape the raving war horse, the donkeys crossed traces and fought against their lines, becoming entangled. They brayed their terror, adding to the pandemonium.

The war horse, huge and black and a wraith of dancing fury, raced to the rear of the van. His rush surprised a man pulling up his pants, oaths and spittle flying from his mouth. Tul'ran swung, his face a mask of contempt, and another soul destined for judgment shrieked away from the battlefield.

After the first stroke of the sword, time for Tul'ran seemed to crawl, with the others moving as if trapped in syrup, just so, and he at full speed. The speed of battle immersed him in each sword thrust, the stench of blood and sweat rising to greet his nose, and his fear goading the urgency of action.

A man behind the van had enough time to cast a spear, which bounced off Darkshadow's breastplate, not even leaving a dent in the leather. The attack enraged the stallion more, were it possible, and Tul'ran braced, knowing what was to come. Darkshadow planted his weight on his front feet, twisted, spun, and drove two large, back hooves into the man's face, crushing bone into the barbarian's brain.

The fourth man was on his hands and knees, scrabbling for his sword. Bloodwing the Blade bit into his neck, spewing vertebrae, flesh, and blood onto the sand. The fifth Gutian rose from the desert behind the caravan, slashing a curved sword at Tul'ran's leg. Darkshadow, a veteran of warfare and well-versed in treachery, skittered away, and Tul'ran swept his sword across his body. Bloodwing bit down into the barbarian's skull and cleaved his brain in two, the blade perpendicular to the man's bulging eyes, and he died.

The sixth? Where was the sixth? Ah, there, running away to the oasis as if the trees would somehow awaken, sweep palm fronds into Darkshadow's path, and save his life. Tul'ran's left hand came up, an obsidian knife balanced between two fingers and a thumb, and he cast, the muscles in his arm and shoulder rippling.

The blade was a black streak of chaos as it glided through the desert air and planted with a wet 'thud' into the coward's spine between his shoulder blades.

Darkshadow wheeled, screaming his wrath and hate and bloodlust, seeking another enemy, but it was done. It took Tul'ran several moments to calm the horse, slapping his neck with affection. He forced a soothing tone into his shaking voice, which was still fueled by adrenaline.

"We have prevailed," he said, stroking the trembling horse's neck and withers, "be at peace, brother."

As interested as he was in the contents of the cage on the back of the caravan, necessity demanded attention to his weapons. He trotted Darkshadow to the man lying face down in the sand, who was spasming now, the last seconds of his life draining into the desert floor. Tul'ran stretched down, almost out of the saddle, and yanked the obsidian blade from the man's back.

Out of a bag attached to the saddle, he withdrew a piece of cloth and cleaned the throwing knife and Bloodwing. As he cleaned the blades, taking care not to cut himself on their merciless edges, he watched with pitiless eyes as the figure on the sand became still.

Satisfied his weapons were free of blood and gore, Tul'ran sheathed them and spit on the Gutian's corpse. He turned Darkshadow's head and walked the horse toward the caravan, the ground around which was stained with the blood of the bodies strewn about the sand.

They would leave the desert, and all the carnivores and foragers claiming it as home, to scavenge the bodies. Tul'ran wouldn't grace them with his sweat to give them the honor of a funeral pyre. Let their bones strengthen the dunes as their souls even now fed the fires of the dominion claimed by demons.

Darkshadow turned around the tail of the caravan, still swinging his beautiful head back and forth as if expecting the resurrection of prey. Tul'ran looked into the cage and stopped, stunned. A woman glared back at him; her legs crossed before her as she sat in the crate.

She was the most stunning woman he'd ever seen.

She wore a torn tunic made of black-green linen covering the length of her body. Something or someone had battered and crumpled it. Dirt littering the bottom of the cage stained it. It had served as a shield for her virtue, and it had, by its look, acquitted itself with honor.

Her hands were long and looked strong, but the heavy ropes binding her wrists locked them into a painful curl. His eyes traveled from her wrists to her face and stopped at her eyes. Eyes as green as her dress, but sharpened as by glass, and framed by charcoal, sat above her high cheekbones. Mahogany brown skin covered the woman's face, a palette of duskiness over a portrait of beauty. Her hair was black, as richly black as the deepest night, and so silken it begged a touch.

She glared at him from those amazing emerald eyes. The captive woman snarled at him in the Tongue, the language he learned at his mother's knee. It was a stiff and formal language, but once the ear became accustomed to its nuances, it flowed like poetry. It was a civilized language gracing an uncivilized era, reminding the listener of a long past age where people still had nobility, courage, and honor. A language of romance and love, or coldness and death.

"I am of no mind to be scanned and assessed like cattle at auction," the woman said, amazing Tul'ran with the cultured tone of her voice. "Are you going to let me out of here, or are you like one of these animals?"

She spat.

"If you are a man like them, I would prefer to stay in this cage and die of thirst."

Tul'ran opened his mouth to retort, insulted by her speech and caustic tone, but his words tangled his tongue and lay stillborn. He drew Bloodwing, and she scrambled back into the cage, uncertain of his purpose. Tul'ran slashed down, and the heavy ropes holding the door in place swept free. The door fell awkwardly, the bottom of it nearly hitting her as it fell to the sand.

With a cluck of the tongue and pressure applied with Tul'ran's knees, Darkshadow retreated from the now-open cage.

The woman crawled from her confinement and dropped to the ground, sweeping straw from her tunic with her bound hands. She glared up at Tul'ran, squinting against the sun draping around his broad shoulders like a halo. She thrust her hands towards him; her face wrapped in a haughty mask.

"Are you a slaver? Will you leave me bound like a dog?"

Tul'ran sheathed Bloodwing in its scabbard. He withdrew from his vest the knife which, only seconds ago, had taken, with great satisfaction, the life of the fleeing barbarian.

"Have a care to not move," Tul'ran said as he reached down to cut the ropes around her wrists. "This blade will part your flesh as easily as it cleaves the rope."

Freed, the woman turned and staggered around to

the front of the caravan, reaching in to dig around behind the seat reserved for the driver of the van. After a few moments of searching, she produced a leather purse and a long, soft sheath. She withdrew from the sheath a thin dagger, which looked like the maker had created it with a purpose inviting havoc.

"Those edges look sharp," Tul'ran said, as if speaking to himself.

She directed a piercing look into his eyes.

"They are, mind you, and I am skilled with them. If these pigs had not taken me by surprise, even now they would feed flies at my door's step."

She slipped the dagger back into the sheath, tucking it into a belt of leather around her waist. The purse also found a place within the belt, and she arranged her tunic so it concealed both purse and blade within its depths.

She turned and looked at the carnage littering the surrounding sand.

"So here are the mighty warriors who dragged me from my abode," she mocked, "handled me like a grain sack, and threw me into a cage for a reason unknown to gods and people."

"Why are there men?" she added with disgust.

"I just released you from your cage, and you want to debate the creation of all things? Very well, then. Why are there goats?"

"Why, indeed?" she said, her voice a whip snap. "Men and goats both smell the same, eat in the same manner and will lie with anything put before them. Men would kill a woman as soon as take pleasure with her. What good are men and goats?"

Tul'ran calmed Darkshadow, who was growing

restless beneath him. The warhorse could feel his rising irritation. It wasn't wise to allow Darkshadow his head when a person angered his master. Men died under this horse's hooves for much less than an insult from a slashing tongue in an angered mouth.

"I have sworn a blood oath to do no harm to a woman, unless I find her blade at my throat. You already make me regret my vow. I had no purpose in the oasis in which I lounged, other than to mind my thoughts. Your screams thrust me into a conflict, offering me no advantage. Even your gratitude lacks convincing."

"Gratitude! I know what kind of 'gratitude' men like you seek, and you are not getting it from me!"

The words stung, in part because they were true. Tul'ran flicked away a fly, which had diverted its attention from the corpses lying on the sand to find refuge on his forehead.

"It is true some women I saved from harm paid their gratitude in full within the confines of a hut, a grove, or some other place of privacy," he admitted warily. "Know you, though, they gave their gifts without coercion, consent flowing from actual words and not perceived through the deed."

She lifted her chin, eyes glinting.

"If such gifts are required by the social standard of the day or by local custom, are they a gift freely given? Where lies the choice in duty? Does a woman truly volunteer her favors if local custom requires her to gift her body to settle a blood debt?"

Her questions stumped him. He never considered whether the social compulsion to reward him with a consensual bounce stripped away consent. Yet one more thing upon which to brood when time permitted, Tul'ran thought, as her words soured his mind. He turned his regard outwards and looked her over once more.

The woman was tall, Tul'ran noticed, now that she was standing outside the cage. She had one forearm's length on him. He couldn't recall if he had ever met a woman so tall, casting an appreciative glance over her slender, well-proportioned form. The look did nothing to lessen her anger.

"Will you just stare at me like a lump on that black monster you call a horse? Have you never seen a woman? Perhaps it is so. It would accord with your depraved gape, I warrant. What are you called?"

What was he called? This one didn't know him by sight?

Without thinking, she provided a vent to the annoyance growing within him, nursed by her acidic tongue and caustic tone. He turned Darkshadow to face her, held her eyes with the gaze of a wolf sizing its prey, and said simply,

"Tul'ran az Nostrom."

The black of the woman's pupils expanded to the very edge of her bright green eyes. He felt satisfaction as the blood drained from her face, which made her skin a less vibrant shade of brown. Tul'ran could see the pulse at the base of her long, lovely throat quicken. Her right hand moved to her neck as if to calm the blood rushing through her veins. Or protect them from the sharp cut of a rage-driven blade.

There was silence for a time. Something passed behind her eyes, cringing at the contemplation of him. She had the look of one staring into the eyes of death. It was the look of a damned soul fleeing from a firestorm threatening to chase it into the afterlife.

"The Sword Himself," she said, when the silence had stretched from seconds to minutes, the words dripping with awe. Another moment passed as she held herself stiffly, waves of expression flowing across her face. Tul'ran could almost see her mind working.

"I would never have imagined myself standing before the Sword Himself," she said, as her voice trailed off.

Then something else flashed in her eyes. In less than a second, her dagger was out again, and Tul'ran gawked in surprise at the shallow red line appearing above his wrist on his left arm. By the stars, she was fast! Darkshadow, a skilled war horse and ever vigilant on the battlefield, hadn't the time to shy from her rapid advance and attack.

"Tul'ran az Nostrom." She uttered the ancient ritual in staccato rapidity, as if afraid he would strike her down before the words could come spilling from her lips. "I commission you in a covenant by the blood spilled between us to lend your sword to my cause. Fight with me for glory."

He stared at her, astounded, for long seconds, which drew out further and further like a shriek. The temerity... the nerve of this one! Her face paled again as she saw him consider the various methods of her death at his hands. He willed his anger silent, not even deigning to look at the small spill of blood on his arm.

"First," he said, keeping his voice low and slow,

though his heart raged, "you do not invoke the covenant by slicing into him who has already answered your peril. 'Spilled blood' is the blood spilled by warriors standing back to back, knee deep in the battlefield's gore, sharing death and glory."

"Second," he said, warming to the subject, "one may only invoke the covenant when death is the only means to bring life to kin and clan. I do not see how you claim on either account."

"Third," he finished, his mouth a grim line, "the last person to cut me screams even now in the deepest depths of hot, comfortless Hell. Wound me again and it will be my fervent desire to have you join him."

He lashed his words to anger, framed them to intimidate her, and intended them to leave her quivering in a mercurial puddle of fear. To his disbelief, they had no such effect. True, there remained a halo of fear behind her eyes, but their depths also reflected defiance and courage. This one was different. Different could be dangerous. And enthralling.

She licked her parched lips. The act was so elegant Tul'ran almost missed her next question.

"Is there one present who can judge between us as to the validity of my claim for a covenant?"

Tul'ran found his eyebrows at the top of his forehead and lowered them.

"You are without sense," he said, "or the bravest woman I have ever met. Or it is possible you are insane. The latter may require further consideration. Are you daft, woman? You cannot invoke a covenant when I know not the enemy, the ley lines of correctness between the positions of you and your foe, and the potential cost to me and my Line. Even if I were to judge you, I can make no Finding when I have no information."

A satisfied smile crossed her face, which once again sent his eyebrows skyward. What had she won, he wondered, making her look so pleased with herself? He didn't have long to wait for the answer.

"Then I demand a Telling. You will hear my tale, Tul'ran az Nostrom, Master of Bloodwing the Blade, Sword of Judgment, Deliverer of Death. You will hear the story of Erianne of Kabolon, as one warrior hearing the word of another and acknowledging it so, after which you may judge if there is to be a covenant between us."

There was a well-laid trap. His estimation of her rose against the lingering taste of anger. He couldn't deny her a covenant on a lack of facts and then refuse her a Telling. If he granted her a Telling, he was bound by oath and duty to consider whether it merited the covenant she claimed, strict technicalities complied with or not.

He looked at her standing there, frightened yet bold, cowering yet determined, desiring to flee and ready to fight. This one smacked of Fate, and he shunned anything smacking of Fate. A wise man would leave her to fend for herself in the desert.

He struggled to recall a time when he walked in the footsteps of the wise.

He could abandon no one in need. Were he capable of doing so, his body would show much less scarring, as would his soul. He was a fool; he decided then. What was left but to journey upon the fool's road?

"Erianne of Kabolon, I will hear your Telling. Let Truth decide our path and whether we take it together in a covenant. If I adjudge in your favor, I shall join my arm and my sword in your cause."

His next words were so cold they would have frozen water were it at hand.

"If I adjudge against you, Kabolon, may whatever gods in which you believe have mercy upon you."

"For I will not."

CHAPTER THE SECOND:
THE TELLING OF ERIANNE
OF KABOLON

Erianne of Kabolon, so gloriously enchanting,
Was a woman of mystery, 'twas said.
Her beauty was exceptional and often lay wondrously
In the eyes of the men she left dead.

Erianne drew a sharp breath. The callousness of his words stung her, as had the icy glare accompanying them. He would hear her; it's what mattered. She looked up at him, his face giving her nothing, and pressed on.

"Then are you ready for me to proceed with my Telling, milord Tul'ran?"

Tul'ran quirked an eyebrow at her question.

"For one so hasty to seek a covenant through a Telling, Kabolon, your knowledge of the custom is sorely lacking. A Telling is more than the lips of one moving and the ears of another listening," he said, as if reciting the words from a script behind his eyes. "It is a ritual as serious as marriage. The Teller becomes an Honored Guest, abiding in such comfort as the Host provides until the tale is told. At once, when the tale is told, several things thereafter might happen, both in the short and long order. As it is here, in short order, it will be necessary for me to adjudge the Telling, with life and death consequences. Be careful what you ask for, Kabolon. I warn you again, if I find against you, your life is mine to do with as I please."

Erianne lifted her chin defiantly, sparks snapping in the depths of her rich green eyes.

"I shall take my chances with the integrity of my cause, milord."

Darkshadow shifted, impatient feet stamping into the sand. He snorted. Tul'ran smiled, though it was thin and without warmth.

"Very well. Have it your way. As my warhorse reminds us, a Telling does not take place in the furnace of a Mesopotamian desert, with flies appearing from nowhere to plunder the bodies of men left rotting in the sun. Put away your blade, Kabolon, and ride with me."

Erianne did as Tul'ran instructed, and he lifted her onto Darkshadow. He was strong, not even straining at her weight as he winched her into the saddle with one arm. She noticed he placed her in front of him, not at his back. She imagined he yet had a memory of the swiftness of her hands with her dagger. Only a fool would put someone as fast as she was behind him, with a temperament and a view of destiny, and him, unknown. From what she had heard of him, he was no fool.

She tried to invoke a covenant and bind him as an ally, but he hadn't tasted the full measure of her character. Dying on a whim is still dying. She expected no less caution, though his attitude ground her nerves. She should've expected no less arrogance as well. Erianne reminded herself to be careful with her tone and language. An arrogant man didn't comfortably accept a challenge from a woman, and this one was a killer. Precisely why she needed him. The last thing she expected to find, though, was the master of killers.

They rode together back to the oasis, Darkshadow tossing his head and snorting from time to time, his black mane dancing back and forth. Time for a little diplomacy and to set the stage for a calmer discourse. Erianne turned her face to the warrior riding behind her back, vocalizing in the softer edges of the Tongue.

"Milord, I am not familiar with your noble steed. He acts as if he were replaying the battle in his mind and seeing his foes fall at his feet. Is there any merit to what I say?"

"Who knows? Mayhap he does. No one hears the thoughts running rampant in the minds of horses. I know many who think of them as dumb animals, to be used and abused as considered desirable. I know horses to be intelligent, sensitive creatures. That Darkshadow has a soul; I do not doubt. That his soul lives in an intelligent mind; I also do not doubt. In my regard, Darkshadow is a better human being than most people I have met."

Erianne smiled.

"It may surprise you to know I feel the same way about horses, and some other animals, as well. Will you allow me to ask a further question?"

She heard him grunt and assumed consent.

"You attacked my captors with savagery, unlike anything I have seen. The attack seemed personal to you. If I may be so bold as to ask, why were you so intent on their annihilation?"

She wondered, in the ensuing stony silence, if she had offended him. When the reply finally came, his voice was cold and emotionless.

"They were Gutians. Their history precedes them and justifies the violence of my attack."

"Milord Tul'ran, forgive me. I am not so schooled in the chronicles of this region, not being from this place, such as to have heard tales of the Gutians. It would honor me to have you sing me their ballad, if you are so inclined."

Tul'ran sighed. Erianne wondered how much conversation he had with people daily. He certainly didn't seem to want one.

"I will not sing their ballad, but I will speak it. Trust me when I tell you my singing voice would drive harpies away, hands firmly cupped over their ears. In the place from which you came, Kabolon, had you heard of the Akkadian Empire?"

Erianne nodded, staring at the oasis in the distance.

"I had, milord. They lost power after the reign of Naram-Sin."

The saddle creaked as Tul'ran shifted his balance behind her.

"Naram-Sin was a weakling, as had been his father before him. The city-states of Lagash and Uruk began reasserting themselves after a succession of milksop Akkadian kings. The Akkadians lost power because the Guti came down from the Zagros Mountains and invaded the land. After they wrested control from the Akkadians, the Gutians controlled Mesopotamia, especially the south, for five hundred years. Gudea, one of their most famous rulers, left statues of himself in temples across Sumer. They made the Sumerian city of Adab their capital."

"The Gutians were an abhorrence, lesser in status and worse than any other creature on Earth. They raped and killed innocent women and children, having no regard for conscience, law, or propriety. Often, they claimed what was not theirs and drove the rightful owners away with curses and the edge of a sword. They were barbarians, and barbarians are not people."

Erianne shifted in the saddle, glancing up at the scorching sun.

"Surely, milord Tul'ran, they were not as bad as their reputation proclaims."

"They were worse," he said. "To say they were a brutal people is to say the desert gets warm under the blazing sun you just admired. The atrocities they committed against the men and women they captured went far beyond employing means to subdue the land. They enjoyed the pain and suffering of others. I have heard, though I cannot say for certain, they sacrificed children to their gods. They earned the designation of being called barbarians."

"Eventually, Utu-hengal of Uruk overthrew the

Guti, and some of the Gutians retreated into the Zagros Mountains. Others scattered throughout the region. Some scouted for new lands to rape and pillage. I give any barbarian whose shadow crosses my path the grace of a quick death, which they do not deserve."

Erianne glanced back at his face again, once more set in stone. There was more, she sensed. The ferocity of his attack was personal, born of pain and loss. She wanted to ask, but checked her tongue. He had yet to judge her, and it was never wise to annoy a judge before they made a finding. Erianne turned to face forward, feeling a trickle of sweat sliding down her ribs. It was getting hot.

They rode in silence for the rest of the way to the oasis, giving Erianne time to rehearse her Telling. It would have to enchant him. She knew much of the legend of Tul'ran the Sword. She was counting on the accuracy of his Ballad. Her life depended on his skill with a sword and her ability to bend words well enough to encourage his skill to her purpose.

When they arrived, though, the Telling still had to wait. The blood of his enemies had spattered Tul'ran's leathers and clothing. Blood splashes were on Darkshadow, his harness, saddle, stirrups, and bindings. Tul'ran dismounted and then lifted Erianne from Darkshadow, though she needed no such aid. He gestured to the oasis.

"You will find the water in this oasis good to drink and pleasant in which to bathe, Kabolon. I must see to the cleansing of my horse, his gear, and myself. I never leave the blood of the dead on my stallion or my person. Blood draws flies, and I loathe maggots. The body fluids of my enemies are not worthy of clinging to me or to Darkshadow."

"There is also the matter of sustenance. Battle makes me and my horse ravenous. I do not know when last you ate and drank. After we have met our most basic needs, then shall I hear your Telling."

His proposal sounded good to her. Erianne was thirsty; she all but dove into the pool of clean water to drink its life-giving essence. The water was as he described: cold and clear and delicious. Even the richest wine never found such favor with her palette, as water did then.

After she drank until she was full, Erianne studied Tul'ran, seeing details for the first time. He was shorter than her by several inches, but you could've put a pole and two buckets on those shoulders and not known where the shoulders ended and the pole began.

He was well-muscled; she thought. She knew men like him wandered a great deal and didn't have the pleasure of regular meals. Protein was in short supply in the arid surrounding lands. Fighters took a minor part in muscle-building hard labor. Their muscles were wiry and strong, not as bulky as the ones she contemplated on her rescuer's body.

'Rescuer,' she thought with a wry twist. If she had had the right tools at hand and if the Gutians hadn't taken her by surprise like a child, she wouldn't have needed the help of a rescue. She uttered curses under her breath. Her capture had complicated things, and complications made for problems. This would upset the others with whom she traveled. They were already unhappy she was on this journey, and this incident would only make their quiet distaste worse.

She walked back to the shade of a large palm tree and sat in the grass at its base, watching Tul'ran take the tack off his horse. He took out a bladder riding at his hip, slung over his shoulder and wound through the leathers, and poured water onto a cloth. With care, loving care, she thought with surprise; he wiped down his horse wherever he saw blood or dust. The massive equine didn't seem to worry about how and where his master touched him, contented to graze at the lush grass.

Tul'ran's legs appeared as strong and well-muscled as the rest of his body. Tight-fitting leather breeches covered his legs and ended in soft shoes worn by the Medes, Sagartians, and Pointed-Hat Scythians. Beside the leather shoes attached to the pants, he wore knee-high leather boots, tied in the front, as was the custom of the time.

He wore on his torso a mid-length belted cloth tunic, or chiton, as it was called, with sleeves covering to mid-biceps and a V-neck neckline, also laced to the front. The chiton was purple and mixed with white, which was very unusual. The wearing of a purple chiton 'shot with white' was the prerogative of a great king, but he looked like anything but a king.

A red leather overgarment covered the chiton. It resembled a thick vest. Leather thongs fastened the back plate to the front plate. They ran down his sides, from the armpits. It was sturdy and marred by shallow nicks and cuts from blades and arrows. The leather armor had a sheath built into it, sitting over Tul'ran's heart, from which the hilt of a long, narrow black knife hung. The armor squeezed across his heavily muscled chest, which had the added benefit of keeping the knife in place.

Slung over those impressive shoulders was a cloak as black as a desert night; silky and smooth. It flowed over and around him like a second skin.

She wondered how he didn't succumb to the heat of the desert, dressed as he was. All she was wearing was a period dress with no undergarments, and she was melting in the surrounding temperature.

When Erianne studied Tul'ran's face, she felt her pulse quicken. His black hair was long and swept back. His face, well, his face was handsome, but in a rugged and not a pretty way. He had dark brown eyes and a long forehead. A large nose, not out of place on his face, centered his intense eyes. He had a square jaw, and she could see the muscles bunched at his jawline. A man who gritted his teeth often, then.

She remembered the teeth he bared in fury when he was fighting, which were whiter than those of the other men she met here. He had crooked incisors on each side of his front teeth. The man's canines were a little longer than what she would consider normal, but, again, the look didn't displease.

Lines etched their channels on his tanned forehead, the corner of his long-lashed eyes, and alongside his mouth. He had no facial hair, which was unusual. She found his lack of a beard pleasing. The contours of his face were strong and didn't need covering. It set him apart from other men. She suspected it was one reason he kept it clean.

He had the face of a man who had seen much calamity and caused a great deal more. The face of

Tul'ran the Sword, Warrior Lord. She knew his Ballad; had, most recently, heard it sung in its entirety by a performer who sang the words with a quiver in his voice, as if afraid the subject of them would walk in from the shadows and cleave tongue from mouth. If he were half the fighter, as his Ballad proclaimed, then he could be of worth to her. A good deal of worth.

She watched as his hands wiped blood and gore from his horse's tack. When they were clean, he reached into a larger leather bag sitting beside another tree and withdrew a vial. From the vial, he scraped out some mush looking like lard and wiped it on the leathers. He did the same for his vest, leggings, and boots. Satisfied, he stood up and stretched before he replaced the vial. The stretch rippled from his waist to his neck, and Erianne again felt her pulse quicken. The gods had sculpted his body with wonder, indeed.

His eyes met hers then, and all such thoughts faded. There was no warmth in them. She imagined all warriors had such eyes; orbs which saw too much violence to caress the face of another with joy. He hooded his gaze, betraying nothing of emotion.

"Do you hunger?" he asked with unexpected politeness.

"I do, milord, and I would welcome a meal. It has been many hours since I fed this body."

"I have only the food of a traveler to offer you," he said, turning back to the big bag. "Dried meat, dates, and some nuts. It is not the fare a noblewoman should enjoy. Notwithstanding its simplicity, this meal will sustain you during the Telling."

She laughed, a quick, short bark.

"You mistake my status, milord, for I am not born of royalty or nobility, but of the working class. I have not such pride as I will shun any food you offer to allay my hunger."

Tul'ran unwrapped a leather parcel and produced smaller packages wrapped in light cloth. The warrior presented the contents of the packages to her and bowed with a nuance she didn't understand.

"Eat then, Mistress Kabolon, as much as you like and can stomach. I have the means to replenish this supply."

They ate in the tree's shade as the sun climbed higher in a clear blue sky. Before them, the wind tossed golden plumes off the dunes, stretching out as far as the eye could see. The air around the oasis felt languid as the heat rose. Even Darkshadow stopped eating. He dropped his muzzle down to his knees in repose; one huge back foot canted against the other leg. She could see tension leaving Tul'ran's body as he ate. His body rested, but his dark eyes pierced the desert and never stopped moving.

When they finished eating, Tul'ran wrapped the remnants and placed them back in the bag. Both walked to the oasis and washed their hands and faces in the chilly water. Satisfied, they returned to the cool embrace of the tall trees and sat opposite one another. She sat legs crossed; her limbs covered in the abundance of the tattered green tunic. While Tul'ran cleaned his horse, tack, and clothing, she had woven her hair into a loose braid behind her head to leave it out of her face.

Tul'ran braced his back against the tree. He could

see the entire small oasis and the desert beyond from his vantage point, she noted. He didn't seem to worry about anything coming against his back. Should someone approach from the rear, Erianne suspected Darkshadow would rouse and alert long before they could get close enough to take the warrior by surprise.

She tried to calm her mind and still her racing heart. This would have to be good.

"May I proceed, milord?"

"Do," came the curt reply.

Erianne turned away from him and produced from her bosom a gold-colored cord. She turned back to him and tied a loop around each wrist; the cord stretched taut between them.

If, at the end of the Telling and the giving of a Finding, he drew a blade and split the cord, then they would establish a covenant between them. His life, his sword, his arm would be hers until they were victorious or one of them died. Only she could claim victory, for he would bind himself to her campaign.

Were her Telling not persuasive, the cord would remain uncut between her hands. It meant he wouldn't join her in a covenant. She would give up her life to him at his pleasure. It also would mean, if he so chose and only at his discretion, that the thin gold cord would be a symbol of her slavery to him. Her body would be his to do with as he pleased until he released her or one of them died.

There were consequences to a Telling; it's why they were rare and not invoked without careful thought. She hoped she hadn't made a mistake.

She took a deep breath, searching for the right

cadence in the words of the Tongue.

"I am named Erianne of Kabolon, and this is my Telling. I stand upon my House's reputation and the honor of my Ancestors; you may accept the ring of authenticity in my sayings. Hear me and judge my expressions so you may discern between me and you. May Truth and Grace weigh your decisions; may your Finding bring honor to us both."

"I hear you, Erianne of Kabolon," he said, his face set in rigid lines. "I will give your Telling the listening it deserves."

She was a little startled by the shortness of his ritualistic answer. Such a curt response didn't bode well, did it?

"I am the one child of my father, Delric of Kabolon, merchant and scholar. I am of eight and twenty turns about the sun." She noted the immediate rise of his expressive eyebrows.

"Once was I married, but before my husband could sire children with me, the Medes struck him down in anger. My husband was not a warrior and should not have fallen with an arrow through his chest, but he was in the wrong place, and anybody in the wrong place can fall to the sword."

He acknowledged her explanation of why she was unmarried at such an old age with a flick of one hand.

"Since my husband's death, I have lived with my father. My mother died when I was yet young, so father and daughter have been companions to one another as he plied his trade, and I assisted where I could. He taught me to read and write."

Another raised eyebrow.

'To damnation with his eyebrows!' she thought.

'How will I persuade him if he believes me incapable of intelligent thought?'

She took a breath, calming her annoyance. Losing her head at this moment would be a grave error. Literally.

"My father, in his time and in his land, was, too, a mighty warrior. He taught me the ways of the blade and the bow. He raised me to fight with hands and feet and contrived me as his arrow. While I never had the mischance of being loosed upon my father's enemies, for he tried always to make no adversaries, yet I possess the skills and discipline to deliver a mortal blow if and where necessity demands."

Her words may have had an impact, but it didn't show in his eyes or face. He likely didn't believe her. Female warriors weren't plentiful in Mesopotamia in 2005 BC. He might have dismissed her last statement as pure bravado. Let him try something, anything, and he would see just how much she had spoken truthfully.

"We left Kabolon and journeyed to this land to seek our fortune, doubtful I, in my advanced age, would find a husband and produce children to the glory of my husband's name. We settled in a city close to this place, some six hours by foot, in my estimation, though I confess I had never heard of this oasis in such proximity to my abode."

She saw her last sentence strike home with him, though she didn't know why. Was it because she said she'd never heard of the oasis? It was true; it was an oddity. In the desert, an oasis was a coveted find. This one wasn't large, but it had clean water and a grove of date palms supplying both shade and food.

There was also a thick carpet of grass for livestock to feed on.

Even if she and her party hadn't come across it, they should've heard stories of this life-saving sanctuary from the nomads who roamed the barren region. Such information was vital. Desert people were fierce, independent, and protective of what was theirs, but never failed to share news which could save the lives of others. A mystery to be solved another time.

"My father and I found peace and a small measure of prosperity in the city. His dealings were always honorable and true. Our neighbors liked and respected him, and rare it was when they were at odds with us. Until..."

She licked her lips. She noted, with interest, licking her lips had some effect on him.

"Until?" he prompted when the silence stretched.

"Until," she said, not looking into his eyes, "One Vebrax thought it his right and duty to take me to his bed, as one of his many wives, out of pity, he told my father, so I should not be unwed into my old age. My father resisted his advances, claiming the honor of our House had withstood his daughter's absence from the marriage bed, and would do so with comfort in the future."

Her father's response outraged Vebrax. He was a merchant of some repute in the city and had taken a dislike to them from the moment they found a place there. The first time she met Vebrax, he let a hand rest a little too low on her hip, and she, just arrived and not oriented, had instinctively slapped it away. His face became very red, and he might have done something more, but the disturbance had found her father's eye.

"My father turned his gaze on Vebrax, how men did when they lived the experience of releasing the souls of their enemies to the silence of death. Men who kill never lose such a look, and Vebrax felt it deep in his heart. Vebrax withdrew, angered and humiliated."

"We thought the vexation solved, milord, and considered no reason to be wary of the merchant and his desires. My father, within the last few days, had to return to our land for a fleeting time to contend with matters of the House, but I remained in the city."

"He left you alone?" Tul'ran's face was a study in disbelief.

"My father left me for a short while, milord, knowing I possessed the skills and wherewithal to care for myself, avoid danger, or deliver it into passing should the need arise."

Tul'ran snorted.

"All evidence to the contrary."

Despite the sting of his words, she noticed the judgment of her father at the back of his eyes, and shuddered. She couldn't forget with whom she was dealing. Yes, he was primitive, but he had a code. A very unforgiving code. This wasn't a man of whom you made an enemy without consideration of the aftermath. Pain and death were the second and third-order consequences of enraging Tul'ran the Sword.

"Before he could return, the rabble whom you killed in the desert beset me in my home. Why they came to choose my house among the many in the city, I cannot say. How I came to their attention, they did not disclose. I only know they burst into my abode, seized me unaware, and threw me into the crude cage the caravan carried."

"The barbarians were careful to take from my body my purse and my dagger. The men were not as careful with their hands during the search as they should have been. They touched parts of me only my husband should touch, had I one, which brought me great shame."

Her words had the desired effect. There was a storm in his eyes now, and she could see lightning dancing in the depths of their darkness. His jaw clenched, and she saw his hand reach for the hilt of his amazing sword. She needed to hold back a bit. It wouldn't do to make his blood boil too soon.

"We left the city in haste before the moon had made its journey halfway down through the sky. Hours have I traveled, with no food or water. I had no cover against the cold of the night, other than a small bed of straw within the cage. We journeyed until dawn split the sky. I heard my captors jabber when the outline of this oasis braced against the sun's rise. It was then the conversation turned to me and to my fate. To me, it sounded as if there was to be no ransom paid. My life was about to be forfeited."

"Why kill her?" one of them asked. "We could sell her in Babylon. She is of fine form and has a comely face. She would fetch a fair price to fill our purses further. Why waste such fine meat?"

"Yes," said another, "but if we are to sell her to the flesh merchants, then we should make certain she will not displease her buyer. We should test the suitability of our wares before we offer them for sale."

Tul'ran was livid now, the knuckles of his hand pale with the grip he placed on the hilt of his sword.

"You know these were not men."

She cast her head downwards. "Milord, I do not weave my Telling to anger you or cast aspersions against all men. I only offer these words as Truth and to support my claim for a covenant."

A moment passed. She could see, as she raised her head, the muscles in his jaw working, and she wondered, worried, if he could control his obvious anger long enough to hear her out. She pondered the source of his fury. His code wouldn't condone sexual assault, she knew, but still she questioned the intensity of his reaction.

"Proceed," he said, after some hesitation, to her relief.

"It was thus you found me, milord. I saw you dispatch my captors with such speed, stealth, and violence of action, I became concerned for my safety. 'What manner of man is this?' I asked myself. 'Has he come to my rescue, or does he satisfy his own dark desires?'"

At the look on his face, she rushed into her next words.

"Recall, milord. I did not know who you were. I saw only the Hand of Death on a great, black beast who himself took life as if it were of no consequence. When the two of you dispensed murder with such ease, I feared for my soul. How was I to know my liberator was the famed Sword Himself?"

Her words appeared to pacify him a little, at least.

"Then you released me from my captivity and allowed me to reclaim my dagger. By so doing, you gave me a measure of confidence in the continuance of my future. I apologize to the greatest extent possible, milord, if my manner and speech did not convey my sincere and humble gratitude. Fear and the dread prospects the Gutians had laid at my feet still ensnarled my thoughts. I ought to have counted it greater your actions in freeing me and then sparing my life."

She again dropped her head downward in a convincing manifestation of abject remorse.

"Think nothing of it." His voice was dry and shaded with irony. "Were I captured in the dead of night, thrust into a cage without knowing the name or face of my enemy and threatened with disgrace, I, too, may have had my thoughts rattled. You acquitted yourself well, given the circumstances. Please continue."

She composed herself again.

"I have been away from bed and home for too long. My father will have returned this dawn to find his door unhinged and his daughter gone. I fear the manner of my leaving may break his heart. Our enemy has not thought twice about having dogs chew at our bones, so I fear for his safety. I would hasten to his side to quell the terror of my thoughts."

She drew a deep breath, which brought his attention to her breasts as they strained against the fabric of the dress. He looked away, but not so quickly she didn't notice.

The glance pleased her. So, he wasn't above

admiration for the female form. It could serve her purpose well. She also noticed how his face flushed as he moved his eyes away from her breasts. Another good sign. He didn't appear to be disposed to force himself upon her against her will. Interesting.

"When you revealed yourself to me as the Sword Himself, I seized upon a plan in hopeful desperation. I knew of the covenant; my father spoke of it in my hearing with his acquaintances. It is clear to me I mistook its subtleties. Otherwise, I would never have drawn a blade against the Mighty Tul'ran and spilled blood in furtherance of my own selfish ends."

"Having done so should show to you, milord, how desperate and anxious my mind was in the moment. I fear gravely for my father and my House. Should you weigh this Telling in balance, and find not in my favor, I beseech you for mercy. I pray you will grant me your leave to return to the city to search for my father and learn of his fate. I would, of course, choose to do this with Tul'ran az Nostrom at my side, for my safety and the fate of my House."

She looked at him, her eyes moist with pleading.

"This is my Telling, milord. I beg you for a Finding in my favor. My Telling is at its end."

She dropped her head again and waited; her bound hands resting on her lap. The wind was playing with her hair, moving the thick strands gently around her face. He had to see her as winsome, vulnerable, a maiden in need of rescue. She slowed her breathing and took deeper inhalations to allow her breasts to move enticingly within their confinement.

She wove the Telling like an artist, painting oceans

of courage mixed with droplets of blood. The texture of it was like a song wherein one could almost hear the weeping of hearts rent in two and mended with love. Surely, he would have to find in her favor.

Surely.

Yes, the Telling was magnificent.

Not one word of it was true, but he didn't know it yet.

CHAPTER THE THIRD:
THE FINDING

Beauty once lived where none dared belong
Like the warmth of a kind summer's day
Then darkness of thought and a covetous heart
Savagely drove beauty away.

Tul'ran watched Erianne with care as she spun her Telling. Her voice was gentle, cultured, and as sweet in his ears as honey on his lips. He marveled at the brilliance of her teeth. The woman's mouth wasn't full-lipped, but her lips begged for a kiss. Erianne's face conveyed anger, concern, fear, love for her father, and hope in a dazzling array of breath-taking expressions.

He had to assess her narrative, weigh it against necessity, and decide. He settled himself to deliberate, but other thoughts set aside her account and filled his mind instead.

Her words had stirred within him an ancient pain

laid upon the dry earth of a parched soul and a desiccated heart...

Mesopotamia, the seventeenth day of the sixth month, 2024 BC... nineteen years earlier

Tul'ran was two and ten journeys around the sun when his joy ended.

He stepped into the day as if it were the present, with no space between then and now. The oasis faded away. It was a pleasant summer's day, with the sun promising an abundance of heat and the cerulean sky offering not a wisp of a cloud.

Tul'ran's father tasked him with slopping the swine, his primary assignment within his House. It was a job he despised with every essence of his being. The hogs stunk and transferred their stench onto him. It seemed no amount of scrubbing with his mother's coarse homemade soap could scrape the smell from his skin.

Instead of attending to his duties, he had fashioned for himself a sword made of wood with his father's whittling tools. He danced just outside the pigpen, slashing and cutting at the post holding the gate. A slice here, a feint there. Tul'ran the boy imagined himself not as the son of the owner of livestock, but as one of the King's men battling for the honor of the King's House and defending the land from distant foes.

His father wasn't just the owner of farm animals. His father was Al'ran az Nostrom, or Al'ran of the Green Trees, as translated from the Tongue. He ruled over a large orchard, producing fruits of many varieties. The fruits of the orchards of az Nostrom were famed for their sweetness and flavor.

His father had learned from the generations of his House the value of fertilizing fruit trees with the solid waste of swine. Another one of Tul'ran's jobs; another he despised.

Tul'ran was about to administer a fatal cut to his imaginary enemy when a blow to the side of his face knocked him to the dirt. He rolled in the dust and looked up, squinting against the glare of the sun and the rush of pain in his skull and neck, to see his father towering above him.

His father's face was livid, a stark portrait of anger, disdain, and hate. This wasn't the proud appearance of a man showering favor upon his only son. His visage suggested he would rather have seen his son dead, or better yet, sold for a few shekels.

Make no mistake, he had wanted sons. He was a tall man, standing head and shoulder above every other male in the nearby village. His back was broad; he had a brawny chest tapering down to a small waist. Tul'ran's sire had light brown hair still full on his scalp, though he was late into the end of the forty-plus years of his life. He had a hooked nose bordered by two sunken, dull blue eyes which never smiled, no matter how far upwards his thin lips moved. He had a square jaw and a square chin, hidden within a full beard.

His height and good looks had drawn his mother's attention well enough.

Ah, his mother. There was great beauty. The wags whispered she was the daughter of the Queen, though not sired by the King. The King had left the throne to his Queen for the journey of one turn and a half about the sun as he fought in foreign lands for more wealth and territory.

He had left his cousin, a Prince, at his palace to provide support and comfort for the Queen. Support and comfort the Prince gave, with gleeful abundance, until the Queen realized one day she was with child. She withdrew from public life for nine moons and emerged again thereafter, claiming full recovery from a dreaded illness which had threatened her life. A child out of wedlock and born of an adulterous affair will, indeed, threaten a Queen's life.

As for the child, the gossips whispered; the Queen gave the girl to a wealthy merchant who traveled far and broad. The King and Queen had prospered at the hands of this merchant, whose own wife was barren and couldn't give them the children they both so desperately desired. In exchange for his silence and a promise the daughter would never know the truth of her lineage, the merchant accepted the child with gratitude. He left the city behind forever, knowing the danger the truth could bring to his Queen and his own family.

The tiny family settled into the village in which Al'ran's father had the great orchard. In time, their daughter, Merenthia, grew into a dazzling beauty. Though not tall, she had a lean, sensuous body, weaving from one pleasing shape into another. She was full of breast and hip but proportioned, so neither seemed out of place on her form.

Her face was in the shape of an inverted teardrop, and held a slim nose, full, delicious lips, and large dark eyes. Her hair was as dark as coal and fell to her waist by the time she was of an age to wed.

Tul'ran's father was a full five and ten journeys around the sun older than her when he bargained for her betrothal. The marriage price he paid was legendary, but he saw within her the chance for tall, handsome sons and deemed the cost most worthy.

But, alas, for the first five terms, there were only daughters. Beautiful daughters, yes, three of whom had already fetched a healthy marriage price for the coffers of the House. Al'ran had not yet committed the remaining two daughters to a betrothal, but they, too, had their mother's looks and gentle disposition. Their prospects for marriage and a wealthy bride-price were secure.

His daughters had been a source of familial pride and prosperity for Al'ran, but inside he seethed even more every time Merenthia announced her birthing added another girl to the family.

When Tul'ran, the sixth and last child, had been born, it was, at first, a source of glorious celebration. The physicians told Al'ran his son was to be his last child, for the pregnancy had been so difficult Merenthia had almost died upon the birthing table. Al'ran didn't care. He had his boy at last.

But as his son grew, joy and celebration turned to bitter disappointment. Tul'ran was small when he was born and remained smaller than other boys as he grew. True, he became wiry and strong as he aged, but it was clear he would never attain his father's height or stature.

As a child, the boy was plain looking. His father announced when in his cups, bitterness dripping from each word, no woman would find beauty in

Tul'ran when he was of an age to marry, raise children, and take over the House and the orchard.

Al'ran came to despise his son, who had no interest in his father's affairs and property.

Tul'ran didn't care at all about the orchard; the ingenuity of emplacing ditches in such a way as to afford the best irrigation of the soil. He disregarded all teachings about the temperament of the climate, and the dozens of other things ensuring the success of the Green Trees. His mind seemed always to be elsewhere, on other things, so much so Al'ran thought the boy stupid or dazed.

This wasn't a boy who delighted in his father's great wisdom, attained through his sonorous teachings. He'd rather spend time with two old, crippled warriors in the village; listening with fascination to their tales of triumph and sorrow, brotherhood and adventure.

He wasn't his father's son, Al'ran concluded, though he bore a striking resemblance to Merenthia and a passing likeness to himself.

It was clear his wife could no longer bear a son worthy of him. So, Al'ran sought the eager, fertile loins of another woman in a nearby village to bring his seed to fruition as a son and heir, much to the pain and shame of Merenthia.

He hadn't yet gained his heart's desire when the barbarians came.

On this fateful day, Al'ran stood, glaring at the piece of refuse Merenthia claimed was his progeny. He looked with contempt at the lad cowering in the dirt from the sharp blow to the head. A blow Al'ran administered out of frustration because the slacker had once more avoided duty in favor of unprofitable play.

He reached down and grabbed the boy's long black hair, yanking the lad to his feet.

"So," he said, his tone a growl, "you would rather dance with sticks than tend my swine. If you will not go into the pen of animals who bring me profit, I shall stick you into a pen of your own until your eyes see their value as I do."

Al'ran yanked his son toward a small, nearby structure made of wood housing the implements of his trade. He thrust Tul'ran into a small cubicle built into the side of the structure. The sun hadn't yet reached midday. There was no water in the structure, and it would soon get hot. Al'ran slammed shut the door and barred it with a piece of wood. The heat might scramble the boy's brains into some sensibility, he told his son. The regular beatings he administered produced no effect, which was certain.

Tul'ran said nothing. The pattern of abuse he received at his father's hands wasn't unusual, though the punishment was always outside the sight and hearing of his mother. He resigned himself to the fact his father despised him, though the knowledge never failed to thrust a sharp icicle of pain into his chest. At least, Tul'ran promised himself, he wouldn't give his father the satisfaction of his tears or his pleading.

He pushed on the door, but his sire had latched it from the outside. He sighed and shrank down to the dirt floor. There was nothing for it then. He was in the shed until his father's rage had subsided or his mother called him for the evening meal. He knew once she had done so, his father would 'seek him out' and bring him to the family table.

It was then, in the middle of black thought and recurring heart-pain, the horses came around the far side of the House.

There were four men on the horses, dressed in long robes. They wore scarves or veils falling from their folded head coverings past their faces. They had curved swords tucked into the sashes around their waists. Their gnarled hands bore many rings of varied sizes and garish quality. They looked tired and dusty, the weight of a long journey bending shoulder and neck.

Al'ran stopped in astonishment at the sight of the four men cantering into his yard. He had never met Gutians; in his defense, neither had anyone else in the surrounding village. His first response was to elevate his anger into an indignant rage.

"What business do you have here to enter onto my property without an announcement or invitation?"

The four men looked at each other and stood for a moment before one nudged his brown, slender horse forward.

"Is this how you greet guests?" The language was in the Tongue but broken and choppy.

"You are no guests of mine," came the retort, "for I have extended no solicitation. Be gone from my land!"

The man looked back at his three companions, then turned once more to Al'ran.

"My friends and I are travelers from a faraway place. We seek food, water, and shelter for one night.

We ask for nothing else, just the necessities for our comfort after a long journey. I see from your orchards you are a wealthy man. Can you not spare us this favor? It will be for just one night."

Al'ran spat onto the ground. "You are barbarians. I would not spare you lodging in the same pen as my swine. Be gone from here!"

The man on the horse frowned, sudden anger burning in the eyes peering from behind the veil.

"You could have saved yourself with a common courtesy to a weary traveler. We have come far to scout this land for our people. We find fertile soil, rain, riches, and women pleasing to the eye. Since you will not permit us the smallest of our asking, we will take all you have." He uttered a sharp command in a foreign language.

Two of the horsemen launched their mounts forward, reaching under the armpits of the startled orchard owner and throwing him to the ground. Before Al'ran could contrive a response, they had beaten him on the head with the pommel of their curved swords. As he lay on the ground, stunned by the blows, they lashed his ankles and wrists with a cloth. His hands were bound behind his back in a method not permitting a simple escape.

The first man got off his horse and walked over to the man in the dirt to put one dusty shoe on Al'ran's head.

"You think yourself better than we. Your warriors come into our lands, pillage our fortunes, and assault our women. Men such as you treat us as dogs, as the very swine you house in your pens. Our gods shall bring judgment on you as you have brought terror on us."

As horror would have it, Merenthia chose this moment to walk out the front door of the House. It startled her to see her husband lying on the ground, trussed before strange men dressed in foreign clothes and wielding strange armament. She gasped, drawing the eyes of the men toward her, whirled, and slammed shut the door.

The leader looked at two of his men, who ran and made tinder of the door as they barged through it. Tul'ran heard shrieks and screams coming from within the house, but in the close confines of the shed, he could do nothing but watch. A dawning terror seized his throat and threatened to squeeze his pounding heart to a halt.

One man dragged Merenthia back into the yard, her shift torn by her struggle to resist the hands of the strange man. The other man dragged out with him Tul'ran's sisters, both of whom were screaming and struggling. The barbarians threw the females to the ground in front of Al'ran. Their leader walked over to Merenthia and yanked back her hair, holding a blade to her throat. He looked at Al'ran with eyes no longer human, so consumed were they with hatred.

"We will take everything you have. It will be more than we would have asked, and greater than we expected you to offer in hospitality. We will let you watch as we defile your wife and daughters. You will learn the measure you could have earned through mercy, for none will we show. When we are done, we will make it certain you will never father children again. Then we will burn out your eyes and leave you to wander through the rest of your life having what we will do to your wife and daughters as the last image in your greedy soul."

Tul'ran's eyes glowed through mists caused by tears as he watched the men savagely rape his mother, over and over. She begged for her life and pleaded for her daughters between agonized screams.

They brutalized her until her face became slack with emptiness and her throat could no longer make a sound. When the barbarians finished ravaging her, they slashed her womb open with one of their curved swords. They left her there, broken, devastated, unable to move as she bled. She had to endure the agony of watching the same treatment of her daughters until she died.

Against the screams, pleading, and impotent ranting of his father, the barbarians administered the same savage treatment to his young sisters. There was Evann'ya, his favorite among his sisters. She was of six and ten journeys around the sun, well past the age of marriage. His father held her back from the many proposals already received, waiting for a Prince to pass through this part of the King's realm. Her loveliness, grace, and kindness made her worthy to be a Queen.

Evann'ya was stunning. She was tall and slender, with sparkling blue eyes set in a face of such beauty men wept from their craving for her. Her long hair was blond, a throwback to earlier times and a rarity in those days. Many pondered whether she was a daughter of the gods, or some other man's child, but never said so in Al'ran's presence, for fear of his wrath. She was Tul'ran's second-youngest sister, and his most staunch defender.

More than once she stood between Tul'ran and his father, when his father was drunk and wanted to beat him. When she couldn't stop him from being beaten, she would hold Tul'ran's head on her lap, wash his face with a cool cloth, and sing to him.

Evann'ya would tell him stories at night about how Tul'ran would grow strong and become a great warrior. He smiled as she whispered about the ballads they would sing to honor his deeds on the battlefield. Often, he fell asleep, even through his pain, in his dear sister's arms.

Despite the favor Tul'ran's father heaped upon the heads and shoulders of his daughters, Tul'ran loved all his sisters. He practically worshipped Evann'ya. His love for her was deeply ingrained in his soul.

Now he had to watch her being violently beaten and raped not twenty paces from where he sat. When he could endure no more, he thought to break down the door and rush to her rescue. She must have known. Somewhere, she felt his heart and heard his silent cries. She stared at the shed, screaming as the barbarians viciously assaulted her body, but even then put her fingers to her lips. 'Do nothing,' her eyes pleaded.

Between screams, her full lips mouthed the words, 'Save yourself, brother.' He stayed hidden, his heart roaring with rage and impotence as they ravaged her into unconsciousness and then cut her as they had his mother. Even in her death, she had protected him. She guarded her little brother. For the last time, she had saved him.

Lilo'eth, the youngest of the daughters, had not even started her cycles, so young was she. She was dark-skinned and dark-haired, carrying much of her mother's beauty in her cheekbones, her nose, and her eyes. Her torment was the hardest to watch because she was just a child, barely older than him. She was but ten months old when Al'ran forced himself upon Merenthia in his selfish desire for a male heir.

Lilo'eth screamed and screamed, trying to claw her fingers into her attacker's eyes, but they just laughed and beat her senseless until she, too, lay dying in the dirt. She had always been a fighter, wrestling with Tul'ran as if she were a boy. Several times, she had pinned him to the ground during their bouts and kissed his cheeks until he gave surrender. She was wild and carefree, making Al'ran worry he couldn't tame her enough to fetch as large a marriage price as had his other daughters. Her wildness had pleased Merenthia, who saw in Lilo'eth a shadow of what once dwelled in Merenthia's soul before her husband broke her.

Tul'ran had not realized until then he was giving each of them a eulogy.

It was more than he could bear. He closed his eyes and shoved his fists in his mouth so he wouldn't scream or cry out at the horror playing in front of his eyes. He tried to shut his ears to the sobs and shrieks of the women he loved. His bowels loosened into the cloth of his trousers as fear and hate rained acid upon his soul.

One barbarian had started a small fire with wood

pieces hacked from the swine pen. Another heated a knife over the flame, staring at Al'ran with a gaze of contempt so dark and filled with hate it could only have originated from a demon living in his soul. Two men held Al'ran as the leader cut away his trousers to expose his genitals to their derision. The man with the knife reached down and cut off the orchard owner's testicles, taking his time and seeming to delight in the man's screams. When the cutting was done, the man used the heat of the blade to cauterize the wound so Al'ran wouldn't bleed to death.

The barbarian leader once more grabbed Al'ran by the hair.

"See what you have done, pig of a man. This is what we saw when your people came to our lands. You ravaged us as we have now ravaged you. For the rest of your life, I wish you to know you could have prevented all of this had you offered us water, a meal, and shelter for one night. The hardness of your heart vented the hatred of ours. Enjoy this image; it is the last you will see."

The third man came back, the blade in his hand heated from the flame. Al'ran screamed, screamed, and screamed again as they forced open his eyelids and pressed the fiery blade against his eyes.

As the orchard owner lay in the dirt, blinded, neutered, sobbing, the men ran into his home to plunder it. After what seemed like hours to Tul'ran, they loaded cloth sacs filled with the treasure of the House onto their horses.

For a time, the four Gutians had an intense discussion in a language then foreign to Tul'ran's ears, with much arguing and gesturing. From what

Tul'ran could gather from their motions, one wanted to burn down the House and the orchard. Another pointed to the village close to them to the west, as if to argue against giving the villagers, and any armed strength they might have, an inclination of what they had done in this place. The leader shouted an order and the four men turned their horses away from the yard, leaving behind a broken, sobbing man and a helpless, trapped boy.

Tul'ran lay in the dirt in the shed. He had soiled his pants. After the men left, seeing in his mind's eye the carnage left behind, he vomited his breakfast onto the front of his shirt and trousers. His eyes were red and swollen from tears, which no longer fell. The savage rape of the women of his family ripped his heart in two.

In utter anguish, his soul howled a silent shriek into the heavens, born of pain, despair, and helplessness.

Someone answered the cry.

The lad felt, heard, sensed a response caressing its way into his mind.

"Tul'ran," said a small, still voice. "Child. Whom do you seek with your wails?"

"Seek?" He sensed the pain he endured had driven him mad. "Whom do I seek? My mother and sisters lie before me, the last hours of their lives ravaged by animals. Whom do I seek? Someone who will give me revenge!"

A moment passed when Tul'ran wondered whether he had imagined the Voice. Truly, he had gone mad.

"Tul'ran, child," then said the Voice. "I do not

desire for you the hatred crushing the hearts of men into charcoal and reducing their souls to ashes. It is well said a man who seeks revenge must dig two graves, one for his enemy and one for himself. I will not give you revenge, but I can offer you justice."

Justice. Tul'ran was of the tender age of two and ten turns around the sun. His only encounter with justice was the cruel hand of his father, who, today, had experienced justice of his own. Or was it?

"Is what I saw today justice?"

"No," came the soft reply, as tendrils of something caressed his brain with love. "What you saw today is born of an ancient malevolence, set forth upon this world by the selfish desires of two hearts. Hearts, I am sad to say, of My creation. They set into motion a venomous disease, which you call 'evil', bringing pain and suffering into what was supposed to be a beautiful and peaceful world. It is not justice."

"I am confused." His agony convinced him he had become insane with grief and anger. "What do you offer me, then?"

"If you will set aside any of your evil doing from before my eyes, I will gift you with righteousness, and punishment for those who bathe in evil. Cease to yearn for evil and do not do it. Learn to do good. I will help you pursue justice and rebuke the oppressor. Together, we will plead for the widow and defend the fatherless. If you are willing and obedient, you will eat the good of the land."

Tul'ran paused, his mind reeling with concepts foreign to his youthful understanding.

"Who are you?"

It was a laugh then, a smattering of pure joy laced with love.

"You may call me El Shaddai," said the Voice. "It was I who created all things from the imaginings of My heart. By My desire you were born and by My will shall you die. I have contended with humans from the time they rebelled against Me. I have sent throughout the land looking for those who would return to Me and restore what evil has destroyed. For many a year have I searched for a People who would be Mine, who I would raise up as a standard for all people. None have presented themselves; yet still I seek."

Tul'ran was afraid to ask a stupid question, but El Shaddai had piqued his curiosity. "What is a year?"

Again, His glorious laughter. "A year, My child, is what you call one journey about your sun."

"I am then two and ten years old."

"You are."

"I am just a boy," Tul'ran said, as bitterness burned his tongue like acid. "I could do nothing as those beasts tortured and killed my family. What could I do for you?"

The Voice answered with stunning certainty.

"Obey me and I will deliver into your hands all you will need to find justice and peace. Walk with Me and I will usher into your arms love and joy. Give me yourself, and I will protect you from all who would desire you harm. You will become My Judge, and I will go before you in power and strength."

When was a decision a choice, and when was it just inevitable? El Shaddai was a god. Of this, there was no doubt. Who else could talk to his mind about creating humans and worlds? Somehow, this god saw him and heard his wail. Somehow, this god could offer him a life where now there was nothing but an endless path of pain.

The Voice was back.

"Who will go for Us to seek justice and render judgment upon this world?"

Tul'ran did not need time to give his answer.

"Here I am, El Shaddai. Send me. I will render judgment."

Judgment. A Finding.

A shudder ran through Tul'ran's body. He looked up into the eyes of Erianne of Kabolon. His reverie had been too long. The rigidity of her form and the stress lines about her eyes told him so.

He could see in her face she was worried his decision wouldn't accord with her heart's desire.

"Kabolon," he said, his words steady and neutral despite the stark memory still lingering in his mind. "I adjudge."

She dipped her head.

"Milord," she said, "Kabolon stands in judgment and is ready for your Finding."

Tul'ran withdrew from his leather vest the long, black knife. The tang of the knife, curved and spiraled, would only fit comfortably in his hand. Its blade was straight, black, and sharpened on both edges. Its maker balanced it perfectly for throwing. Not just a knife, it was a thing of dangerous beauty.

The blade came down and rested against the cord binding her wrists.

"Kabolon," he said, in a tone stern and grave. "I

have adjudged your Telling and do not find it wanting. It is worthy of covenant, and thus do I enter one with you. I shall lend my sword and my life to your cause. Your adversaries shall be my enemies until you have laid to rest the strife between you and them, or until one of us shall die. This I swear on my honor and on my sword, as if we spilled blood between us."

The cord parted at the slightest nudge of the blade. Sharp, it was, indeed.

"Milord," she said, gratitude and relief welling in her heart. "I thank you for the mercy of your Finding and the covenant into which we enter today. I shall work with all speed to lay to rest the strife between me and my enemies, so you will not have to lend your arm, sword, and life to my aid for a time greater than what is necessary. You have my oath: I shall not abandon you until death."

"Until death." Tul'ran repeated, his face solemn.

Then he smiled.

His smile scared her more than anything else had that day.

"So, tell me, Erianne of Kabolon, in what direction do you point my sword?"

CHAPTER THE FOURTH:
CONSEQUENCE

Into the depths of the deepest dark thought
Did the mind of the Warrior dwell.
Judgment he cast with his mighty right hand
Against those he cast into Hell.

Erianne leaped to her feet, the epitome of fluid grace. She extended her right arm forward, away from her body, her arm loose, her hand pointed down at the wrist, forefinger pointed straight, and the other graceful fingers arched inwards as she spun in a slow pirouette.

Her actions roused his curiosity.

"What do you do, Mistress?"

She closed her eyes and kept turning, but wasn't so occupied as to answer him.

"An unerring sense of direction has always been one of my talents, milord. It is as if my heart can sense true north. If I extend my arm outwards, in this manner, it will find my direction of travel by sheer inspiration. My fellow travelers think of it as a parlor trick. I, myself, am not sure it will work in this place."

She stopped, her hand straightened now, as she pointed at a certain route across the dunes.

"There," she said. "In the direction of my finger shall we find the city from which the barbarians took me. There shall I find my enemies, or the path to their domain. It is there I point Bloodwing the Blade and his master's arm."

She side glanced him, misinterpreting the odd expression on his face.

"'Tis a gift, milord, given to me by a Power unknown to me, so I might always find my way, even when the sun kisses the horizon and darkness shelters the night."

He nodded, appearing to be nonchalant about her ability to discern direction from the edge of a fingertip. She had half expected him to proclaim her a witch, presenting a knife as a warding force against her sorcery. There was something about him she found strange; he accepted the strange far too readily.

"Then it is there we shall journey, Kabolon," he replied, making no move to rise.

"Let's go!" She said, turning to stride with exuberance towards Darkshadow. It only took her a moment to realize he wasn't following. She turned and saw his bemused face; his right eyebrow canted upward over his long-lashed eyes. She cursed at herself, though not aloud.

His presence, as daunting as it was when he was killing everything in sight, made her feel comfortable. Comfortable made her relax, and relaxing made her forget where and who she was.

"Forgive me, milord, but my circumstance is one begging for resolve and crying for urgent action. As the seconds troll by, so increases the danger in which I might find my father. I would go to his aid and stand with our common enemy as quickly as we can journey."

He shook his head in one emphatic negative.

"Kabolon, we cannot travel through the desert during the day. The sun is now at its highest point. You do not feel it because a slight breeze washes us, and these palms lend shade to gentle the heat. According to your own testimony, we would travel on foot for at least six hours. There is no water or shade between here and any place in every direction you might so eloquently point. If we journey by day, by the time we arrive in the city, the heat will consume us and we would be near to death. It is not a state in which to confront your enemies."

That wasn't good. Time wasn't on her side.

"I cannot help but notice your lordship has a magnificent steed, tall at shoulder, wide of girth, and firm of feet. I am but a shadow of your frame. Such a gallant mount could convey us both."

Tul'ran looked with affection at the black beauty sleeping without a care in the shade of three closely grouped date palms.

"Your assessment, mistress, is correct. He could carry us both. He could, but he will not. Mark me, Kabolon, and hear the wisdom gleaned from the bitter end of experience. A warhorse is only as good as his strength allows; exhaust him and while his heart would strive to deliver his greatest effort, his body, stroked too long by a scorching sun and more than accustomed weight, would not rise to meet his mind's expectations. When we travel hence, we shall walk beside Darkshadow and only mount when we near the city itself."

Which ends it, she thought. She couldn't question his statement, spoken with the surety of one who has seen war and conquered its nuances. If he said his horse couldn't make it across the desert carrying them, then he couldn't. Full stop.

"And in the night, milord? Will Darkshadow (what a great name for a black horse, she thought) not be able to convey us then, when the sun rests in its journey and the evening winds bring solace to the parched sands?"

He smiled.

"I perceive the urgency of your quest, Kabolon, but when we depart it shall be the three of us trudging through the sand borne by our own feet, as inadequate as they might be to your necessity," he said, with an undeniable finality.

She sighed, deflated.

"Until then, milord? I see the sun has a way to travel before its journey is at an end. What do you propose we do to fill the remaining hours?"

A part of her, the cynical part never trusting men in full, no matter how superficially gentle they appeared, half expected a wink, a nod, and a meaningful gesture to the grass beside him. So bridled was she by the thought, his next question took her unaware.

"How long did you sleep before the barbarians

took you?"

She blinked.

"Sleep, milord?"

"Yes, sleep," he said, mild irritation showing on his face. "In your Telling you spoke of many hours of travel beyond your doorstep before the dawn crept in to greet you and bring me to your side. I misdoubt you slept in a filthy cage in a caravan not designed for human cargo; at least not comfortably. You have had no occasion to sleep since last night. I would wager you exhausted and gamble securely."

She was tired; she admitted. He was right. The night had been a grueling ordeal, and the day so far had been no better. The adrenaline had seeped from her veins, leaving her more than a little weary.

"What do you propose, if may be so bold as to ask?"

He rose then and reached into the large sack sitting at the base of the palm tree next to his. He withdrew a big roll and cast it down with a well-practiced flick of the wrist. The bundle revealed itself to be a large, thick sheepskin, wide enough for them both.

How convenient, she thought. Some things never change.

He noted the look on her face and shook his head.

"Kabolon, never in my years have I joined with a woman in passion against her consent and willing participation. I am of no mind to seduce you into a hard bounce. As long as we are in covenant, and even after, should it so be your will, I will touch no part of you that your husband would caress in the throes of passion. But we are bound by covenant, and covenant decrees necessity."

"We sleep," he finished.

He turned away from her and, with a flowing cast of his shoulders, his cloak swirled away from him like a black fog. With practiced fingers, he released the leather thongs binding the sides of his vest, and it, too, dropped away. Next came the wide belt at his waist, after he removed various tools and objects from it. Reflecting on the warmth, he reached back, grabbed a handful of cloth, and pulled the chiton over his head, revealing rigid muscles rippling like half-molten rocks.

Erianne drew a deep breath as she felt her face flush. Someone eternal had sculpted his body beautifully! There was a slight hint of fat about his waist, but the rest of his upper body denied fat as if it were a thing of contempt. Scars, there were. Many scars. Several were white with age, but some were still red, as if angry with their estate.

"M-m-milord," she said, unable to keep a stammer from her voice, "Do we undress? I have but this smock you see as my covering, and it is not my desire to bare my body for any eye to see."

He sat down and began removing the cords on the sides of his leather pant legs.

"I see your dilemma, fair lady, and I am not without sympathy. But how long can you remain in your shift without feeling as if it is wearing you and not you it?"

He reached over with his left hand, gathered up his cloak, and swung it in her direction. She caught it and brought it to her chest.

"I will avert my eyes," he said, "to give you such

a measure of privacy as you may attain in the open, as we two are. When you have removed your clothing, wrap yourself in my cloak. You will find it woven with a material to keep you cool as you sleep in the shade. My loincloth will remain on my body so my nakedness will not dismay you."

Nude now, except for the loincloth, he rolled over on his left side to the farthest edge of the sheepskin and lay still.

For a moment, she was unsure of what to do. It annoyed her. Why was she acting like an inexperienced virgin? Erianne had been naked with other people many times in the past, in less private places than this oasis in the middle of nowhere. As for any lasciviousness her naked form might inspire, her instructors trained her well in the art of hand-to-hand combat. He wouldn't find her an easy mark, even if he was the Lord of Death.

She watched him, though, as she removed her tunic and wrapped the cloak around her naked body. He didn't even stir. In fact, she thought with suspicion; it looked from the rise and fall of those amazing shoulders he had already fallen asleep. Here she was, naked under his cloak, and he just passed out. It irritated her to no end.

She laid down on her right side at the farthest end of the sheepskin and closed her eyes to the barren wasteland just beyond the oasis, an outsider in a strange land to which she knew the rules but had yet to feel its essence take root within her soul.

Tul'ran's mind drifted not only to sleep, but back to the scene nineteen years earlier, with him a lad of twelve years of age and his mother and sisters bleeding in the sand; his nightmares willing, despite the revulsion of a pain-filled, scarred spirit, to return to the day of his greatest horror and loss.

He was lying on the floor of the shed, drained of tears, wracked with unending pain, even after the gentle ministrations of El Shaddai, when he felt a pressure in his right palm. He looked at his hand, startled to see his fingertips wrapped around the whorled hilt of a black dagger. The grip, knotted and twisted, fit his hand as if it were a glove. He changed the knife to his left hand, and the grip astonished him; it fit his left hand as easily and completely as did the right. When El Shaddai gave gifts, they were exceptional indeed.

El Shaddai's Knife, as he would forever know the blade, was half the length of his forearm. It was double-edged and ended in a sharp point. He examined the blade; it was sharp, while purposed to be hearty and strong. He felt the balance and approved of where it sat on one extended finger. It would throw well and with accuracy. It was a gift fit for a king, not one who only recently tended swine.

He staggered to his feet at the thought and found yet another surprise to rattle his distressed mind. He was clean. The front of his tunic and trousers, upon which had rained most of the vomit exploding from his mouth only minutes earlier, looked as if it had just come off the drying line. His right hand moved to his buttocks, but again, there was no sign of excrement or the disgusting after-smell of the same.

In fact, Tul'ran thought, as he inhaled through his nose, the only odor he could detect was a faint smell of Spring flowers. The lad shook his head. He would ponder these things at length when there was time and a desire to muse, but for now his duty lay elsewhere.

Tul'ran looked at the knife nestled in his left hand and turned his gaze to the wooden door covering his cell.

He thought there to be no doubt he could use the blade to secure his release, but was loath to undertake the task with it. It was too fine, too beautiful, too new to risk failure and damage. So, he moved backward, pressing his back into the wall of the enclosure, and then lunged forward with all his might, kicking at the door with his right leg. The door burst open in a shower of splinters, and Tul'ran was free.

If freedom was ever this, he thought with bitterness. The barbarians had arranged the naked bodies of his sisters and mother in a half circle around his father, who lay like a baby in the dirt, feet tucked up and arms wrapped around his torso, sobbing and wailing still. Tul'ran ignored him.

He walked to where the nude body of his mother lay, his mind soaked in deep shame for the need to look upon her in such a state. The Gutians had covered her in bruises and blood. One barbarian had torn out some of her hair by the roots and cast it to the ground near her face. They had used her body to hurt and humiliate her in front of his father, and Tul'ran almost lost the contents of his stomach once more. The revulsion was kindling an anger such as he had never felt. It was an anger demanding release with each second of memory of what his poor mother had to endure.

He couldn't look at the bodies of his sisters yet, as his mind wouldn't reach out and touch such trauma, so fresh it was to their terrible and haunting screams.

Without having said a word to his father, Tul'ran shuffled into the House. He found a cleaning bucket, some rags, and clean linen.

Tul'ran dragged the bucket to the well and drew water. He returned to his mother's corpse. Gently, silently, tears raining from his eyes, he cleansed the blood and dirt from her hands, legs, and body. When he got to her face, he realized her eyes were open and staring into the heavens. He closed them and bent to kiss her forehead, the kiss of a son to a mother who was his champion, his friend, his confidant, and the greatest source of love in his life.

He almost fell backwards when he smelled Spring flowers on her skin. It was the same smell permeating the tool hutch when he had his brief and rapturous encounter with El Shaddai. Was this His way of telling Tul'ran that even now Merenthia, in soul and spirit, enjoyed the same loving ministrations as had he, but in the Elsewhere, beyond the now? He closed his eyes and contemplated this new mystery. Where before there was belief, for he couldn't deny the encounter he had with the Elsewhere, now there grew the small seed of faith.

When he finished cleansing his mother's corpse, he covered her with fresh linen, so the world wouldn't have to look upon her broken body and suffer his pain.

He then turned to his sisters and wept further.

They were innocent. His mind raged. What value did their rape and death have even to the greatest evil?

Despairing, he cared for his sisters in the same loving way as he had their mother, wondering if ever the burning pain lancing his heart and bleeding his eyes raw would ever subside.

Done with the gruesome deeds, he turned his attention to his sire, still squabbling and moaning in the dirt.

He set the bucket aside and filled his right hand with El Shaddai's Knife.

"Father," he called out in a hushed tone. Al'ran bolted upright into a sitting position.

"Tul'ran?" he croaked. "Tul'ran, my son, my joy, do you still live? Praise the gods, it is so!"

He struggled to rise, but Tul'ran held him down with one hand to the shoulder. His father ranted, not noticing the hand restraining him.

"Tul'ran, by the gods! I shall now have my vengeance on those animals! There lies buried beneath the twisted tree in the orchard a box of silver. It contains enough treasure to take us away from here. I shall hire a warrior to train you in the might of arms, for as much as it will do a runt like you. I know of one such man, named Quil'ton az Peregos, in a village far from here called Gilgesh. You shall become my sword, and with hatred will you cut down the beasts who have so viciously maimed me. With you as my eyes and my arms, we shall kill the barbarians and return here triumphant to start a new life, accck..."

The ebony blade in Tul'ran's hand cut his father's voice short as it entered his sire's throat, drove through the back of his mouth, and lodged in his brain. Had Al'ran's eyes been whole, they would bulge now. Tul'ran watched with a coldhearted stare as the last moments of life left his patriarch's body.

This man's rage and stony heart had authored the last chapter of the lives of the women he loved; a chapter filled with unspeakable pain, terror, and anguish. But for this greedy, thoughtless man, his mother would be here, wrapping her arms around him, instead of lying in the dirt with his sisters. Even now, his sisters should laugh and tease him with gentle delight as he washed for the nightly meal. Had Al'ran a thought or a word for his wife and beautiful daughters? Nay, all he could rage about, as if he still had his manhood, was money and revenge. Death was even now too good for him.

As Al'ran died, Tul'ran spoke his first vow.

"It will be I, father, who will hunt to the ends of the world for these men. When I come upon them, they shall die, but not before I recount the horror of this day in their ears, and they understand the full measure of their shame. Tonight, you prepare the table where they will come to dine."

Tul'ran saw a trickle of blood seep down the blade and spoke again.

"By the blood of he whose life I end at my hands, thus do I covenant. I shall not leave this life until I have avenged myself in full. Let all who come to know these words hear and despair. I shall never take from a woman what she does not give without consent. Nor shall I raise a hand or bring harm to any woman from this day forth unless her blade is at my throat and mine to hand. To those who stand as my adversary, know you this: I am Death, and I am born this day for you."

It was a strange feeling to know his first kill was his father, he reflected, as he withdrew the blade and cleaned it on his father's clothing. He knew he should feel something for it, but, he thought, correctly, his time for nightmares would come.

He wrapped his father, clothed and unwashed, in a blanket used for the horses and set to prepare a fire to burn their bodies and honor his dead.

It was a long, arduous task. He was strong for his age, but only two and ten years old and slight of body. It took every ounce of his will and strength to leverage the bodies of his family onto the small, crude platform he had built. The time would come soon to light the fires to consume the corpses and turn them into ash.

The sun was touching the horizon when he completed the task. Feeling the want of time, he grabbed a plowing tool and ran out to the twisted tree at the edge of the orchard. The tree had endured a savage blow from a lightning strike, taking its life as surely as Tul'ran had taken his sire's. Tul'ran dug around the tree until the blade of the plowing tool hit something other than dirt, stone, or root.

It was a box carved of wood, simple in appearance.

He struck it open, amazed at the contents spilling out. Tul'ran counted fifty-two small silver bars. He remembered the instruction of his mother on money and its value, which she gave to him on the day of his twelfth birthday.

"A shekel is a unit of weight," she had said, her

voice as sweet as figs. "For as long as I can remember, we have used the shekel as a unit of weight to balance fragments of bronze. Bronze was used to buy things. One shekel pays for one moon of labor. Twelve shekels of silver are worth twelve moons of wages to the man who labors in our orchards to pluck the fruit and make it ready for sale. Your father can buy a slave for ten to twenty shekels. Your father buys slaves to work for the House instead of hiring laborers. It is cheaper over many journeys about the sun to buy slaves and feed them than to pay a neighbor for twelve moons of wages."

Merenthia had slipped a ring off her hand.

"This *har*, or ring, is worth sixty shekels. Those who work silver cast *har* with various shekel weights. It is the weight of this ring which gives it its value. A *har* can come in different shapes and sizes; larger ones have triangular ridges and others are just thin coils."

She had run her fingers through Tul'ran's long, thick hair and smiled.

"We are fortunate people, my child. Your father's father was a man of great wealth, and your father inherited this fortune with the orchard. People poorer than us pay for their food and goods with less valuable money made of tin, copper, or bronze. Sometimes they pay in barley. We can pay for our things with shekels of silver. Though we are wealthier, never deal poorly with those who have less than us. Should anyone ask you for money for food, drink, or lodging, always give what they ask. In this way, you shall measure your wealth in far more than silver and bronze. Your reputation will be your fortune."

Tul'ran pondered her words, his forehead crinkling.

"Mother, is a shekel the most amount of money a person can have?"

She smiled at him; her face glowing.

"No, my astute little son. If you had sixty shekels, you could exchange them for a mina. If you had great wealth, you could exchange sixty minas for a *kakkaru*, which some people call a talent. I will show you something, but you must keep this our secret."

Merenthia gracefully stood from where she had been weaving and walked to one corner of her bedroom. She dug in the dirt until she found a small pouch made of cloth. She opened the cloth and pulled out a small silver bar, which she handed to Tul'ran. He raised his eyebrows at the heaviness of its weight.

"This, my darling boy, is a mina. You must not tell your father I have it. A merchant gave it to me on my wedding night and told me to keep it hidden as a way of feeding the belly and clothing the body if ever our family fell into distress. Remember where I have hidden it; it will be yours on my passing."

Tul'ran looked at the pile of small silver bars in his cupped hands. Fifty-two minas were equivalent to three thousand, one hundred and twenty-two shekels. He was holding almost a kakkaru of silver. It was a fortune.

The gentle women in his family could have ridden in a fine cart drawn by horses, instead of taking the long walk into the village for supplies. They could have entertained in fine clothing and bejeweled ears instead of the same rundown smocks time after time. Tul'ran studied the money with dark thoughts, wondering if it was possible to raise his miserly father from the dead for the pleasure of driving a blade through his heart. Then again, his heart may have been too small to find, even with the majestic knife gifted to him by El Shaddai.

He carried the bounty back to the House. He strode into his father's private room, the room from which he banned all others, and prepared for his journey. There was a large leather bag beneath the rudimentary table. He dumped the contents of the bag on the floor, for nothing of his sire would stay with him. There was a hidden pouch on the interior wall of the bag. He placed into this place of secrecy the minas his father had hoarded beneath the twisted tree.

He then went into his mother's room and dug in the dirt until he found the cloth. The mina was where his mother returned it eight moons earlier. With the sharp point of El Shaddai's Knife, he drilled a hole through one side of the bar. He found a length of leather cord and patiently fed it through the crude hole. Tul'ran tied the cord around his neck and touched the bar snugged against his chest. For as long as he lived, Merenthia's mina would stay near his heart.

He searched for the *bar* earlier adorning his mother's hand. Tul'ran raged again when he couldn't find it, knowing the barbarians had stripped it from her body. They had not stopped at robbing her virtue, but robbed her remains too. Tul'ran spat on the ground and rubbed the place where dirt and sputum met with his right heel. Again, he repeated the vow he had made over his father's corpse.

They would pay. They would pay in blood, and urine, and feces, and death. Fear would consume their souls in the last moments of their lives.

Tul'ran shook his head. It was time to pack. Into the bag he put the wondrous Knife, the only three loincloths he owned, a clean tunic, and clean trousers. If he were careful with his money, he could buy any other articles he required. He would live well.

Several pieces of fruit found the bottom of the bag, as well as a striking stone with which to start fires.

When he finished packing, the bag was too heavy to walk with for any length of time. He had to have the bag for his necessities, and his bag demanded transportation.

There was only one mode of transportation available to him; a mode which strove to injure any person who sought his back, and he was just outside the House.

In the enclosure, just past the point where his family's bodies had lain, was an enormous horse. He was two years old to the day, and as black as his father's soul. His sisters had commented when their sire first brought the horse home: there would be a danger of losing the stallion within its own dark shadow. The name took root and held, and he and his sisters anointed the stallion as Darkshadow thereafter.

As much as he was a beauty, he was also without respect for any person who sought to set a rope around his neck or attempt to leap upon his back. He was fast, strong, and his heart was wild. All attempts to bend him to harness or saddle had left men long schooled in the art of training steeds to leave their yard muttering, rubbing sore backsides and possessed of assorted bruises.

Tul'ran stood in the enclosure now, not twenty paces from the beast.

"Darkshadow," he said in a calm and even tone. "Hearken to my words, for I covenant with you this day and forevermore. Should you bend your will to mine, I shall take you with me wherever I go. I will see to your stomach before mine. I will give you the first drink of the finest water to slake your thirst, and I will defend your life as I would my own. Should you disdain this offer, then watch as I set another path for you."

Tul'ran walked over to the gate, barring the exit to the enclosure, and flung it open. He walked five paces in the opposite direction and turned once more to the stallion, who scrutinized him closely, ears flickering, as if in puzzlement.

"There is your freedom," Tul'ran said, "for as long as you might have it before someone throws a rope about your neck. Follow your feet to the left to freedom, if you so desire, or follow your heart and bind it with mine to glory."

Tul'ran left the enclosure and turned right to amble toward the shed which had earlier imprisoned him. The day was still not barren of amazement, it seemed, as he glanced from the corner of his eye and saw the stallion following him, head down, his jaws moving back and forth in a chewing motion.

As if it were always so, and not a now cloaked in frightening newness, Tul'ran draped a rope about Darkshadow's head and formed a halter of sorts, and reins, of sorts. He took a thick blanket, the last in the shed, and flung it over the horse's back. Then, acting as nonchalantly as if he had done it a thousand times, he gripped the stallion's long, black mane and flung himself onto his back.

A few seconds passed, and Tul'ran decided it would be in his best interest to breathe again. Another gift. By all appearances, Darkshadow had decided there was no merit to a dubious freedom and cast his lot with the slight boy on his back. Perhaps he heard the oath taken by the lad, and it stirred the wildness in his own heart. It was possible a deep part of his mind knew no one destined him for the cart, but for the carnage of battle and chasing glory.

Maybe he was simply crazy.

"Come, brother," Tul'ran said. "We are away, for once the funeral pyre is lit, the village will come with haste."

Tul'ran dismounted on the left, grabbed the bag in which he had stuffed sundry items, and walked to the pyre. He curled Darkshadow's lead about his wrist and bent to the pack to retrieve the striking stone. Once he lit the pyre, he knew the villagers would come, some with concern, others with curiosity. His elder sisters' husbands would contest to inherit the orchard, so naught would go to waste. The House and orchard were his by right of being his sire's only son, but he would never return, much less run a business from the ground forever stained with the precious blood of the women he cherished.

The wood from the funeral pyre caught flame. Soon, it would set the bodies ablaze. Tul'ran looked up to the heavens, straining to see beyond the vast pale blue sky into the home of the God Who offered him purpose.

"El Shaddai," he whispered, "Lord. I pray for the souls of my mother and sisters and place them in Your tender care." His voice broke, a sob closing his throat as tears once more dripped from his eyes. "To You I send my sire for judgment, for I cannot judge between him and me. Hatred consumes my heart for him, and I would condemn him harshly, without regard for those things inviting Your mercy. You have treated me with love and kindness. Only You can be fair with his judgment."

Tul'ran looked at the funeral pyre, the flames catching and rising higher against the dry wood.

A part of him wanted to put El Shaddai's Knife to his own throat and cast his dying body on the pyre. He wouldn't. His life had purpose now, and his arm was bound in service to the God who gave His Knife to an orphaned waif. He reached out a hand to his mother; the linens surrounding her catching the flame, and shed his last tear.

"Goodbye."

Tul'ran mounted Darkshadow, again without incident, and froze. To this point, necessity had dictated his movements. Now destiny would set his face toward his travel, but he had no inkling of his destiny.

As if in response to his consternation, the Voice came back to his mind, caressing it as a parent caresses the face of a toddler.

"Tul'ran, child," said the Voice, as it set tingles running up and down Tul'ran's spine. "Set your face to the South and East. I will command my servants concerning you to guard you in all your ways. On their hands they will bear you up, lest you strike your foot against a stone. Follow me and I shall renew your strength. I tell you the truth; you shall mount up with wings like eagles; run and not be weary; shall walk and not faint."

"Fear not, for I am with you; be not dismayed, for I am El Shaddai and there is none like Me. When you pass through the waters, I will be with you; and through the rivers, they shall not overwhelm you; when you walk through fire, it shall not burn you, and the flame shall not consume you. No weapon fashioned against you shall succeed, and you shall make dumb every tongue rising against you in judgment."

The Covenant stunned Tul'ran. The promises were too much to absorb in the youth's staggered mind, but he accepted them, as promised, and turned Darkshadow's head to the South and East. When they were almost through the orchard, he couldn't resist a look back. There was a string of torches coming from the village. The villagers saw the blaze and raised an alarm. They would think of him as one more body on the pyre, if they thought of him at all. No one would consider that a boy slight of build and tender of years would have ridden away to seek Justice.

The dread of his loss once more settled like a weight upon his chest.

There was a weight on his chest.

Tul'ran woke, eyes opening to the dusk of nightfall, alert, his body tensing for action. He lay silent for a moment, listening, assessing, all senses alive. Everything was still. Not frozen still, just still.

He glanced down and discovered the source of his discomfort. Erianne had rolled over to him and placed her head upon his chest, a wide swath of black hair obscuring his vision of her face. She had flung one elegant arm about his waist and was deep in sleep. The sensation was pleasant. Tul'ran grinned. Her reaction to this predicament promised to be entertaining.

For a moment, he didn't stir. He didn't want to rouse her yet. Tul'ran struggled to recall when it was he had last experienced such a feeling of warmth in the cold recesses of his soul.

A sharp breath knifed into his lungs. Those thoughts roused demons who inflicted pain beyond endurance. It was best to let them lie.

"Kabolon," he called, loath to cast sound into the stillness of the dusk air. She didn't so much as stir.

"Erianne," he said more sternly, "Arise."

"Noooooo." She murmured, sleep thick in her voice, speaking in a language he didn't understand, "*It's too early. Go back to sleep.*"

"Kabolon!" He hissed. She startled awake, rising to a sitting position like a deer leaping from a hiding place, curling the cloak to her chest. He noted with delight, she at once became as flustered as he had hoped.

"Milord Tul'ran," she gasped. "My apologies, I did not, meant not to insult or presume..."

He raised a hand to silence her.

"Peace. Not only was there no insult, but the manner of your sleeping was pleasurable."

Her breathing increased, a hint of panic touching her widening eyes.

"Did we...?"

"No! Nothing happened between us other than two companions bound by covenant securing needed rest before passage. Do not trouble your mind on this account."

"Are we away, then?"

"We are away. Let us refresh ourselves in the oasis and pack our things. When we are ready, you have but to point, and there shall we journey."

Tul'ran turned his back to give Erianne privacy and scanned the desert under the glow of the last rays of daylight. He put on his armor, wrinkling his nose at the faint, pungent odor of the chiton. The time to wash his clothing would have to come soon.

Once they had dressed, Tul'ran and Erianne strolled to the oasis without speaking. Eyes averted, they took care of bodily functions and splashed water on their heads. As Erianne finger brushed her long hair, Tul'ran packed the sheepskin before tacking up Darkshadow. He moved quickly but efficiently, his mind distracted by the thought of the cloud of his covenant-mistress's hair laying scattered across his chest.

A terrible curse: imagination.

It promised things reality rarely delivered.

The Hunter watched them, satisfied.

Intel describing where the Hunter could find

Erianne had been correct. Their only logical option was for the two of them to proceed across the desert toward the city. The Hunter would find an ambush point in their path and kill the woman. The predator would do nothing to injure the warrior, for his wellbeing was necessary to preserve the Purity. Of course, should this Tul'ran person become a distraction, necessity could also dictate the end of his life.

Either way, the Hunter promised silently, one or both of a woman and a man would lie dead before the sun rose into the sky again.

CHAPTER THE FIFTH:
AWAKENINGS

By covenant bound, did the paired duo
Make their way through the cold desert sand
Where treachery sat, with bated breath,
To end their lives with a night-shaded hand.

Mesopotamia, the second day of the eighth month, 2005 BC, after midnight

A sullen silver half-moon hung above the shrouded desert, a gleaming jewel in a star speckled night sky. It shed enough light to give wary travelers a place to set foot without fear of disturbing the denizens of the night carrying poison in fang or stinger (and waiting to use them with eagerness). The restless wind, ever-present, stirred, gathering away the last of the heat hoarded by the sand and replacing it with a dry chill. It was a good night to journey.

Tul'ran slung the leather pack across Darkshadow's back and checked again to ensure the tautness of cinches and straps. It wouldn't do to have Darkshadow startle, unlikely as it may be, and cast weapons and other necessities into the night-shrouded desert dunes.

Satisfied, he turned to Erianne and stopped cold.

"Kabolon?" he asked, his eyebrows near flinging from his forehead. "Where are your foot coverings?"

Erianne looked down at her bare feet, flustered by their nakedness.

"Milord," she said, "the barbarians took me from my home while I was at the beginning of my nightly preparations, bare of sandal or shoe. They took me with great haste and violence, having no regard for the necessities of a lady or consideration for comfort. I fear I am without foot coverings."

Tul'ran shook his head. Not noticing her lack of footwear bewildered him. He considered himself astute and observant. His awareness of her, her intelligence, her manner of speaking, her form, and her beauty hadn't extended, apparently, to a consideration of her feet. He shook his head again, as if to clear away silken, seductive webs distracting thoughts from purpose.

"You cannot journey through the desert bare of foot. Even without the harshness of the sand grating across your skin, your foot could fall upon a stone sharpened by wind and time, resulting in an injury. Unhealthy feet will cripple you."

He considered further, examining her with a critical eye before expelling a gust of air.

"There is naught to do but let you ride, mistress, for we cannot have you lamed before any action requiring firmness of stance or fleetness of foot."

He ought to be forgiven for thinking her greatest threat was a cut to her foot or painful arches. He had yet to learn she had much more to dread than such trivialities.

Erianne bit down hard on her lips to prevent them from exploding into a giggle. She was delighted she could ride instead of trudging through the desert. She wanted to hug him for the suggestion, but chose against it. He had reflexes which may have interpreted such a gesture as a threat, and she wasn't sure she would survive his response. It was an accurate assessment.

"Come then. Let us mount you."

She whipped her head around, startled, the words of one culture clashing with the values of another. But he was already moving to the left side of Darkshadow. She shook her head. He didn't mean what she thought he just said, even in jest.

Tul'ran adjusted the leather bag backwards to give Erianne room in the saddle. When she walked to his side, she gave him the pretty foot of her left leg, and he hoisted her upwards onto Darkshadow's large broad back, causing the horse to lean his head to the side to eye her. The Sword Himself noted his stallion's response.

"Be careful, brother," he said, with an admonishing slap to Darkshadow's neck. "She is a friend and ally, and we are not so rich in both to see you send this one flying into the night."

Tul'ran moved forward and to the right of Darkshadow's head and began the long journey across the sand. He kept both Darkshadow and the Mistress of Kabolon in the periphery of his vision, while flinging his awareness outward in search of all who might offer harm.

A fleeting time after they set out, Tul'ran noticed a subtle shift in Erianne's body, and he turned in time to see her suppress a shiver. He cursed himself as a fool. All she wore was her tunic, and while it was sturdy, it lacked the protection his attire gave him against the cool night air. Perhaps he should have his vision checked, he thought, or, further, his heart for its failure to see her discomfort. It was just him and Darkshadow traversing the wide expanse of the region on most occasions, secure in their own ease. Isolation wasn't an excuse for thoughtlessness.

He moved to Darkshadow's rump and removed the sheepskin roll from the leather bag. He handed it to Erianne.

"Forgive me, Mistress," he said with a murmur. "I have failed in my duty to see to your comfort. Pray, drape the sheepskin about you. It may offer you solace against the cold."

Erianne smiled, her lips curling in such sweetness it sent a delightful shiver down Tul'ran's spine.

"I thank you, milord, for your kindness and generosity. Although I should traverse this sandy plain on foot and at your side, you have bidden me ride. You have given thought to my comfort and granted me some measure against the cold. How could it not be true you are a man worthy of your reputation as a mighty lord?"

She couldn't say for sure in the dark, but she thought he may have blushed. He spun away to lead them forward, hiding his face from her.

They walked through sand radiating a faint glow

in the Mesopotamian night, under the gaze of a disapproving moon, with only the sound of feet sloshing through the silica disturbing the silence.

After the first thirty minutes of solitude, Erianne sighed.

"Milord, the night is long, and our journey is far. It shall feel longer if we travel in silence. I would beg a further token from you. May I ask questions of you for my edification and in pursuit of knowledge?"

She had a pretty way of speaking; he thought. Her words had the unusual effect of loosening his lips and calming his guard. The possibility existed she might be a witch, for she had definitely charmed him. Yet, the prospect of it wasn't sufficiently dire as to silence his renegade mouth. The part of him guarding his heart against others remained strangely silent. So much so, he agreed to her request without even the slightest qualm.

"We are bound in covenant, Mistress. Question and I shall answer, but beware; you shall have my truth and may regret the asking."

She nodded.

"Then I shall steel my heart and guard my soul against your candor and my imaginings."

He laughed. She giggled in response to his laughter, and Tul'ran found her giggle delighted him. He grinned, though the darkness didn't show it.

"What questions do you have, Erianne of Kabolon?"

She paused for a moment, pondering.

"I could not help but to notice, milord, the fierceness of your response to my captors' attempt to steal my virtue and trample it beneath their feet. It is a response I have rarely seen in men. I neither offer nor intend insult by those words. It is my deepest desire you should share with me the arrow which struck your soul and scarred your heart of hearts."

It didn't take long for her to go there, did it? His smile faded. Well, he said he would tell her the truth, didn't he? Where was his famed suspicion of a person, his legendary restraint on speech and lip? Ah well, let her have it then, and into the wind the costs. Without slowing his pace, he told her in a quiet tone about the worst day of his life.

Whatever Erianne expected when she asked for his story, she'd never imagined this. She cringed at his father's treatment of him, a twelve-year-old boy who just wanted to spend some time in play. Tears flowed from her eyes as she heard of the rape of his mother and sisters, and her stomach roiled with nausea when he described their wounds. The tears threatened to break into outright sobs as Tul'ran spoke of the gentle way he cleansed their bodies and covered them for cremation.

The hellish memories trampling trenches of darkness in his soul now found a way into her own despairing heart.

She almost swore aloud when he recounted, with no emotion in his voice, driving a blade into his father's throat and brain. It horrified her a twelve-year-old child had been so driven by his pain, outrage, and hate, he would kill his own father. On the other hand, she was happy his sire had met a just result on the very ground into which his wife and daughters bled.

With his words, Erianne shared the thrill of his bonding with Darkshadow and the exhilaration of sitting on the stallion's back for the first time. She felt the heat from the fire of the funeral pyre, which raised the sting of tears on her cheeks once more.

She looked back at the scene near the House from the edge of the Orchard and mourned.

He was a superb storyteller, for his revelations were rich and adorned with intricate layers of complex emotion.

The recounting bled an hour from their trek across the desert. His Telling spent both their emotions by the end. They journeyed on in silence for another few minutes before Erianne spoke again.

"Milord." She swallowed, her voice threatening to crack. "Had I the power to send you back into the place and day to warn your father of what was to come, I would do so without hesitation or fear of consequence."

He looked at her, and she could see a bitter half smile in the moonlight.

"To what end?" he asked. "Even had you such a power, would you think my sire would listen to his whelp? More like he would have slapped my head against the nearest stone to loosen my thoughts and provoke clarity. What has passed is done once, now, and forevermore. We carve our past in granite, and there it lies like a gravestone: immovable, irrefutable, unfailing. I could not change it, no matter how deep the desire of my heart may be."

His wisdom left her eyes wide and her mouth open. She closed her mouth and moved on.

"Then let us set aside the subject of the demise of

your loved ones, milord, for I confess it distresses my heart. While I told you, in jest, I would steel myself against your truth; I did not expect a blade of pain to enter my ears and worm its way into my soul. Speaking of blades, milord, is there a story gracing the legend of Bloodwing the Blade, and how you gained it?"

He smiled again, more fully this time, and added an exuberant nod.

"Indeed, mistress, indeed. Mark me now, there is amazement surrounding this story, and you may find it hard of belief. Ridiculously hard of belief. I will tell you the truth, but finding confidence in it will stretch your mind to unthought of limits."

"I will run my chances, milord, and with gladness."

"Have it your way. When I rode away from my home, Darkshadow and I wandered for weeks in the general direction of south and east. We came upon the village of Gilgesh, near the city of Lagash, wherein lived a retired fighter. He was a master of arms, strategy, and tactics, nimble of limb and strong. I begged him to train me in the ways of war, but he looked at me as a mere boy, and a small one. When I told him of my roots and the strength of my labor, it was only then he relented."

It had been a tough negotiation. Quil'ton az Peregos, the very man mentioned by his father, was unmarried and lived alone. Once Tul'ran realized he had found the man whom his father wanted to hire to train him, he slyly asked around about the fellow. Quil'ton's neighbors were eager to gossip about their reclusive warrior.

Quil'ton despised cooking and cleaning his hut, they said, having had someone to do those things for him while he was engaged in campaigns of arms and might. He retired from military service for a time and then some, so he no longer had the funds for the luxury of a servant. It aggravated his spirit to no end.

With the information Tul'ran gathered, he formed a plan of approach.

Tul'ran encountered Quil'ton outside the man's hutch one morning, as Quil'ton was cursing over a small bucket of milk he had just purchased and now spilled by accident at the step of his door.

Tul'ran advanced toward Quil'ton while walking; Darkshadow was at his back, as always, observing with wariness. Darkshadow had adopted the boy as his own, and the part of his brain, which didn't think like others of the equine persuasion, looked upon protecting the lad as his foremost duty. An intelligent horse is a true prize; an intelligent horse bordering on murderous insanity is lethal.

"I give you good morn, Quil'ton az Peregos."

The man whipped around and snarled his response.

"Good morn, is it? This milk, even now nourishing the dirt at my stoop, cost me a piece of bronze and a favor. Now I have you pestering at my heels like a pup. Where in my words do you find a good morn? If you are hungry, I have food. If you thirst, I have a well in the back of this hutch. What will it cost me to be rid of you?"

Tul'ran grinned, mouth stretched wide, with an impudence born of a courage refusing to quail before the grizzled warrior.

"Why, only your time, Master. I have a desire for war; it sings in my bones like the falcon keening after its prey. Yet I am undone, for I have neither the training nor the skills to see me survive any length of engagement on a battlefield. I seek your time and skill to start my journey upon the road to glory."

Quil'ton glared at him from under bushy eyebrows, blue eyes framed with ice.

"You younglings are all the same. You come to me singing songs of treasure, and maidens, and honor and glory." He spat. "There is no glory in war, boy. There is only blood and guts and pain, belonging to you or another man, which someone far away from the battlefield has decreed your enemy. Glory, pah! There are only the pitiful shrieks of your brothers as they lie gushing their lives into the dirt, casting their eyes into the abyss, and knowing they will never see father, mother, wife, lover, or friend ever again. What you seek is a storyteller, not an instructor. Be gone!"

Tul'ran saw the necessity for a change in tactics.

"Master, I am young, and though I appear as but a shadow compared to younglings my age, I am strong. I lived my first twelve turns about the sun on a farm where I tended my father's herd and bent my back to chores. My mother and sisters taught me to cook and mend; to clean and make tidy those things coming undone. I offer you the services of my back while you train my body."

Quil'ton paused. He inspected the boy standing in front of him. The youth was skinny and not tall, but looked strong enough. He clothed himself well and somehow had come into possession of a magnificent horse.

As he was examining the boy, his gaze went to the boy's eyes. And stopped. The boy had a haunted look lying behind the piercing dark stare. While the eyes were not hostile or insane, they held within their depths a knowledge gained by men far older than the youth. Quil'ton knew the look well. The lad had killed.

One more time, he tried to get rid of the boy.

"I have no need of a whelp to lie about my home while I attend to my affairs."

Tul'ran smiled with a faint pursing of his lips.

"Perhaps, but while you tend to your affairs, what harm would come from returning home to a warm fire, a cheerful host, and food on the table?"

"A fire I can start, a meal I am capable of preparation. I have no need of company!"

The smile on Tul'ran's face never wavered.

"Yes, but these tasks bring no joy to your face or gladness to your heart. I am young and strong and do not shun labor. I will bond myself to you for five turns about the sun, and you will train me in all the skill and knowledge you yourself possess. At the end, we will part our ways. You will have lost nothing and gained some measure of comfort and camaraderie."

The older man stood without speaking for a few moments, considering.

"And who will pay to feed the noble beast who walks at your back like some fearsome rearguard?"

Tul'ran inclined his head, knowing he had won, and granting the elder warrior the favor of a graceful exit from the field.

"My father was a wealthy man." True. "He did not think in ways martial." Also, true. "But he did not despise me for my dreams." False. "When I pronounced the path of my destiny, he recovered from his treasure a modest sum and bade me take it to allow me to find my legend and fund my own campaigns." Really false. "I have sufficient funds to pay for my lodging and the lodging of my horse." True.

Quil'ton ran an appreciative gaze over the horse.

"A mount such as yours could fetch you a pretty sum, were you to sell him."

Tul'ran sighed, adding a little theater to the sound.

"Alas, even if my heart were so inclined, my honor would not permit me. I have sworn a covenant with Darkshadow, wherein he gave me his life for his comfort and peace. The pact binds us unto death."

"And if someone seeks to separate you from your Darkshadow in negation of your desire?"

"They die," came the icy response.

Tul'ran stared into Quil'ton's eyes, and the older man felt his blood go cold. There was an offer of death and eternal torment in the look, which wasn't an idle threat, but a gift of shadowy certainty.

Another pause, this time longer. Quil'ton nodded and asked,

"To what name does my recruit answer?"

"I am hight Tul'ran az Nostrom, and some day legend will declare my feats and ballads proclaim my repute."

Quil'ton took him in, and Tul'ran's training began with vigor. He had tasks within the hutch, which he completed to his master's satisfaction. In return, Quil'ton invested in the lad all his considerable skill and talent in the art of returning men's lives to their gods.

The boy grew and filled out. He reached his present height by the time he was six and ten turns about the sun and would grow no more. Muscle, though, ah, it was another matter. Tul'ran worked his body hard, and his physique responded by layering muscle upon muscle, strength upon strength. The youth became powerful, fast, and skilled beyond measure with bow, spear, sword, and dagger.

Quil'ton secured a friend who had ridden horses into battle and survived the encounters. His friend, Ragar, trained Tul'ran and Darkshadow in the art of fighting as a pair. The two of them, Ragar confided to Quil'ton, were a force beyond measure. They thought almost as one, fought as seasoned warriors, and gave no quarter.

As fierce as Tul'ran had become, his mount was even more so. Darkshadow delighted in battle, feared neither man nor beast, and lusted for killing more than anyone would think capable. Or reasonable.

On one such day of training, Tul'ran, mounted on Darkshadow, was attacking two poles around which Ragar had tied clothing stuffed with straw. Each had a head, of sorts, which was more clothing filled with straw and shaped in the same dimensions as a human skull. Both horse and human had worked themselves into a lather and were coming to the end of the exercise. Darkshadow raced forward, and Tul'ran cut at one foe with a forward slash, reversing it into a backlash as they surged by.

Then Darkshadow, enraged to the fullest extent by the temerity of their second enemy to continue to exist, lunged forward, planted his forelegs into the ground and spun, driving his back hooves through the second opponent and the pole to which they tied the cloth and straw. Tul'ran wasn't expecting the move and flew over the horse's head in a wide arc before hitting the ground and rolling, as his master taught.

He stood up and looked to watch Darkshadow scream a whinny and drive his front legs repeatedly into the straw man on the ground. Tul'ran glanced over to Ragar and Quil'ton, who seemed stunned by the horse's pummeling of the pile of cloth and the stallion's insane anger.

Tul'ran limped to the raging horse, calling in a soft cadence. Quil'ton went to rise and shout a warning, but Ragar restrained his arm.

"Let's see what he will do," Ragar said in a whisper. Quil'ton allowed himself to be guided back into his seat, but not without reservation.

"Darkshadow, brother," Tul'ran called, drifting towards the horse and keeping his eyes on the ground at the horse's feet. "Battle has passed, and we have won the field. Peace, brother, peace. There is no further need for your might. Look, you are frightening the children nearby."

Darkshadow stood, quivering and snorting, as the young man approached him. He dropped his head, flickering his ears back and forth, and chewed, moving his jaws from side to side.

Tul'ran continued talking in soothing tones as he

approached the horse's head, rubbing his hands on the beast's neck and withers.

"There, brother, there. You see? Our enemies lie vanquished at your feet, and you are the champion. The villagers will sing songs to your glory this night, while your enemies keen their laments before their loved ones. Come, let us go to rest. You have earned your grain this day, my friend."

Tul'ran turned and limped back to the men, without taking a grip on Darkshadow's halter, and the stallion followed as meek as a kitten.

Ragar sipped back a drink of wine and saluted rider and horse as he watched Tul'ran put Darkshadow away for the day.

"You'll want to attach your name to him," he said, in a low tone, to Quil'ton.

"Huh? What are you talking about? Or can you even create a thought with a cup to your teeth? How many of those have you had?"

Ragar grinned, the parting of his lips revealing a sizeable gap where the butt of a spear had separated tooth from mouth in a long-forgotten conflict in a distant land.

"I'm not so far in my cups I can't see what's in front of me, you old motherless son. Mark me, Quil'ton az Peregos. Someday, balladeers will sing melodies to the lad's glory at the same time as widows lament the death of their husbands lying at his feet. His name will be on the lips of every man who can speak, and they'll speak in whispers for the dread of it."

Quil'ton pushed Ragar off his stool, sending the other man sprawling onto the dirt, and laughed.

"You're not so sober you can find balance on your perch, old man. I think you see what you want to see and not what the future portends."

Ragar got up, smiling his gap-toothed smile again.

"It may be as you say, old friend, yet I persist. Someday the name of Tul'ran az Nostrom will delight the ears of women yearning for a hard bounce and wilt the hearts of their husbands at the telling."

Both had a hearty laugh then, leaving the conversation while they watched, bemused, as Tul'ran, without a horse, completed his training.

Five seasons came and fled like a nightingale chasing the dawn. The day came when Tul'ran stood before Quil'ton, strong and honed. Not just a warrior turned true, but a weapon in his own right.

Tul'ran bowed and, to Quil'ton's dismay, his eyes misted over and set his vision of the younger warrior askew.

"I take my leave of you, Master. Thank you for your time, patience, and training. I came to you as a boy; I leave as a man, placing feet on the road to destiny. Should ever you have need of my arm, should ever you find an enemy at your back, you have but to send word and I will return with all haste to stand with you. Your friends shall be my friends and your opponents shall be my enemies. Your friends shall I honor, and your enemies shall I send to kneel before the god who would judge them."

It was a noble speech and threatened to squeeze shut the older warrior's throat as well as to cover his cheeks with water.

Quil'ton cleared his throat.

"I am grateful to you, son, for you have reminded me I have yet purpose in life and gifts to give. And speaking of gifts, I have one for your leave-taking. It is a tradition in the world of war, requiring the instructor to gift his student with a blade when all training is complete. I would honor this custom, but I do not possess a sword worthy of your arm." He hesitated.

"There is a place I would send you for your blade. I will not impart to you how I came upon the knowledge of this place for fear you would think me a lunatic, but I ground my belief in reality, not fanciful visions."

Tul'ran looked puzzled.

"Point me as you favor me with the kindness of your heart and words, to this place of wonder where I might gain a blade suitable to my arm and purpose."

Quil'ton nodded, his stomach a little queasy. He wasn't sure if he was pointing the young warrior to his destiny or his death.

"Follow the base of the ridge beyond the village until you come to a place where the rock casts shadows within itself. When the sun takes its rest in the sky and greets the land, you will find your way to the place where you will have your sword."

There was nothing left to say then, although both men longed to tell the other of the feelings engendered by their bond as instructor to student, bondsman to oath sworn, veteran to recruit... and father to son.

For indeed, as the days flew by, Tul'ran and Quil'ton took great enjoyment in passing the time after the evening meal with stories and gossip, laughter, and song. Tul'ran was honest about what happened at his father's hands, although he could never find the courage to relate his relationship with El Shaddai. The treatment the boy received from his sire and the horror he was required to endure by his father's stupid decision outraged Quil'ton.

The instructor didn't lay his hand even once on his young charge in anger, nor did he ever speak a caustic insult to the boy's face. Quil'ton became the father Tul'ran had dreamed of while lying on his bedding on the farm, his body wracked with pain from his sire's beatings. Master and student began as strangers, bled as brothers, and then found the bond of father and son.

Tul'ran felt a heavy weight on his heart as he once more left behind him a father, though this one hearty, alive, well, and true. The young warrior mounted Darkshadow in one smooth motion, the leather bag set on the back of the saddle, nodded to the man standing before him once more, and turned his horse to the hills.

He did as he was told, following the base of the ridge for some time until he arrived at a place where the rock seemed to fold in upon itself and left a dark stain on its face. Tul'ran dismounted, walked up to the rock, and pressed against the granite outcrop. The rock didn't yield to the pressure and ignored his efforts. The young warrior looked to the sky and noted the sun hadn't yet reached the prescribed point.

Resolved to patience, he found a place worthy of perch and sat down to wait.

When the sun kissed the ridge before it, something shifted. The rock face, which had been as dark and solid as the inside of a well, seemed now to glow. Intrigued, Tul'ran walked to the rock face and found, to his enormous surprise, there now appeared a gap in the granite, one large enough to accommodate himself and Darkshadow. Tul'ran returned to his stallion, grazing with contentment nearby, and took up the reins. They ventured inward together, as always.

The young warrior stepped into the cave's entrance, daunted but not afraid, and followed the winding passage deeper into the ridge. After the passage of some time, the cave opened and led into an enormous cavern consumed by a bright white light. He halted, his mouth hanging open as if the sight before him had rendered his brain stupid.

The center of the cavern held the largest man Tul'ran had ever seen. He was double Tul'ran's height and girth. His forearms alone were as large as the young warrior's thighs. A fine white linen tunic covered the man from head to toe, though it bunched at the back as if covering a massive hump. Power emanated from him in waves and with such strength as to make Tul'ran want to fall to his knees. The man gazed at him out of bright, pale eyes piercing Tul'ran's soul, a faint smile on his lips.

"Tul'ran az Nostrom. At last."

Tul'ran shook his head, as if coming out of a daze.

"Your favor, I beg of you. I know we have not met, for I would not forget a man of your stature, no matter the circumstance. Am I to know your name?"

The giant shook his head with a pleasant

expression on his face.

"You are not, though it would not dismay you to learn the name of him whom I serve. You are to be given a magnificent gift to further your purpose and advance your destiny."

The man, if he was a man and not some god, reached out a massive hand to the workbench and laid aside a linen cloth covering the bench. Unwrapped, the linen gave up its prize: a long, black sheath covered in archaic runes and glistening with the kiss of promised glory. The giant put his hand to the hilt of the sword, and the blade withdrew from the sheath with a soft, leathery hiss. It was long, black, and double-edged. The metal of the blade was a deep black, almost as if it reflected the bottom of the ocean. As the giant raised it vertically, something in Tul'ran's soul sang a greeting.

"Behold," the giant said in a deep, even voice. "Bloodwing the Blade. My kind have held it from time immemorial. It has graced the hand of one who was once far mightier than I. It is a gift to you, for you have proven true to your word and steadfast in your practices."

The being, Tul'ran could not think of him as a mere man, reversed the sword and offered the hilt to the young man.

"Take it up and feel its balance."

Tul'ran stood completely still, pursing his lips.

"You have said it once graced the hand of one far mightier than you. I cannot comprehend one greater than you. Who am I to take up such a sword?"

The being smiled faintly.

"You are Tul'ran the Sword, not so named

because people will confuse you with a weapon of war, but because you are a living instrument of death. He whom I serve judges you worthy. Take up the sword."

After another moment's hesitation, Tul'ran reached out and grasped the hilt. Immediately, something went out of him and into the amazing blade, for the edges of it, before a shining black, now glowed an intense blue. It was as if Bloodwing became part of his body, seizing his soul and burying it in its depths.

The massive being nodded his satisfaction.

"Be wary of it, Tul'ran az Nostrom. Its edges are beyond sharp, for this blade will pass through anything it touches. You need never put a stone to it, for it does not require sharpening. Nothing can withstand its touch. Handle it with great care."

Tul'ran turned his body and looked up at Erianne, as if to make sure she remained awake.

"The words of this great man spoke true. At his insistence, I took a mighty swing with Bloodwing against the granite bench upon which he had rested the sword. To my astonishment, the blade parted solid rock with indescribable ease, and returned to me from the stone without impingement."

"I turned to the giant and asked him how the scabbard could contain a sword with such edges. He but smiled at me as if I had inquired of a great mystery far beyond my knowledge and comprehension. Fairly so. He told me I was not to be bothered with such a thing, as neither sword nor scabbard would fail me in my lifetime."

"He bade me leave then, offering me good wishes for campaigns filled with glory and honor. I took the hint and wished him farewell; the wondrous blade now sitting on my hip. As I left the cave, I turned back to inquire what should be done with Bloodwing the Blade were I to near my life's end. I almost fell off my horse. For where there was once a cave, glowing with invitation, there was now again only a sheer rock face."

"I departed with haste, for the mystery of the place scared the wits out of me. For the past four and ten years, Bloodwing has not left my hand. With it, I grew my legend, and against it, nothing can stand. This is the tale of how I came to gain Bloodwing the Blade. I swear it to be true as if I uttered my words on blood spilled between us."

Erianne sat still and very straight on Darkshadow's back, feeling the strong, comfortable gait of the war horse beneath her hips.

"Thank you, milord. It was a wonderful telling, and I am more than half a mind to believe it. May I ask yet one more question?"

He cocked an eyebrow at her. Now what?

"Proceed, Mistress."

"If it should not be impertinent to ask, what is your age?"

He snorted. "As if you place impertinence at the forefront of consideration before you ask questions! No, no, it was not for avoidance, I said as much. I am one and thirty years old."

She was about to open her mouth for another question and froze.

Literally.

Time froze.

Everything around him ceased moving, ceased breathing, ceased thought. Tul'ran ripped Bloodwing out of its sheath and spun, piercing the cloak of darkness around him with his dark eyes.

Time only froze when he was in immediate danger of his life. It was another gift from El Shaddai, one saving him from death on countless occasions. It was a gift only given when an attack came unawares, with surprise leaving the Sword Himself wounded unto death if not countered with speed beyond the pale. This was his closest held secret and the foundation of his Legend.

Tul'ran wasn't as truthful as he could have been when relating his history to Erianne, being careful to avoid talking about his encounter with El Shaddai and the gift of His Knife. El Shaddai was his secret to keep close to his heart, and he wasn't yet in a place where he would give away such confidences.

Tul'ran spun another tight circle. He didn't see anyone around him and couldn't perceive the threat giving El Shaddai such distress as to bring the world to a halt. Tul'ran drew the Knife with his left hand, Bloodwing in his right hand, and walked a circle around Darkshadow. Nothing. Mystified, he walked another circle in a wider pattern, seeking, yet not finding, an enemy.

Tul'ran sloshed through the sand to Darkshadow, who was turning his head back and forth, his ears twitching. A time freeze no longer startled the warhorse or upset him; so many had he endured with his master. Tul'ran caressed the horse's face.

"Brother, the woman who sits on your back has value to me. If you move, you may cause her injury when Time resumes. Bide here patiently while I search out the cause of this threat. I will return, I promise."

Darkshadow whickered and nudged Tul'ran's hand with his nose. Tul'ran grinned and reached into a pocket for a date. The warhorse snatched the morsel out of his hand and began chewing enthusiastically. It made the warrior grin.

"Ever the glutton, even in the face of mortal danger. What am I to do with you?"

Receiving no answer, Tul'ran began a second search for the cause of the time disruption. He was on his third pass when he came upon it. It was an arrow on a direct line to Darkshadow, some ten paces away from his steed's nose. The arrow sat high off the desert floor, though just within his reach. It sang with malevolence and tasted of evil. He looked back from the butt of the arrow down its length towards his party and could just make out Erianne and Darkshadow in the light's dimness. Whoever notched the arrow and set it free had the eyesight of a night flyer. Such an enemy would be formidable.

Tul'ran examined the arrow from all sides, planning against the most immediate threat. He knew from experience he couldn't dislodge it from its path, but he could disrupt it.

Taking care not to touch the arrow's head, which the archer could have glazed with poison, Tul'ran reached behind the barb and snapped the shaft. He proceeded down the shaft to the butt, snapping the length into as many sections as possible, bending the broken lengths into different angles. The push of the bow would continue to direct the arrow in its intended path, but it would be in pieces and tumbling, instead of intact, straight, and deadly. Considering further, Tul'ran withdrew his dagger and put the tip to the point of the arrowhead. When he made solid contact, he pushed the nose of the barb down, exposing the broadside of the arrowhead to the flight path.

Satisfied he had caused as much damage as he could to the feathered menace, he walked forward along the flight path, searching for the archer.

He just about missed the Hunter.

It was only because of Tul'ran's habit of turning and scanning for enemies behind his back did he make a startling discovery. Hanging in the middle of the night was a small, glowing circle. Within the circle, yellows, oranges, and reds outlined Darkshadow, with Erianne on his back. Tul'ran inched closer.

Even with his eyes within a hand's distance of the circle, he couldn't see how or why the circle presented itself, suspended in the air. He reached out a tentative hand and found it attached to the riser of a bow. Even in this light, he should have been able to see the bow shaft.

The warrior looked to the left of the circle, and all he could spot was the pitch-black outline of the desert under a moonlit sky. Tul'ran could see nothing of Erianne and Darkshadow. He turned his head back to the circle and marveled at the precision of the outline of woman and horse, though dressed in the colors of warmth. This time, he noticed a vertical green line crossed by a horizontal green line intersecting at the point of Erianne's left breast.

Assassin.

A chill ran down his spine.

He reached out again and found the bow, traced it to a hand, the hand to an arm, then the shoulder, then the neck and head. Tul'ran traced the body with his hands. A soft material, which didn't feel like cloth, covered the body. The maker colored it well. It blended into the surrounding environment to such a degree Tul'ran couldn't differentiate the body from nature. How wondrous indeed. Tul'ran would have parted with more than a few minas to buy such clothing.

Tul'ran considered his next move. He could do so patiently; there was no doubt. Time wouldn't resume its course until he returned to his place and fit himself into the position he was in when Time came to a halt. The forces bringing Time to a screaming halt would, if he relaxed and permitted it, mold him into his return place with precision.

He walked back to the circle and traced with sensitive fingertips the outline of the thing and found where it connected to the bow. Maintaining his left hand on the riser of the bow where the edge of the thing touched it, Tul'ran removed his Knife. The Knife could cut any material as easily as could Bloodwing.

He rested the blade against the riser of the bow, taking care to keep his thumb and fingers far away from the sharp edge, and sawed. He had a small, cylindrical thing in his hand when he finished cutting. Tul'ran put the thing to his eye and swept it across the desert floor. He saw no other living bodies other than the outline of a scorpion resting about ten paces away, stinger curled high.

He turned and looked through the cylinder into the area where he knew the assassin stood, and felt astonishment again. Either the assassin possessed no warmth to kiss the object's eyes, or something blocked the body's warmth from its gaze. He swept the device back to Erianne and Darkshadow and saw them bathed in the colors of fire.

While he didn't know what the cylinder was or where it came from, he was loath to lose something like it. He found a pocket in the wide belt around his waist and tucked it away, while also replacing El Shaddai's Knife.

His doubts didn't extend to what he was going to do to the assassin. He withdrew Bloodwing with his right hand, found the assassin's arm with his left hand, and traced back to the assassin's neck. The warrior put Bloodwing to the assassin's neck and sawed until the blade had exited the other side. He also pushed as hard as he could on the head. Tul'ran knew he couldn't pull off the head while frozen in Time. The push he exerted would leave behind enough force to dislodge head from neck when Time resumed.

The Hunter didn't know it, yet, but the days of stalking human prey and killing them were no more. In this sense, the Hunter had been prescient; one or more of a woman and man would lie dead on the desert floor before the sun claimed dawn's attire.

Tul'ran cleaned Bloodwing as best he could on the assassin's clothing, which he couldn't even see in the dark, but didn't return it to the scabbard. There might yet be some blood on it he couldn't observe in the dim light. He would clean it once he returned to Darkshadow.

Satisfied he had accomplished the assassin's death upon Time returning to its course, Tul'ran withdrew the cylinder from his belt and sought his party. The warm lights gave him direction. He walked back, mindful of the arrow hanging poised in the air between him and Erianne, ready to dispense its evil purpose.

As he got closer, Darkshadow whinnied a loud greeting and tossed his head, still in the same place as when his master had left. The Sword Himself patted the enormous horse's neck and fed him another date.

"Good boy."

Tul'ran hid the cylinder once more. As he moved back into his place before Time froze, he set Bloodwing in his left hand and struggled to push it into a position in front of Erianne's left breast, where he had seen the focus of the intersecting green lines. It was an effort to get the blade into position because the forces squeezing Time to nothingness struggled against his attempts. When he felt he had provided as much protection as possible to the beautiful woman astride his horse, he relaxed.

Time snapped back into reality. Erianne screamed as the head of the arrow clanged against Bloodwing, with other pieces smashing into her body. Darkshadow startled at her scream, but his well-trained instincts translated the startle into a shiver rather than a lunge.

"*What was that!*" Again, the strange language.

"Forgive me, mistress, but I do not understand the language you just spoke."

"Something hit me," she yelled, in the Tongue.

"Something did," he acknowledged. "Are you injured, Erianne?"

So consumed was she by checking her body for injury, she failed to notice he had used her first name and cloaked it in concern and warmth.

She dashed her hands over her body.

"N-no. I think not. I remained unharmed. What was that?"

"I am grateful you are unharmed." Tul'ran reached down and passed up pieces of the broken shaft to her shaking hand.

"It was an arrow destined for your heart, but which found its destiny end on my blade."

She looked at him, goggling.

"Milord, an arrow is fast. To have time to recognize it in the dark, register its flight path, draw your sword, and place Bloodwing between my body and the incoming missile is astounding. Gods, just how good are your reflexes?"

She looked at him with wide, wary eyes. Tul'ran gathered she was genuinely frightened. He was uncertain whether her fear came from the weapon, almost dissecting her heart, or the man preventing it from happening. He couldn't let her dwell on her fear.

"Are you sure you are well, Kabolon? Did the startlement of the arrow cause you to vent your bowels into your tunic, onto my saddle, and over my horse?"

She choked on a surprised laugh and shook her head.

"No, milord, I have not soiled myself and desecrated your tack and the fine horse upon which it rests."

Darkshadow turned his head and whinnied loudly. She giggled and put her hand to his neck.

"Did I misspeak and say 'fine' horse? Nay, my tongue, more fully loosed, ought to have said, 'magnificent stallion, with bearing and might far over those of his kind.'" Darkshadow turned his head forward, mollified.

Tul'ran smiled, gladdened to see his impertinent and unpalatable question had distracted her, at least momentarily, from her apprehension. He very much didn't want her to be afraid of him.

"We have an enemy, mistress, who waits not for our coming into the city, but wishes to lay our stiff bodies at its gate. They have forewarned us; the fools. Let us venture forth and see what awaits us thirty paces ahead, for it is unlikely our foe could see well enough in the darkness to launch a strike from a greater distance."

He knew his words to be false, what with the cylinder lying warm in his belt, but wasn't ready to share its wonders just yet.

Tul'ran led them to within paces of where he knew the body of the assassin lay. Heedless of rocks in the sand, Erianne threw herself off Darkshadow's back and walked to where Tul'ran stood. Shoulder to shoulder, they advanced... and stood rooted to the spot.

The Sword Himself had expected to search in the sand for a body not easily seen for some mysterious reason. Instead, they found a cloth wrapped head laying there, still oozing blood from the severed neck into the desert floor. Nothing else remained, whether it be bow or body.

Erianne made a shocked sound, and Tul'ran reached out a comforting hand, but the Mistress of Kabolon moved forward. She leaned down and touched the severed head, feeling along its back, finding a catch, and releasing the black shroud from around the face.

It was Tul'ran's moment to swear, uttering several oaths in rapid succession.

The assassin was a woman. A woman strange in appearance. Orange hair lay short, cropped on top of her head, and she shaved the sides of her hair to mere stubble. A ring of metal looped through her right nostril, and many rings and studs adorned her ears. On her neck, just above where Bloodwing sawed through, was a picture of a flying bird painted on her skin.

Tul'ran looked at Erianne to seek her reaction, and she amazed him again. Shocked she was, but not, he thought, at the woman's appearance. It was the shock of recognition. She knew the face of her enemy, and it distressed her greatly.

"Do you know this woman?" he asked, seeking confirmation.

Erianne shook her head.

"No," she lied, standing quickly to her feet. "I do not know this woman."

For a moment they stood there, Erianne consumed in thought while looking at the head lying in the sand and Tul'ran filled with suspicion by her response. What reason would she have had to misstate the truth? The assassin had, as Tul'ran knew, clearly targeted his covenant-mistress. He didn't doubt she was distressed, but why not share what she knew?

"Forgive me for pressing, Kabolon," he persisted, "but if you know the identity of this woman and for whom she wages war, you must impart your knowledge to me as befitting our status within the covenant. I must know my enemy. It is not enough to know one face."

She shook her head, unhappy. "I tell you the truth, milord. I do not know the name of this woman."

It may be true, he thought, she didn't know the woman's name. What didn't pass her lips was the knowledge of who held this woman's oath, and why they frightened her beyond measure. A seed of mistrust worked its way into the part of his crying, 'Beware.'

"Let us then go to the city, which should be just ahead, judging by the time we have traveled. Come, I will set you to horse."

Once he saw Erianne firmly seated, he reached into a small bag for the only cloth capable of cleaning Bloodwing without being ripped to threads. After carefully wiping the Blade, he returned it to the scabbard before walking Darkshadow past the grisly scene of the bodiless head in the sand.

His mind was in turmoil. They had a foe with

access to strange things, permitting them to see in the dark. Their enemy had clothing fading body into nature so convincingly as to make them near invisible, except it didn't seem to work if the bearer died. And where was her body?

Only minutes had passed since the assassin released the arrow, and they trekked to the place of the ambush. There were no disturbances in the sand suggesting others had taken the body and fled. If they had, why would they leave the head exposed to his scrutiny? Was it their way of acknowledging his skill and their defeat? Or was there something sinister at play?

Tul'ran thought there to be far more to this maelstrom than appearances suggested, and now suspected Erianne to be not just standing victim at its center.

He was right.

CHAPTER THE SIXTH:
MERCY

Oft, it is said, the wail of the dead
Yearns for pardon where Love does not go,
Out of the shadows rode Warrior and Beauty,
To release running blood before Mercy could flow.

The city of Ur in Mesopotamia, the second day of the eighth month, 2005 BC

They walked the remaining hours to the outskirts of the city in silence, both their minds in turmoil. Soon, the sun would rise, and they could make their way into the city. A wall surrounded it, and sentries stood at the gates. They would join the lines for entrance when the sun kissed the sky, but until then, were required to wait in the desert.

Tul'ran and Erianne had stopped at a rise, enabling them to see into the vast city of Ur. This city sat near the mouth of the Euphrates, and its first king, Mesannepada, established it as a city-state in the 26th Century BC. Ur-Nammu founded the Ur III Empire and conquered the Sumerian region. Ur dominated southern Mesopotamia after the fall of the Akkadian Empire. It controlled the cities of Isin, Larsa, and Eshnunna and extended as far north as Upper Mesopotamia.

Under Ur-Nammu's son Shulgi, state control over industry reached a level never again seen in the region. Shulgi, historians said, created the Code of Ur-Nammu, one of the earliest known law codes three centuries before the more famous Code of Hammurabi. He took steps to centralize and standardize administrative processes, archival documentation, the tax system, and the national calendar. He captured the city of Susa and the surrounding region.

Ur's current King, Ibbi-Sin, came into power long after the empire rotted from within. By the time he took the throne, the empire had prospered for ninety-one years. Ibbi-Sin didn't have the military prowess of his ancestors and would rather indulge in the pleasures of the flesh than in strategizing the next campaign. Like all great empires, it fell because it rotted from within.

The city Tul'ran and Erianne purposed to enter was a bustling port on the Euphrates River, and canals wove through it like laces in a bodice. A massive, stepped pyramid, or ziggurat, rose above a city filled with merchant ships, warehouses, weaving factories, markets, and residential areas. Large factories produced wool clothes and carpets for export abroad. Ur was the center of a wealthy empire drawing traders from as far away as the Mediterranean Sea, 750 miles to the west, and the Indus civilization—called Meluhha by ancient Iraqis—some 1,500 miles to the east.

The expansive city was home to over sixty thousand people and included quarters for foreigners. It was a key trading partner with Babylon, located to the north and west of Ur.

For Erianne and her people, it proved to be a perfect place for a base of operations. It was far too busy a metropolis to concern itself with the sudden arrival of a few strangers.

The bright half-moon glowed into Ur as it crept away the remaining minutes before dawn. Here and there, torches shone, suggesting roving patrols or merchants setting out to set up their wares for early morning trade. It seemed peaceful, very much unlike the turmoil embroiling the minds of the two watchers.

Tul'ran sat near Erianne, who wrapped herself tightly in the large sheepskin throw. When Erianne had spun her elegant way-finding in the desert and came to rest, he knew full well to which city she pointed. It was Ur. Of course. It would have to be Ur.

Again, he tasted apprehension at the back of his throat, a lingering sliver of acid left by Fate's cloying tongue.

Tul'ran knew this city well. He had almost died in it.

After Tul'ran left Quil'ton, he searched for the Gutians who had ended his childhood with terror and pain. He knew they mostly dwelled in the Zagros

Mountains in the northeastern portion of Mesopotamia. The scholars he encountered told him the Gutians had widely dispersed after their empire fell, and some welcomed the anonymity of the cities.

As he worked his way south and east, he came across other villages and towns. He sold his arms to merchants and farmers seeking protection from robbers. He did so likewise for various trade caravans, which feared armed assailants in an inhospitable desert offering no protection from attack. Common criminals were no match for his military training, and none could stand against his amazing blade.

Tul'ran added gold and silver to his purse until it became too cumbersome to bear them on Darkshadow. It was then he devised a system of secreting away lesser amounts of treasure in various places, against a day when he could no longer swing his fearsome sword.

Ten years after he fled from his home as a terrified boy, he came into Ur and found the subjects of his long search. He had done as he had sworn. Gathering the four men in one place within the city, he recounted the blood chilling tale of the raping of his womenfolk and the desecration of his father's body. The second the last word left his mouth, he attacked the four men, sweeping blood back and forth across the street with savage fury until the men lay dead at his feet, carved into pieces.

The Gutians designed the meeting as a trap, something Tul'ran had not expected. A score of men started pouring into the square in which the four slaughtered Gutians lay, their minds bent on vengeance and a quick end to Tul'ran's life.

The fighting was brutal. There were no rules of fair play where Tul'ran fought one at a time.

They came at him from all sides, viciously swinging swords at his back, head, chest, and legs. With every swing of his arm, Bloodwing carved through the swords, flesh, and bone of his enemies, yet sharpened bronze found its way through Tul'ran's unearthly protection. The cuts led to bleeding, and the blood flow weakened the young warrior. Though he was two and twenty years old and strong, well-trained in mind and body, he couldn't long withstand such furious attacks from multiple quarters.

One of the attacking men threw a spear, striking him in the center of his chest, toppling him from Darkshadow's back into a lethal melee. While he kept his grip on sword and knife, he left his mount behind as the mob focused its murderous intent upon him.

A sword slashed horizontally across his left shoulder, above the biceps, and Tul'ran nearly fainted from the burning pain. The same sword slashed vertically from the top of the shoulder down the biceps, though not as deeply, and Tul'ran almost fell, barely able to swing around to carve through the man's weapon and cut through his face from right ear to left.

To his horror, as he grew weaker, Bloodwing seemed to lose its edge, no longer cutting through metal, armor, and clothing as easily as it had done. He realized then the sword's strength drew on what lived within his own body. As he grew weaker, so did

Bloodwing.

Now he knew what would happen to the mighty blade upon his death. The powerful sword given to him by a being which may or may not have been human would drain the last of his energy, feed it into the desert sand, and become just like any other dull, useless weapon long past the glory of its early years.

Tul'ran panicked. He was dying. He could feel the lifeblood sink from his veins and knew this day would be his last, and soon. In a final, desperate measure, his soul reared back and screamed his second prayer.

"El Shaddai, save me!"

Time froze.

It was the first occasion Time froze. Tul'ran looked on in bewilderment as everything around him ceased moving. The blood continued to seep from the many cuts on his body, but nothing else moved. There was no sound.

"Am I dead?" His throat, dry from caked dust, could only utter the words in a whisper.

For the first time in ten years, the ghostly tendrils he associated with the touch of El Shaddai wove their way into his brain.

"You are not dead," said the Voice, in a whisper caressing his exhausted mind. "Tell me, My child, why did it take you so long to call upon Me?"

Tul'ran dropped his head, his face covered in blood and shame.

"I forgot." His voice was soft and hoarse, pain filtering through the words.

The Voice stirred, changed, became a little sterner.

"My child, why do you kill these men?"

The question caused Tul'ran to whip his head up.

"You were there, El Shaddai. Did You not see what these men did to my mother and sisters and father? Was it not You who came to me offering me Your protection and Your gifts? I am Your oath sworn, and I have given over my life to You for pursuing justice and rebuking oppressors."

The Voice became sad, though it continued to stroke his mind with loving kindness.

"This is not justice, Tul'ran. This is vengeance. Did I not direct you vengeance was mine and only I would avenge?"

"The four men you killed who had desecrated the bodies of your family, their deaths fit within My call for justice. These other men who now lay dying at your feet were not at your farm."

"These other men have wives who rely upon their strong backs to bring home food every day. Their children look to these men for wisdom and guidance, for peace and security, for a home and sustenance for their bellies. Who will give them those things once you have shed their blood to their last heartbeat?"

Tul'ran's shame deepened. He saw the wisdom in El Shaddai's words. When the other men attacked, he only had to turn Darkshadow's head in a different direction and run away. Instead, these men became the focus of his pain, and his hatred of them led him to plunge headlong into battle.

"I'm sorry, El Shaddai. I repent of their deaths

and seek Your forgiveness. Will You extend to me Your mercy?"

"You are my Chosen Judge in this age," came the grave reply. "I will not end your life this day, but know you thusly. When you have won this battle, you shall lie in fever and pain for four and ten days. At the end of those days, you shall wash yourself in an oasis I shall provide for you. The waters of the oasis shall baptize you and make you clean in mind, body, and soul. For as long as you obey me and keep my commands, ever it shall be so. No matter where you travel, there shall be an oasis waiting for you when it is time to rest and heal. When the oasis has healed you, take half the fortune you have secreted away and give it to the widows and children of the men you have killed this day."

"Thank you, El Shaddai," Tul'ran said, relief flooding to the core of his bones. "I shall not fail You again."

"What have you learned, My child?" There was a slight edge to the prompting.

"I have learned to temper justice with mercy," he said, humility cascading in his heart. "Once I thought You to be a God of vengeance. Now I see You as a God who tempers vengeance with mercy, One who is quick to forgive and generous to provide."

The Voice stroked his mind with tender approval.

"You have learned well and grown in wisdom. When I resume Time, it will move much more slowly for your enemy than you. I will give you enough strength to kill the rest of these men, for they have all offended Me with the careless use of their swords, with the women and children they raped and abused, and with their faithlessness to their wives. But know you always it is only within My domain to avenge against those who have offended Me and not yours unless I set you on the path to their destruction. If ever you are uncertain, you have but to ask."

Tul'ran dipped his head once more. "I hear and obey, Master."

"When you have finished this ghastly task, mount Darkshadow and ride two days into the desert. I will provide sustenance there for your stallion. He, too, is my creation. For as long as you shall live, Tul'ran az Nostrom, so shall Darkshadow live and remain in his youthful vigor and strength. It was I who brought the two of you together, and it is I who will keep you whole, for I designed both of you to fulfill My works."

Then, in an instant, El Shaddai was gone. Tul'ran could feel forces around him molding his body back into the same place and form as it was before the suspension. Time moved again, although at a much slower pace, as promised. It still took a grueling effort for Tul'ran to wade through the throng of men. He killed them as he passed them by until no one remained. It took every piece of energy he had to stagger to Darkshadow, who watched him with large, luminous, worried eyes. He barely dragged himself onto the saddle, and he almost lost his place when the horse lunged away.

In a doorway, nine and ten paces away, a young Gutian crouched, protected by the shade cast by the frame, shaking and crying. His leaders had ordered him to take his place in the fight, but fear seized his heart and squeezed all desire for battle from his brain. He cowered now, in fear and shame, watching the magnificent beast carry away the monstrous warrior who had killed four and twenty men.

When he could return to his feet, he ran into the area of the city housing the Gutians. It took a large cup of wine and a sharp slap to his head to put him in a place to tell the tale.

The Gutians were far from their mountainous homes in the Zagros, and their numbers were small. Half of their fighting force lay dead in another part of Ur. Tul'ran had announced himself to the four men he had first killed, and the youth remembered his name with a vividness which would never leave his memory.

Soon, they would utter the name of Tul'ran the Sword from mouth to ear in fear and trepidation. The youth couldn't recount whether they had injured the Sword Himself in the fighting; so great had been his fear. The elders put together their heads and came to the only plausible conclusion. They had to leave before the warrior returned.

During the night, before the gates closed, all the remaining Gutians fled Ur, carrying with them the possessions with which they could travel with ease. They left behind their households, their goods, and their dead. They would spread the word of the massacre everywhere.

Not only were they talented storytellers, but their balladeers were among the best in Mesopotamia. With sweet singing voices and creative wordsmithing, they built the Ballad of Tul'ran the Sword on the backs of the dead, and it became more popular than the Songs of the Kings.

Careless with the truth, the balladeers freely embellished the tale of the Massacre at Ur with each shekel tossed at their feet by an enraptured audience. The number of the Gutian dead and the fierceness of their enemy swelled with each telling until the listener no longer knew if Tul'ran the Sword was human or demon or a mixture of both.

He might as well have been a demon. Over the next six and ten days, Tul'ran felt like he was in a place reserved for the condemned. After two days of riding, man and horse stumbled into an oasis he had never seen in the area. Tul'ran had only the strength to strip the tack and packs from his horse before he collapsed in the grass under a large date palm. The young warrior lay there for hours in agony before he could summon the strength to remove his clothing and leathers to wrap himself in an ebony cloak El Shaddai or His servants had spread out for him on the grass before he arrived.

Tul'ran endured the full measure of his punishment for four and ten days. He tried to bandage his wounds as best he could, but he couldn't reach those on his back. They became filled with pustules, and the inflammation caused further pain. Though in agony, he never once called out to El Shaddai to relieve him of his torment, knowing the punishment for his disobedience, though harsh, was fair given the lives he had taken.

After his first night of feverish dreams, he found a skin bladder at his side, filled with icy water. He drank and washed his face. Near the bladder was a very thin cake, round and colored beige. He put it to his lips and tasted it. It was a pastry laced with honey.

He ate and fell back to sleep. Each day it was the same: frosty water and the thin cake appeared at his side and nourished him for the day.

Several times, fevers wracked his body. His teeth chattered from shivering. Tul'ran was feverish to such a degree that hallucinations gathered before his eyes and tempted him with fantastic tales. On one such occasion, his mother and sisters sat around him whispering words of comfort and promises he would make a full recovery. They washed his face and fed him hot soup. Over and over, they expressed their love for him and their pride in the man he had become.

He cried when he saw their exquisite faces; asked for and received their kisses. It was the first time in the entire ordeal he could fall asleep amid the pain.

At the end of the fourteenth day, the pain vanished. He raised his head and saw a pool within two hand spans of where he lay. Tul'ran crawled to the waters of the oasis. He climbed into their chill. The broken warrior drank, floated with his face to the desert sun, and luxuriated in the water for what seemed like hours.

When he took himself out of the water, he noted with shock his wounds had healed into thin scars. El Shaddai had shown His goodness and kindness, Tul'ran thought. He had learned his lesson well. He now understood the difference between justice and vengeance, mercy and unforgiveness. It wouldn't be a mistake he'd commit again.

"Milord Tul'ran." The soft voice of Erianne of Kabolon brought him to the present with a start. So deep in thought was he, the rise of the sun against the morning sky didn't come to his attention. It was time to learn the fate of her people.

He glanced at her sitting in the morning sun; the sheepskin draped around her shoulders, a worried look on her face. He gave her what he hoped was a comforting smile and nodded.

"Please forgive me, Mistress, for losing myself in the trappings of my thoughts. Are you ready to journey forth and discover what has become of your father?"

"Indeed, I am," she said. "Do we walk or ride?"

Tul'ran looked once more to the sky and adjudged several hours had gone by. The time they sat waiting to enter the city would have refreshed Darkshadow.

"We ride. Arise, Kabolon."

Tul'ran asked for and received the sheepskin covering her shoulders, whereupon he rolled it and placed it back into the large leather bag. He swung the black cloak from his back and leveraged it about her. The cape was long on him, but with her three-inch advantage over his height, the cloak came to the bottom of her ankles. It would do.

Again, she presented a shapely foot to Tul'ran's cupped hands. He hoisted her into the saddle. Once sat, he arranged the cloak around her so it covered her tunic and some of Darkshadow's rump. With her beauty and her poise, Erianne looked regal.

Tul'ran undid the scabbard from about his waist. One of the wondrous gifts of the scabbard was if he tied it, thus and so, he converted it from a belt around his waist to one about his shoulders. Such a configuration held Bloodwing almost vertically, with the hilt splitting the gap between his head and right shoulder.

Tul'ran preferred to cross draw the Blade from its scabbard at his hip. Erianne's presence behind his back made the movement more awkward than usual. Also, drawing Bloodwing from the scabbard at his back produced a long, dramatic arc. It emphasized the danger of the moment for those whose life he would measure in seconds if they the wrong decision made. Intimidation saved lives.

Tul'ran slipped onto Darkshadow's back in front of Erianne and turned the great stallion's nose to the city's entrance.

"Ur," he said, lethality dripping like shards of metal from his teeth. "I come."

Erianne heard the words and shuddered. She didn't understand the context behind the utterance or the venom dripping from the words, but it was a threat, to be sure. The peaceful city laying in the desert below was about to get a visit from darkness born of a world filled with horror.

Their ride through the gates was uneventful. Though they stood out from the throng, no one sought to challenge their passage. All made way for the horse and its riders. Tul'ran and Erianne wound their way through the tight city streets, cramped with people and outdoor displays. They ignored the beseeching cries of the merchants, as Erianne guided him with subtle nudges to his sides in the direction they should go.

Darkshadow had not quite neared her hutch when Fate chose again to raise its serpent head.

"There she is!"

Tul'ran brought Darkshadow to an abrupt halt as a large merchant, a living fountain of arrogance, stepped in front of the warhorse. Erianne's body tensed behind him. The merchant was taller than Erianne, which made him much taller than Tul'ran. He was a large man, but fat, instead of muscle, made up his bulk.

The shopkeeper dressed himself in a blue tunic running from head to toe and wore about his substantial girth a sash made of silk. They would make good funeral clothing, Tul'ran decided.

The merchant had long, oiled hair, and a thick, brown beard covered his face. His eyes held a strange mixture of anger, jealousy, and want.

The merchant wasn't a pleasant sight, but then again, Tul'ran had killed worse.

He replied to the merchant in a smooth, agreeable tone, containing not a bit of the impatient irritation he felt at being brought to a halt in such a way.

"Merchant, I am on urgent business. Stand aside."

The merchant didn't budge, nor lessen his anger. He seemed to get more incensed with Tul'ran's casual dismissal of his presence.

"Listen, you half-wit gnome, the woman seated behind you is mine! I offered payment for the bitch and staked my claim with her father. Give her to me, now! She is my property!"

Tul'ran's body tightened, and his energy grew colder. His pride wouldn't let him tolerate insults to either of them. This fool was giving Tul'ran's sword arm more than enough incentive to let loose.

The thought gave him pause. If he killed the merchant, the King's guards would come in such quantities not even a legendary swordsman could overcome the onslaught. They would have to flee the city before Erianne had one word of what happened to her people. He reminded himself his duty to Erianne outweighed a prideful desire to part the merchant's head from his shoulders.

He also remembered full well the number of dead at his hands, so displeasing to El Shaddai the last time he was in this city. It wouldn't serve his reputation, however, to leave the slurs unanswered. Tul'ran shifted in the saddle to give greater freedom to his drawing hand.

"Merchant," he said, the serenity in his voice belying the tension in his body. "We perceive differently, you and I. A woman is not property to be bought and sold with abandon. She is a free and independent person with the same rights as you. To this woman behind me have I pledged my protection in covenant. Your claim, whatever you think it may be, is subordinate to my covenant with her. Stand aside and let us pass."

"I am Vebrax of Ur!" the other man said with a roar, fully enraged. His loud shout drew the attention of the hawkers and vendors standing nearby, and several turned to watch. "You will give me what's mine, or I shall take it over your broken little body!"

Tul'ran's eyebrows pitched up. He had had enough. Boosting the volume of his voice so the entire square could hear it, he answered with icy shards of despair-filled eternity glistening from each syllable.

"*I* am Tul'ran az Nostrom, the Sword Himself, Master of Bloodwing the Blade, Taker of Souls!"

"I am Death and I have come for you."

Tul'ran uttered the last words so coldly, so deeply, Erianne shivered despite the warm cloak enwrapping her. As he spoke the last words, Tul'ran reached back and drew Bloodwing in a mighty arc, and brought it to bear at his side.

The words had an immediate effect.

Vebrax turned white. His eyes became enormous. He seemed to shrink within his frame as his mouth dangled open. They knew his name here. His legend started here and, as the ensuing seasons passed, became larger with each excited telling. Death sat before him on a horse colored the night sky, and he had called his doom upon himself by failing to see it sooner. Vebrax couldn't move. He couldn't speak.

He wasn't alone.

The entire square had stopped its bustle, and everyone stared at the confrontation, transfixed, as if they were rabbits waiting for a snake to strike.

Tul'ran nudged Darkshadow forward and brought Bloodwing's tip almost into contact with Vebrax's chest. Vebrax wanted to throw himself on the ground, plead for mercy, beg for forgiveness, barter for his life, but his body and mind had abandoned him, as if he was already in the paralysis of death.

"Vebrax of Ur, I give you one chance for life. *One* chance! Answer this, my next question, with every shard of honesty you may have left in your corrupt, covetous body, and I shall let you live. Deceive me and your wives shall be widows and your children shall mourn for a father who was too stupid to live."

"I have pledged my sword to this woman by

blood oath. Blood oath! Someone took her from her home near the place where your life now stands in peril. Six Gutians, whose designs for her included rapine and death, stole her from her father. It should not surprise you those barbarians even now scream for mercy in eternal flames, for into my hands destiny delivered them and by my hands were they slaughtered. I am told you laid claim to this woman with her father, and her father had turned you aside."

Beads of sweat had formed on Vebrax's forehead, and he agonized as he felt a gush of urine spray down his leg.

"Here is my inquiry, Vebrax. Your life depends on the truthfulness of your answer. Did you hire the Gutians to pursue this woman and return her to you, or sell her to the flesh markets of Babylon if she would not have you of her own free will?"

The merchant convulsed his head back, willing every other muscle in his body to stay still for fear of antagonizing the blade set almost against his chest.

"No, milord Tul'ran, Mighty Lord, no, I did not! By every god in this world and in every heaven, do I swear I had nothing to do with the abduction you have described! I abjure it, for only animals would do to a Lady what you have expressed."

Tul'ran looked into the man's eyes and could smell the stench of fear off his skin. Afraid he was; terrified of his promised death. But there was no duplicity in him. Vebrax didn't know about the plot to seize Erianne. Tul'ran was sure of it.

The insults Vebrax had hurled at him and Erianne angered him. While they stung his ego and wounded his pride, they, in themselves, were not sufficient reasons to send the man to stand before El Shaddai. He had no feeling El Shaddai needed this man's life this day to judge him for his sins. Tul'ran sighed to himself.

With a nudge of his heels, Darkshadow stepped back, and Tul'ran replaced Bloodwing into its sheath. He could feel Erianne's relief vibrating into his back. Vebrax stood rooted to the spot, still uncertain as to his future.

"Merchant, I find you have spoken the truth. Heed my warning. Never again let your shadow cross mine or this woman's, for should it do so, I will kill you within the space of one breath and spit on your corpse as you fall. Stand aside!"

Vebrax didn't just stand aside. He lunged sideways and threw himself face first into the ground, relief flooding through him in waves. The Sword Himself had humiliated him, yes, and tattered his status in the community, but he had looked into the face of Death and lived.

He would tell this story well, even though it made him sound lesser in the ears of the hearer, but it would be a warning ballad, a clarion call, to all who failed to recognize Tul'ran az Nostrom when they came under his gaze. He could once more measure his life in years.

The team hunting Erianne of Kabolon planned to end her life in hours and minutes, not years.

They followed the warrior and the woman through Ur, keeping to shadows and enclosures. Trained to stay out of sight until the moment was right to strike, they kept a distance between themselves and their target.

There were four of them now. They found the headless body of their colleague in the desert, and it outraged them. Their training couldn't answer the question of how their quarry killed a skilled assassin, which elevated their rage further.

Erianne would answer for her death.

Soon.

CHAPTER THE SEVENTH:
TREPIDATION

Between Erianne the Dark and Tul'ran was made
A covenant of blackest desire,
A wrong to avenge, justice to serve,
And enemies to cast in the fire.

"Would I insult you if I said I am relieved, milord Tul'ran?"

Tul'ran turned his head to inspect Erianne's face, as Darkshadow stepped jauntily through the crowded streets.

"In what way are you relieved, Mistress?"

"Forgive me, milord. I do not know you well enough to understand the limits of your anger or the dimensions of your patience. I was certain Vebrax was a dead man when he challenged you."

Tul'ran grinned, but there was more savagery than mirth in it.

"If I killed every fool who stood in my path and thoughtlessly hurled insult, the physicians would no longer have custom. Who am I to deny them their wealth?"

Erianne leaned forward and pressed her body against his back, mindless of the pleasant sensations she sent coursing through the warrior's veins.

"I thank you for staying your hand. You know how eager I am to see what has become of my party, which eagerness escalated with the discovery of the assassin now lying dead within easy riding distance of this city. I feared the intercession of the fool, Vebrax, would delay the satisfaction of my need to know what happened to my people."

Erianne had felt apprehension and excitement building within her as they came within minutes of the small clay structure her group claimed as home. Enwrapped in her thoughts as she was over unification with her party, she hadn't seen the merchant lunge in front of Darkshadow.

As Vebrax acted the clown and insulted her in front of the Sword Himself, Erianne panicked. She thought the idiot would ruin everything. She had held her breath when Tul'ran drew his sword. Erianne was certain the merchant wouldn't put another morsel of food into his fat belly.

To her amazement, the Prince of Death stayed his hand. She had heard Tul'ran was dangerous, not merciful. His dangerousness came from a mind twisted by hatred, vengeance, and grief. Erianne couldn't fathom where he learned mercy.

She remembered watching him when he was brooding upon her Telling. He had sat long in one position, wrapped up in dark thoughts that blackened his face and twisted it into something almost not human. It had filled her with dread.

She thought at the time it was her Telling forcing his face into such harsh lines. Even though he had been looking down at his hands the whole time, she sensed the powerful emotions in his stare. She couldn't glean whether he was upset at her situation or if she wasted his time with a story he wouldn't believe.

Her fear of him had tempted her to just stick her dagger in him while his dark reverie ensnared him and take her chances with his horse. It was well she had thought better of it. This was Tul'ran the Sword, Deliverer of Death. She would have gained a quick end to her life down such a path and nothing more.

She had watched him in the desert before they entered the city, as another grim trance consumed all his attention. Erianne wondered about the things she didn't know about him. She knew, now, what had set a young boy to hunger for death and vengeance. There was more darkness to his story, she suspected. The depth of the cost to his mind and soul was unfathomable. She shook her head to return her mind to the present.

"Milord, at the next vendor, turn to your left, I beg of you. At the end of the row of residences is my hutch."

Tul'ran reached down to stroke the sweaty neck of his stallion.

"We are near the end of this night's journey, brother. Soon you will have food and drink, and a place to lay your head."

The stallion snorted and tossed his head, as if decrying a mighty war horse such as him needed trivialities such as food, drink, and sleep. Tul'ran laughed and clucked at him.

Erianne returned to her thoughts. Tul'ran was a mystery, but not the fun kind. There were things about him that made little sense. His relationship with his horse was a part of it. When he told her how old he was, something in her brain rose to the surface like a whale breaching the water. He was thirty-one years old. His confessed age meant the glorious beast of a horse upon whose back she rode was eighteen years old. Despite his age, the warhorse was powerful and had the energy of a colt. Something was wrong and, as always, it was in the math. Even his reference to his age was off. In this culture, people referred to their ages as 'journeys around the sun' or similar allusions. Tul'ran used the word 'years,' as did she.

After he recounted his history, she felt dazed, uncertain, and her head spun, just a little. Especially after the tale of how he gained his sword. 'Unbelievable' wasn't a strong enough word for his yarn.

He wasn't what she expected. The threats to her life were not what she expected, either.

Erianne trembled.

Tul'ran turned to glance back at her again.

"Are you well, Mistress Kabolon?"

"Forgive me, milord. I felt a trembling of fear tug at the edges of my mind as I reflected upon the grisly sight of the decapitated head we left behind on the sand."

"Ah, yes, our enigmatic and unknown enemy."

What did he mean? Did he know she had lied? She told Tul'ran the truth when she said she didn't know the woman, but she knew very well the name of the group to whom the woman belonged and what they wanted.

"My enemy desires my death; there is no doubt. My adversaries, whoever they may be, found me with ease and had enough time to set a hunter in my path. The thought makes my heart quail, milord."

She couldn't say to him these were people fanatical in their beliefs and they joyfully plunged into pursuing their fanaticism, heedless of the threat to self and mortality.

"How I became their enemy, their target, I do not know. I fear my father and his party may know extremely well. I feel as skittish as a colt, looking for ambush in every shadow."

"Fear not, Kabolon. You ride with me. Nothing more will transpire this day."

There he was, tempting Fate again. 'When would he learn?' she thought.

The rest of the short ride turned out to be uneventful. People passed word of what took place in the square at the speed of lightning. As they rode, the crowds parted in front of them as if they were the bow of a ship splitting the sea. No one interrupted them again as they approached the doorway to a small clay structure.

Erianne found the door, which the barbarians had shattered from its place when they broke in to take her, restored and whole.

"Milord, I am happy to report my relief. I can tell

from the edgings and frame of the door my people took steps to repair it. They had returned without harm. Whether they remain safe is yet a question to be decided."

Tul'ran slid down from Darkshadow's back and surveyed the area behind them.

"All appears calm and peaceful, though we know well the dangers concealable in serenity."

He offered a hand to Erianne to help her down, which she accepted despite the lack of need.

"I will enter first, Mistress Kabolon. Should you hear combat from within, mount Darkshadow and ride away quickly. If our enemy lies in ambush, I will deny them their prize."

The warrior drew Bloodwing and pushed open the door, sliding in fast, vigilance high, expecting violence, and meeting only silence. After a moment, he came out and gave her a nod. Erianne entered the place and looked around in various areas, touching several things.

Her party had left her clues. They positioned subtle signs in the way they placed things, so, and moved, thus, to impart a story not plain to the undiscerning eye. Her people had returned and found the door shattered, with her gone, taken by violence. They couldn't follow nor mount a rescue.

It was ironic the Gutians targeted her for abduction because she was the only one with the martial skills and training to protect the party. A shudder rippled across her slender shoulders. Or maybe her capture was by design. The rest of her group were scholars, skilled academicians, not gifted with physical strength or martial training. They would be as helpless as children against an enemy bent on their harm. She had to find them.

The telltales they arranged with purpose told a straightforward story. They left for the other camp at once after ascertaining the violence of her disappearance. The party would wait for her there. If she failed to return within a specified time, they would, out of necessity for their own safety, leave.

She had to catch up with them. They were her only way home.

She whirled around to see Tul'ran watching her with a look of keen interest on his face. She composed herself to the Tongue and spoke.

"Milord, with the state of this house, I am gladdened to say my father and others traveling with him arrived in safety. Not finding me here and captured, they abandoned this house to return to the place of our origin. I fear they are in grave danger. Last night, we found an assassin intent on ending my life. I fear persons such as she may be intent on ending my father's life as well. I must go to them with all haste, to preserve them from harm."

A shadow fell across the face of the Sword Himself.

"Your father left without mounting a rescue?" he asked in a calm enough tone, but there was no mistaking the condemnation in his voice nor the offer of violence against a man who would leave his daughter to the fate promised by the broken door.

"My father no longer has your physical capability, Mighty Warrior. His charges are scholars who have never known a blade, much less swung one. Were he to recruit them to a rescue, they would have been more likely to injure themselves than anyone else."

To her relief, he smiled.

"I have met men such as those you have described, and I can understand your father's reluctance. Even so, when would he have responded to the violence he found here and the abduction of his daughter?"

'Never' was the answer she couldn't give him. The Protocols were clear. She either returned on her own or not at all. She expected even now the phrase "I told you so" was flying around at will, where her party camped.

"It will take much time for my father to gather a force of sufficient might and worth to challenge an enemy of strength and numbers unknown. I am certain he works the challenge even now."

Tul'ran nodded, his face an impassive mask.

"Do you continue to bind me to your quest, Kabolon?"

The question startled her. She hadn't considered their covenant might end when she returned to this place. She looked at him standing in the doorway, taller in spirit than his physical height. He was a living anomaly, Death captured in human form with such precision Fear itself was afraid of him. He held Bloodwing as a man might hold a beautiful but deadly lover. Blade and Warrior, as much one as metal and man could be. Desire rushed through her as she took in his rugged face and serious dark eyes.

She definitely didn't want him to go.

"Milord, I fear my enemy is still before me, though I know not their want or design. My life is forfeit if they should find me, and I would not wish them to find me without the comfort of your strength at my side."

He nodded, his face pleasant.

"I am your oath sworn, Kabolon. I am yours until you release me or until one of us dies. What is our next action?"

"We must go with haste to my father's camp, a two-day journey hence. But not through the day, if I am of the requisite understanding?"

He smiled.

"You are. We ought to partake of food, water, and sleep while the sun beats down upon the sand. Is there a place where I might stable Darkshadow?"

"Indeed," she said, gesturing to the back of the place, "we were careful to gain an abode with accommodation for horses. There is a small alley between these structures, which leads to a tiny enclosure in the back. The previous owner covered half the compound with a thatched roof. It should have hay and water. While you attend to Darkshadow's needs, I will find us some nourishment."

Tul'ran saluted her with Bloodwing and left through the front door, making sure he closed it. After sheathing the blade, he led Darkshadow to the narrow alley between structures and through to the back. He found a small enclosure with a rudimentary gate. It wouldn't hold a horse determined to leave, but Darkshadow wouldn't leave without him.

Tul'ran removed the tack from the tall, black horse and set it aside. After taking off the blanket, he withdrew a brush from the leather bag and brushed the stallion. He checked Darkshadow's legs and feet.

Then he found hay in a wicker basket set aside in one corner of the enclosure. He smelled it and rubbed it between his fingertips. It was of good quality. There was water in a container near the hay, and he invited Darkshadow to partake of both hay and water, which the stallion did with eagerness.

Darkshadow plunged his nose into the feed. Tul'ran stroked his neck.

"Do you know the depth of my love for you, my fearsome brother? You bore a new person on your back today, the first since me, with grace and forbearance. I am ever in awe of your intelligence, strength, and might. Know of all my treasure, you are my most-valued jewel."

Darkshadow snorted and tossed his head, sending dust from the hay rising into the enclosure like the white seeds of dandelions. Tul'ran laughed.

"Ever one for terse conversation, are you? I leave you to your meal, you great lout."

Satisfied he had taken care of his horse's needs; Tul'ran picked up the leather bag and moved to return to the house. As he passed through the enclosure, he noted with interest another set of tack laying on a blanket, neatly folded, in one corner. It would do for a medium-sized horse.

Erianne moved to a corner of the hut right after the warrior had left. There was a hole dug into the earth in which her group had placed several clay jars. The shade afforded by the structure made the earth beneath the hut cool. The clay in the surrounding soil added insulation, which kept chill the contents of the clay jars. Such a system of jars and clay cellars acted as a refrigerator, although nothing stayed fresh for long. Erianne opened each clay jar and found only one to have something in it: fresh water. Her compatriots had done a thorough job of sanitizing the hut, including removing all the food they had stored underground.

The front door opened as Erianne withdrew the jar of water from the clay shelter. She turned to present the jar to Tul'ran.

He raised one inquiring eyebrow, and she said, "I have water to offer you, milord, but little of anything else. I fear there is no food within this dwelling."

The corners of his lips moved upward in amusement.

"Then it shall be necessary for us to return to the marketplace to buy sustenance. Perhaps Vebrax will supply us with food. It would be an amusing sight, though I hope he has changed his tunic since last we saw him. It will also be necessary to purchase a horse for you because I am loath to walk the desert one more night."

She looked at him, a little alarmed.

"Forgive me, milord. I fear my purse will be inadequate for the task. While I have some means by which to buy food, there is not enough to purchase a horse of abundant vitality to take me through the desert."

Again, the eyebrow.

"We are bound in covenant, Mistress Kabolon. Should you not have the means, I bear the expense, and gladly. I am sure we will find ways for you to repay the debt."

The last sentence startled her, but he spoke it as

he was turning to the door, and she couldn't see his expression. The implication of his words confused her. She hoped for a meaning which wouldn't cause her stomach to clench in anticipation of unwanted sexual advances.

A disturbing thought then crept its way into her mind. Would they be so unwanted? Had she not looked at him and lingered her gaze on his face, his body, and arms? Oh, those arms! Would it be such a terrible thing if those dark eyes turned to her inviting passion, and would the asking be unwelcomed?

She shook her head, a brief longing casting her mind into confusion. There were rules, she knew, very, very strict rules against contemplating a physical relationship with this man. Rules, which, if broken, would be used to break her, truly.

Before they left, Erianne glanced down at herself and halted. Tul'ran spun to look at her, concern creasing his forehead.

"What is it, mistress?"

She felt the tinge of a blush touch her cheeks.

"Milord, I have wandered through the desert all night, though riding, by your grace. This tunic has seen better days, and I fear it will bring unwelcome attention. Might I have a moment to splash water on my face and adorn myself in clothing less damaged?"

Tul'ran half-bowed at the waist.

"Who am I to deny the necessity of my covenant-mistress? Pray, continue. I will wait outside, for I see nothing in this abode giving you privacy once you divest yourself of your clothing." He turned and walked out the door, closing it behind him to take up a post on the right side of it.

Erianne turned to the spot where she kept her bag. She was distressed it wasn't in its place. She knew the barbarians took nothing with them when they seized her. Perhaps a thief took it, taking advantage of the busted door. Or perhaps her party had taken it to leave no evidence of their stay behind. She felt a little frantic as she cast her gaze around the room until her eyes rested on a small pile of detritus lying in one shadowed corner of the hut. It wasn't there before.

She moved the detritus aside and saw, with relief, her black leather bag under the pile.

Those who made the bag constructed it in such a clever way it would unfold into a garment bag, but looked ordinary when bound up. She laid out the bag and opened it. She sat, stunned for a moment. Her possessions were gone. There were only two different garments in the bag.

The first was what she termed, with affection, as her "battle gear." Before she left for Ur, she found a description of Tul'ran's battle leathers. She had copied them without shame, having regard only for modifications to her height and delicious curves.

Leggings of leather covered her entire lower limbs and ended in a soft leather shoe of sorts. Over the shoes went a pair of long leather boots, designed to end at the knee. She couldn't resist adding a flair; she made the top of the boots a little longer and wider so she could overlap the top of the boot over her knee. The leather breeches and boots enhanced the effect of her long, supple legs, much to the consternation of the men in her party.

While Tul'ran's tailors dyed his chiton in royal

colors, hers was a plain beige. Overlaying the chiton was a leather vest in Tul'ran's style, but in a plain brown leather as opposed to the red. As well, the collar at the back of her vest rose higher, to the base of her skull, to supply protection to the back of her neck. Both the chiton and leathers were light, supple, and much, much stronger than they looked.

She toyed with putting on her battle gear and discarded it with a muffled giggle. Erianne could only imagine the look on the fearsome warrior's face as they promenaded through the city as twins.

The woman laid her battle gear aside, pulled away a black cloth covering the second item of clothing, and sat bewildered. This she hadn't brought with her from the other camp. It was a tunic dyed in royal purple, with a white hem the width of her thumb encircling the base of the throat and cascading down the front of the tunic in a vertical line. There were a multitude of precious gems sewn within the hem: rubies, sapphires, diamonds, and emeralds.

Her party left her a waist chain of solid twenty-four karat gold links. Though made strong with a subtle alloy, she could separate each link from the chain and then, without effort, break them into pieces for use as currency. Her party had left her a dress fit for a Queen.

What they took away with them was a disaster.

Her coin was gone.

Erianne felt panic grab her throat and squeeze her chest as her breathing became labored. She wanted to scream in abject terror.

They were going to abandon her.

The dress and jewels were a survival kit. She held

in her hands a massive fortune by the day's standards. She could hire a small army and live in comfort for the rest of her days. Her panic increased. The rest of her days without family, loved ones, children, alone. Alone!

Just as her mind started a downward spiral into grief and despair, she heard a discrete cough from the doorway.

"Mistress," Tul'ran said, amusement plain in his voice, "May I remind you I yet stand here exposed to the heat of the midday sun?"

Her fear and despair popped like a soap bubble. 'Have some sense,' she scolded herself. The voice at the door was proof positive she wasn't alone.

The bejeweled dress and gold she held would only be necessary if she didn't make it to her party in time, and it wasn't a foregone conclusion. Of course, they would take her coin with them. Its value far exceeded the value of its base metal. It wouldn't do to have the coin fall into the wrong hands if she hadn't returned to the hutch.

"One moment more, milord, I pray thee. I am almost ready."

She discarded her dirty, tattered black-green shift and left it near the bag. She would need it again; such was her misfortune. One didn't ride through the desert on a horse dressed in Queen's livery.

She noted with a flare of gratitude her party had left her several pairs of underwear. They were considerate, at least. Within a few minutes she dressed in regal accoutrements, complete with a waist chain and a set of shoes both practical and fashioned for the period. Her hair would have to stay loose, she decided. Her escort was baking in the sun, and she didn't have time to put up her hair. Nor did she have time to apply charcoal around her eyes, which was the local custom for women.

Erianne opened the door and stepped onto the street with a flourish. Tul'ran turned, a smart comment bubbling on his lips, but no sound passed. He stood there for a moment, eyes wide, gaping at her. When he found his brain, lost as it was in wonder at the sight of her, he spoke with an undeniable warmth.

"Erianne, you are exquisite."

She blushed to the full depth of her cheekbones. Erianne noticed, this time, not only did he say her first name, a sign of intimacy, but he spoke it with affection. She curtsied.

"Milord, you flatter me with your kindness."

His expressive eyebrows danced on his forehead.

"If it is kindness to acknowledge beauty to be the subject of every ballad from here to the end of time, then am I pleased to extend such compassion to you."

His words, his look, flashed warmth through her body and bred feelings she had to deny if she were to survive this place.

"I have heard it said warriors melt if exposed too long to the heat of the day," she said, coyness shading her words. "Should we not go forth?"

He laughed, but took her direction. He turned aside to allow her to walk a half pace ahead of him, as was her right. A warrior escorting a Queen would never walk at her shoulder. Erianne turned to his left side and touched his shoulder without thinking, still distracted by the feelings racing through her body. He glanced at her, amazed at her touch, but said nothing.

"Milord, ought we not find some way of securing Darkshadow, or bringing him with us? He is a magnificent horse and may have fallen under the gaze of covetous eyes."

Tul'ran nodded. "I have your point, Mistress, and you make it well."

He turned to face the houses on the cramped street, knowing there were ears behind doors and shuttered openings. His voice once more rang with crystal clarity into the street, the words plain and the meaning clear.

"Ur. I, Tul'ran the Sword, declare the following oath."

Tul'ran spat into the earth at his feet, mixing the fluid of his body with dirt in a ritual as old as the ground itself.

"We return in short order to this abode. Should anyone take, touch, or interfere with my horse, then I shall find that person. Even if it takes my entire life, I shall track him to the ends of the world. I shall stake him under a desert sun and slowly cut open his bowels so the creatures living there will have sustenance for days. As he dies, in pain reserved only for the deepest depths of the demonic realm, I shall recount to him how his wife, father, mother, sons, daughters, nieces, nephews, and cousins will lose their lives at my hands because of his greed and stupidity. All of this I swear, as if I make this oath on blood spilled between us."

Erianne looked down at him, wide-eyed. She

gazed around the street, seeing no obvious response, but could imagine the oath was already being transmitted as fast as they had heard it.

"Well, your speech should do it. Let us pray we do not fall into circumstances preventing our return. It would be a shame to have Darkshadow starve to death because no one dares to come within one hundred paces of this place."

Tul'ran grinned, a pleasant sight on his relaxed face.

"We will not tarry long enough for it to be a concern. I am rested and armed. We have already met one fool. Should there be others who might have thought of crossing swords with me for my horse, they would have laughed at the folly of Vebrax of Ur by this time, and will think twice on their reckoning."

Realization dawned.

"You made an example of him."

"I did, for I have no desire to take the lifeblood of any man in Ur if I can avoid it. There was a time when the arm of Tul'ran the Sword made blood run like a river in the streets of this city. I have no desire for a repeat."

Intrigued, Erianne sought his gaze, which roamed through the streets ahead, to the sides, and behind.

"I would have the tale if it were within your desire to tell it."

"Perhaps another time," he said, his mind taken up with his surveillance of their surroundings.

The marketplace was alive with people churning about, their shouts and pleading cries clashing like gulls over the ocean. There was much activity, as people rushed from place to place to sample wares and bargain prices. Erianne saw rugs of diverse sizes and bright colorations thrown at the feet of a prospective buyer, the merchant expounding with excitement on the quality of the weave and the thread count. Others were hawking pots and cooking utensils right next to beggars sitting in rags, reeking of unwashed bodies and breath, holding out scab-encrusted arms for some pittance.

Here and there, ladies dressed in the time's fashion and guarded by armed men whose eyes scanned the marketplace without resting, would touch some fine jewelry presented by anxious artisans. As the gems lying in their delicate hands tempted them, they wondered just how angry their husbands would be if they were to add more jewels to their already bounteous collection.

The market was alive with trading, haggling, anger, joy, hope, and despair. It offered every flavor a city could extend. It was exhilarating.

As Tul'ran and Erianne walked, people watched them, but with side glances and not open stares. They were an oddity. She, with her regal dress, stunning beauty, and height, standing taller than the warrior. He, with his broad shoulders, scarred leather, and the ever-present blade positioned high above his back.

The two of them commented on wares, laughed at playing children, and complimented artistic pieces. Women swooned over her dress and jewels. Men re-directed their wives' attention with haste. Were Tul'ran and Erianne not Killer and Queen walking with purpose, one might have thought them a couple out for a mid-afternoon stroll.

They stood, after wandering for an hour, before an enclosure holding four horses of different ages and conditions. Tul'ran gazed with the eyes of an expert over the lines of the horses in the cage, noting their age, health, and physical condition. His eye settled on a mare of medium height, dressed all in a coat of brown with legs and feet to accommodate her frame. She was young, strong, and a beauty in her own right. She would do.

Tul'ran caught the eye of the vendor and gestured him forward with a tilt of the head. The vendor scrabbled to him, inclining his shoulders toward the earth, and lowering his eyes.

"Milord Tul'ran, Master of Death, how may I be of service to you?" the merchant said, not daring to look the famed warrior in the eyes.

"I would have the brown mare with the long mane and tail. How much will you take for her?"

The merchant raised his hands, palms outward, on each side of his face.

"I would not presume to bargain with the legendary Sword Himself," he said, a grimace of fear in the rat shaped face. The mare was young and healthy. He had been counting on her to fetch a profit for his family. With a sinking stomach, he foresaw his profit trotting away at the end of a lead held by the most fearsome warrior in the region. "The mare is yours, mighty lord, my gift to you. Take her with my blessing and the blessings of my house."

Tul'ran shook his head. He read the merchant's face and knew the reasoning behind the merchant's offering. "I have not rendered service to you worthy of such a present. Nor will I render service to you while I am bound by oath to the woman who walks at my side. Therefore, I will pay a market price for the mare."

The merchant shook; the encounter had lasted far longer than he would have liked.

"If it must be a price," he said, his voice unsteady, "then pay me two pieces of silver and she shall be yours."

Again, Tul'ran shook his head.

"You deny yourself profit where it is unnecessary. Were you to sell this mare in Babylon's markets, you could, with a little haggling, get seven and ten pieces of silver for her. Of course, you would have to care for her well during the travel. You would face the uncertainty of her arrival in good health and condition. The cost would be at least one shekel of silver to take her to market, leaving you a profit of six and ten shekels. Such is the price I offer you for this mare: six and ten shekels of silver."

It was a generous offer. Tul'ran had overstated the price of the mare by at least eleven shekels of silver, but he had noticed the gauntness of the merchant's form and correctly surmised the merchant's earnings worked first to feed his family and then to feed his stock. What money remained, as little as it was, found its way into the merchant's skinny belly. This offer would give the merchant a sound profit for the month, if not for the year.

The merchant was nodding, his head bobbing up and down with eagerness, and held out his hands. "If your lordship will be so kind as to fill these hands with six and ten shekels of silver, then the mare is yours with my blessing and the blessings of my family to the third generation."

Tul'ran fought to keep a smile from his lips. A smile wouldn't do. He didn't want to diminish his reputation as a predatory dealer of death while he and Erianne were walking without warriors at their backs in this city. He counted out six and ten shekels of silver and placed them in the merchant's hands. The merchant entered the enclosure, put a rope around the mare's neck, and led her to the Sword Himself.

Tul'ran took the lead rope from the merchant's hands and passed it to Erianne.

"Now you have a horse to call your own."

The gesture touched Erianne deep within her heart, and tears threatened to mist her eyes. She looked down at the merchant and nodded her thanks.

"Does she have a name?"

The merchant looked flabbergasted. "I beg your pardon, Your Majesty. Do you inquire if I named this animal?"

Tul'ran took Erianne's left elbow and turned her away, saying in a quiet voice, "Perhaps Your Majesty will honor this horse with a naming rather than having it chosen by someone who had not the presence of mind to appreciate her beauty and baptize her with identity."

Erianne took her cue, lifted her chin, and led the mare back towards the vendors of food. She couldn't resist sending a jibe in Tul'ran's direction.

"Surely the reputation of Tul'ran the Sword suffers this day."

He glanced at her, raising an eyebrow.

"How so?"

"When last I heard your Ballad, milord Tul'ran, the singer's voice wavered as he sang about a man over six cubits in height, with shoulders as wide as the stave on a cart. Fearsomely long are your fangs, according to legend, from which blood drips as you bite into the hearts you remove from your kill. Your eyes are as red as coals, and fire bursts from your mouth when you roar. How shall the image prevail against the story of a sweet man who purchased a horse for triple her worth from a vendor who counts his profits as thinly as his frame?"

Tul'ran boomed out a laugh, startling several merchants nearby.

"You are astute in your observations. I was not aware I had become such a monster in the eyes of the people. To overcome your fears, Your Majesty, I will strive to glare at even the children playing at our feet."

Erianne giggled.

The sun was warm, but not uncomfortably so.

She walked through crowds of people who were quick to show their respect with friendly, if slightly fearful, smiles and a bend in the neck and head.

The merchants offered them free food, which Tul'ran and Erianne declined with grace. Both knew how hard these people had to work to bring their products to market, and neither was minded to take advantage.

They paid generously for unleavened bread, a block of goat cheese, a clay jar of goat's milk, and some sort of dried meat. They left behind them broad smiles and merchants eager to show their profits to their competitors and brag how they came to be in the service of the Mighty Tul'ran.

Erianne didn't fail to notice the skinny children following them, running away to their parents with shekels of silver subtly pressed into their hands by the Sword Himself. He really was working on ruining his reputation.

Successful in their venture, Erianne and Tul'ran returned to the hut, the crowd once more parting before them in waves. Tul'ran took the food into the house to set a place for their meal, and Erianne led her horse to the enclosure in the back.

It didn't surprise her to see Darkshadow in the enclosure, still munching on the hay. After the curse Tul'ran had laid down on the people of the street, she doubted any of them were so foolish as to come near the place.

As she brought the mare into the enclosure, Darkshadow perked up his ears and stared at the mare with an intense gaze. He whinnied and pawed the ground with his massive right front hoof.

Erianne knew at once what the look was about. She stepped in front of the mare, raised her right forefinger toward Darkshadow's face and said, with firmness,

"No! There is to be no intimacy between the two of you. I need this mare fit to ride tonight, and you shall not molest her!"

Darkshadow looked at her with obvious wonder in his eyes. This was new. In his entire life, only one had commanded him, and it was the man who approached warfare with the same devotion and intensity as did the stallion. In his limited mind and understanding, Darkshadow knew his master placed some value on this woman who threatened him with a stern voice and an upraised hand. Darkshadow shook his head and returned to grazing. This would require some further consideration.

Satisfied she had made her point, and feeling more than a little foolish at the thought the stallion had understood her, Erianne returned to the hut. She opened the door, expecting to see a legendary warrior performing the domestic duty of setting out a midday meal, and stopped in abject horror.

There was blood. Everywhere. It cascaded over the walls and ceiling. It covered the floor, and the coppery stench of it was overwhelming. There were four bodies in the hut, carved into various pieces, clothed in the same cloth as had been the assassin in the desert.

Her eyes found Tul'ran standing in the center of the room, and her heart fell to her knees. He looked as if he had bathed in blood; it matted his hair and face. If they hurt him...

She stumbled to his side and found his hard gaze looking up at her face, noticing the fear in her eyes melded with concern.

"Be at ease, Kabolon," he said, seeing the rise and fall of her rapid breathing and the throbbing pulse in her neck. "I am without harm. These people were waiting for me when I arrived. Their clothing has a strange quality, making them blend into their surroundings such as to make them invisible to the eye."

His toe nudged a mysterious object sitting on the

floor.

"They tried to press this into my flesh when I walked through the door, though I am uncertain whether it was to render me dead or unable to assist you when you arrived. They didn't expect the swiftness of my reaction and fell to Bloodwing's desire. Of this, however, we may be certain."

He looked at her, a look conveying unknown nuance and meaning, but was as serious as the grimness of the scene and the finality of the death littering it.

"Our enemy is upon us, and we must flee."

CHAPTER THE EIGHTH:
DEVASTATION

Tales of wonder, kindness, and love
All interwoven with sonnets of death,
How would the Warrior survive his heartbreak
When his sweet Love drew her last breath?

They stood in the blood-spattered abode for a long moment, a dissonance from reality twisting in their minds. The two of them had just left. They hadn't been away for more than two hours. Within the time, four of their strange enemies discovered them and tried to kill them.

Once more, Erianne found herself flabbergasted by Tul'ran's ability to survive against impossible odds. The dead people framed the ambush perfectly, with guaranteed success. What manner of man could pick out their nearly invisible forms, avoid their attempts to subdue him, and react with the lightning speed required to overcome them?

"Tul'ran," she said, so shaken she spoke his first name in a familiar and culturally insensitive mode. "What are we to do? How can we escape into the desert with little food and no sleep?"

"We have no choice," he said, his voice grim, his tone emphasized by the drying blood drenching his hair and face. "It will not take long for their masters to recognize their failure and set out against us again. We must be away as quickly as we can gather our things."

She nodded, as her stomach threatened to release itself onto the floor at the sight of the ghoulish carnage around her.

"I will change again."

"Wait! Perhaps you should not."

She turned to look down at him, her forehead crinkling.

"I cannot ride pell-mell into the desert wearing the garments and jewelry of a Queen, milord."

He nodded, a glimmer of thought lighting his eyes.

"Nor should you, milady, for it would be inappropriate indeed." The glimmer turned into a glint. "However, it would not be untoward for a Lady of high station, or a Queen from a distant land, to ride through these streets in a stately manner. Our enemies have struck from ambush, in the dead of night or from seclusion. I think they would be loath to strike in daylight, in crowded spaces, before a multitude of eyes. It might bring unwanted attention to them from the King's guard, especially if the victim was royal. You saw how the people in the market reacted to your manner of dress and disposition."

"Would it not be unseemly for a Queen to have only one warrior in her retinue?"

He grinned like a wolf through the blood on his face, which only enhanced his next words.

"Not if the warrior is Tul'ran az Nostrom."

She grimaced. He had a point. He had proven the foundation for his legend several times over in her sight. So much so she felt the balladeers understated his prowess with a sword and his willingness to kill.

"You cannot ride with me fresh from battle. The gore encrusting you will raise eyebrows!"

He nodded in agreement.

"Pack your things, milady, and fast. I will wash the blood of our enemies from my sword, my vestments, and my person. When you judge me clean, we shall set forth in boldness to claim the day."

Once more, with little inhibition or vanity, Tul'ran discarded his clothing, save for the loincloth. He poured as little water as he could spare into a wooden bowl. He reached into the leather sack for a clean strip of cloth, dipped it into the bowl, and cleansed his skin. When he removed the blood from his face, neck, and arms, he threw the blooded bowl of water on the floor with nonchalance.

Erianne raised her head in irritation when she saw him discard the water within the hut, then checked herself. The scene was already a gruesome mess, and she was never coming back here again. What should it matter?

Erianne scooped up the object their attackers intended to use against Tul'ran and packed it in her bag. She finger-combed her long hair as best she could and put it up. She didn't have a crown, but she could create the semblance of one with her hair.

Tul'ran refilled the bowl with a smaller quantity of water and began the arduous task of cleaning the blood out of his gore-encrusted hair. He had no means by which to see himself because the bowl was small and the water in it lost its reflective quality as soon as the blood touched it. He had to cascade the contents of the bowl onto the floor and refill it several times before the water ran clear from his head into the bowl.

The warrior removed a plug of caustic soap from the leather bag and scrubbed the bloodstains out of his chiton. The soap was crude and not perfumed, but it was effective. When he finished, the chiton was wet but clean. The leathers were much easier to clean, and soon he dressed.

He turned to get her approval and was stunned, again, by her appearance. She stood tall in her royal purple tunic, which was so well tailored it hugged every sensuous curve of her body. The gold chain enfolded her small waist, and the long length dangled to one side. She had piled her black hair upon her head to resemble a crown, with strands of hair cascading down to frame her delicious brown face. Erianne had smeared charcoal above and below her eyes, and her green eyes shone brilliantly through her darkened lids.

"Do I look like visiting royalty from some distant, foreign, and exotic land?" She asked, her tone as sweet as honey. The dazed expression on his face delighted her.

He swallowed hard. Tried to say something,

swallowed again, and nodded.

"You are the very essence of royalty, my Queen. You make me feel inept and foolish, and flustered all at the same time. I want nothing more than to bend my knee to you and pledge service for as long as I live, so entranced am I with the vision of majesty standing tall, proud, and beautiful before me. Have I removed all the bloodstains from my person and clothing?"

Erianne was so lost in his words and the emotion in his eyes, it took her a moment to hear the end of his sentence. His question jarred her back into the reality of the surrounding bloodbath. She walked up to him, carefully avoiding the small pools of blood scattered around the dismembered corpses. Erianne scanned his hair, face, neck, and body, front and back.

"Indeed, milord," she said, satisfied. "What next?"

"We eat, for we need our strength for the ordeal to come. We can stand in the far corner and turn our backs to this hideous scene to have our meal. It will not be comfortable or appetizing, but we must not eat outside, and we cannot go without food."

Erianne looked at the small wood table and was astonished to see their purchased food standing there, not looking worse for wear. Even the goat's milk hadn't spilled. How on earth had he managed it? Her head swam again as peculiarity and anomaly collided violently within her brain. She had studied this man and thought she knew him. There was something else going on with him she was powerless to fathom.

She helped him carry their foodstuffs into a corner of the hut, where they stood, presenting their backs to the mess behind. Neither wanted to eat, but both knew they could carry none of their meal with them. They ate rapidly, without enjoyment, without tasting, piling food down their throats as fuel, not as a pleasurable meal. It was necessary and thoroughly dissatisfying.

When they finished, they grabbed their bags and scanned the interior of the hut in a last survey. Nothing of theirs remained behind. If their enemies didn't come to reclaim the bodies of their dead, the King's guard would. In the desert heat, the corpses would spread the putrid odor of decay throughout the entire marketplace in swift order.

When they arrived at the horse enclosure, Tul'ran made Erianne wait outside the small corral so she wouldn't dirty her fine dress. He saddled Darkshadow first, for one always prepared their weapons quickly and thoroughly when in anticipation of warfare. After he saddled the stallion and placed upon his back the large leather bag, Tul'ran checked the horse's legs and feet. Satisfied, he moved to Erianne's horse and dressed her with the tack he found within the paddock, checking cinches with the same repetitive thoroughness.

We are a fine pair, Erianne thought. We no sooner leave danger at our backs, and it rears up again before us. How long can we keep this up? How long can people run, riding on the razor-sharp surface of destiny's edge? Destiny's Edge.

"Milord," she called out, just as he bent to check her horse's hooves. He glanced up at her with curiosity, as her voice didn't alert him to danger.

"Milady?"

She was "My Lady" now, not "Mistress," she observed, delighted. Somewhere, some when since she met him, he had elevated her station from wealthy middle class to nobility.

"I would beg a favor of you; when you address my magnificent horse, it should be by her name, which you should know to be Destiny's Edge."

"Destiny's Edge," he murmured, feeling the rightness of it roll with delight on his tongue.

He turned to put one affectionate hand on her horse's neck.

"Will it please you, Destiny's Edge, to have a friend check your legs and feet for any impediment threatening to lame you in your travels?"

Erianne stifled a giggle, not so much from his fine speech towards her horse, but with her expectation Destiny's Edge would answer the query. Her brain was going native all too fast.

Saddled, loaded, checked, and re-checked, Tul'ran led the horses from the paddock. He glanced at Erianne up and down and frowned.

"I could not help but notice, Lady Erianne; your tunic, while elegant, is not suited for riding."

She smiled. He thought her dress was too tight.

"Fear not, milord, for who would design a dress for a Queen without accounting for such a necessity? Behold."

She turned and Tul'ran saw a gap etched in the center of the fabric from the top of her thighs down to the ankles. Erianne parted the gap and Tul'ran saw a large volume of fabric expand into the part.

Brilliant. She could mount a horse as normal, stressing no point of the tunic, while it continued to fit her form in a way most pleasing to the eye.

He returned her smile.

"I see. Well thought, milady. In what direction must we make our way?"

Erianne glanced around her, searching for movement or anomaly, and concealed eyes. Satisfied, she closed hers and once more extended her right hand, bent at the wrist, forefinger extended, the rest curled loosely to her palm. She turned until she felt the suggestion deep in her mind and stopped.

"There," she said.

North and East. North and East lay Lagash and Susa, with enough dangers for them there without regard for the other mysterious, persistent threats against them.

He helped her up onto her horse, Destiny's Edge, he reminded himself, and then mounted Darkshadow. Tul'ran gestured Erianne to lead, as was befitting her station. He would ride just behind and to one side to protect her and guide her with spoken suggestions.

Ride they did, with leisure through the city, in regal display. Tul'ran was grateful their path didn't, at least, take them near the palace. He knew well the reputation of the King of Ur, who considered it his duty to bed any beauty coming under his gaze, much to the Queen's chagrin.

As they walked their horses through Ur, Tul'ran dismounted from time to time to refresh their travel supplies, making purchases as Erianne watched the frantic nature of the marketplaces. It was less pleasurable now. She scanned the faces of the people, searching for a threat. Fear touched her heart, and she hated being afraid. It was a relief when Tul'ran jumped onto Darkshadow and they rode on.

Erianne projected well the very essence of royalty. To such a fine degree, the citizens of Ur didn't just make way, but bowed low before her as they passed. By morning, all would know throughout Ur a foreign Queen, resplendent in dress and astonishing beauty, had ridden out of the city followed only by the Sword Himself. One man, as they passed, commented on the dearth of an armed guard. His friend cuffed him on the head.

"Have you no eyes? Do you not see who rides at her back? It is Tul'ran az Nostrom, the Taker of Souls. Who would be so foolish as to threaten Her Majesty with harm when the Prince of Death rides at her side?"

Erianne overheard them and glanced back at her entourage of one. Tul'ran sat tall on the back of Darkshadow, and waves of menace drifted away from him like the ripples made by a poisoned lance cast into a pond. He set his face in a death mask. In the midday sun, his muscles glistened with sweat, enhancing the ridges they made under his skin. As always, his cold, cold eyes scanned the crowd for threats, while Darkshadow pranced and tossed his head as if yearning to leap into combat. Who, indeed, would be so foolish as to threaten her with harm when such a man rode at her back? Her pulse quickened as she wondered how long she could keep him there.

It would take four days for the King to hear the

rumors a foreign Queen had ridden through the length of his city with no one notifying the King of her coming and her going. It caused him deep shame his advisers hadn't given him the opportunity to extend honors and hospitality to the ravishing beauty, including the distinction of sharing the pleasures of his bed. So distraught was the King, he ordered the beheading of three of his advisors.

The head of the Commander of the King's Guard wasn't one of them. He returned home the night Tul'ran and Erianne left Ur to his wife and children, kissed them as they lay sleeping, and offered a prayer of thanks to one of his gods. Tul'ran the Sword had entered his city quietly and left peacefully. None of his men rested on a funeral pyre. He had one thousand men under arms and at his disposal, but the Commander feared deep in his heart he would have needed twice the number to capture or kill the Prince of Death.

Such was the strength of a balladeer's song.

By the time dusk dropped, Tul'ran and Erianne had escaped the confines of the city, and both felt relieved. They rode in silence for a time before Erianne cleared her throat.

"Milord, the night is long, and our journey is far..."

Tul'ran burst out laughing, and Erianne giggled at the loud guffaw. He shook his head and looked at her from the corner of his eye.

"Ask and I will answer, milady."

"You have delighted me with your history, milord; a history I have found fascinating. All things martial have you imparted to me, so I now seek a different thread. Long have I heard of the exploits of the Sword Himself in the bedchambers of the women who fell headlong for your charms. But what of love? Will you weave for me a tale of your first love?"

There was silence then. A heavy silence, marred at the end by a deep sigh.

"I have sworn to tell you the truth, Lady Kabolon, and the truth you shall have. Hearken to the tale of Katja of the Gutians."

He couldn't believe he was once again baring his soul to this woman. By what right of Honor and Code did she claim access to the darkest, deepest recesses of his heart? A large part of his mind screamed at him for his foolishness and disregard for his customary reticence. A smaller part of his mind chided him for his cowardice. His covenant-mistress demanded a telling. What right did he have to refuse her? The threat it would cause pain to the Mighty, Heroic, Indestructible, Tul'ran the Sword?

Mind made up, though threaded with unease, Tul'ran turned to face forward and spun the tale into the night.

Tul'ran honored his promise to El Shaddai. After he recovered in the desert, he returned to the hidden places and retrieved half his fortune and, if the truth be told, a fair amount more. It took him a year to find the location of the home of the Gutians he had killed, but find it he did.

When he rode Darkshadow into their village, panic ensued. Tul'ran was hoarse from yelling, and

Darkshadow was near exhaustion by the time he had rounded up the citizens of the village and convinced them he wasn't there to kill them.

When they had calmed to less than sheer panic, he addressed them as a crowd.

"I have committed a grave injustice against you, people of the Gutians, and I am here to make right what my arm made wrong."

For a start, he explained to them how four Gutians had attacked his family and left him orphaned, though he could see there were many ears closed to the accusations against their men. The warrior confessed his obsession to avenge his family's torturous deaths and how it had led him to Ur. He acknowledged with humility his failure to ride away once his revenge was complete, instead of taking the lives of their men.

"And so," he concluded, "I have come with restitution. I know silver cannot replace the lives I have taken, but I have naught else to offer you. If you will but name for me the widows of the four and twenty men who fell at my feet, I will deliver to them, here and in this place, the blood price for their husbands' lives."

The crowd stood, unbelieving, restrained, until a woman walked forward, rubbing her hands on her tattered clothing.

"I am hight Vendolyn," she said, with timidity. "My husband was Corvins. He was a kind man, but easily persuaded by tales of duty, honor, and glory, especially when in his cups."

The crowd murmured in assent.

"His glory has left me penniless and with three

children to raise on my own. I am not too proud to take what you offer me, Killer of Men, though I will confess it will not be with gratitude in my heart."

Tul'ran declined his head.

"I hear you with shame, Vendolyn, and honor your courage. Name your blood price and you shall take it with you this very hour."

"Fifty shekels of silver, Lord of Death, will not warm my bed at night or comfort me when I sorrow, but it will pay for food for my table and clothing for my children as they grow. It is almost five years' wages and gives me time to find a husband to care for me and my family."

The price pierced Tul'ran's heart like an arrow. So little for a man's life, for the dreams entrenched in the heart of a husband and father left to die in the dirt of Ur.

He had brought with him two donkeys, upon which he had laden his treasure. He dismounted from Darkshadow, and the crowd gave way, wary.

Tul'ran walked back to one donkey and returned with a sack filled with three minas and sixty shekels of silver, the equivalent of two hundred and forty shekels. It still wasn't enough, he felt, but far more than what she had the courage to ask. It would provide for her and her children for the next twenty years.

He handed the heavy bag to the woman, who fair staggered under its weight.

"Here are three minas and sixty shekels of silver for your loss, your pain, and the suffering of your children."

The woman stared into the bag; her mouth

rounded into an "o". She looked up at Tul'ran.

"For me, milord, truly, without condition or the return of favor?"

"For you," he said, "truly, without condition or the return of favor."

Then it moved faster. Two and twenty more widows asked, and two and twenty bags he gave, leaving the widows scrambling away to hide their new bounties. It delighted some of them to know not only were they free of husbands who were lazy, stunk from too few bathings, and made frequent, obnoxious demands for sexual intercourse, but they were now in possession of a small fortune ample to make them independent of other such men.

Tul'ran raised his head into the lull. The experience of hearing the stories of the women, the losses they felt, and giving them inadequate recompense exhausted him.

"There is one more. Stand forward so I may pay you and take my leave."

Quietness descended on the crowd. After a few moments, three young men made their way to the front of the gathering. The man in the lead bowed with just a slight nod of the head to Tul'ran, his body stiff, his gaze unrelenting.

"Prince of Death, Killer of Men. There is no widow remaining in our family. When news of my father's demise reached her ears, my mother fell ill. Her spirit left her, and she would not eat or drink. Within a matter of weeks, we lost her to death as well. It agonized us to watch her starve herself. She was but bones and skin when we laid her to rest."

Tul'ran sighed.

"Leaving yourself and your two brothers."

"Leaving myself, two brothers, and a sister."

The man stepped aside, and a woman presented herself from behind him. She was short, lithe, and pretty. She had light brown hair tied tight to her head, and her eye color was a tawny brown. Her lips were full in a wide mouth, currently turned down in a severe frown. She folded her arms across ample breasts and looked him up and down.

When she spoke, her voice was a melody, pleasing to the ear in pitch and sound.

"You look as though you have traveled long and far, Tul'ran az Nostrom."

"I have, mistress, for I have driven hard to find this village and pay my dues for taking its men."

Tul'ran became uncomfortable when the woman stared at him silently for a long time. She spoke again, as if she had decided and was ready to put her decision into effect.

"I am hight Katja, of the People of the Mountains. My father was not the wealthiest of men, but his means exceeded those of others in this village. We will not take your blood money, for it exceeds our necessity."

She held up a hand against his protest, which died on his lips.

"Keep your silver, Prince of Death. My brothers and I will not take it, but I perceive you will have no further need of the donkeys following your horse's lead."

Tul'ran felt his eyebrows lift, and a smile threatened his lips.

"You perceive correctly, Mistress Katja, of the

People of the Mountains. The donkeys are yours, and the silver as well, if you are of a mind for it."

Katja turned to her brothers, who stood at her back.

"Remove the remaining silver from the donkeys and place it at the feet of the Warrior's horse. Take the donkeys and stable them, giving them food and drink."

Her next question floored Tul'ran.

"When have you last had a hot meal, clean water to drink, and a roof under which to sleep, Tul'ran az Nostrom?"

A murmur rustled through the crowd, and she turned to them, uttering with a sharp tongue,

"Silence! Do I come into your homes and tell you to whom you should offer hospitality and aid? Do I mind your business and interfere in your affairs? This man has come into our village without brothers-in-arms to defend his back, even though he brought with him a vast fortune."

"He has distributed his wealth to the women who lost their husbands and the fathers of their children, including the families of the four men who raped and killed his mother and sisters. Should those four families have benefited from his generosity? Would you have paid a blood price to the family of a man who raped your wife and daughters? He has removed the burden of the care of all these widows and their children from your backs. If I should choose to offer him some small comfort in return, it is on my conscience and not yours to judge."

She spoke well, Tul'ran thought, awed by the confidence and force of her speech. All murmuring ceased in the crowd, and some of them nodded their heads in agreement.

She turned back to him, eyes contemplative again.

"What say you, milord? Will you accept comfort and aid from your enemy?"

"Are you my enemy?" he asked after a moment of uncomfortable silence. "If there yet exists strife between us, then I would rather be away. If I perceive danger or feel the kiss of a knife at my throat, I will respond with the ferocity for which I am famed. Let us be clear with one another before I consider your kind and generous offer. If war yet girds the ground between us, then let us part on friendly terms and see each other never again."

Another silence ensued. When the woman spoke, the edges in her voice had softened.

"Let there be peace between us, Warrior. I tire of placing my dead on a funeral pyre and watching the ashes of those I love ascend into the heavens. Come into the joy of our home without fear or dread of open left palms on your heart and right palms closed over knives at your back."

And so it was. After Tul'ran stabled Darkshadow, Katja treated him to the first hot and quite delicious meal he had in some time. He wondered if the Gutian woman was going to poison him but fell back on the reassurance his supernatural protections would yet prevail if such were the case. They cleared a spot for him in one corner of the house, laid straw down as a mattress, and gave him plenty of bedding on which to lie. He fell asleep quickly and slept the sleep of the innocent.

The next morning, he arose and dressed in the

silence of a house which hadn't yet awakened to meet the dawn. He folded the bedding as best he could and made his way to the door.

The morning was cool, for the sun had barely risen. Tul'ran stood on the stoop and inhaled a deep lungful of fresh mountain air. He hoped Darkshadow had slept as long and hard as his master; they had an arduous journey ahead.

A scraping sound to his right caused him to whip his head in the direction, muscles tensing in anticipation of action.

The elder brother, Gilgon, was it?, was sitting there. He had a blade in one hand, but he raised it in an open palm with fingers spread, in as non-threatening a manner as possible.

"Peace, Warrior. The blessings of sleep often deny me. When sleep refuses me sanctuary, I come out here to carve, so it does not disturb my family."

A block of softwood was in his right hand, various cuts and whorls shaved from its form.

"What do you make?" Tul'ran asked, striving to be polite.

"A bird in flight, for my sister. It will be a hawk in the mode of seeking prey. Why are you leaving, Lord Tul'ran?"

Tul'ran blinked at the sudden change in topic.

"While I am most grateful for the hospitality of this house, I fear my continued presence here will be of such discomfort for your neighbors and friends as to bring little peace to you and your family. I thought to leave ere the hour should come."

The older man smiled ever so slightly.

"We made our house of firm stock, Warrior. We

do not fear the wagging of tongues set on gossip and slander. I invite you to stay. Learn of our ways, for knowledge leads to understanding, and understanding leads to peace."

So he did. He tarried with them far longer than expected. Tul'ran learned to relax his suspicions of them, for they were open-handed with their time and holdings. He spent a great deal of time in their company: the three brothers and one sister.

From Gilgon, he learned to set a knife to wood and produce from it something functional or pretty. The first task he set for himself was the creation of a wood box. Gilgon showed him how best to carry out the task. With an ax, he neatly chopped a section a thumb's width in diameter from a log of softwood.

"The lid," he said, showing Tul'ran how to cut the section and shave it to make a clean rectangle. He then showed the Warrior how to shape the inside and outside of the rest of the block to accommodate the size and shape of the lid.

When Tul'ran completed the task, he asked the older man, whose talent and patience he admired, how he could fix the lid to the box. He had received a grin and a gentle cuff on his shoulder in answer to the query.

"It's what ribands are for, my young friend, as you shall see."

From Shervon, he learned how to extract fish from the clear streams generously bordering the village. The middle brother in age was a font of laughter, always finding humor in something or another. He took great enjoyment when Tul'ran's feet slipped on wet rocks and his catch pulled him into the freezing icy water. He was a teaser of the first order. Tul'ran learned how to get into the game of playing practical jokes; the two of them constantly sought to one up the other.

The youngest brother, Eluth, was a hunter of some renown despite his youthfulness. He delighted in tracking wild game, spending hours following his quarry through the brush, and waiting for the precise moment before launching an arrow into the beast's heart. Eluth, the serious one, taught Tul'ran the subtleties of tracking signs: a broken branch here, a leaf torn from its perch before its time there, and the meaning of delicate indentations on the earth. Many a day did the two of them leave the village to forage for meat, for they fed not just their household, but those in the village who didn't have the means to forage for protein themselves.

With Katja, he spent the most time.

Until then, Tul'ran had had very little experience with women. War, the knowledge of war, and the acquisition of both had filled his brief life. He had put no thought to the delight women offered and had known none in a carnal way.

He spent countless joyous hours in the company of the vivacious young woman. They walked together in the mountains, hunting for the vegetable sustenance the slopes offered freely to any who would spend the time and effort in the gathering.

Over an ale by the fire, when the nights were cool and sleep had settled the rest of the village to quietude, they spoke of their lives, though avoiding the delicate and painful subjects of their families' demise.

Twelve full moons, Tul'ran lived with them. Katja taught him to read and write, for she was astonishingly conversant in the three languages common in Mesopotamia. Her brothers had hovered nearby at first, but gradually faded away to other tasks when they observed Tul'ran's conduct with Katja to be honorable and decent. Together, Tul'ran and Katja cooked the game Eluth killed, the fish Shervon caught, and the vegetables they gathered. Katja taught him the mysteries of spices and seasoning.

Tul'ran came to love Gilgon, Shervon, and Eluth as brothers. He came to develop quite a separate set of feelings for Katja.

Tul'ran found in Katja an intelligent woman who delighted in conversation on any subject and who found pleasure in teasing him incessantly. Her eyes danced when she spoke, and her smile lit her face like the sun at midday.

As the days passed into the flight of many moons, Tul'ran became increasingly enamored of her. He noticed her form on a different level and had difficulty keeping his eyes from the movement of her bosom and the sway of her hips when she walked. Feelings rose, unbidden, from the deep and liquid depths of desire.

He recalled the day they first kissed, near the end of eleven moons after he had arrived in the village. They were standing on a hillock overlooking her house, their fingers intertwined in the way of those whose captured hearts sought linkage through the means of touch. As they stood there, the wind rustling their long hair, Tul'ran stared at Katja and realized his heart was no longer his alone.

He held her gaze and uttered the words to change his life.

"I love you, Katja."

Her eyes shone with delight, and she raised her hands to his cheeks.

"Finally."

She brought her mouth up to his for a deep and abiding kiss.

They found many an opportunity thereafter to bring their lips together and pour into each other's spirit an outcry of love. Eventually, Tul'ran's youthful body sought a deeper intimacy, but Katja would fend off his advances with a laugh.

"Would you dishonor me, Tul'ran, by taking from me what I have given to no man? What potential husband would have me in wedlock should I give to you the gift in which only he should delight?"

After one such occasion, his body frustrated and patience exhausted, Tul'ran looked at her and said with certainty, "No other man shall have you, Katja-love, for you are mine and will be until death finds its way to our door."

"What are you saying?" she asked.

"Katja, I would have you for my wife if you find me the object of your desire and wish our hearts linked to destiny's end."

She leaped into his arms and squeezed her arms around him with such force he nearly left his feet.

"I will take you as my husband, Tul'ran, and pledge you my troth until our life's end."

They were married a few days later under the brightness of a full moon, the twelfth since his arrival. In the moons passing since Tul'ran entered their lives, having seen how quickly he became embedded into Katja's family, the villagers grudgingly accepted him into their social circle. It was no wonder the entire population of the village attended their wedding, all bringing their well wishes to the happy couple.

Before Katja and Tul'ran left their house to attend the ceremony, he presented her with his bride-price: three minas and sixty shekels of silver in a wood box he had carved under her older brother's tutelage. Gilgon had taught him well; she took great delight in it and laughed aloud at its contents.

She shook her head. "So, you put this silver into my hands, after all."

He smiled at her, his eyes shining. "You certainly put me through my paces to arrive at a place where I could present it."

She laughed again, coyly. "Wait, my soon-to-be husband, you have yet the full measure of the paces I will put you through on this, our wedding night."

Tul'ran sauntered ahead of her to the center of the village, leaving her in the care of her three brothers. A length of time passed, and he worried she had changed her mind. Eventually, she and her brothers entered the center of the village, much as they had when Tul'ran first met them. Gilgon, taller than Katja, led the procession with Katja in the middle, followed by Eluth and Shervon, all dressed in finery.

When her brothers stepped away from her, Katja glided forward into the light of the torches. A shawl of linen draped around her body, overtop a skirt. She decorated it with tassels at the edges and fine thread. His bride wore bangles of silver on both wrists, and she decorated one ankle with a band of gold. She was stunning, and Tul'ran couldn't have felt happier if he tried.

An elder had versed him in the ritual. He took from behind his back a veil her mother had gifted to Katja for the day she would marry. Tul'ran walked over to Katja and draped the veil over her head and face.

Tul'ran stepped back, admiring the woman, and looked around at the surrounding crowd, who were awaiting the ritualistic phrase with uncommon eagerness.

"She is my wife," he said, and it was done. They were husband and wife from the moment of the utterance forward. The village then sat down on blankets and carpets Katja's family had arranged for them. Servers presented food and wine, and the ensuing merriment lasted for a long time.

Tul'ran was engaged in hearty conversation with another man from the village when he felt a tug on his ear. He turned his head to look at the face of his wife, who had an eager look in her tawny eyes. She pressed her lips against his ear and whispered,

"It is time for you to receive the reward of your patience and perseverance, my husband and my lord."

Tul'ran jumped to his feet, all enthusiasm, and she laughed as he took her hand. He started towards the house, but she restrained him with her left hand to his chest, an open palm against his heart.

"I have a surprise for you, husband, which you

will not find in our marriage bed in the house."

Mischief danced in her eyes as she drew him away from the feast. Torches lit a path winding down the side of the hill on which they had built the village. Tul'ran was grateful he had abstained from consuming too much wine, for it would have been easy to become dizzy and pitch forward off the cliff.

They arrived at a place of wonder. A band of torches encircled a natural pool, and steam rose like the wisps of a dream from the surface of the water.

"What is this?" Tul'ran asked as he reached down to dip his fingers into the pool, surprised by the heat his hands met.

"The heart of this mountain feeds warmth into this pool," Katja said in a seductive voice. "Its salts are pleasant to the skin, and the heat will soothe your muscles to the depths of your soul."

Tul'ran stared at her, lust coursing through his body. Desire shone in her eyes; an eager anticipation of what was to come danced upon her lips, enthralling him.

"Take off your clothes, husband, and enter the pool, if you favor me with your love."

The Warrior did as he was told, gingerly at first because he had not, before then, disrobed before a woman. After the initial hesitation, he undressed with greater confidence as she smiled and giggled with delight at the removal of each piece of clothing. When he cast aside his loincloth, he entered the pool, taking pleasure in its warmth, and set his back against the rock.

"It's my turn," she said, lust dripping like an elixir from her throat.

She slowly unwrapped the shawl from her body. Her eyes focused on his every expression, watching his face tighten with desire and longing. She maneuvered the wrappings to leave her upper body covered until, at last, she casually flicked the shawl away.

She stood in the torchlight, momentarily allowing him to feed the hunger in his eyes as he roamed his gaze over her face, her shoulders, her breasts, and her waist. A seductive smile again seized her lips, and her eyes brightened with the expected fulfillment of her desire.

She removed the skirt in one deft, quick maneuver and stepped into the pool, immersing her lower body to the waist, leaving for the moment her upper body exposed.

Time froze.

It took Tul'ran several blinks of lust-filled eyes to understand what had happened. Time had stopped. Her breasts no longer rose and fell with every breath. Time's stasis locked her eyes open, pupils wide and begging for desire. The air was still, and there was no sound.

Bewildered, he looked around, but could see nothing beyond the torchlight. It took him a moment to realize the configuration of the torches, their proximity one to another, took away completely his vision of the night beyond their encirclement. As if it were so by design.

He slowly raised himself from the pool, disrupting the frozen tendrils of steam arising from its surface. The young warrior stepped out beyond the torches and gave his pupils an opportunity to become accustomed to a night lit only by the full moon overhead. There was an enemy about and their designs were not peaceful.

It didn't take long to find them. Three men crouched in the bushes beyond the torches, behind the frozen form of Katja. Each man had a knife in his hand, and as Tul'ran approached them, blood rushed into his ears, so consumed he was in disbelief.

Katja's brothers, Gilgon, Eluth, and Shervon, were crouched in the shadows. There was enough light for him to see the contortions of hatred on their faces and the ugliness of their grimaces.

Stunned, he fell to his knees, mind and heart refusing to believe the threat so evidently poised behind his ladylove's back.

"El Shaddai. El Shaddai, what is this?"

The Voice touched his mind, the tendrils deeply immersed in sorrow.

"They betrayed you, My son."

"B-betrayed." The tears flowed. "But how? Why?"

"By their hatred for you and as vengeance for taking the lives of their parents."

Tul'ran shook his head, unable to grasp, unable to believe these men whom he loved as brothers were crouching before him, ready to seize him and kill him. Then, as horror dawned, trivial things sprung to his mind from all the days passed; the cessation of intense whispered conversations when he entered the room, the bite of some of the teasing, and the harshness behind a playful shove or blow.

"What am I to do with them?"

"You must send them to Me for judgment," came the soulful reply.

"They must die? Why must they die? Since I am warned, I can easily disarm them, for there is not a warrior among them trained as I am. Those knives are for cooking and cleaning, not taking the lifeblood of a well-trained man. Wherefore must they die?"

"Is it not enough I have set them aside for judgment?"

Tears were streaming down Tul'ran's face as his heart slowly ripped to shreds. The agony of loss was beating against his soul like a persistent drum, casting echoes of pain from his past into his present.

"They are the brothers of my beloved, and beloved of me as well. How can I kill them?"

"My son," came the firm reply, "it is not meet and right I should explain Myself to you, for you are my Chosen Judge. It should be enough for Me to point your sword and seek your obedience in fulfillment of My conviction. But because I see your pain and understand the depth of your sorrow, I will answer."

"These are the things you do not know about these, your brothers. Do you recall the widow Vendolyn?"

"I do, El Shaddai. She left the village two moons ago to journey to the place of her family, for she had no relatives left in the hamlet after I poured her husband's blood into the dirt."

There was anger now in the Voice.

"She did not make it to her ancestral home. Gilgon followed her into the desert and there did he lay open her throat and the throats of her children for the silver you had paid as blood price."

Revulsion filled Tul'ran in a wave.

"He killed her for a bounty?"

"He killed her for her silver, valuing her life and the lives of her children as nothing, not even gracing them with a funeral pyre."

Disbelief, shock, and a gut-wrenching emptiness cycled through Tul'ran's mind in waves, tears pouring in a steady stream from his eyes.

"And the other two brothers? What of Shervon and Eluth? What have they done to incur Your wrath, Mighty Shaddai?"

"Do you remember the widow Shiraz?"

Oh, no. No, no, no, no, no.

"The widow Shiraz." Tul'ran said, fearing what he knew was to come, "A foul beast set upon her as she washed her garments in the river. It slashed her to ribbons, and she died on the side of the stream. Her parents took her children in and care for them still."

The Voice in his mind writhed in pain and anger.

"Shervon and Eluth beset the widow Shiraz. Gilgon had confided in them what he had done with Vendolyn, and they lusted for their own fortune. It was they who tore the poor woman to shreds after they tortured her for the hiding place of her blood price. When they announced to the village, a beast had attacked her, all the people ran down to her rescue, giving Shervon and Eluth time to recover her wealth."

"Do you know what it is like to love the children of your creation so much you would die to save them from torture? Do you know what it is like to hear their screams, to feel their pain, and to sit by as they expire?"

Huge sobs were racking Tul'ran's chest now, as he sank lower to the earth. He dug his fingernails into the dirt, focused only on the desire this cup would pass from his hands.

"Then why do You allow it, El Shaddai? Are You not the Creator? Do You not hold the stars of the heavens in Your hands?"

"I am the Creator; I hold the stars of the heavens in My hands. All My creation is beloved by Me, especially the men and women I have made in My image."

"But more precious to Me than even them is the gift I made to them of free will. To each man and each woman, I gave the power to set their feet on the paths of their own choosing. Sometimes, the evil desires of some break like massive waves on the shores of the lives of others, wreaking havoc."

"I cannot offer free will and interfere when the exercise of free will grieves Me. Vendolyn, her children, and Shiraz abide now with Me in peace and comfort eternal. The actions of their murderers I now adjudge, and you shall be the executor of My judgment."

The tears ran unabated, but the sobbing had subsided.

"Why did You not tell me this before this day? How is it I must learn these things only now, on the night of my greatest joy, on the day of my nuptials with the woman I cherish and love?"

The Voice echoed with a tremor of grief.

"When did you ask, My son? Before you became ensconced in a village consumed by hatred for the measured way in which you took the lives of their sons, brothers, nephews, uncles, and husbands, did you inquire of Me as to the wisdom of so doing? Before you took unto yourself this woman as your bride, did you speak your desire to My ear and seek the wisdom I could offer?"

When would he learn? He was a fool. He sought El Shaddai when his life was in shambles or near to an end, but spoke to Him not at all in moments of joy and peace.

"I plead ignorance and stupidity, El Shaddai. Once again, I seek your forgiveness. May I ask of Your wisdom now?"

"You would inquire as to the disposition of your bride," came the soft, knowing reply. "Know you thus, child of My heart; every decision made by a man or a woman extends a thread into the tapestry of their future life. I see not only the threads of every decision made but also those of choices considered and rejected, past, present, and future. I know the desires of your bride's heart and the lengths she would go to fulfill them. Do you think you would be in this place, at this moment, without the knowledge and acquiescence of your wedded wife?"

It crushed him. She had seeded love in his heart, replacing the pain of his childhood. It now lay trampled beneath the cloven hooves of betrayal. Her deception shattered his hopes and dreams. He understood devastation beyond devastation.

Tul'ran moaned and writhed on the ground, beating his chest and sobbing. He could no more deny the Truth than he could deny the knowledge he failed to see it. Love had blinded him.

"What am I to do?" he asked, his hoarse voice rent by anguish.

"Go up to your lodging and pack your things. Prepare Darkshadow for the journey and lead him down to the water's edge behind you. Bring with you my Knife and Bloodwing and lay them at the water's edge. I will then bring Time back into its course."

"And what of Katja?"

Tul'ran wiped tears from his cheeks while he waited, in agony, for the answer.

"You are My Chosen Judge. I will leave the decision as to her fate in your hands. Choose wisely, My son, for the lengths of chain forged by hatred and revenge are long and will send all to the grave. I foresee in many of the threads of her future where her hatred will cause her to pursue your death at the expense of her life."

Tul'ran's relief was palpable. He could choose to not kill her. He could divorce her for cause and leave her and this village in his dust forever. She wouldn't have to die.

"By your command," he murmured, as El Shaddai left him.

He rose awkwardly to his feet, staggered by the burden placed on his soul. Tul'ran rubbed tears from his eyes and cheeks and walked over to Gilgon. He removed the knife from Gilgon's hands, hands which had taught him to shape wood from its natural state into items of usefulness and joy.

Tul'ran plunged the knife into Gilgon's chest three times in the area where he knew the heart to be and, on reflection, cut deeply into each side of the man's neck. He knew a large amount of blood

194

flowed in the neck and cuts to those places would lead inevitably to death.

The bereaved man moved to Shervon, and a sob caught in his throat. Shervon, who laughed so easily, but hid so well the acid hatred in his heart, suffered the same fate as his older brother.

And, at the last, the youngest, Eluth, his favorite of the three brothers. Eluth, who would never again feel the kiss of the morning sun upon his face as he left the comfort of his bed to chase wild game in the brisk bite of dawn's breath. Tul'ran wondered if his heart could break any further.

When he had cut Eluth as he had cut the other two of his brothers, Tul'ran threw the knife down at Gilgon's feet and hiked up to the lodging to do as El Shaddai instructed.

Everything, the village, the people, the wind, the leaves, the trees, were all frozen in silence as he placed his things in the leather bag. He left behind the pieces of silver, for they were no longer a bride-price, but blood money.

He took the leather bag to the enclosure where Darkshadow stood, watching him and pawing at the ground with nervous tension. It was as if he could feel the depth of Tul'ran's sorrow and felt helpless by it. Tul'ran uttered words of encouragement, patting the horse's flank as he dressed the war horse, all the while tears carving rivulets in his cheeks.

Having gathered his clothing, his weapons, and his horse, he led the stallion down the steep slope and maneuvered him opposite Katja, beyond the torchlight. He stood within the circle of the torches and looked once more upon his bride. For a few moments, he considered staying there forever, with time frozen in its place, ever contemplating her beauty and grieving his loss. Instead, he bent himself in obedience to the will of El Shaddai and crawled back into the pool.

Time snapped back into play with a splash as Katja dropped into the pool. At once, a loud series of crashes sounded in the bushes behind her, and she turned, startled. She turned back to Tul'ran.

"What was...?" The words stalled on her lips as she noticed the grief engraving its marks on her husband's face. It took her another moment to realize his hands were outside the pool, Bloodwing in his right hand and the wicked obsidian knife in his left.

"What transpires, my husband, which brings you into my arms with weapons in hand?" she asked, licking her lips.

Tul'ran looked at her with grief washing from his eyes in floods of pure agony.

"Do you not know, wife?"

When she wouldn't answer him, he pointed his chin to the brushes behind her.

"Did you not know your brothers were lying in wait in those brushes, weapons in hand, their hearts set to murder, and their eyes focused on the desires in which demons rejoice?"

Katja gasped and launched herself from the pool, but Tul'ran was no longer interested in her naked body. She wrapped the shawl around her wet skin and rushed towards the bushes beyond the firelight. Seconds later, a shriek split the air. She came back moments later, eyes wild, brandishing a bloodied knife in her right hand.

"What have you done?" She phrased the question as a demand; her face contorted in rage.

Tul'ran leveraged himself out of the pool, his mind a testament to sorrow beyond human tolerance. He stood before her, naked, vulnerable, and asked the question to which he knew the answer and dreaded it falling from the lips he wanted to kiss.

"Did you know?" He asked, his voice raw with emotion.

Her face contorted, changed, and twisted into something wicked.

"Did I know?" She shouted, half-hysterically. "Who do you think conceived the plan, you despicable piece of excrement? Who do you think plotted your death even as you were appeasing the weak women of my village with your silver? I planned this from the moment you rode all proud and haughty into our midst, casting out treasure as if it could compensate for the lives you took without thinking. You are a selfish, ugly beast. Were it within my power, I would kill you, raise you from the dead, and kill you again and again for all eternity."

He shook his head in disbelief.

"You planned this? You carried your plan in your heart for twelve moons, plotting my death even as you pressed your lips against mine and pledged your love to me?"

Katja laughed harshly.

"You pitiful fool. Only now do you understand the depth of my hatred for you! Your heart was so easy to manipulate, 'Mighty Warrior.' You were just a boy when you came to us, and you're still a boy now. Do you know how many times I stood over you while you slept, aching with the desire to plunge a knife into your throat? I waited for this day to strike you down with your greatest joy. Men are stupid, and you are not even a man yet."

Pain. Pain burrowed deep into his heart like the head of a spear. Life didn't equip him for this level of betrayal. His heart wasn't strong enough to bear this level of pain, this depth of hatred from a woman who owned his whole heart.

"So be it," he said, his voice ragged with agony. "In my foolishness and the inexperience of my youth, I did not see the deception in your eyes and your heart before this day. I divorce you, Katja. And leave you to your hatred."

Her eyes glowed with something akin to insanity. She walked towards him slowly, bloodied knife in hand.

"Do you think to be rid of me so easily, Butcher? Do you think the bodies of my brothers lying behind me lessen my hatred and desire for your death?"

Tul'ran raised Bloodwing to chest level, and she paused, inches away from destruction.

"I love you," he said, already mourning the loss of her. "Do not come further. I do not wish to wet this blade with your blood."

She nodded, understanding smoothing the lines from her face.

"You love me, truly. I can see it in your eyes. I can hear it in your voice. Do you know how much I bear the agony of longing for a kiss from my parents, the gentle touch of their breath on my cheek and the warmth of their embrace? The pain of loss is a torture which rises with the sun and endures through a sleepless night. It is a judgment, this prison of loneliness and grief. How fitting it is you should know this, Tul'ran az Nostrom. You have now found the place where you can kill what you love."

She lunged forward, and he watched, unbelieving, as she impaled herself on his blade. He couldn't move, so horrified was he by her suicide. Her eyes were bright with hatred. Katja bared her teeth. Her mouth warped in a snarl as he watched, unblinking, while the light of life left the eyes of the woman he loved deeply, passionately, desperately.

All this, he told Erianne, as they rode through the desert, again not mentioning El Shaddai. Tears streamed down both their faces.

"Erianne, I do not remember how I left the place. I do not remember traveling through the night or the nights after it. For the longest time, I felt nothing. I numbed my mind and heart to life and everything in it. When my cognizance returned, I set about to fulfill my destiny."

"You are correct when you say in the last number of years I took to my bed many women. But from the day of Katja's death to this one, never again did I give a woman my heart to keep. In all my life, love was pain; an agony I never wished to experience again."

There was nothing more for either of them to say. They rode long into the night, both immersed in regret, both longing for the dawn to find them, and both awash in the dread their hearts would never know the light again.

CHAPTER THE NINTH:
REVELATION

The Queen and the Warrior fled to the desert
And pointed behind them, fierce hounds of Hell,
But the pursuers were the captors, hate resurrected,
And in the furnace would they soon dwell.

Mesopotamia, the third day of the eighth month, 2005 BC
What is it about the break of day? As the eastern sky turns to light and chases away a recalcitrant moon, what is it which greets opened eyes with tidings of joy and hope for the new day? How is it the demons haunting the resting hour, hiding in shadows, foretelling harm, and threats of harm, flee from the resting mind as the sun sends ahead glimpses of its glory over the darkened horizon?

All questions of great import and worthy of philosophical debate, but neither of Warrior nor Queen could have answered any of them this morn.

Erianne and Tul'ran were exhausted.

They had traveled through the night before entering Ur and missed their sleep on the following day. They rode again all night, which stretched long and tedious before them as they plodded along in melancholy silence. Here, at the break of dawn, they and their horses were weary to the point of collapse.

"Milady," Tul'ran said, his voice croaking. "We arrive at our waypoint."

Erianne had been riding with her head tucked to her chest, fighting to stay conscious and in her saddle. Destiny's Edge had a soothing gait, and it threatened to lull her into a dream state.

She jerked up her head and squinted into the rising sun. Just ahead, an oasis loomed in the desert, silhouetted against the bright red sky. It wasn't large, but it looked to have a pool of clean water and a grove of date palms providing both shade and food. There was also a thick carpet of grass for their horses to feed upon...

Erianne reined Destiny's Edge to a sharp halt, a startled cry sounding from her lips.

Tul'ran whipped around in his saddle, scanning the desert for the source of her distress.

"What is it, milady?"

She pointed ahead, flabbergasted.

"The oasis. That oasis. It is the one we left behind after we first met. Somehow we turned around, we have gone the wrong way, we..."

"Peace!" Tul'ran said, stopping her unnerved tirade. He glanced up at the last fading stars.

"We have traveled north and east, my Queen, as directed by your hand, and we have not strayed from our course. Check your senses. You know this to be true."

Erianne, her head whirling from confusion and fatigue, closed her eyes and centered on her internal gyroscope. He was right. It was impossible, but he was right. She opened her eyes and calmed her breathing.

"Forgive me, milord, but I would swear on my life we ride into the very oasis in which you took me after my rescue."

He wouldn't meet her gaze.

"All oases can look the same after a long night's ride. Even a welcome sight can read strange to fatigued eyes."

They rode on, but Erianne couldn't shake a feeling of incongruity, a sense of *déjà vu* plaguing her mind. Look, there was the large date palm under which Tul'ran had reached into his bag for their meal. There, a smaller group of trees close to the water where Tul'ran had tethered Darkshadow. She didn't have an eidetic memory, but it was superb. It was telling her they were in the same oasis one day and two night's ride from their last sojourn at water's edge.

She had expected some disorientation before she came to Mesopotamia. Her instructors told her how different everything would be from her perception. Mostly, she had found things were as she expected. But the anomalies she had experienced with Tul'ran were not only unexpected but almost impossible. Part of her brain wanted to explore those thoughts, to chase them down the rabbit hole, but she was far too exhausted to care.

They rode into the oasis just as the sun completed

its leap into the sky, and they dismounted. Tul'ran removed the packs. She went to remove her horse's tack, but Tul'ran held up a hand in dissent.

"I imagine you would like to get out of your finery and into the tunic you wore on the day we met. You have my apology for not stopping in our flight to give you an opportunity to rid yourself of a Queen's livery. Why not change while I occupy myself with tending to the needs of our horses? I give you my word: I shall not cast my gaze upon your naked form."

"I accept with gratitude, milord. This regal dress is far less comfortable than my tunic."

She took her bag and settled it beneath the tallest tree, out of habit glancing back to ensure he wasn't sneaking a peek. He was not.

Tul'ran moved the horses to the water and allowed them a deep drink. He then led them to the abundance of grass surrounding the pool. While the horses plunged their muzzles into the green profusion, he removed their saddles and blankets. He produced a brush from the leather bag and scrubbed the sweat and knots from both horses before checking their legs and feet. By the time he stowed their tack between the roots of the smaller tree, a quick glance showed Erianne turned back into her black-green tunic and waiting for him near the largest tree.

They strolled together to the oasis and drank from it, enjoying the richness of the liquid gliding down their parched throats.

Tul'ran looked up at Erianne, fatigue etching lines on his face and around his eyes.

"I hunger, milady, and would indulge my stomach before I bathe. What say you?"

"I'm starving! Let's eat!"

The enthusiasm produced on him a boyish grin, and they walked back to the shaded area beneath the large date palm. Tul'ran retrieved the traveler's fare, which he had replenished as they rode through the streets of Ur.

"I wish I could offer you more lavish fare for your consumption, milady. It seems our destiny is to dine sparsely."

She wolfed down her first bites, her mouth not able to keep up with her stomach's desire.

"It is true, the food is plain, milord. Yet it tastes better, in this moment, than a royal banquet. I feel wealthy beyond measure."

Her heart noted his warm smile, which pleased her.

After they ate, Tul'ran spread the sheepskin roll on the ground and settled onto it with a "whoomph!" He gazed at her with bleary eyes and gestured to the pool behind them.

"I offer you the first opportunity to bathe, milady. You have my assurance; I will not offend your naked form with my eyes."

She curtsied.

"You are a gentleman of note, milord, and I am sure rewards await you in your afterlife for the courtesy you have extended to me since we first met."

He grinned at her, and she turned to the oasis. Stripping off the tunic, she edged into the cool water and luxuriated in its silken kiss. She had no soap, so the water would have to leach away as much sweat, grime, and stench as it could, unaided. She stayed there a good long time, until she felt a shiver rippling through her body, her mind reminding her of the misfortune which came to people who fell asleep in pools of water.

With reluctance, she extracted herself from the pond. There was nothing with which to dry herself. After checking to make sure Tul'ran wasn't watching her, she presented her naked body to the already blistering sun in shameless supplication.

Once the moisture had evaporated from her skin, she picked up the tunic and gave it a distasteful look. There had been no time or place to wash it. She hadn't thought to ask Tul'ran for his cloak again, and she couldn't walk back to him stark naked, could she?

Mischief danced in her eyes. The look on his face might be worth it. Then again, why tease the man? She didn't know what length she could push his desire before it would overcome him. There was no merit in chancing an encounter they'd both regret.

Clothed, refreshed, but for the grimy feeling of wearing dirty clothing against her cleansed skin, Erianne strode back to the large palm. She stopped short of the sheepskin roll and shook her head. Tul'ran had removed his clothing, but for the ever-present loincloth. He was fast asleep, a snore rolling from his nose and mouth.

She noticed the dark edge of stubble on his face and wondered how he shaved. Perhaps he waited until the end of his wanderings, when he could enjoy a maiden's touch running a razor across his skin.

Maybe he would let her shave him?

She tossed her head, sending loosened hair flying. Idiot! Get your head in check! You'd think you'd never seen a man before, she chastised herself. Rules, remember?

It was only after she dragged her eyes from his semi-naked form did she notice the oddity on the roll next to him. He had removed and folded his cloak in the spot where she would sleep. She shook her head. Very few men were so thoughtful where she was from; she might get used to this place. She changed out of the tunic and wrapped herself in his cloak. Erianne laid down on the roll, perhaps just a little closer to the sleeping warrior than the first time she lay with him, and fell into a dreamless sleep.

Darkshadow screamed.

Tul'ran bolted upright as the shrill whinny cut through his sleep-entrapped brain. Confused, he stared at the sky. Half a day had passed into the mid-afternoon, and his mind protested it was far too early to arise. He looked everywhere around the oasis and found the source of the warhorse's cry. Galloping across the desert in the distance, twelve figures in black tunics and headgear approached, curved swords held high above their heads.

Erianne was sitting up, blinking the sleep out of her eyes, holding his cloak tight to her chest. He didn't spare her a glance and barked,

"Get up and get dressed! Our enemy is upon us."

He cursed them, in at least three different languages she understood, and sprang to his feet. He looked at the approaching men, gauging time and distance. There wasn't enough of both. He ran to Darkshadow and released the warhorse from his tether. As rapidly as he was able, he threw the saddle and breastplate on his stallion, casting furtive glances at the approaching men as he did so.

When he finished tacking Darkshadow, Tul'ran grabbed Bloodwing and El Shaddai's Knife. He turned to receive his second shock of the day.

Erianne had dressed. She had in her hands a slender sword and the ever-present dagger, but it was the manner of her dress that threw him. The woman dressed as a female version of himself, with different coloration, perhaps, but there was no mistaking the cut and styling of the leather breaches, the knee-high boots, the chiton, and the leather vestment.

He walked towards the edge of the oasis, clad only in a loincloth, Darkshadow following behind. As walked past her, he threw an odd glance at her face, undiscernible in meaning, and growled,

"We will speak of this if we live the day."

"Milord," she said, hurrying to his side as he walked past the edge of the oasis into the desert sand. "Do you not dress?"

"There is no time. Our enemy is upon us."

And they were. They had ridden hard all night and were even now pushing their horses to the limit in the scorching desert heat, but they were almost upon the oasis.

Tul'ran reached out his hand to grasp Darkshadow's muzzle and turned to look into the horse's large right eye.

"Kill them all."

Darkshadow leaped ahead, riderless, and charged

into the oncoming men. Fatigue had also dulled their senses. They hadn't thought to spread out their forces. The stallion slammed into their midst, biting the oncoming mares with sharp teeth, drawing blood, and kicking out with his massive hooves.

The mares added their whinnies to the din of the shouting men. Two horses collided, flinging their riders headlong into the sand, one shattering his leg. The man shrieked his pain into the pandemonium as the charge became a melee of confusion.

Tul'ran strode into the chaos, Erianne one step behind. A rider charged the Sword Himself and Tul'ran chopped. Erianne saw Bloodwing pass through the rider's right clavicle, down through the midline and exit left of the man's body, severing him in two. It startled Erianne to the point of almost not blocking a scimitar aimed at her head.

As she frantically parried the flurry of scimitar hacks, a part of her mind reeled in disbelief. When he told her he had sliced a granite block in half with the Blade, Erianne thought it to be an exaggeration. It was a fantastical story. It seemed also to be true.

The rider besetting her gave her an opening, and she cut deep into his abdomen, unhorsing him and leaving him bleeding to death in the sand. She turned in time to see Tul'ran cut another man in half at the waist, his face a mask of murder and unquenchable fury. Blood already covered his nearly naked body.

Erianne watched as Darkshadow came up behind another rider, seized him by the collarbone and flung him, screaming, from the saddle before rising and pounding hooves into the man's writhing form.

Then there was no time to watch. A man ran

towards her, swinging his scimitar viciously. She countered the blow, which almost staggered her, so hard was it delivered. Her counter had dropped the man's sword beneath the waistline, so she turned with a spinning back kick and delivered a thick leather heel to the man's temple. He fell to the sand, stunned, and was only briefly aware of the sting of her blade as it entered his neck.

Erianne's instincts caused her to drop into a crouch and spin backwards, sweeping her feet around her body. The foot sweep caught a man coming up behind her by the ankles and tumbled him to the ground. He crabbed backward as fast as he could move. She struck at him with her sword, not giving him a chance to recover his footing. He left his thigh open, and she swung into it. The slice sent a stream of arterial blood arching from the wound. He yelled, dropped his hands to the wound, and her blade cut across his throat.

Again, she spun just in time to meet a rider bearing down on her. It was hot. Her tongue felt glued to the roof of her mouth. She was sweating; the salty essence ran into her eyes and threatened to blur her vision. Her heart was pounding with the force of combat, and she could hear the blood singing in her ears.

Rather than countering the rider's vicious swipe, Erianne danced away from the cut and stabbed the man in his posterior. He grimaced with pain and tried to raise his arms for another swipe, but a slender, obsidian blade sailed into his heart. He looked down at the knife, disconcerted, confused by how it came to find its way into his chest, pitched from the horse, and died.

Another man came screaming at Erianne, uttering curses. His eyes were wild with hatred and battle rush. He was taller and heavier than her first kill. This man was more adept with the scimitar. Erianne's world became a blur of counter, parry, lunge, and counterattack. Her body ached and her muscles screamed with fatigue. The man hacked at her, but miscalculated the shifting sand beneath his feet.

Her enemy slipped, overextending his attack. She cut him on the side of his temple and over his right eye, not a clean blow, but one gaining her instant advantage. Wounded heads bleed. A lot. The gushing blood poured into his eye, obscuring his vision. Erianne pressed, hammering away at exposed points on his body until he, too, fell, dying in the oppressive heat.

She turned, desperate to find her partner or his stallion, hoping beyond hope he had not fallen. She need not have despaired. Tul'ran was fighting two men, if fighting is what it could be called. They had brought with them shields, which the Sword Himself was hacking apart with his ethereal blade.

She didn't see the end of the fight because another man was upon her. Perhaps he had seen she was a woman. Perhaps he had noted her slender form and presumed weakness, notwithstanding her height. He raised his scimitar high above his head with both hands as he ran to her, as if to cleave her in two.

His face ran into a front kick she snapped off the desert floor and into his scarf-covered nose, crushing it. This man, though, had fought before and was no stranger to being struck and having to endure pain in battle. He staggered backwards, wiping tears from his eyes, before Erianne launched her attack at him. They fought with desperate purpose, sword clashing against sword with a tinny, clinking sound. A bloody grimace masked her face as she fended off the blows and returned the favor.

She didn't know how long she could keep this up. Trained, she was, and trained well. It had been a while since she had the chance to train, though, and she was more than a little out of practice. And breath.

Her opponent exposed his left knee. She kicked, catching him flush on the soft part below the kneecap. As he fell, he swiped at her and she caught the blow on her sword, but the dagger was in her left hand, and it found his throat with a most-satisfying gurgle.

All was quiet. All movement had ceased, but for the milling of frightened, riderless horses. Some horses, whose fighters dismounted early into the fray, not all by choice, had wandered to the oasis to drink of its chilly waters. The sand was littered with the broken, bloodied bodies of the men who had ridden so hard through the night and day to catch Tul'ran and Erianne as they slumbered. For their diligence, they died under a scorching sun.

She stood there, panting, sweat drenching her leggings and tunic, her hair a frantic mess, exhilarated and terrified. Grateful to be alive and ready to collapse. They had won. When the realization of their victory cemented itself in her brain, she doubled over and vomited.

She righted herself, wiping her mouth, and

watched as the man with the shattered leg hobbled away from the battle space as fast as his good leg could take him. To his misfortune, he caught Darkshadow's attention. The stallion was in full blood rage, beyond hatred, beyond sense, beyond restraint. She could see Darkshadow's intent. The warhorse had no sense of mercy.

"Darkshadow! Enough! Leave him be!"

She tried to remember the words Tul'ran had used in training.

"Darkshadow, brother! The battle has passed, and we have won the field. Peace, brother, peace. There is no further need for your might!"

The shouts fell on empty air. Darkshadow charged at the fleeing man, reached out with bloodied teeth, and ripped at the back of the man's neck. The man screamed as he fell face first into the dunes. Darkshadow was upon him, pounding him again and again with those massive hooves until there was nothing left but a pile of tunic and flesh drenched in gore.

A part of her watched in horror as the beautiful horse sent one last kick into the downed man's head, her stomach reeling again. She had difficulty reconciling the savagery of the attack with the sweet and docile temperament she had known on their long evening journeys together.

She thought of Tul'ran and turned to search for him.

He was there, standing before her, a tangle of blood, sweat, and sand, death dancing in his cold, cold eyes, and the long, slender, midnight black blade at her throat. A voice from the rawest part of his anger and pain clawed its way out of his throat. "Who are you, and why are you here?"

CHAPTER THE TENTH:
THE TELLING OF
ERIANNE DE MI CORAZON

Erianne the Dark was not who she claimed.
Her treachery made the Warrior's heart roar,
What foul betrayal had been set afoot
Bringing the goddess to Death's very door?

Erianne stood frozen to the spot, mortified, watching as icy waves of fury danced in his eyes. Her breath, hindered by the battle, gasped inwards and held as her lungs refused to move. She didn't answer because she couldn't, so hypnotized was she by the fatality promised in his eyes and the knife at her throat.

"Speak!" He commanded her, his voice harsh and unrelenting. "And truly, for if I hear falsehood passing through your lips, if I read deception in your eyes, I. Will. End. Your. Life."

He meant it. Every staccato word enforced it. Her death burned in his face, as did the strength of his purpose.

"Milord," she stammered, willing her body to not move so much as a hair. "How have I deceived you into some foul circumstance?"

"You would dare to play word games with me, woman? Do you think me unintelligent? Do you strike me as a fool?"

"You have, at least twice, by my count, spoken in a language I have never heard. For a long time, I have lived in this region. I have fought many men of different languages and dialects. I am proficient in most of those languages. Never once have I heard the one you have spoken."

"You knew the name of your assassin in the desert, or, if not her name, the name of the one who sent her. When I asked who she was and whence she came, you deceived me. You deceived me, your covenant-mate!"

"When we were in the city, you flinched when you thought I would strike down Vebrax. You wished for my restraint when you should have felt outrage at his insult. Did you demand his death? No! When you did not, the suspicion born in the desert grew into mistrust."

"Three times have our enemies found us and struck us from ambush. Three times in short order did they know where to come and how to set forces in our path."

"No sooner had I spilled my heart into your ears and told you of Katja of the Gutians than twelve

Gutians attacked us in the desert."

It was a terrible coincidence, but he would never believe it, she knew, fighting to compose herself.

"You have told me your father was a mighty warrior, but he did not rescue you. Nor did he make any effort to do so. You told me your purse was too lean to purchase a horse, yet I have seen the vast wealth dripping from your body as we rode through the streets of Ur. You would have me believe your father would not spend a tenth of it to raise an army and campaign for your release in one of the largest cities in this region. A city flooded with men starving for shekels and a chance to wage war."

"You fight in a style I have never witnessed, using less your weapon and more your arms and legs. In all my days, I have not met a fighter like you."

"You are not who you said you were, and I will have your truth or your death. Now!"

'I'm dead, I'm dead, I'm dead,' Erianne thought frantically. If she didn't tell him the truth, which he could apparently discern more readily than she thought, he'd kill her. If she told him the truth, and if she made it home, they'd sentence her to death. There would be no defense to violating an oath she swore on her life.

"Milord Tul'ran, I beg your mercy. I have given an oath on my life I would not disclose to a living soul my true identity and purpose. If you force this from me, I shall surely die."

"You shall surely die if you do not," he said, pressing the blade up against her throat. She could feel the skin part where the blade met it. A tiny trickle of blood formed beneath the blade and scratched its way down her sweaty neck.

Erianne closed her eyes and surrendered to her fate. Yes, she was dead. Her death was a certainty written in stone. If she lied, he'd know it and kill her. Her superiors would sentence her to death if she told him the truth. If she stayed with Tul'ran, her common enemy would continue to hunt them. All wanted to end her life.

It came down to the question: by whose hands did she want to die?

She thought of the time Tul'ran had used her first name, with warmth and affection. Erianne recalled all his surreptitious glances at her, some in admiration, some carrying a faint glow of lust. She remembered how he walked beside her in the market in Ur, proud, like a man showing off to the world his beautiful bride. The woman in her was not, could not, be certain, but if there was any possibility she was right...

She couldn't have him kill, again, someone with whom he might be in love.

She steeled herself and opened her eyes to his ferocious gaze. Her bloody blades fell to the desert floor when she released her grip on the hilts.

"Tul'ran az Nostrom, the Sword Himself, Prince of Death, Master of Bloodwing the Blade, Sword of Judgment, Deliverer of Death. I beg you for the mercy of a true Telling. By the blood you have drawn from my throat this day and against my life, I swear I shall tell you the truth, the whole truth, and nothing but the truth. Even if it is hard for you to hear and harder to trust. Once you have heard me, I will wait upon your judgment and accept whatever fate you decide, be it life or death. I ask only your permission to give a proper Telling this night as we ride once more."

She swallowed. Heat and effort had parched her throat. The knife threatening to slice it open wasn't helping, either.

"I will speak with honesty and deliver veracity from my heart. To show you this, I will now tell you my first truth. Know as I speak this, I give up my life. I swore an oath to others I would not impart this information on pain of death. As soon as I utter these words, my oath holders will know and sign a warrant for my execution."

She looked at him, eyes glistening, and took a deep breath.

"My true name is Erianne de mi Corazon. Four thousand years into your future, I was born. I am trained as a scholar. I have returned to this Age to study you. You have noticed things about me ringing falsely, not because I am a woman out of place, but because my place is out of time."

Tul'ran's face became blank as he regarded her with a gaze screaming with incredulity and disbelief. He stared into her lush green eyes for what seemed like an eon.

"Corazon, or whoever you are, your words make me dizzy. The future? What madness is this? And four thousand years! Never have I even contemplated such a number. You are eight and twenty years old; I heard you say so yourself. You want me to believe you are four thousand years older than me? Am I going insane? How is it possible for you to travel backwards through the years and stand before me as if you were born into this place? Surely it must be impossible."

It was getting harder to breathe. She noticed his hand developing a slight tremor. A shaking hand and a sharp knife do not a happy couple make.

"I am sympathetic with your disbelief, milord Tul'ran. I would not attribute credibility to this tale were I not standing here with a man who died four thousand years in my past. Milord, I speak the truth. Can you not read it in my eyes?"

"I do not know whether I can trust myself to read your eyes. I do not know what to trust at this moment. My mind whirls like the wind in a desert storm. It is too easy to speak the truth to you. I do not readily share the thoughts and experiences you have drawn from me. You have somehow cast a net of insensibility over the part of my mind normally reserved for caution. You have proven to be deceptive and cunning. When I consider how you have deceived me so well to this point, I am given pause. I see you have noticed the tremor in my hand. Fatigue and shock are about to have their way with me. This I know for certain: it would not do to cut your throat before I have my answers."

To Erianne's incalculable relief, the knife blade came away from her neck and Tul'ran backed one step away. He lowered El Shaddai's Knife to his side. Erianne's legs were shaking so hard she could barely stand.

"Erianne de mi Corazon," he said in a grave, exhausted tone. "I accept your oath. I will hear your Telling this night as we once more ride the dunes, for it is so we must be away from this place as quickly as possible. Once I have heard, I will adjudge."

Erianne raised her hands outward, wrists close together. He looked at her, uncertain of her intent.

"I am your prisoner, milord. I offer my wrists for binding unless you will accept my parole until the appointed time."

He blinked at the woman standing tall before him. He could see the weariness on her face, the fear in her eyes.

"You fought hard and well; you were a worthy ally against the Gutians. I lost count of the number of times you stepped between my back and an approaching foe. You saved my life this day, and more than once, I warrant. I accept your parole. Between now and the time appointed for a Finding, let there once more be peace between us. We remain bound in covenant until you release me or one of us dies."

He cocked his head at her.

"Or do we? Do you even have covenants in your time? Do you feel bound by our covenant, or was it merely a device by which you secured my cooperation to fulfill your desires?"

Yes, he was intelligent, she noted, while relief washed over her body. His ready acceptance she was a time traveler amazed her.

She bobbed her head.

"Yes, milord, we have covenants in my time. I express to you with all my heart I remain your covenant-mistress, our lives bound until release or until death. As you have protected me from harm, so will I protect you, whatever you need and whatever I can provide."

Satisfied, he turned away, then checked the turn.

"It would seem titles do not apply as between us. It would be best if you simply addressed me as Tul'ran and I, you, as Erianne. At least this should be done when we are alone. When with others, we should continue as before so as not to raise suspicion as to your true nature."

It was too much.

Too much adrenaline, too much heat, too much fear, too much relief, and too much belief from a man who should by all rules of logic and sense never have accepted any of the words pouring from her mouth.

Erianne fainted and dropped onto the sand.

The cool, damp cloth felt good against her skin. She was laying in the shade, her upper shoulders draped across something soft, yet firm. Someone was murmuring her name as the cool, silken touch danced against her forehead, cheeks, and face.

She opened her eyes to look into the concerned dark eyes of the man who, most recently, had wanted to kill her. One of his eyebrows quirked.

"Hello, Erianne. Do you wish to regain the joy of living?"

She snorted, noting he must have dunked himself in the pool because the blood was gone from his hair and face.

"In what ways have I most recently experienced the joy of living, milord?"

"Tul'ran," he chided.

"In what ways have I most recently experienced the joy of living, milord Tul'ran?"

Laughter moved his chest.

"Have you always been this impertinent?"

They were under the tallest palm, his back pressed against it, and her head and shoulders resting on his thighs. It was late afternoon. The air was peaceful. In the background, flies buzzed about the broken, bleeding bodies of their enemies.

Erianne nestled a little further into his thighs.

"My friends know me as a pleasant woman, calm in disposition, and faint of temper, never rushing off to go where lions fear to tread."

He couldn't restrain another laugh.

"Whoever has given you this impression, milady, has lied through teeth with a wicked tongue."

"Erianne," she chided in a tone of mock severity.

"I have something to show you," Tul'ran said when their laughter subsided. He reached behind him and produced something from within the folds of his clothing. It was a black cylinder with a dull, matte finish. Erianne's eyes grew wide as she snatched it from his hand.

"What is it?" he asked, noting the immediate recognition on her face.

"It is a *thermal imager*," she said. She explained further when she saw his forehead wrinkle. "It is a device mostly used at night. It senses heat in darker, cooler places and displays them to assist a hunter in finding his prey. Where did you get this?"

"The female assassin whose head we left in the desert had attached it to her bow. I cut it from the riser of the bow after I noticed it hanging in midair, with an outline of you sitting on Darkshadow painted in colors of warmth: yellow, orange, and red."

A puzzled look crossed her face. "When did this happen? How did you see through the thermal imager from where you were standing beside me? You deflected the arrow from my body with Bloodwing. When we journeyed to where the assassin lay; only her head remained."

"Forbearance, Erianne. I will explain all. You have my word. But not now. We must pack and ride once more into the desert. Night will soon fall, and we must be away from here before more of our enemies ride out to seek us in this place. I show you this thing because I am most concerned with the ease with which our enemies find us. Can our enemies track us through this thing you call a thermal imager?"

Erianne examined the imager. It was of a make and model with which she wasn't familiar, but she knew very well who their enemies were and the resources at their command.

"It is possible," she conceded. "I am not familiar with this device, but our enemy has the means to track their warriors through their clothing and equipment. Though not readily plain, they may have inserted such a means into this device."

Erianne reached into her battle leathers and pulled out the object she'd scooped off the floor of the hutch.

"In my time, this is called a stunner. It will send a force through your body of sufficient strength to immobilize you completely while keeping your life intact. Our enemies sought to disable you with this and then capture or kill me. It, too, may allow them to track us."

"Then they must go," Tul'ran said. He went to rise, then checked himself. He looked back at her face, deep into her eyes.

"Erianne de mi Corazon, I have done you a great injustice. I have put a blade to your throat and drawn blood. I confess, with great shame, I harbored an intent to end your life. Will you offer me grace and forgive me?"

She did the unthinkable.

She wrapped her arm around his neck, lifted her head, and planted a long, soft kiss on his lips. The kiss startled him at first, but he settled into it well enough. When they disengaged, a long while later, her eyes were shimmering.

"Tul'ran az Nostrom, you have favored me more this day than has any man in my life. You heard me, accepted my oath, and stayed your hand. You drew only enough blood to clear my head. I remain in your debt."

Despite his weathered and tanned skin, she could see a blush rise to the roots of his black hair. He tried to stop a grin, but was unsuccessful. He dropped his head.

"You honor me, milady. The debt is mine. Thank you for the delightful acceptance of my apology. I would continue this delight further, but it is best not to do so when I am clad in only a loincloth. I would not dishonor you with my body's response to your kiss and your beauty. To further our good fortune, I must seek at once to rid us of these things we have collected belonging to a place far in time from here."

He eased her off his lap and strode to the horses

grazing near the oasis. Erianne watched him go, smiling. She didn't know where the kiss came from. Erianne would seduce him to save her life, were it necessary, but the thought had been nowhere near the forefront of her mind before her mouth touched his. She ran a fingertip over her lips. He was a good kisser.

Tul'ran walked toward the horses milling about the oasis, pausing when he found a mare suitable to his purpose. He led the mare to the edge of the oasis, thermal imager and stunner in hand. After finger-brushing the knots out of the mare's mane, he braided the devices into her hair.

Erianne jumped to her feet and walked over to where Tul'ran stood. She reached out to touch the hand skillfully knotting the horse's hair.

"I cannot permit what you are doing."

He paused, looking at her with mild surprise.

"Why for not, Erianne?"

"My laws forbid any person from my time leaving behind any item from the future. We made the law to prevent someone in our past from discovering such an item. I see what you are about to do. You would set this horse free to return to Ur and give our enemies false information about where we ride."

She let his hand go. The contact was taking her mind to a place most inappropriate.

"If someone discovers the thermal imager in the horse's mane, the consequences could be dire for both this era and the future. We could change the future by a casual act, and many could die or simply never exist."

Tul'ran's forehead crinkled as he struggled with

the concepts she described. He stood for a moment, deep in thought.

"What if they were not to discover it?"

She looked at him, puzzled.

"What is it you propose to do?"

"Observe."

Tul'ran walked into the desert and found one man she had killed in combat. Her kills were much cleaner and the bodies less torn apart than his. He threw the bloodied body over his shoulders and brought him back into the oasis. Tul'ran searched among the packs on the barbarian's horses until he found a length of rope. He took the small devices and shoved them down the dead man's throat as far as he could reach, then further yet with the tip of the Knife.

She approved. No one conducted autopsies in this era. Someone would find this man and bury him in an unmarked grave. No one would study this region of the world for thousands of years, if ever, so no one would discover his body and the devices. If they burned him on a funeral pyre, which was the custom of the day, the heat would reduce the devices to ash.

While possible, it was highly unlikely anyone would ever find the devices. Unless they were sending signals monitored by their enemies. In such a case, the Order of the Purity would retrieve the devices in short order. As careless as they were in targeting her in antiquity, their enemies would never leave the devices to pollute the timeline.

After Tul'ran tied the dead man to the horse, he led the mare from the oasis, pointed her nose toward Ur, and gave her a sharp slap on the rump. The horse at once ran away, though after a while her pace slowed to a walk while keeping a course towards the city.

Tul'ran returned to the oasis, noting Erianne was busy gathering their things for leave-taking. He walked to the pool, stripping away his loincloth and plunged in, the chilly waters almost taking away his breath. The warrior scrubbed his body and limbs vigorously for a few moments before climbing out. He stood still to let the warmth of the waning day dry him, too tired to worry whether she was watching him standing fully naked under the sun's rays.

When he was dry, he wrapped the loincloth around his waist and returned to his leather bag to pull out a clean covering. He caught Erianne's eye and cocked one eyebrow. She turned away to give him privacy, fighting back the urge to sneak a peek.

After several minutes, they dressed and loaded the horses. Tul'ran lifted an eyebrow, and she pointed east.

"I am relieved to note you are pointing away from Babylon, Erianne. Your hand gestures to a ridge of mountains we will find in the distance. I have had my fill of cities for the time being."

When they set out from the oasis, darkness had fallen. The moon had lost its fullness, but still glowed in the cloudy, star-filled sky. They rode silently before Tul'ran broke the peace.

"Milady, the night is long, and our journey is far..."

She grimaced at the phrase she had used to open his heart and pour out a torrent of thundering pain.

How ironic the phrase offered in jest had now become a warning shadow of discomfort to come.

"Then I to my Telling, Lord Tul'ran, the Sword Himself, Avenger of the Innocent, Master of Mercy."

"I must, however, begin with a Telling of my parents, Luke Manyfeathers and Priya Sharma Pillai, for it was their story which led to the reason people of my time come to yours."

"I will start with my father."

Luke was a scholar of Indigenous descent, his line originating with the Anishinabe people, formerly known as the Ojibwe, in Manitoba, Canada. He had high cheekbones, dark hair, the solid green eyes of his ancestry, and an uncommon height. When he was sixteen years old, he was six feet eight inches tall, though his height was built upon a skinny body devoid of muscle.

His family pressed him to get a scholarship playing basketball, but he lacked the desire and physical coordination to play the game. Luke secured his own entrance to places of higher learning through his incredible intelligence. At a pace much faster than those of his peers, he earned a PhD in theoretical physics. He was working on his second PhD when he met Priya.

"My mother and father were much in love until their last days. The two of them could not be less alike."

Priya's parents were both of East Indian descent. In the year her parents met, the population of India arrived at a breaking point. The government passed strict laws denying children to its citizens unless they achieved a suitable rank or status within the country. Rank or status was based upon academic achievement or research and development contributing towards the growth and development of India. It wasn't based, at all, on wealth, fame, contribution to the arts, or achievement in sports.

Government enforcers rigorously monitored and promptly investigated childbirth records for fraud, deceit, or bribery. The courts sentenced offenders to death. To ensure respect for the law, government-controlled physicians removed the ova of all females who reached menstruation. They froze the ova for the unlikely event the government would allow them to have children.

Priya's father was a physician who discovered a path towards the genetic treatment of cancer, still under development when he accepted an arranged marriage to his wife. Priya's mother was a brilliant physicist, blessed with great beauty. The two of them had dedicated their lives to pursuing knowledge and the secret desire their achievements would allow them progeny. Eventually, their superiors rewarded them with permission to have one child, Priya.

Priya was shorter and rounder than her parents and lacked her mother's intense beauty. She had a wickedly playful sense of humor, which allowed her to make friends easily. As a youth, she excelled in soccer and cricket. Her selection as class valedictorian came as a surprise to no one.

Priya developed into the intellectual equal of her parents. Eventually, she made her way from New Delhi to Oxford University, where she secured a PhD in physics, with a focus on quantum mechanics.

Erianne had the beginning of a headache at the end of the brief description of her parents and their careers. She deliberately skipped mention of the topics of physics and quantum mechanics because she couldn't translate such esoteric concepts into the language and understanding of his era.

Tul'ran was clever and curious. He wasn't afraid to ask questions about the things he didn't understand.

"I am amazed the world arrived at a place where leaders deny people offspring. If individuals may not have children, then how did you come to be?"

"Patience, Lord of Impatience," she teased. "I promised to tell you my story; I did not promise it would be brief."

She was pleased to hear him chuckle. Throughout her first Telling, he had wrapped himself in such an aura of darkness she feared for her life. She should be equally afraid now, for he had yet to adjudge her after the Telling was complete.

Somehow, though, this occasion was different. Had she not awakened on his lap with him washing her face, with tenderness in his eyes, she would have been far more concerned with the prospect of dying. Things had changed between them; they were closer in heart and mind. Shedding blood together on the battlefield meant a lot to a warrior like him.

They weren't just bound by the glory of battle and the restraints of the covenant. There was something deeper connecting their hearts, too. Especially if the delicious kiss meant anything. He had warmed towards her as they rode away from the oasis, suggesting their linkage was still intact.

Enough linkage, she hoped, to keep her alive when the sun rose to greet the darkened sky.

"My parents met in a place of education, called *Oxford University*, where others gathered to exchange thought and promote ideas. After a common friend introduced them, the two of them became instantly enamored of the other."

Yeah, right? They jumped into bed faster than the speed of light. They were the unlikeliest of couples: him with his immense height and quiet, somewhat somber disposition, and her almost half his height, a happy social butterfly. Their joint intellect overshadowed what they lacked in physical similarity. They spent many a night dissecting the secrets of the universe while exploring the secrets of their entwined bodies.

After only one term of study, Luke Manyfeathers journeyed back to India with Priya and begged her parents for permission to marry their daughter. Her parents had become non-traditionalists, which made the path easier. It was effortless to like the giant Priya introduced into their midst. After all, everyone loved Canadians.

And so it was Luke and Priya were married in her customs. The guest attendees at the wedding bit their lips hard to restrain laughter on seeing the tiny, plump bride escorted from the wedding ceremony by a skinny mountain wearing a sherwani at least one size too small.

Luke and Priya returned to England to recommence study and research. Luke secured a lucrative government grant to study the effect of dark matter on the mechanics of the universe. It was a topic so close to Priya's area of expertise, she enthusiastically joined him on the project.

"My parents described to me their happiness during those days. Peace endured throughout the world. They had food, water, shelter, and friends."

Tul'ran stroked Darkshadow's neck.

"All they yet needed were horses."

Erianne giggled.

"Indeed, there were not so fortunate."

Luke and Priya's lives orbited each other within the bubble of academia, and it seemed as if their joy would never end.

Until it ended, when disaster struck. Not just a disaster for them, or England, but a disaster of global, epic proportions: the First Cataclysm. Ironically, the First Cataclysm started on Good Friday, March 27, 2065.

For years, the effects of global warming had translated into unusual weather patterns in unexpected parts of the globe. Some with dangerous and life-threatening consequences. The sea levels rose with the melt of the polar ice caps, and coastal cities were under constant siege. City planners continually engineered and built walls, levees, and drainage systems to prevent catastrophe.

During the First Cataclysm, catastrophe bloomed like a thermonuclear bomb.

For thirty days it snowed or rained ice cold *everywhere* in the world, all at once. The rain came as hurricanes and monsoons lashed coastal areas and deep inland. Tornados cascaded from the storm systems like field mice running from beneath bales of hay, with lethal effect. Wind, rain, and snow pounded every part of the planet Earth.

By the end of the First Cataclysm, the Earth was two degrees cooler and a lot wetter.

"What we described as the First Cataclysm was a disaster of weather. Moisture fell from the skies in overwhelming amounts, destroying cities and homes alike. Many died."

The destruction was unimaginable. Tides bulldozed their way into crowded coastal cities, flooding and damaging them immeasurably. People lost homes, businesses, and lives. So many lives. One-tenth of the entire global population died in the brief span of weeks. Sicknesses sprang up all over the world and decimated the population further, as besieged health centers couldn't cope with them.

The weather damaged electrical grids in many countries beyond repair. It ravaged fossil fuel development and production facilities so much it would take decades to bring them back online.

The only good coming out of the destruction of oil and gas was the development of cold fusion technology to power electrical systems. Such technology was rapidly and generously shared around the world.

For years, people had petitioned governments and corporations to save the environment and protested in cities around the world. They need not have wasted their precious moments. The environment coldly reset itself with no regard for the people who called the world home.

"Such disaster befell us it brought the people and their means of earning a wage to their knees."

Nation-states lost the rigidity of their identities

when the First Cataclysm shattered the world. No country was so unmarred it could recover on its own. The excesses nature had unleashed upon the world had an unexpected effect. Countries cooperated better than at any time in history, and the world moved toward a one world form of government. A single global currency merged the economies of every state, including what had been strong, independent nations.

The only country continuing to maintain independence was the United States of America, which firmly kept control of its currency, economy, and military. While their level of cooperation with the world government increased substantially, America remained firmly and fiercely independent. Canada looked to its big brother on its southern border and maintained its independence, too, placing its trust more in the longstanding relationship than in the emerging structure of the Global Legislature.

"You must remember, Tul'ran, I am describing a world far in the future from the present. The learning of our scholars is very advanced. The people of the world clamored for the scholars to find the means to control the weather and avoid a repeat of the devastation."

Tul'ran looked up at the night sky, having in it but a few clouds.

"If I can accept you have traveled through thousands of years to ride at my side, I can believe your people could devise a means of stopping rain. I ascribe truth to your words."

Erianne looked at him, an odd expression on her face. Again, she found his level of acceptance extraordinary. What did she not know about him? This was far too easy.

Destiny's Edge took the moment to whinny and toss her head, as if she, herself, couldn't fathom the warrior riding on the beautiful stallion walking at her side. Erianne smiled.

"I thank you, gracious and kind lord of all he surveys."

He grunted.

"The night is not so long you should discontinue your Telling."

"I shall continue with haste, milord, with haste."

Luke and Priya answered the global call for a scientific solution and pooled their intellectual resources to find an approach to controlling the environment through the quantum realm. They discovered something far more incredible. While not the means to control weather, they discovered the possibility of traveling through time. As an afterthought, they proved the mathematics of how a sufficiently financed company could engineer such travel. On October 1, 2065, Luke and Priya published their findings and sat back to wait for the response of their fellow scientists.

The discovery created a firestorm. While governments and corporations rushed to implement theory into practicality, scientists, philosophers, and religious leaders hotly debated the merits of traveling back in time. Many argued the world had already subjected them to a great disaster and wondered whether future time travelers caused it. 'Causality' became the word of the day, and the ensuing intellectual debate was enough to guarantee a lifetime of migraines.

"As you can appreciate, Tul'ran, my parents' pronouncement of their discovery left people frightened and amazed. My mother and father insulated themselves from the furor as best they could, but could not avoid fame. With their fame came recognition and reward."

Luke and Priya quietly received only one of the many bonuses following upon their discovery: the permission to have a child. India's laws had held her ova hostage, but the government of India was more than happy to release an ovum to the couple who were the darlings of the world. Priya received her ovum gratefully and cherished it like the world's priciest gem. Shortly afterwards, Priya's physician gave them the most joyous news of their lives: Priya was pregnant with their child.

"On February 14, 2067, I was born."

In answer to his follow-up question, she explained the current years rolled down to zero and restarted upwards. It was in this manner the number of years between their eras was over four thousand. Tul'ran rubbed his temple as if he were getting a headache, she noted with sympathy.

"My birthing was one day late, Tul'ran. My father would often proclaim it was the only day I was tardy for a meal. This is how my parents conceived me and brought me into a world of turmoil and promise."

"Are you named after your father or your mother?"

She laughed.

"Neither, if the truth be told."

Before she was born, her parents, knowing they

were having a girl, hotly disputed what she should be called. Luke had favored a combination of names blending both their cultural histories and families. His suggestion ended up being nine names long, and Priya would have none of it.

"We'll name her Erianne de mi Corazon," her mother laid down, with gentle ferocity, "for she truly is the child of my heart." At least she had picked one name favored by Luke.

"But love," Luke protested, though not nearly as firmly, "she won't have the names of either of our families. Your parents will be furious. Mine now live with the Creator, but yours has been waiting for a grandchild for as long as I can remember."

"I'll handle them," Priya said, and she did. So came into the world Erianne de mi Corazon, Erianne of my heart, as the Spanish would translate it into English. The blessing of the birth of their child so moved Luke and Priya; they became Christians. At Erianne's christening, the pastor of their new church baptized all three.

"I confess, Tul'ran; to say they spoiled me as a child is to say the surface of the sun, midday, is a little warm. My parents loved me, doted on me, and spent every waking moment with me."

The Nobel Prize awarded to them in physics, as well as the lucrative jobs offered by Oxford University, gave them an enormous source of funds. Their wealth allowed them to spend every waking moment with their daughter.

They were with her when she took her first steps, claimed independence from the potty, fed and clothed herself, and rode her first bicycle. Not for her the plebeian public school system. Luke and Priya took upon themselves the education of their daughter, while giving her plenty of opportunity to meet and make friends and take part in sports. She gained her mother's athleticism and shone in soccer and, to the horror of her parents, rugby. She learned to ride equestrian and became very proficient in the saddle. Erianne loved horses, and horses loved her. She was driven, as her parents were driven, and she excelled.

Erianne grew into a tall, graceful woman. She had a goodly portion of her father's height, his green eyes, and his lean body. From her mother, she inherited dusky brown skin and jet black hair. Her grandmother's genes blessed her with exceptional beauty. All of them contributed to her amazing intelligence.

They vacationed together, of a sort. Luke and Priya couldn't take her to beaches in the Caribbean because many of them were gone or still trying to re-establish themselves after the First Cataclysm. Instead, they invented a holographic program in their home, rivaling the realism only offered previously by fictional television shows. Almost as an afterthought, they secured a patent on their holographic technology. A group of engineers built the holographic imagers under license and sold them to the world.

"When I reached three and ten years, my family was wealthy beyond ridiculous. On the day celebrating my birth one year later, the leaders of the world announced rules by which people like me could travel backwards in time."

They created the Time Accords for protecting the present when researchers launched into the past. Only accredited Historians could travel through time. These were scholars as eager to preserve the purity of history as the fanatics who loudly protested any incursion into antiquity.

Authorities locked up the engineering specifications for the time travel devices tighter than the gold in Fort Knox had once been. The One World Legislature permitted only a small, select group of men and women access to the technology. Nothing existed online, exposed to infiltration by the denizens of the Dark Web. All means and methods of time travel were a tightly held secret: governments didn't have it, corporations didn't have it, and individuals didn't have it.

"Keeping the information secret was uppermost in the minds of our leaders."

The One World Legislature created and funded the Time Travel Initiative. It also built an artificial island in the Atlantic Ocean. To this island, they sent the engineers and quantum physicists who jointly created the time travel network, including Luke, Priya, and Erianne. TTI essentially imprisoned anyone who worked for them.

A penitentiary it was, but a more lavish one never existed in history. TTI paid the scientists significant sums of money, provided sumptuous housing, and supplied them with lifelike androids for their entertainment and amusement. They provided all this within the geographical confines of the ocean-based facility the residents called Atlantis. Their extended families profited from their wealth, but never again from their company.

"Anyone working for my group, Tul'ran, is not and will never be free to travel the world in the future. It is the only way to prevent a malevolent force from gaining their knowledge."

He spun his head toward her.

"Does this also apply to you, Erianne?"

"It does, but as I shall explain, I chose this life with such knowledge."

From her earliest years, Erianne dedicated her life to becoming a Time Historian. Besides her intelligence, she had another advantage: she was an empath. Strangers opened their hearts to her and exposed the deepest secrets of their souls. People trusted her immediately and shared openly. For someone who wanted to research history, it was an invaluable asset.

She studied hard and excelled in all the areas needed to achieve Historian status: history, mathematics, physics, cultural sensitivity, and political science. She, like many other prospective Time Historians, wanted with all her heart to journey back to the area once described as the Middle East.

Her parents watched with unease as she pursued her dream. If the Time Travel Initiative accepted her, Erianne would take up residence on Atlantis permanently, and she could never leave to see the rest of the world. They loved their daughter a great deal and hated the thought her career would be a life sentence in a remote location. Yet they also loved their baby girl so much they couldn't deny her the future she desired. The world rained rewards on them because they had had the freedom to make choices. They would do no less for their child, no matter how much it hurt. So, they encouraged Erianne and opened doors for her into all the fields of study available to assist her in her quest.

Erianne learned much information about the people, the geography, the languages, the cultures, and the politics of the Middle East. She became fluent in the Sumerian, Babylonian, Akkadian, and Amorite languages.

"I can translate for you with anyone we meet in this area."

Tul'ran pursed his lips.

"I will remember your kind offer. Once I mention my name, however, translation is often not required."

Erianne bit her lip. There she was, getting too comfortable with him again. How many times would she have to be reminded he was Tul'ran the Sword, the renowned Prince of Death, before she would remember with whom she dealt?

"I also had to learn how to survive in a culture made alien to mine by the passage of thousands of years. Historical records always had to be treated as suspect because the author brought with him and her their own biases, understanding, and perspective. The victor often writes history. I could not truly achieve a pure appreciation of what took place in history unless I experienced it for myself."

"I learned to be cautious, careful, and adaptable so as not to offend someone because the author of a historical book thought a tradition too minor for inclusion or so commonplace it did not merit special mention."

Erianne was twenty-three years old on June 17, 2090, when TTI sent the first object into the past. Only inanimate objects were in the first transition to evaluate what would happen once the TTI attempted to retrieve them. They sent a box back one hundred years to a remote spot in the Sahara Desert. The controllers left it there for twelve hours, Origin Time, or OT. When they commanded it to return, it did, promptly and with no problem.

Microscopic analysis showed the box had accumulated microbes one hundred years old.

The microbes' presence sent the Time Travel Initiative's adversaries into another tizzy. The world, they proclaimed, could suffer another global plague with deadly consequences if time travelers brought back a virus for which there was no immunity or vaccine. Here, the politicians agreed with the anti-Travelers, insisting upon TTI creating a strict regimen of quarantine and testing after the return of each Time Team.

"Two months later, the Controllers sent a human team of two young, active military people, a man and a woman, back to the same date and location."

The couple were a breeding pair; a marker against the prospect they might end up in a dimension devoid of human life. They were, after all, traveling through the quantum realm.

After twelve hours of OT, the two returned healthy down to the cellular level. The program was a success. When the first human test team transitioned out, Erianne held her breath and crossed her fingers, then celebrated with gusto when the two returned without harm.

"I watched with envy as Time Teams traveled into various periods throughout history. They came back with proof of their findings, and almost all the world celebrated. Places of learning set up entire new departments to pour over the treasure trove brought back from antiquity."

Tul'ran pulled Darkshadow to a halt, a troubled look on his face.

"Do you mean your Time Teams take people from this now to yours?"

Erianne chopped the air with her hand.

"No! To do so is forbidden expressly. Our direction is: we are not to interfere with the lives, comfort, and safety of those who live in the past."

This amused Tul'ran to no end.

"How are you doing so far?"

Erianne laughed aloud as she looked at the man who had saved her life daily since she arrived in antiquity, placing his life in jeopardy.

"Not so well, milord, not so well."

At the end of her academic studies, and having achieved her twenty-fifth birthday, she felt ready. She had absorbed all the knowledge available to her and felt confident she could excel as a Time Historian. Her father noted her confidence, and while he was proud of and very pleased with his daughter, he felt the necessity to draw her aside before she applied to the Appointments Board.

"Tell me, daughter, lifeblood of my veins, what have you left to learn?"

She had frowned, uncertainty creasing her brow.

"I don't know what you mean, Dad. You've seen how hard I've worked and what I've studied. There's not much more I can study about Mesopotamian language, culture, and values."

"True," he acknowledged, his eyes serious but warm. "What distinguishes you from every other candidate who is as qualified?"

It stumped her. She thought hard for a few minutes and shrugged her surrender.

"You have me, Dad. I know you're driving at something, but for the life of me, I don't know what it is."

He smiled.

"You wish to go into an era and study a culture rife with misogyny and violence. How will you protect yourself without drawing attention?"

She knew the answer to the question and supplied an immediate answer.

"Every Time Team has a Protector; they take care of security."

"I see. How many of those Protectors are Historians?"

She pondered his question for a moment, casting her mind over the specifications of the Team construct requirements.

"I don't think any of them are. They're retired military; most have Special Ops training."

"So then, how much more valuable would you be if you were not only an accredited Historian but also trained in martial arts and the use of the weapons of the period?"

Understanding dawned. She surrendered by making a half bow to her elder.

"What do I do?"

Her father arranged for her to be trained by one

of the Security officers on Atlantis who had survived a full career on a Special Air Service team. He also arranged lessons on the use of a sword, dagger, and throwing blade, as well as martial arts instruction.

For three years, she trained hard. She learned how to survive in any environment without food and water at hand, even suffering through a one-week survival course with nothing but a knife and an incorrigible refusal to quit. Erianne achieved a black belt, proficiency in using almost any blade, and two scars, which made a lasting impression of the dangers of carelessness. She became, in every sense, a scout: intelligent, cautious, adaptable, and more than capable in a fight.

"Tul'ran, this is the training to which I referred when first we met."

"I would like to thank the people who trained you, Erianne. You are a demon on the battlefield. I would not wish to face you when you set your mind on destruction. Indeed, I invest upon you a new station and title for which you well deserve: the Princess of Destruction."

"You are most gracious for a Lord of Death."

"Laughter is distracting me from your Telling. Pray, continue."

It was a tough three years. She watched the coverage of the progress of the Time Initiative. The debate had continued to rage on social media and in the scientific community about the dangers and morality associated with time travel.

Scientists who demanded protection of the timeline argued the theory of the Butterfly Effect, arguing any change made by time travelers could alter the timeline with devastating effect. Avid proponents of time travel argued the theory time travelers couldn't alter the timeline because the past was inviolate. A serious error by a time traveler would create an alternate reality for the traveler only, separate from the timeline they left, because *this* present would be *their* past. No one knew which theory was correct; there was no way of confirming either theory even after they began time tunneling.

Erianne watched each newscast with increasing jealousy as she struggled for patience during her training. As she trained, she continued to pour over anything written about the area and period to which she fervently desired to travel... and found an anomaly.

"You were the anomaly, Lord Tul'ran. Historians from my era describe you as a prolific military man, accredited with single-handedly slaughtering overwhelming numbers of foes. What made you stand out from other such men was one very odd detail. You disappeared from the timeline."

Not killed, not retired to a small village with a wife and umpteen children, just... gone. Vanished. He was there, and then he wasn't. His story excited Erianne to no end. If she could find out what happened to him, and if it were unique, well, a Nobel Prize in history couldn't be impossible, could it? She was sure her parents would swoon with happiness if the Stortinget draped the medal around her neck.

She became so enamored with her historical anomaly she commissioned period-specific clothing the same as his, with one major difference: the chiton material and the leathers would be bulletproof.

Literally. She had the manufacturer reinforce the fabric and leathers with fibers capable of withstanding the blow of an arrow, spear, or sword without cutting the material or her skin.

It would still hurt like nothing else, and there would be a bruise, but she'd survive. The exposed areas of her head, neck, and throat would remain vulnerable to attack, but her gear would ward off most other weapons available to the people of the age. When the manufacturer delivered her battle gear, she showed it to her father, who expressed his pleasure at her foresight.

She had just finished her training when TTI announced a second time trip to Mesopotamia for the period of history she had studied with such diligence. Erianne applied as soon as TTI opened the call for applications.

They denied her.

She was livid when she received the rejection.

TTI Appointments Boards advised her in the rejection comm she was on an alternate list, first on the list, mind you, because they selected twelve experienced time travelers for the team. The Team would transition in only forty-eight hours after the announcement. She realized TTI selected the Second Team well before the announcement. A determined Erianne had to move fast to remedy the inequity.

She spent much of her personal savings to arrange an emergency hologram meeting with the Appointments Board to plead her case, pointing out she could satisfy the role of Time Historian and Protector. They met her pleas with stony silence. The Board was unmoved.

Erianne arm-twisted her father and mother to call family, friends, businesspeople, and politicians to exert their influence to get her on the Second Team, with the same results. The final blow was a call from Second Team Leader-Mesopotamia, who acidly informed her if she continued in her efforts to force her way onto his team, TTI would issue a permanent ban preventing her from becoming a Historian. She would have an opportunity on another occasion to join the Team, were she to take her rejection in humility and with patience. Deflated, she accepted her fate.

Then Fate intervened only two days later, on, of all days, Easter (Resurrection) Sunday, exactly 30 years after the First Cataclysm.

"Tul'ran, the Second Cataclysm was more extensive in emotional toll than the first. While the First Cataclysm was horribly destructive, it was indiscriminate. It didn't differentiate between a rich nation or poor, wealthy people or impoverished, technologically advanced or not. The Second Cataclysm was far, far choosier. In the space of a heartbeat, almost nine hundred million people disappeared from the face of the Earth. My parents were among those who vanished."

"Your parents vanished?"

"Indeed."

"You have my deep sympathy, Erianne. It must have devastated you!"

"Our devastation was beyond belief. The Second Cataclysm took people from every social class, every profession, every place in the world. The worst was the loss of the children. Every child eleven years old or younger disappeared. It did not matter where they were from or who their parents were. Thousands of babies vanished from their mothers' wombs. You cannot imagine, Tul'ran, the grief of millions of parents who lost their children in the blink of an eye."

The Second Cataclysm seemed to draw more from the poorer nations, particularly in South America. A sizable number of vanished people were from Canada, the United States, and Mexico.

The expansive reach and abruptness of the Second Cataclysm caused a worldwide uproar. Particularly incensed was the group of scientists who argued for the sanctity of the timeline and against time travel. Once more, they proclaimed to any listening ear alterations to the timeline created by incursions into history caused the disappearances of millions of people. They created the Order of the Purity and vowed to use every means at their disposal to disrupt time operations.

"TTI suspended all operations pending a review. I did not care. Grief consumed me at the loss of my parents. They had loved me like a precious gift. They taught me, traveled with me, and gave me anything upon which I set my eyes. Their sudden disappearance gutted me, especially since they left me alone on a prison island in the middle of the ocean."

The next six months were a blur. She vaguely recalled the funeral for her parents, while wrapped in the tender arms of her parents' co-workers. It was a massive funeral, attended by scientists, dignitaries, politicians, and businesspeople from around the globe, though most of their appearances were virtual. The virtual funeral was understandable; TTI forced almost everyone who came to Atlantis to remain on the island.

She could barely focus her intellect during the reading of the will, an estate making her wealthy beyond her wildest dreams. The sympathy of well-wishers, who did everything they could to help her through her mourning, flooded her. If you asked her to remember a specific day or act of generosity during those months, she couldn't describe it, so buried she was under her misery.

It was into those dark depths of grief, a quagmire of despair, a light shone. The Leader of Second Team-Mesopotamian called her with the news. A review of the timeline and measurements within the quantum realm didn't reveal any changes or disruptions. Whatever caused the disappearances of millions of people wasn't because of the actions of any Time Historian. Time travel operations were to continue, and she was to be added to the Team.

The Second Cataclysm had claimed one Time Historian and two Protectors from the Second Mesopotamian Team. They added her to the Team to fill both roles. She would be their only Protector; TTI could train no one else into such a role to fit their parameters in short order. Erianne was so excited she didn't recognize and question why the Second Team had needed two Protectors instead of one. She sensed some urgency in the need for the mission to go ahead on October 15, 2095, but the Controllers wouldn't give her any reason for the urgency.

"I am disappointed to say, Tul'ran, the other members of the team were not happy to see me join them. They felt I was a spoiled, privileged child who bought her way onto the team through money and sympathy for my losses. They resented me from the very beginning of my brief training with them."

Tul'ran cocked an eye at her.

"Is it necessary for me to tell you they were fools? I have only known you for mere days, and I would go to war with you without a second thought."

Erianne smiled. In his way, Tul'ran had paid her the highest compliment he could give.

"It was not the only difficulty I faced."

Before being allowed to travel, Erianne attended a medical clinic for boosters, vaccinations, and the removal of her ova. The announcement of the latter procedure startled her. When she made inquiries about the necessity for it, the nurse primly informed her if she became lost, by grave mischance, they couldn't very well have her running around and having babies back in antiquity.

They implanted organic nano robots on her optical nerves, which recorded everything she saw once she activated the recording system. The surgeons attached similar bots to her auditory nerves to record sound. Her body powered the bots. If she died, the bots dissolved into nothingness after twenty minutes.

"You have kept a record of everything you have seen and heard between us?"

She bit her lower lip to not laugh at his question, laced as it was with a hint of outrage and horror.

"No, Tul'ran. Things have been so tumultuous, I

never thought to set a record in motion. I have recorded nothing passing between us."

A little white lie.

She didn't want anyone to know how badly she screwed up this mission, which is why she never started documenting. Once she started a recording, she couldn't shut it off. A computer stored everything she saw and heard from the point of initiation onward. Only a TTI tech could retrieve the footage.

Her right lower molar housed a microcomputer with a one-exabyte molecular drive. An exabyte is the equivalent of one million terabytes. When a Time Historian concluded a mission, the techs wirelessly accessed the drive and downloaded all the audio and video collected by the Historian throughout their interaction with history. A human eye recorded the video; therefore, it was of the highest definition possible. Techs translated the record into three-dimensional holograms for distribution to the world.

While at the clinic, physicians also implanted a tiny bot next to her heart, a Traveler Identification and Retrieval Accessory Device, holding all her information, medical and otherwise. The TIRAD identified her to the Temporal Scepter, making time travel workable for her.

Tul'ran interrupted, a note of worry in his voice.

"Erianne, is it possible our enemy may have access to this thing lying next to your heart to follow us where we go?"

She pondered for a moment and then shook her head.

"I think not; indeed, I am certain such could not

be the case. My heart powers the device, and the signal coming from it is very weak. I must be within fifty long footsteps of its master for it to have any effect."

He nodded, satisfied. A moment later, he asked another question, this one with a slight bite to the words.

"Tell me, milady, was your abduction by the Gutians a fiction to ensure I would come to your aid, and you would have the contact with me you so ardently desired?"

"No! In all truth and sincerity, milord, I did not know of your whereabouts in these regions. It was never my plan to place myself in your hands. I was to make inquiries of you in Ur, to gather more information, and to satisfy my curiosity about what became of you in the annals of history."

Tul'ran was silent for a moment.

"Did you know the woman I killed in the desert?"

"No, Tul'ran, I did not, but I knew who owned her arm. I could not tell you the name of her employer without disclosing I travel through time. I know she sold herself to the Order of the Purity. Their goal is to terrorize people in my era to end the Time Travel Initiative. I do not know why they target me, specifically. The assassins in my house and the assassin in the desert are all connected to the Order. They coordinated the Gutian attack upon us while we lay sleeping in the oasis. I am a lower-level Time Historian. I have no secrets beyond those of any other person on my Team. Why would they kidnap me? Why would they try to kill me not once, not twice, but thrice now? Were you to have these answers, milord, I would beg you for them and give you anything you asked in return."

"Your first Telling recounted your father, who traveled with you. Was your account of him true?"

"No, Tul'ran. It was not. No such man exists. I confess to you the entirety of my first Telling was a fiction. My Team established this fiction before I came to your age. The fiction's purpose is to gain the trust of those in your era, so they would accept us without question."

He pierced her with a sharp glance.

"It was effective. You convinced me."

"I am so sorry, Tul'ran. I was very desperate. It displeases me I offended you with mistruths and half-lies. I pray you will forgive me."

"What was the true purpose of our covenant? To protect you from this Order? To reunite you with your Team?"

Erianne took a deep breath.

"Tul'ran, my Team is my only way forward to the future. They have something of mine permitting me to wander the streams of time at will. Should they keep my Coin from me, my people will strand me here, in this Age, until my death or until I am rescued. We travel to the mountains with a purpose. It is the Insertion Point, which connects your age to my age, or what we call Origin. I came to this Age from a canyon in the mountains, and it is to this place I must go if I am to return home."

"Would it be so bad to be stranded in this Age? With me?"

The question startled her. She heard within it a heart-cry and thought again his feelings for her transcended their covenant. Tul'ran never loved again after Katja suicided on his sword, but it was seven or eight years ago. Did he find in Erianne the motivation to move on? It was tempting to pursue a conversation with him about his feelings, but to what end?

"Tul'ran, I do not belong here, in this Age. I would be the one displaced in time, with consequences I could not foresee. While it is a pleasure to visit this era, and it has been an honor to become bound to you in covenant, as shield mates, I must go back."

Silence, but for the sound of hooves shifting through the sand and the creak of leather.

"Erianne," he asked after many minutes passed, "did your historical records say when my name became unattached to the grasp of time?"

"No! They did not! For all I know, you might live another one hundred years before the event takes place."

He chuckled.

"I am relieved, but you have seen the way I live and the dangers I encounter every day of my life. I would be shocked beyond measure if I have another one hundred more years of life."

Later, Erianne would reflect on those words and wonder if they had presented a temptation far too great for even Fate to ignore.

Seven shapes suddenly erupted from the sand in front of them in a rough semi-circle, howling at the top of their lungs.

Time froze.

Erianne screamed.

CHAPTER THE ELEVENTH: THE MYSTERIES OF TUL'RAN THE SWORD

Tul'ran the Sword was a man of his word
And his soul and his mind of one part,
Erianne the Dark lived by her learning,
And her soul was as black as her heart.

Tul'ran whipped his head around in utter astonishment. Destiny's Edge shied badly when the figures erupted from the sand, and more so with Erianne's screaming. The woman fought to control the mare and keep her seat while staring at the immobile figures and shrieking. Her panic wouldn't do, Tul'ran thought frantically. She shouldn't be able to even do so. Time should have frozen her with the others!

"Erianne, Erianne, peace! Stop screaming! Be calm, and your horse will calm as well."

Her voice was stark with terror.

"What's happening? What's happening? I don't understand what's happening!"

Tul'ran made placating gestures with his hands and said with urgency, "Nothing good will come of Destiny's Edge throwing you and stepping on you in panic. Calm yourself!"

The last phrase came out as a sharp order and had the desired effect.

Erianne forced peace with herself and spoke soothingly to Destiny's Edge. The mare calmed before standing in place, trembling and snorting. Darkshadow looked on as if bored. He had been at the epicenter of a stoppage of Time on so many occasions they no longer held him in thrall.

"How are you doing this?" She demanded, an edge of hysteria lingering on her tongue as she stared in disbelief at the seven figures motionless before her. Even in the moonlight, she could see where the sand shifting from their bodies had stalled in midair.

Tul'ran chewed his lower lip.

"Ah, you seek a Telling which moves the edges of reality beyond comprehension and belief."

"Try me!" she yelled, startling him again.

He had not yet seen the full measure of her anger and fear, but was feeling the force of it now.

"Erianne, I will tell you all. I give you my oath. For now, when I face a threat so dire, so unexpected, and so immediate, Time comes to a halt. It is a gift for my protection, and one I have received sparingly in the last four and ten years. If the truth be known, it is a gift given to me more often in the past three days than in the past three years."

"A gift from whom?" Her voice was still a little shrill, an echo of her terrified confusion.

"Again, I will tell you all. Be patient. Let me dispatch this threat and reconvene the flow of Time. We have yet several hours before the dawn rises to greet us. It will be more than enough minutes to reveal the mysteries of Tul'ran the Sword."

Tul'ran dismounted from Darkshadow and drew Bloodwing, preparing to kill the shadow warriors who had erupted from the sand to disrupt their lives.

Erianne sat rigid in her saddle for several long seconds. Thoughts clashed in her mind as disbelief warred with reason. She felt out of control. To this point, everything had been relatively normal, if one could ever describe time travel as such. She loathed what she had to do next, fighting against a feeling she was about to betray someone with whom she had developed a close bond. The covenant relationship demanded trust and faithfulness; Erianne felt like Judas. What choice did she have? Tul'ran had frozen time; unless she was losing her mind, this was a first.

As Tul'ran left her, she reached into her mouth and squeezed the molar containing the microcomputer. She heard a chime in her ear, confirming the recording had started. Erianne recited notes, her lips not moving, her voice subvocal, like a ventriloquist of old, so Tul'ran wouldn't hear.

She didn't need to mention the date and chronometer settings. Micro wireless technology connected the computer in her tooth to the TIRAD near her heart. It automatically logged the date and settings on the clock from mission start to mission end.

"SMP. Start Memo, Personal. Mesopotamia, Mission Two, Erianne de mi Corazon."

"I found the anomaly, Tul'ran az Nostrom. He's showing attributes he shouldn't have. Tul'ran can freeze time. He can *freeze* time. Once time freezes, he moves through physical space when others can't. No one can freeze time. While it's possible to move within time, the technology to freeze time in place, or slow its passage, doesn't exist. Such technology certainly didn't exist in this era, unless Tul'ran az Nostrom is not who I think he is. I confess I'm freaking out. This was the last thing I expected to encounter here. End."

As the subject of her clandestine narrative raised Bloodwing for the first strike, he called out to her.

"Erianne, will these of our enemy convey with them the means by which they found us?"

"Yes, yes, they will have a tracker, a device to show them the way."

He moved from one frozen silhouette to the other, searching their bodies until he found on the wrist of one a thing having upon it a red dot. He cut away the thing and walked it over to Erianne, noting as he did so how the dot increased in illumination.

"Is this such a device?"

She took it from his hand, hers still shaking.

"The device is an *omnidirectional signal sensor*, and it seems pointed at me. This is not possible. I checked my clothing carefully before we left Ur to make sure there was nothing sewn within it capable of leading my enemy to me. The signal from the thing near my heart should be too weak to be found with this device."

He pondered for a moment and then took hold of her mare's reins.

"Erianne, please dismount your horse, for I would see something."

She cocked her head at him, shrugged, and jumped off Destiny's Edge. He bade her walk away five paces, and his eyebrows raised as the dot didn't move or decrease in intensity. He ran the device along her mare's head, down her neck and back towards the crude saddle. The light turned from red to green.

He swore loudly.

"What is it?"

"I am a fool! I thought the tack to be a gift from your departed father, for your use if you returned and needed a horse. The opposite is true. Our enemies, contemplating your return, left the saddle behind and infected it with a device by which they could follow us. Come hither and take from me your horse's reins."

She complied, running her eyes over the immobile figures in the sand and recording them as she passed by. Tul'ran removed the saddle from her horse's back. He flipped it upside down and scanned it as carefully as he could within the limitations of the dim light. His fingers searched for something that shouldn't have been there. He found it: the tiniest bulge along one seam.

In retrospect, it would have been better had they buried the device deeper in the saddle's structure to make it harder to find. Then again, no one in this

Age would search for or expect to find such a thing. Its location allowed for easy removal.

He cut out the device with minimal damage to the saddle and set it on his boot. He applied pressure to it with El Shaddai's knife until it emitted a sharp spark and the green dot on the wrist thing blinked out. Their enemies couldn't track them any further by this means.

Tul'ran replaced the saddle on the back of Destiny's Edge, checking the cinches carefully, and Erianne mounted again. He looked at her grimly.

"I tire of these creatures who follow and attack us from a distant Age. Let them have an example of what faces them in this one."

She watched as he prowled around the shadow warriors frozen in Time. Her stomach lurched a little as he cleaved through their bodies. Tul'ran cut each person in many places, so when Time resumed, there would be nothing but blood, guts, and chunks of meat falling onto the sand.

"Milord, I cannot help but notice the damage you do to these bodies bears a striking resemblance to the state of the enemies I found when I returned to the hutch in Ur."

He looked up at her, Bloodwing glistening with the blood it carried as it sliced through flesh, intestine, and bone.

"An astute observation. When I entered the hutch, Time froze as soon as I opened the door. I could not even see the source of the threat. I was confused. When I laid our food and drink on the table, I bumped against someone. Again, they were wearing clothing, blending them so completely in the room I could not distinguish the room from the enemy."

"I cut one apart and sought others. It took me hours searching around the room to find the other three. Even after I cut them down, did I yet search in fear I missed one. When Time resumed its course, I waited for an attack, but none came. Shortly afterward, you came in."

He resumed his grisly task while she pondered further.

"Did Time also pause in its course in the desert when the lone female sought my life?

He nodded once, sharply.

"You have it so. When Time paused its course in the desert, it took me several moments to find the arrow. I could not move it from its trajectory because whatever is translated from bow to arrow, I cannot easily displace."

Erianne subvocalized again.

"SMP. Additional. I am watching az Nostrom carve up our attackers into pieces. Factors are adding up. A man who may not be who he says he is. Possibly a sociopath who carves bodies as easily as cutting up a steak. A man who can stop time. He has a grasp of the law of conservation of energy. My theory is coalescing. End."

Tul'ran couldn't hear her words; he continued as if uninterrupted.

"I broke the head of the arrow from the shaft and the shaft in multiple places. With my Knife did I turn the barb downwards, so its point was no longer aimed at your breast. Once I did my best to disrupt the form and function of the arrow, I traced it back to its source."

Understanding dawned.

"Then you located the thermal imager."

"Indeed. I am not sure if you can understand the magnitude of my shock. There, in midair, hung a depiction of you and my horse, dressed in the colors of a wood fire: yellow, orange, and red."

"Did you not accredit it to magic, milord?"

He looked up from his macabre task.

"I do not believe in magic, Erianne. While I have heard of people manipulating power, I am wary of them. I have spoken with healers and the wise people of the desert, who tell me the power source for sorcery comes from within the very depths of Hell. I do not align myself with the legions of Hell, to whom I consign into the category of 'enemy.'"

"SMP. Additional. Further factor supporting my budding theory. Tul'ran believes in Hell, which, arguably, is more of a modern concept than an ancient one. End."

Then, out loud.

"My apologies, milord, if my question interrupted the flow of your thought. Please continue with your discourse."

Speaking calmly, he resumed hacking apart the bodies frozen in Time.

"I found the thermal imager attached to a bow, the arm holding the bow and the head directing it. I cut off the woman's head, though I did not yet know her to be a woman and returned to you. As an afterthought, when I came back to you, I placed Bloodwing between your breast and what I hoped was the path of the arrow. It is very difficult to move in such circumstances because the forces bringing Time to a halt demands the placement of the body in close to the same position as when Time ran. When I achieved my purpose, Time resumed its course, and you know the rest of the narrative."

Erianne shuddered.

"I wore the black-green tunic that night. My people did not design it with the same protections as my battle gear. Had you not been there, I would have died."

He met the statement with a wide grin, his teeth shining in the moonlight.

"For which I claim the reward of a kiss when we are safe, and if you are so inclined. The last kiss you gave me will not leave my mind and left me with the desire for many more."

Erianne winced. The recording picked up his statement with the same clarity as she heard it. There were going to be consequences to pay for her indiscretion. Her stomach lurched a little as she wondered who it was she had kissed.

Was he a warrior from this era or a psychotically deranged traveler from hers?

Tul'ran finished cleaving the bodies. They showed no sign of the carnage to come, yet. He walked away from the bodies in ever-expanding circles around Erianne and the horses.

"What do you do now, milord?"

"I seek the cleverness of an enemy not satisfied with the chances of success these seven had, notwithstanding the certainty of surprise."

About ten minutes passed before he called out of

the darkness.

"See here, if you can, Erianne."

Tul'ran was behind her, off to the left, at about seven o'clock.

"I cannot see you, milord," she confessed. Her voice had an odd tone, which surprised him. Tul'ran attributed it to the fear arising from her first experience with the stoppage in Time. Surely she would get used to the experience, just as he had. Surely.

"There is another here, with a bow, the arrow notched and drawn, ready to let fly. You should know it is not your image I find in this thermal imager; it is mine. Our enemy tasked seven in the ambush with attacking and killing you, while the eighth was to put an arrow into me so I could not move to defend you. The ground attackers rose too soon; they ought to have waited for the archer to maim me before they started their attack. Then again, they could not have possibly known Time would stop and leave them at their knees. You told me it was improper for them to take a man from this now to your now. Is it proper for them to kill a man in this now?"

"No! They are targeting a human living in this era. You are part of a sacrosanct timeline. The actions they take violate very serious time travel precepts. I am afraid my dangerous enemy is becoming a desperate one."

A dangerous and desperate enemy. Tul'ran didn't like it at all. Such enemies are to be avoided, not baited. The warrior returned to where Erianne and the horses stood. He accessed a bag attached to his saddle, retrieving a cleaning cloth. It looked silken and was a brilliant white. He carefully cleaned his Knife and Blade on the cloth before returning it to the bag and his blades to their sheaths.

"What kind of cloth did you use to clean your weapons, if I may be so bold as to ask, milord? They are so sharp, I am surprised they do not reduce a mere rag to tatters." Erianne asked.

Tul'ran looked up, a frozen expression on his face.

"It was Katja's wedding shift. She wore it on our wedding night when we sought to consummate our nuptials. When I killed her, I tried to wipe Bloodwing on her shift, as is my custom, and found, to my astonishment, the Blade would not penetrate the cloth. I tried to pierce it with my Knife, but also to no avail. Only Katja's dagger could cut it."

A shard of pain stabbed into his soul, and a tear threatened the corner of his eye. Erianne had a talent for ripping his heart from his chest.

"I cut her shift to pieces with her own blade, and I have carried it with me ever since. Once merely dipped into fresh water, the stains disappear. It is a reminder of how the eyes can deceive the heart to its eternal sorrow. Her wedding dress was to have been the banner of our love. It now serves the purpose of keeping clean the sword she used to end her life."

After the last bleak sentence, Tul'ran vaulted into his saddle. Erianne felt soft, firm tentacles wrapping around her body, moving her hands, shoulders, and back into the position she had been before Time froze. She held her breath.

Time snapped back into motion; the bodies in

front of them collapsed into heaps of blood and gore. Destiny's Edge shied again, but Erianne was ready, and she steadied the mare quickly.

Tul'ran led them around the gruesome mess, and they resumed their journey.

"While our enemies can no longer track us, they will have seen our direction of travel. There is nothing ahead of us but mountains; no villages or cities. If your enemies are aware of your destination, they will wait for us there."

She acknowledged his words with a twist of her right hand.

"We address those circumstances when they arise, milord. At least for the remaining length of this night, we should be safe. Why did Time not stop for you when the Gutians rode against us yesterday in the afternoon? You were ill-prepared for their attack and forced to fight without armor."

"I had sufficient notice of their coming. It was deemed that between us, we could hold off our enemy and defeat them. As we did with flair, Erianne."

"Deemed by whom?" she pressed. "Who brings Time to a halt for you, Lord Tul'ran?"

He hesitated. He had a keen sense he must tell her the truth, but realized it would require a retelling of the parts of his past where El Shaddai had intervened, and he hadn't mentioned it to her. Ah, well. There were several hours of darkness left in this night, and it would be difficult to ride them in silence. Each of them had a tale of disbelief to tell. His story was no stranger than hers.

"El Shaddai," he finally said.

"Who is El Shaddai?"

"El Shaddai is *a* god, if not *the* God."

"There is no God."

Tul'ran whipped his head around, astonished.

"What mean you when you say there is no God?"

"There is no God."

"And how, pray tell, do you come to such a conclusion with such confidence?"

"When we confirmed the safety of time travel, there was a large push by religious leaders to have Historians travel into the past to corroborate the existence of the gods of various religions. Time Historians confirmed the presence and lives of Mohammed and Buddha, as well as the authors of various other religions. The Time Travel Lens denied them access to any period related to the Holy Bible of Christians. We tried. The Historians attempted first to travel to the Age of Jesus, the Son of God, who Christians claim died as a sacrifice to save people from their sins."

El Shaddai had a Son! Tul'ran never knew this, but then His Children had never come up in conversation. He wanted to ask questions of Erianne about this Jesus, but she had pressed on, and he remained silent.

"There were many attempts to go back in history to any period of Jesus's life, but the machine would not transport the Historians. They tried to go to the various periods in which Jesus's followers had supplied personal testimony to Jesus's life and teachings. Again, the machine would not send them. The Time Travel Initiative could confirm nothing of the Son of God's life and teachings because the machine could not find a day or place in which His disciples taught of Him."

"Eventually, the Time Historians announced since they could not access the history of Jesus and his followers, the Son of God did not exist. It caused a great upheaval in the world, and many lost their faith. A remnant of the faithful persisted in their beliefs. My parents were among them."

"Did your parents, who were the architects of time travel, explain why the Historians could not access those eras?"

"Yes," she said, hearing the words in her head as if they were original thoughts, "they said God asked for faith, whereas man demanded proof."

"Ah. El Shaddai blocked your efforts so people would not come to believe in Him only because your machine offered them evidence. El Shaddai wanted to be chosen in faith, not proven, in fact."

"Your statement is insightful. It matches the verses my parents quoted to me from the Holy Bible. I remain unmoved and unbelieving. I need to experience God personally before I give my faith to Him."

Tul'ran cocked an eyebrow.

"Did you not just experience His power when He stopped Time to permit us to kill those who desired our deaths?"

She shrugged irritably. "I do not know what it is I just experienced."

"Do you have with you this book called the Holy Bible? If it is in a language I understand, I would very much like to read it."

"I do not. It comes into being many years in your

future. To bring such a thing into the past from the future..."

"Is forbidden," he finished for her, a tone of exasperation in his voice.

"On how many occasions have you traveled into your world's history, Erianne?"

"This is my first journey, milord Tul'ran. How many times have you experienced the halt of Time in its normal course?"

Tul'ran told her. He repeated his narrative of the carnage at the Orchard, without recalling the horrible details, but telling her the fullness of his account with El Shaddai and how he came by the Knife.

"Before I set my face to the South and the East, El Shaddai made me these promises, which I remember as if it were yesterday. He said,

'I will be your shelter, your refuge, and your fortress. I will save you from the fowler's snare and from the deadly pestilence. I will cover you with My feathers, and under My wings you will find refuge. My faithfulness will be your shield and rampart. You will not fear the terror of night, nor the arrow that flies by day, nor the pestilence that stalks in the darkness, nor the plague that destroys at midday.'

'A thousand may fall at your side, ten thousand at your right hand, but it will not come near you. You will only observe with your eyes and see the punishment of the wicked.'

'If you say, "El Shaddai is my refuge," and you make Me your dwelling, no harm will overtake you, no disaster will come near your tent. For I will command my angels concerning you to guard you in all your ways; they will lift you up in their hands, so that you will not strike your foot against a stone. You will tread on the lion and the cobra; you will trample the great lion and the serpent.'

'Because you love me, I will rescue you; I will protect you, for you acknowledge My name. You will call on Me, and I will answer you; I will be with you in trouble. I will deliver you and honor you. With long life I will satisfy you and show you my salvation.'

"There are many things in those words I do not understand," Tul'ran confessed. "Does El Shaddai have wings under which He would shelter me? What are His angels? What I gleaned from His words was a covenant of protection. He has never failed in His word to me in all these years, nor I to him," Tul'ran finished.

Erianne shook her head. Subvocalizing once more, she said, as he continued his Telling:

"SMP. Additional. I'm confused, which is compounded by disbelief. You've just heard az Nostrom quote Psalm 91. I know it well. When I was a child, my father made me memorize it and recite it as part of our evening prayers. The author of Psalm

91 will not write it for hundreds of years. A suspicion is growing inside me at an alarming rate. I'm becoming certain az Nostrom may not be from this era. End."

Tul'ran continued his account of his trip to Ur and talked about his first experience with a Time freeze. He told her the entire story of the night his wife died, again relating how El Shaddai stopped Time to save his life and tried to comfort him with His words.

At the end of his discourse, both fell silent. Erianne was struggling with his account, Tul'ran saw, but he left her to her thoughts. It was strange he could so easily accept her word she was from thousands of years hence, but she couldn't accept his account of his relationship with El Shaddai.

"SMP. Additional. Could it be az Nostrom is insane or delusional? He hears voices others do not; is he schizophrenic? The man speaks to God, and I don't know what to do with his story. He's so confident, so sure of what he's saying. az Nostrom does not display any other signs and symptoms of mental illness, although I suspect some psychopathology given his willingness, if not eagerness, to kill."

Erianne continued subvocalizing for her audience in the future, knowing others would edit her words if they felt she went too far.

"I posit he may be a time traveler lost to history by some accident. He may be amnesic to his past and delusional about his present. If such is the case, he could've tried to build a device using ancient technology to return. Instead, he invented a means to stop time. My theory would explain a great deal."

"Time Historians have disappeared in the field suddenly and inexplicably. The most notorious case involved a Jewish Time Historian who traveled back to record Hitler's youth. Despite his training, the Historian did the unthinkable. He tried to assassinate the future Führer. Just as the knife was falling and before his horrified fellows could stop him, the Historian blinked out of existence. TTI tried to find and recover him, but all to no avail. The event set a precedent for extensive psycho-social evaluations of every Time Historian to ensure against a second incident."

"I've heard rumors of other cases of Historians not returning. TTI classified the details, a by-product of the media sensationalism and public outcry over the attempt on Hitler's life. I can now believe Tul'ran is a Historian who suffered a psychological schism because of not returning home. End."

She turned her head in his direction.

"Did God, I mean, El Shaddai, speak to you when Time froze back there?" she asked, gesturing in the direction from which they had traveled.

"There was no need. Once Time froze, I comprehended and addressed the threat. The situation bore no risk of emotional harm, and I did not need El Shaddai's counsel or comfort."

"Can I speak to El Shaddai?"

He looked at her, surprised.

"Why for not? You need but ask for converse. But know you this: you may not play El Shaddai for a fool. If you seek converse as proof of His existence, He will meet you with silence. He does not offer proof. He accepts faith."

Erianne took a deep breath.

"Tul'ran, how clearly do you remember your past with your family?"

An uncomfortable silence ensued.

"My earliest memory is of my mother singing to me when I was of the age of seven years. I became ill with a disease so virulent, it spread death like a wraith through my village. My father feared the illness; he commanded my mother to remove me from the house and place me in a shed on the far side of the Orchard. My mother complied but would not leave my side."

"For three days I lay bathed in sweat, my lungs straining to draw air through wetness and coughing, obstructing my breath. That she did not fall ill and die was a blessing. I remember her face to this day, wreathed in love and concern, as I hovered between life and death."

"I remember the day of her horrid demise as if it happened yesterday; each scream torn from her throat by those unholy beasts. As she begged for her life, I listened. I heard as she pleaded for the lives of my sweet sisters. My eyes watched her life leave her body. I agonize over the death of my sisters as if they lie in front of me, even now, begging me to burst from my confines and ride to their rescue. I see them as plainly in my mind's eye as I see you riding at my side. Does this sound as if it comes from the mind of someone who does not experience the world in which he lives with clarity of thought and memory?"

Again, a long silence. Ahead, the darkness of the night took on a lighter hue.

"SMP. Additional. I want to slap myself right now. I consistently underestimate his intelligence just because he was born in an era four thousand years earlier than mine. Or was he? He saw right through my query and now understands I'm questioning his sanity."

"If he was born in this era, how would he come to this conclusion so quickly? I'm not a psychoanalyst. How can I be sure he's from this era and not immersed in a psychologically protective dissociative state? Perhaps the reason he disappeared from this timeline is because he transitioned home. Maybe I'm the reason he made it home. If he's from this era, he has to stay here. If he's from my era, I must take him home. Even if it's against his will."

"I'm getting a headache. I must know who Tul'ran the Sword really is and I have to know soon. The sun just popped up over the horizon. We have arrived at the foot of the mountains in which the Insertion Point lies."

"We're out of time. End."

CHAPTER THE TWELFTH: ATLANTIS

Marjatta Korhonen wasn't happy. She should've been, though. While not the richest person in the world, she was easily one of the most powerful. Marjatta keenly desired to keep her power, well, forever. She rose from humble beginnings to the top through hard work and a willingness to use her mind and body to excel. Her parents would be proud of her if they were still alive.

Marjatta's Finnish parents immigrated to the United States before she was born. Her parents brought with them a small fortune, which they worked into a comfortable one when Marjatta was a teenager. She grew up in New York City, with all the excitement, distractions, and incentives the grand city could offer.

'Too bad it no longer exists,' she thought.

Her childhood desire was to become a lawyer.

She studied well enough to get the grades entitling her to apply to any major law school in America. She chose Harvard. Harvard rejected her. She rushed into the arms of her mother, who loved her daughter and gave her whatever she desired. Marjatta's tears gushed from her eyes when she gave her mother the rejection letter. After a sizable donation, the selection board for Harvard Law realized they made a profound mistake. Marjatta started in the Fall.

Still feeling the sting of the first rejection, Marjatta doubled down on her studies. She rejected attempts to join sororities, clubs, and relationships. She dedicated her life to studying, and it paid off: Marjatta Korhonen graduated at the top of her class.

The new lawyer received many offers of employment after she passed the Bar. She chose a multinational firm, allowing her to set up a practice in international and commercial law. She was very selective in her choice of clients. Some of them were not wealthy, but all of them gave her access to powerful people worldwide. She reversed the pattern she created in law school, spending enough time to represent her clients with diligence while seeking every opportunity to socialize with the wealthy and powerful at home and abroad.

Marjatta maintained her policy of isolation from relationships. While her parents had a good marriage, the statistics for the prospects of a successful marriage had dipped significantly after she graduated from law school. Divorces, she saw, often came with scandal, bitter battles over children, and loss of wealth. It wasn't for her.

After seven years with her firm, she made partner.

Fifteen years later, she was the managing partner of the firm's global enterprise. She was in the fourth year as managing partner when the First Cataclysm struck. Fortunately, she'd been skiing in the mountains when moisture cascaded from the sky. The mountains allowed her to stay safe. All the members of her exclusive ski club watched with her in horror as the flood, tide and, of all things, tornadoes systematically destroyed New York City. In one fell swoop, the operating center of her firm washed away.

She was still trying to rebuild her law firm when the One World Legislature announced the Time Travel Initiative. Several hurried and well-placed calls gave her the answer she hoped to get: TTI needed an administrator to oversee operations.

Everything she had done in her life came into focus. She applied immediately for the Administrator position. Marjatta called in every marker, begged every favor, bribed every person who would accept money (and blackmailed those who wouldn't), all to make certain her application to become the Administrator would be successful.

It was.

Those first days in her new role were heady. While lawyers from across the globe argued about the legalities of time travel, she stood up the administrative structure of the Time Travel Initiative.

She was in the control room when they sent the first box into the past, crossing every appendage she had in the hope it would succeed. The champagne flowed when the box successfully returned, and she woke up the next day with a massive hangover.

She authorized the mission for the original traveling pair ('Adam' and 'Eve', as she wryly designated them in her mind) and celebrated again with their safe return. It was she who selected the Team Leaders and tasked them with choosing their teams. The missions brought back a ton of historical data. The Time Travel Initiative was an impressive success.

Until Mesopotamia.

She picked up her transparent tablet and stared at the image of a man with black hair and light blue eyes. He was decidedly handsome; she thought.

She was looking at Chief Petty Officer (Retired) Lamek Davis, a Navy SEAL who had distinguished himself in combat. When they placed the first box on the Transition Lens, Chief Davis became hooked on time travel, said the notes in his electronic file.

He surmised such travel could be dangerous, considering transitions were to be made to hostile civilizations. They would need security on those missions. He studied history with diligence and became fascinated for some inexplicable reason with Mesopotamia in the era of 2100 to 2000 BC. He learned as much as he could about the epoch, including studying some languages of the era.

On June 30, 2092, Davis retired from Naval Special Warfare after eight years of service. When the TTI selection board announced open slots for Protectors, he applied as fast as he could. The day of his selection, July 30, 2093, was both a triumph and a tragedy.

His wife, Kelci, had been patient and long-suffering while Naval Special Warfare deployed him on dangerous mission after dangerous mission. She refused to have children while he was with NavSpecWar. Kelci told him she wouldn't be a single Mom. When she found out he applied for and TTI accepted him into the Initiative, she was furious. The ensuing argument was epic.

Lamek pointed to the wealth they would get, the status they would achieve, and the opportunity they would have to raise a family. She pointed to the watery prison they would inhabit for the rest of their lives in the Atlantic, never to see family and friends again. They would make new friends, he argued, and she didn't even like her family, outside of her brother.

The argument escalated to the point where Kelci stormed out the door. "To go for a ride." The ride in question was their new conveyance, a vehicle which was a combination of an automobile and the drones he used to fly as a child. They were all in vogue and affordable by the middle class. Kelci earned the certification to fly the conveyance even though the salespeople reassured them a child could fly it given the robust and redundant automatics.

They failed.

The conveyance wrested control from Kelci and drove into a hillside, killing three campers who had the misfortune of being in the wrong place at the wrong time. When two police officers and three naval officers came to Lamek's door later in the night to break the news, he was inconsolable. The police officers had to taser him twice to prevent him from getting a weapon and killing himself.

Lamek spent twenty-one days in a private hospital reserved for TTI members and their staff. TTI psychiatrists assessed and reassessed him continuously. Remarkably, although he continued to grieve, Lamek centered himself quickly, and his psychiatrists declared him fit for duty. His superiors attributed his recovery to his SEAL training and the successful completion of multiple missions during his career. After they released him from the hospital, Davis deployed to Atlantis. He performed flawlessly.

After eighteen months of intensive training, TTI assigned Protector Lamek Davis as an observer to a thirty-day mission in ancient Greece as part of a study to find and record the stored ancient writings of Socrates. They transitioned out on April 18, 2095, at 1400 hours. The mission came out well, and he returned with the team, as planned, twelve OT hours after transition. Davis had to clean up a mess within two hours of coming back, but it had nothing to do with his mission.

Hmmm. Interesting. Marjatta made a mental note of the last entry as a seed of thought planted itself firmly in her brain.

She returned to her reading.

Two days later, on April 20, 2095, Davis joined First Team-Mesopotamia as their Protector. It transitioned on the pre-planned date. His Team's job was to establish an Insertion Point at the location selected by the AI. First Team-Mesopotamia was to explore and gather data about the Ur III Empire, centering in the city of Ur.

The city fascinated the world because it was where Abraham, the forefather of the Jewish people, originated. Abraham lived between 1813 and 1638 BC. The closest the Lens would allow them to get to Abraham's epoch was 1900 BC. TTI's planners situated the first Team in-country in 2025 BC to give later Teams a chance to go back and study as much as they could before they hit the denial barrier.

The Team would enter the city as middle-class locals, arrange accommodations, and secure a foothold. It was a ninety-day mission. They checked off every task on their list, making the operation a resounding success. Until the last two days.

The night before they were to return, Lamek Davis disappeared.

His Team remained in-country for five days beyond their scheduled mission run, carefully looking for him and making inquiries as best they could. They searched for the TIRAD imbedded in his chest, to no avail. They knew if Davis's heart stopped, the TIRAD would cease to function. Forty-eight hours post-mortem it would dissolve so no one would, by any conceivable means, encounter futuristic technology.

First Team-Mesopotamia arrived back at Origin and delivered the gut-wrenching news: they lost one of theirs in Antiquity. They had been away for 95 days, subjective time, but to the other employees of the TTI, they returned as scheduled twelve hours after they left.

The subjective time elapsed was strangely disquieting to Time Historians, which is why TTI didn't allow a mission to go beyond ninety days. Psychiatrists and physicians performed a careful analysis of the returning teams to protect against the development of psychiatric schisms. The team members had aged ninety days physically while in-country and didn't regain lost time when they transitioned back. No one could imagine traveling into Antiquity for years and returning to their families physically older. It would be enough to blow anyone's mind.

Lamek Davis made Marjatta's stomach hurt. She was under a lot of pressure from her superiors. Some of them were questioning her ability to lead the Initiative, especially after the Weinstein incident. That was bad. Someone leaked the attempt to take out Hitler, and the world media globally publicized it. They were down for a long while. It was necessary to psychoanalyze every Time Historian, Protector, and candidate for any tendency to repeat the attempt on Adolph or any other figure in history.

After the investigation, TTI eliminated nine personnel; all of them were Protectors. One of them wanted to go into history to save John Lennon's life by interfering in his untimely assassination. It took Marjatta a bit of research to discover John Lennon was a famous entertainer in his era, which caused her to shake her head. Why would anyone risk their life over a musician? Especially one who had been dead for hundreds of years?

Marjatta put new protocols in place after the Weinstein incident to avoid any further adverse publicity. She ordered every mission classified, including the gathered data. They only released the data to the public after someone had thoroughly assessed it. Of course, they didn't alter or sanitize the historical record. History was history, after all. If the public couldn't stomach it, well, they didn't have to watch the holo feeds.

Marjatta classified beyond top secret anything bad. Only she and members of the Oversight Committee knew what had gone sideways. No one else. Continuation of the program demanded it.

The search for Davis continued after the Team returned by scrutinizing the timeline for any hint of him... and the researchers returned a hit.

Records disgorged the history of one Tul'ran az Nostrom, a fierce warrior in the same era to which Davis had traveled. az Nostrom had the singular distinction of having disappeared from the timeline without a trace. Examination of every known historical record showed az Nostrom to be of approximately the same height, hair color, and build as Davis. It was certainly the case he was an uncanny and successful warrior. He mounted kills against overwhelming odds, say, like a SEAL would if faced with foes who were less talented and less trained.

Marjatta slapped together a Second Team and ordered them to be ready to transition within five days. This Team included two Navy SEALs who had served with Davis and could recognize him. Their relationship might be enough to convince Davis to come home or give the Team a fighting chance to recover him, willing or unwilling. One was a medic, which gave them some ability to treat a wounded Davis.

The debate then raged on when to insert the Second Team. Nobody knew the science behind time travel. They were still working it out. No one wanted to make a mistake. The consequences could be devastating. The initial plan had been to arrive one day after the First Team had transitioned to Mesopotamia, grab Davis, and bring him home.

Others argued by doing so, they would create an anomaly because in their present-day, Davis was missing. Marjatta heard so many discussions about time fractures, distortions, spacetime disruptions, and displacement anomalies she was afraid her own mind would suffer a tear in the continuum.

As it was, traveling back into the past violated one of the most fundamental premises of physics: causality. Advisors argued going early could cause a predestination paradox. The Second Team's arrival could trigger Davis to escape and evade, creating the very event the Team was trying to prevent. No one wanted to create a temporal causality loop.

Others argued the timeline protection hypothesis, pointing to what happened to Weinstein. He had disappeared out of every known timeline, vanishing without a trace. The timeline acted on its own accord to prevent interference in the most direct manner possible: eliminate the threat.

Marjatta finally pulled the plug on the hours of discussion and directed the Second Team to insert into Ur one hour, Antiquity Time, after the First Team left to return to Origin. This meant Davis was missing for at least six days Antiquity Time, when the second mission was on the ground. She couldn't help it. Marjatta wasn't about to risk acute damage to the timeline for one AWOL sailor.

Two hours after she decided, the Chief Programmer was in her office, handing her a memory chip.

"This won't work." His voice was defiant, although he wasn't feeling brave enough for defiance.

"What won't work?" she said, snapping at the man who so blithely had interrupted her day.

"I can't send a Second Team back to the same date as the First Team returned to Origin, one hour later."

She shook her head, beyond irritated.

"The Group talked this over at length. Why not?"

"The Group talked it over at length." He snorted derisively. "Maybe the Group should've had a Programmer present when they talked it over at length."

"Just tell me what the problem is," she said, already hating this conversation.

The Chief Programmer sat down; an unhappy look etched deeply into his face.

"The Lens in the Main Building creates a bridge through the quantum realm from our present, Origin, to the past at a certain time and place: Insertion Point. When a Team stands on the Lens, the machine slips them out of Dimensional Space, or DS, through the quantum bubble, and back into DS at Insertion Point. They plant a Temporal Scepter there, which stays at the Insertion Point to keep the quantum bubble between Origin and Antiquity connected. Then you don't have to create a new quantum bubble when you want to come home. The returning Team brings the Scepter back with them, which is what the First Team did, thus closing the quantum connection."

"I know all this!" Marjatta said, her voice a feral

snarl.

"Yes, I know you know all this, Administrator. I need to give you this background so we can get to the problem. A Navigation Coin contains space and time travel coordinates. Each Traveler carries a Coin unique to them. Whenever they travel, they have to insert their Coin into the Scepter and the Scepter slips them through the quantum realm to their destination. If they need to change the time to which they must travel, or the location, they need a Programmer to make the changes. The Programmers are the only ones who can calculate the space and time coordinates for travel."

Marjatta was drumming her fingers on her desktop.

"Are we finished with Time Travel 101 yet?"

"Yes, yes, fine. The problem is, the First Team brought the Scepter back to Origin. Had they left it there, we could have sent the First Team back, or sent in a new Second Team to recover Davis."

Marjatta's frustration was riling the contents of her stomach.

"We can't leave a Time Scepter in antiquity, even if someone gets left behind. We can't have advanced technology lost in Antiquity. If someone in the past discovered it, reverse engineered it, or derived technology from it, the consequence to our present could be frightening."

"Right!" the Chief Programmer said. "So, now we can only send a Second Team by creating a new quantum connection. There must be a twenty-year gap, Antiquity Time, between First Team insertion and the return of a Second Team to be sure we don't create a paradox. If we go sooner, we might trigger a temporal causality loop; a circular loop of events coming into existence to ensure the traveler won't alter history. We designed all our machines as 'one-hit' machines to add a buffer of protection against a loop. The programmers made the AI put a twenty-year distance between quantum bubbles established in the same location and in the same era. It would take months to reprogram the computers to remove the protocols."

Marjatta mulled it over in her mind for a few minutes.

"What if we were to insert a new Team into Babylon instead of Ur?"

The Chief Programmer wiped the sweat accumulating on his upper lip.

"It's the same Insertion Point for both cities, tucked up into a crevice in the nearby mountains, safe from prying eyes. A new team would have to emplace another Temporal Scepter after we create a new quantum connection. It must be far away from Babylon. Like I said, the Ur IP creates a quantum bubble connecting their time to our time through the quantum realm. Just because we closed the connection doesn't mean we made the bubble go away. We don't know how long it takes for a quantum bubble to disperse. It could still be there. We're not exactly sure of the dimensions of the bubble because we haven't designed the instrumentation to measure it. We're certain of one thing. If IP quantum bubbles merge, it could cause a dimensional displacement."

"Meaning?"

"Meaning our good old planet Earth could leave this universe and find itself somewhere else entirely. Pop! Goodbye, Terra."

An icy shiver ran through her body.

"How far away would we have to go with the new IP?"

"No one has tried it in the same era. After we examine a piece of history, we pull out the Temporal Scepter, close out the Insertion Point, and leave nothing behind. We can return after the area cools off. We could set another Temporal Scepter at the same IP, as long as it's twenty years later, Antiquity Time. If you need to do this within an hour of the First Team's exfil, I suggest you put the second IP at least two thousand miles away."

Marjatta shook her head. It was as good as halfway around the world. His solution would never do. It would take the Team months to traverse two thousand miles by horse, donkey, and wagon, going only one way.

One of the other protocols developed by the Time Travel Initiative was to refuse to transport modern technology through the lens. Other than recording devices, tracking devices, and MetaMaterials (so-called "invisibility cloaks"), they disallowed anything in the way of portable electronics, transportation technology, and modern weapons. It would take too long to reprogram the existing set of protocols and build a lens large enough to transport a stealthy anti-gravity plane.

"Fine." She exhaled her surrender. "Program it for twenty years and one hour after the First Team returned."

The Chief Programmer obediently designed the mission for insertion on April 24, 2095. It was, coincidentally, on Easter Sunday. The Team was ready to go, and the timer was running when the Second Cataclysm hit. Both Navy SEALs and one Historian vanished from the deck of the Lens with no reason or explanation. And without clothing. For the only moment in mission history, their physical bodies were gone, but their clothing remained. The mission was immediately scrammed, as technicians frantically tried to find where and when they sent the missing personnel.

They spent hours, then days pouring over the data before concluding the machinery had not sent them anywhere. They just vanished.

Marjatta had not. She wished she had. The entire world was reeling from the instantaneous loss of millions of people who had left errant pieces of clothing and jewelry in their wake. The panic had worsened when all the children, eleven years old and younger, disappeared without a trace. She lost many key personnel from the Initiative; personnel who would be hard to replace.

Word came down from on high: scrub all missions. A detailed analysis had to be conducted of all hardware and software components. No other mission would go until they certified the time travel missions hadn't caused the disappearance because of a temporal rift. It took another six months to examine temporal history with a fine-tooth comb, to sift through the quantum realm for any changes within the quantum flow, and to examine their equipment down to the molecular level. Ultimately, they satisfied, first, the Oversight Committee, and second, the world, they weren't the cause of the disappearances.

Having already disregarded some wingnut religious theories about a biblical "Rapture", the world had no answers. The world needed answers to feel safe, and they were ready to listen to anyone who could provide them.

But it wasn't Marjatta's problem. Davis was her problem. She finally received authorization to resume Time Missions on October 11, 2095. Four days later, she reconstructed the Second Team and sent them back to IP Mesopotamia circa 2005 BC. The Team had secret mission orders, known only to a few of them, to find and return Lamek Davis, dead or alive. They were to pay special attention to one Tul'ran az Nostrom, with the thought Davis had assumed his identity and remained in it twenty years later, Antiquity Time.

Her file review was three days ago. Now she was staring at the pale face of the Second Team Leader as she pondered shooting him in the chest with the gun in her desk and walking away from this stupid job.

"You lost another one?" she asked quietly.

She saw he didn't like her tone. He shouldn't like her tone. He should look for a place to hide.

"We didn't lose her; someone broke into our hutch and took her!"

"Where was your Protector?"

"She *was* our Protector. While we traveled back for supplies, we left her at the hutch to secure it. We arrived back at the hutch two days later. Someone had kicked in the door. There were signs of a struggle. We patched the door and fled to the IP after we sanitized the place."

"Leaving her behind." Marjatta's voice was even quieter now, and rage danced in her eyes.

"Someone came after her," the sweating man protested. "We thought someone was coming after all of us! It could have been Davis, and if he had a screw loose, he could have killed us all. TTI trained none of us to fight a SEAL. We stayed as long as we could. When she didn't come back, we transitioned out."

Marjatta closed her eyes and contemplated the legality of requiring the man to undergo survival training in the Atlantic in the middle of winter, buck naked.

"Leaving the Temporal Scepter behind."

The man was sweating profusely now. Marjatta felt no sympathy for him. At a minimum, his career was over. He had better pray the maximum didn't involve a brief tenure as shark food.

"We had to. We're not monsters. If she makes it back to the IP, she can come home. We left her Coin where she can find it and use it to come back."

There was that, at least. Except they had breached their most important protocol by leaving behind technology some civilization could find and use at any point in history, to disastrous effect.

"Get out of my office!" she said, the gastric juices in her stomach starting a tempest of their own. "I'll figure out what to do with you later."

As the new garbageman-for-life fled her office, Marjatta sat still for ten minutes and thought. She remembered her conversation with the Chief Programmer six months earlier, and it unsettled her. She very much wanted to speak with him again, but he, too, had mysteriously vanished.

The steps to save her job she was considering now could risk the destruction of the entire planet. Then again, what choice did she have? She wouldn't face imprisonment if the planet popped into another universe and killed all life on Earth.

She stabbed an icon on her transparent tablet. When her assistant answered, Marjatta said,

"Get me Special Projects."

Once she ended the connection, Marjatta searched in her drawer for anti-acids.

She was having a dreadful day.

On the other side of the world, someone else was having a dreadful day. Her name was Darian O. and she was the Controller of the Order of the Purity. Someone had just handed her the latest in a series of spine-chilling reports.

A recovery team found eight more of the Order's acolytes butchered in the desert after they didn't return from their mission to kill Erianne de mi Corazon. This following the dead assassin in the desert and the four slaughtered acolytes in the hutch where they intended to capture the woman. Thirteen dead!

The Order of the Purity was small. Thirteen dead acolytes of the warrior class were a terrible loss. Many people believed in the Order, but very few wanted to join a terrorist organization. A terrorist organization! The One World Legislature took the equivalent of seconds to apply the brand.

"Sheep!" Darian O. sneered with vitriol. The fools were so concerned with protecting their simple lives and incomes they couldn't bring themselves to appreciate the danger to the Purity of the Timeline.

It was ironic the Order, so dedicated to keeping the timeline in its pristine condition, didn't consider by returning to the same era, within days of each mission, they placed the entire world in jeopardy of annihilation.

Another came into the room, shuffling. His head was down in obeisance.

"*He* summons." The man croaked hoarsely.

Darian O. felt a chill run down the depths of her spine. There was only one "*he*" in the entire Order, and everyone feared *him*. Being summonsed meant the genuine prospect of pain. Perhaps even death.

"I come." Darian O. hastened to follow the acolyte.

The Order had hidden themselves deep within caverns, inaccessible to authorities who didn't have a map of their convoluted subterranean systems. It was dark, damp, and poorly lit by torches. There was no electricity. Authorities could find and track the electro-magnetic fields cast by electrical systems. The Order lived simply, striving to stay outside of any official notice.

The acolyte approached a door, painted black, and gestured to the two grotesquely shaped guards. Reluctantly, they opened the door, and Darian O. grudgingly stepped inside. The air was clammy, hot, and fetid. She at once fell to her knees, crawling the rest of the way towards a chair. A chair looking very much like a throne.

A man sat on it, dressed in a black suit. The dull light obscured his face, but there was no mistaking his deep, gravelly voice.

"Darian O., my servant, you have failed me."

Darian O. shuddered and tried to crawl deeper into the stone.

"Forgive me, my Lord," she moaned, "I offer you my life in service and strive mightily to carry out your Lordship's every..."

"Silence!" The man eyed the simpering acolyte with distaste. This was all he could manage for help. He hadn't yet ascended to a place of power in this world. The moment was coming, and soon. The Second Cataclysm was the opportunity he'd been waiting for, and before long, he would step into the position of power he craved and deserved.

Unfortunately, his reign was going to be short.

He read all the prophetic texts and practically knew them by heart. They promised him ultimate power for a few fleeting years, then imprisonment and torture. He knew this to be true. He couldn't escape his destiny... in this world.

It had been difficult to steal the time travel technology from the Initiative. He carefully emplaced one of his most trusted servants within Atlantis. The Order was in grave danger every moment his servant lingered. The servant successfully transmitted most of the schematics for the time travel lens and almost all the software before TTI security discovered him. He suicided.

There were scientists who spoke against time travel and deplored its use. They completed a time travel device for the man, at considerable expense and effort. They thought the man would travel back and kill Luke Manyfeathers and Priya Pillai, ensuring they'd never discover time travel.

The man had other plans. Luke and Priya were brilliant scientists, but they had failed to fully grasp the implications of their breakthrough. Time travel required going through both time and space using the quantum realm. The solar system wasn't on a static display in the galaxy. The sun moves through space at the speed of 447,387.258 miles per hour, dragging its planets with it. The orbits of the planets resembled forward-projecting spirals more than circular shapes. It wasn't enough to calculate *when* you wanted to go. You also needed to calculate, with extreme precision, *where* in space you wanted to go.

It took years of computing and ingenuity, but TTI scientists worked out the problem. The Artificial Intelligence transporting people through time solved the equation of when and where in time and space the teams should go. It also constantly attenuated the calculations in anticipation of a return at any moment. The AI transitioned people through the quantum realm instantaneously.

What they failed to appreciate was the technology wouldn't apply only to travel anywhere on Earth, to any time. With the right coordinates, they could travel anywhere in the universe, to any time. It was unknown how long it would take to travel to distant planets through the quantum realm. Time travel on Earth was instantaneous. The man imagined it would equally be so throughout the cosmos.

The writings predicting his demise didn't mention

time travel. It was, he thought, a loophole. Perhaps he and his followers could yet escape their capture and a torturous existence by fleeing to a planet elsewhere or else when.

His people adapted the Initiative's technology, and he sent scouts into the universe to find such a place. Their return would provide an answer. Hopefully, it would be on schedule.

He looked at the pathetic excuse of a human groveling and whimpering before him and contemplated the nonperson's death. If only he didn't have such a shortage of humans to use! He would torture this one over several days, bathing in her screams, until the ripped and dismembered body could no longer sustain life. The fantasy pleased him immensely.

"I gave you one small task, Darian O. All you had to do was kill a girl and make it look like an unfortunate accident in the past. You should have done so using local resources. I find you have squandered thirteen, thirteen!, of my best warriors! For nothing! Tell me, Darian O., how do you wish to exit this life?"

Darian O. covered her head with her hands and shrieked her pleas for mercy.

"Enough!" the man roared. "Quit your screeching. Do I strike you as someone who offers mercy?!"

"N-n-no," Darian O. blubbered, "But your servant can fix this!"

"How? How do you propose to fix this?"

"Your servant has found the location of their Insertion Point, with an operating Temporal Scepter.

The direction in which the woman was traveling was towards the site. We can locate our people outside of the Scepter's fifty-yard transition radius and intercept her! This servant will kill her, if it pleases you, my Lord."

Right. He was going to send this moron to complete such a vital task.

"No. Go into the past and arrange for a group of Gutians to travel to the IP site before the woman arrives. Pay them with a bag of kakkaru and promise them three more if they succeed. They will be rich beyond their wildest dreams. Once we have confirmation of the woman's slaughter, we will send our warriors to seize the Temporal Scepter."

"A good plan, an excellent plan," Darian O. blabbered, grateful she would live another day. "Your servant will set it in motion immediately, Excellent Lord."

"Get out! And do not fail me again, Darian O. If you do, I will decorate my hallways with your guts!"

Darian O. scrabbled out as fast as she could go on hands and knees, and the man leaned back into the chair, an evil smile on his lips.

He had it on good authority Erianne de mi Corazon had the potential to thwart his plans to leave Earth forever. How it could be, he couldn't fathom.

For the potential, though, she would die.

CHAPTER THE THIRTEENTH: PREDESTINATION

Into the canyon strode Warrior and Lady,
Shielded by courage and followed by kin,
Long would blood flow at the heart of the mountain
From the barbarian army they found there within.

Mesopotamia, the fourth day of the eighth month, 2005 BC
Tul'ran and Erianne paused at the foot of the mountain and watched as the sun played orange and pink hues over the peaks and danced gradually downwards. Erianne should've felt happy to be close to Insertion Point, but her state of mental unrest denied her the pleasure.

She thought she knew the man who rode beside her; a man whose history she learned as well as she could have, given the Age in which he lived. At this moment, there was nothing about him of which she could be certain. She'd come for answers; she was leaving with nothing but questions.

The biggest question was what to do with him.

She could take him back with her if she could convince herself he was a lost Historian. Time displacement psychosis could cause his strange beliefs and homicidal behavior. He was intelligent; perhaps enough to have invented a means to stop time. Most Historians were intelligent; some were brilliant physicists. Tul'ran az Nostrom could be Bob from Atlantis, a Nobel Prize winner in quantum mechanics.

She watched Tul'ran scan the mountains for a sign, any sign, of the presence of the enemy. He didn't have the demeanor of a displaced genius. He was a well-built fighting machine, not a desk jockey. Things made no sense.

Tul'ran turned Darkshadow toward her, the black stallion a proud extension of his master.

"Erianne, I confess to unease. Normally, my keen eye and instincts serve me well in rooting out the positions of those who would do us harm. The knowledge my enemies wear clothing making them invisible unnerves me. How am I to react to a foe I cannot see coming?"

"Milord Tul'ran, I acknowledge your concern. You have bested our adversary, invisible to the eye, in our recent past. I have confidence in your ability to do so again."

He didn't look convinced. She plunged onward.

"Milord, we face the prospect of engaging an adversary of unknown strength from this point to the area I know as Insertion Point. Our lives will depend on our ability to trust one another completely. I must know; do you have a Finding after hearing my Telling in its fullness?"

The look of shocked disbelief on his face made her wonder what she had just said.

"Erianne, the decision has been made for us."

She shook her head, confused.

"Who has decided for us?"

He shook his head.

"Erianne, think. Never in my martial history have I experienced a pause in Time including anyone else. You should not have been able to move when Time stopped in the desert, nor had any perception thereof, save for the ensuing carnage. El Shaddai included you, where before He had excluded all others. He has passed judgment on you and found you worthy. There is nothing left for me to adjudge."

He was back on El Shaddai again. How was she going to get to the truth of who he was if he wouldn't give up his delusions?

"It is with all gratitude I receive your Finding, milord. Do you have a thought about how we should proceed?"

"We must nourish our bodies in anticipation of combat. We have had little sleep, but the rush of warfare should keep us fully engaged in the task. As well, our horses could use some rest."

She canted her head in his direction, in a formal half bow.

"You are wise, milord, as I would expect of a great warrior of your stature. Let us repose."

They dismounted and removed the gear from their horses. Tul'ran shrugged the ebony cloak from his shoulders, folded it carefully, and placed it into the leather bag. She saw him with eyes conditioned to his presence. There was no panache in the movement to remove his outerwear.

"Milord, have you no further need for your cloak?"

"If we are to do battle, it may be a hindrance in the close confines of yon crevice. I will have no need of it when we fight. Perhaps never at all again."

He was beyond somber; he was glum.

"Erianne, there is a bit of grass near the entrance to the pass and a small stream falling from the side of the slope. It is enough to appease our horses' thirst and hunger. With no oasis to greet us this morn, we will have to make do with such terrain."

"At least we will not have to eat the grass, milord. We have our provisions on which to dine."

No cocked eyebrow, no smile. No response at all.

Erianne and Tul'ran spread the sheepskin on the ground and sat down upon it; she cross-legged and he with legs spread akimbo. They shared the last of the provisions in silence.

She could sense his uncertainty and unrest and understood them. Before last night's events, she felt they were growing closer. They endured danger together and fought as a unit. Their intimacy grew into something suggestive of a deeper bond than mere friends or shield mates. Then there was the kiss, which kept introducing itself to her memory, with an accompanying rush of confused pleasure.

She sat within feet of him, not talking, his face a featureless mask. Their conversation last night had driven a wedge between them. She knew his discomfort came from her. She snuck a glance at his face. This wasn't the confident, almost arrogant, face of the man who had saved her life in the desert. It wasn't the face of the man who stared down a merchant to defend her honor. Her uncertainty in him had bled into his poise.

Mentally, she gave her head a shake. This warrior was about to dive into chaos, risking his life for her yearning to go home. And the best she could do for him was to freeze him out because she was uncertain about him? This was a terrible strategy. She was demoralizing her shield mate right before a potentially lethal fight. Her feelings counted, but perhaps she should give them precedence after they survived. His morale had to be fixed and right now.

"Milord, I must confess I am insulted."

He jerked his head up at her, a surprised crease knotting his forehead at the haughty tone.

"How is it I have given you insult, milady?"

"We have been together for four days now, and I have borne the burden of watching your beard bloom on your face as black as the midnight sky. Yet not once have you offered to put a blade in my hand and bid me scrape it across your skin to rid it of whiskered invaders. Insulted, I am, in your lack of faith in the sureness of my hand and the purity of my heart!"

"It is not from a lack of will, milady. You address me as 'milord' and not by my given name, as I asked. I feel I have fallen from your grace and know not why."

"Which tells me how little you interact with women from my time. We tend toward the sullen when a man's face darkens with stubble."

A smirk was creeping over his countenance. It warmed her. She leaned over from where she sat cross-legged in front of him and stretched out her left hand. She ran her hand delicately over his stubble, perhaps lingering a bit more than what was purely necessary.

"Verily, milord, were you to throw your cheek against Darkshadow, you might cut him to the bone."

Tul'ran laughed aloud in his big, booming laugh. She giggled. Carefully, so as not to give him the wrong impression, she drew out her dagger with her right hand and placed it across the wrist of the hand caressing his face. She cocked an eyebrow at him, in his style.

Still grinning, he rose, reached for his large leather bag, and rummaged around, returning with the vial he used to clean his leathers. He handed the vial to her and sat down in front of her.

"We have no hot water and there is little with which to soften my beard except this. It is not of the sweetest essence, it is true, but it will help to keep me from looking like a skinned rabbit, ere you are done."

She giggled again.

"What little faith you have in me, Tul'ran! Whence I am done, not even your magnificent steed will recognize you, so handsome you shall be!"

"It will take more than a dagger scraping the beard from my face to achieve the goal," he replied wryly as she removed the lid from the jar. The lard-like substance inside didn't smell like roses. She wrinkled her nose at the smell.

"Are you certain you wish to have me make use

of this, Lord of the Black Stubble? Although, I warrant, the stench alone should be sufficient for our enemy to sue us for peace."

He laughed again. It was working. The dark cloud hanging over his head was dissipating. The Tul'ran she had become accustomed to was back.

She dipped her long fingers into the goo and moved her hand to his beard. She used as little of it as possible and could achieve a form of oily lather on his skin. Tul'ran repositioned himself so his legs were straight out. He pinioned his arms behind him as he stretched back, exposing head and neck to the sky.

Erianne picked up her dagger and kneeled over his hips. With more certainty than she felt, she began ever so gently scraping the sharp edge of the blade across his skin. It helped that his face, exposed to years of sun and weather, was leathery and resisted the blade. She carefully scrubbed away all the dark stubble scattered over his face and neck while he, all the while, closed his eyes and gave every appearance of a man at perfect peace with a knife to his throat.

She could see he was luxuriating in the opportunity to rest as she spoiled him. This was warfare as a warrior like him understood it: long cycles of calm and silence followed by short, intense intervals of terror.

When she finished, she leaned back and looked at him critically. He opened his eyes and tilted his head forward to present it for inspection.

"It is unfortunate, my covenant-master, to know women do not entirely make up the enemy force."

"Why is it so?" he asked, another smile threatening his lips.

"Because one look at this face and they would verily swoon at your beauty, casting down their swords and beating at their breasts out of their lust for you."

He burst out laughing and ran a hand over his skin, still slightly greasy. There was a definite twinkle in his eyes.

"All the temptation, and yet not one drop of blood spilled. I thank you for your kindness, milady."

"Erianne," she said, her voice severe, trying hard to keep from smirking while he again laughed. "And thank you for asking me to shave you!"

There was the expressive eyebrow again.

"When did I ask, Erianne?"

"When you confronted me with a beard so dark I feared I was in the presence of Vebrax himself, why, for certain, did you ask!"

He stood up, his grin stretching his cheeks wide, and helped her to her feet.

"You are a treasure, Erianne de mi Corazon."

They were standing close, staring at each other, almost sharing breath. They looked into each other's eyes, seeing depths of emotion neither expected. He lost himself in the brilliant green of her eyes while she drowned in the darkness of his. They were the entire universe, all the stars in the sky, all eras of time, and nothing else existed. Endless strands of possibility wove an undefined pattern around their minds and hearts.

Erianne wondered if again their lips should or would touch, when a movement behind him caught her eye. She stiffened. Tul'ran noticed right away, and before she opened her mouth, he whipped around. Both Bloodwing and the Knife were in his hands.

'Gods, he's fast,' she thought, once more impressed by his reflexes.

A single rider was approaching from a distance, with a donkey in train. Tul'ran squinted against the morning sun. It was a man; he was certain, and appeared to be in the dress of a warrior, though dated. The horseman drew closer.

Suddenly the Sword Himself let out a loud whoop and ran towards the horseman, sheathing his weapons as he ran. The interloper had just enough time to get off his mount before Tul'ran tackled him. The two men rolled on the ground for a brief time, beating each other with their fists, which confused Erianne considerably. Either they were friends, or they were trying to kill each other in a most peculiar way.

Eventually, the two rose and strode back to Erianne, dusting themselves as they walked. Both men were grinning from ear-to-ear. Erianne had a moment to assess the stranger. The newcomer was taller than Tul'ran by several inches, and less broad across the chest and shoulders. His hair was almost solid white, and deep lines burrowed into his skin. He walked with a trace of a limp, which Erianne didn't know was because of a past wound or Tul'ran's attempt at playing linebacker.

As he drew near, she saw a twinkle in the other man's pale blue eyes, framed with ice. She rose to her feet, stretching herself to her full height, taller than both men. The stranger half smiled and sketched a bow, and Tul'ran gestured toward him.

"Lady Erianne of Kabolon, I have the honor to present to you my old Master, Quil'ton az Peregos. Here is the man who honed my body into the blade you see today."

Erianne sketched a curtsy, her face impassive, not reacting at all when Tul'ran spoke her cover name.

"It is my honor to meet you, Master az Peregos. Know I am deeply in your debt."

Quil'ton's bushy eyebrows rose in surprise.

"The honor is mine, Lady Kabolon, though, in truth, I know not how you may have come into my debt. I have a keen memory, milady, and I am quite certain I have never met a woman with your beauty."

Her smile rewarded him for his gallantry.

"In having trained your student so well, Master, you prepared his arm for my defense. He has wielded it mightily in my aid, saving my life time and time again."

Quil'ton looked her up and down and scanned Tul'ran as well.

"I adjudge by your dress you are no stranger to combat yourself, milady."

Then, to Tul'ran,

"You have a most peculiar manner of clothing your women, Tul'ran. She would look much nicer in a tunic."

They all laughed, and Tul'ran again maintained her cover with aplomb.

"The Lady asked, my friend, in what manner she should flatter me, and I advised her, in jest, she could accomplish this admirable goal by adorning skins like mine. It was a matter of great surprise to me when she did so."

Erianne had to bite her lip. Tul'ran's last sentence was truer than Quil'ton would ever know.

Quil'ton grinned at her.

"Precocious, then."

"I believe, milord Tul'ran used the word 'impertinent,' if the truth be told."

The men laughed loudly, and Erianne felt herself relax.

"Master az Peregos, you look famished and parched. We have not much to offer, but what we have is yours."

He bowed to her and smiled.

"Milady, your kindness shines as a testament to your generous heart. Fear not. I have just returned from Babylon on my way home, and I am well-stocked. Let me be your servant and provide sustenance."

He was well-stocked indeed. There was meat, smoked to perfection, and a cheese which had endured the desert heat well. He had unleavened bread, dates, and grapes. The three of them feasted, joked, and laughed to a point where Erianne almost forgot the threat they had yet to endure.

"So," Quil'ton said after they finished the meal and put the remnants away. "You are a long way from home, son. How is it I find my ward here, so far from anywhere?"

Tul'ran cocked an eyebrow at him in response.

"I should ask the same of you, Master. How is it I find you so far out into the desert, a great distance from the comfort of your house? What brings you this far hence? I did not know you to be a man to wander when I was yet your ward."

Quil'ton snorted.

"When you were yet my ward, I had a fear of wandering out of a grave concern I would return to find my asses starving and my hutch burned to cinder."

Laughter ensued.

"But to answer your question earnestly, do you remember one Ragar, the man who taught you to fight with the splendid horse of yours?"

"Indeed I do, Master, and with great fondness."

"He was fond of you, too. He told me ere he left us you would be a great warrior one day and I should attach my name to yours. Over time, the song made its way into Gilgesh of a dauntless fighter named Tul'ran the Sword, who, balladeers sung, caused Death itself to cringe away from his shadow."

"Ragar took it upon himself to let slip from tongue the Master who trained the famed swordsman was none other than one Quil'ton az Peregos, living at their very feet. Clamor found its way to my doorstep, followed by shekels, as fathers begged me to train their sons. Others came to our village from further places."

"One day a man approached me, one Malibar of Babylon. He offered to fund the creation of an academy in his great city, where the Instructor to the Sword Himself might find students and secure a pension worthy of his stature. Who was I to refuse such an offer?"

"Over the past three and ten years, I have trained young men in the art of war and young women in the art of defending themselves against old men seeking to stain their virtue. My academy has grown to the point where my former students now train the neophytes, while I wander back and forth to my village as my whim pleases me."

"I am returning this day to Gilgesh after satisfying myself most recently my students have done less damage to my good name and reputation than I feared. This route provides fresh food for my horse and donkey, and water trickling from the mountain's ledges. It takes longer to get home, but it pleases me to arrive with livestock showing bellies instead of bones."

He, too, was a wonderful storyteller, Erianne thought. Maybe Tul'ran learned it from him.

"Will you to my question now?"

Tul'ran glanced at Erianne, choosing his words carefully.

"If truth be told, Quil'ton, an enemy pursues us. They do not show restraint in their pursuit or desire to kill us both. Did you hear of the Gutians?"

The older man nodded somberly.

"They sing your Legend from Babylon to Uruk, from Nippur to Nineveh, from Assur to every humble village in between. May I say, son, I grieve your loss of Katja and offer you my consolation?"

Tul'ran dropped his face so the emotion in it wouldn't show to his mentor, and Erianne quickly picked up the narrative.

"The Gutians, Master, seized me in Ur, with a design they should sell me in the flesh markets of Babylon. Milord Tul'ran interrupted their despicable scheme and laid their bodies to waste in the desert. Since then, he has been my stalwart guardian, securing me against further harm. Our enemies' losses do not daunt them. They pursue us relentlessly. We had hoped so seek refuge in yon canyon, but we fear our enemies have surmised our destination and wait inside for us to come."

A pall fell over the three for a few minutes, while Quil'ton nodded thoughtfully.

"Well, there is nothing for it, then. I will join my blade to yours and leave those barbarians to die in their waste."

Quil'ton's statement caught both younger people by complete surprise.

"Master," Tul'ran protested, "we could very well be entertaining the prospect of our deaths. We have no illusions about our chances, for the numbers against us may be overwhelming. We can offer you no reward for your service because a dead man cannot spend shekels. By what design would you choose to risk all?"

Quil'ton looked Tul'ran in the eye.

"By what design? The question brings me great shame. It tells me I have not conveyed to you properly the fullness of your worth to me."

Quil'ton drew a deep breath.

"You are my son."

His eyes narrowed.

"Not by blood, 'tis true, but by the bonds of war and mighty arms, and the affection we hold for one another. I remember you, a small, skinny youth of two and twelve journeys around the sun, standing before my hutch with your big black monster at your back. I saw the determination in your face, the seriousness in your eyes, the pride in your stance. My heart knew then you were the son I never had the privilege of spawning from my loins."

"Never once did I lay a hand on you in anger; never once did I speak ill to you. When you told me the story of your father, the man who should have borne greater love for you than I, and how he mistreated you, well, I wished for nothing more than to journey back to your orchard and spit on his ashes."

"You are my *son*."

"If the Gutians threaten *my* son with death, then they shall know the fullness of the wrath of Quil'ton az Peregos, Instructor to the Sword Himself! The last thing they shall see will be father and son standing over their dying bodies and jeering their brief journey into Hell."

Quil'ton's soliloquy powerfully moved all three of them. The men were blinking back tears, trying very hard to show their masculinity through stoicism. Erianne did nothing to hide her tears, but they were for an entirely different reason. They expressed intense relief.

Tul'ran had been telling the truth.

Though Quil'ton's arrival smacked of coincidence in the extreme, the two of them clearly had no time to concoct Tul'ran's history between themselves. Quil'ton's heartfelt recitation confirmed everything Tul'ran had told her. She left aside for the moment the consideration of the existence of El Shaddai and how he interacted with Tul'ran. It was enough to know she could place faith and trust in her man again.

Tul'ran clapped the older man on his left shoulder, then stood up.

"You are my father. If the Gutians fear Tul'ran az Nostrom, the Sword Himself, Prince of Death, then how much more will they know dread with my father at my back, sword raised, and fangs bared? Let us go and give them a quick death."

Quil'ton rose, more stiffly, and dropped his hand on Tul'ran's left shoulder. They stood there silently for only a moment, sharing the certainty together they were the storm, and may the gods shelter all fools who sailed in their way.

Erianne, looking on, felt hope. They might pull this off. Quil'ton may have been older than Tul'ran, but he looked to be in excellent shape. He moved like a fighter, and if he taught the Sword Himself everything he knew, well, their enemy was in for a nasty surprise. The thought cheered her up immensely.

"Father, I would have a moment to speak with Lady Kabolon, alone, if you would grant me the grace."

Quil'ton smiled, misunderstanding the desire for the privacy of their conversation.

"I will re-pack the provisions and ready my stock for war. Call me as you need me."

When Quil'ton walked away, Tul'ran turned back and sat beside his covenant-mistress.

"Erianne, I need to know what awaits us in the canyon. We need some sort of plan, rather than rushing headlong into battle."

She nodded and quickly drew upon the sand a large circle, under which she drew a neck to a smaller circle, under which she drew another narrow neck to the mountain's edge.

"We are near the entrance of the canyon, which is yon tall, thin seam in the rocks. It will only accommodate two people walking together, with little space between the walls and the outside of our shoulders. There will be not much room to maneuver, much less react."

"The large circle is Insertion Point, where our team gathered ourselves and our stores upon arrival. *MetaMaterials*, the invisible cloth, screens the Insertion Point from view in the narrow neck. Our foe will not perceive the entrance to the Insertion Point. If our enemy lies in wait, it is within the smaller circle. Indeed, my superiors chose this location for this reason. The smaller circle offers an excellent point of ambush for any invasion force. We may travel safely from here through the narrow neck leading to the second circle, for the mountain's walls are too sheer and the gap too narrow to allow for combat."

She brushed the circles away as Tul'ran pondered their strategy. After a moment, he turned his head and sounded a piercing whistle. Quil'ton returned and sat with them.

"Subject to your advice, Father, I offer the following proposal for our incursion into the mountains. Erianne and I will lead, swords drawn in readiness for combat. You will follow, leading Destiny's Edge and your stock. Horses and donkeys are far too valuable in the desert to leave them behind. Darkshadow will take up the rear, for he will not allow our stock to panic and stampede from the mountain. I expect we will arrive at a place of opening where the battle will begin."

Quil'ton was nodding.

"It is an excellent strategy, son, and allows for the most favorable deployment of our forces. As you have said, let us go and give them a quick death."

In short order, they saddled their horses and secured their gear. Before they entered the mountain, Tul'ran took Darkshadow's face into his hands and spoke.

"This day you fight rearguard, brother, for the canyon is too narrow to permit us to fight as one. Do not allow the other horses to retreat and defend us from any enemy who would sneak up on our backs."

Darkshadow whickered, and Erianne looked at the two of them oddly. She wasn't quite ready to believe the horse understood what Tul'ran said. Then again, with all the weirdness surrounding them from the onset of their journey together, she wasn't prepared to discount it entirely, either.

Thus, did they advance into the mountain: the famed Sword Himself, walking with Bloodwing held in a ready position, its edges lusting for blood. At his shoulder marched the winsome Erianne, wielding her sword, who had also withdrawn her dagger and held it in her left hand, tucked along her forearm to not expose it to a disarming strike. Only paces behind them walked Quil'ton az Peregos, Instructor to the Sword Himself, blade in hand and death dancing in his eyes, leading the stock. Darkshadow stalked at the rear, tense and poised to fight, ready to unleash the fury of his rage upon any enemy who dared to cross his path.

For the first fifty strides into the canyon, all was quiet. Quiet, until they came to a clearing in the mountain. The attack, when it began, was sudden, as multitudes of armed Gutian men erupted from behind rocks and jumped down from ledges. Peace became war in less time than it took to blink.

With lethal grace, Erianne and Tul'ran danced a choreography of death.

Shoulder to shoulder and back to back they fought, as one, as if in their whole lives all they had done was train and make war together. Their movements were fluid, mercurial, and fatal. They rained life's end upon their foe with fierce determination and incomparable skill.

Quil'ton grinned as he saw Tul'ran slice his first opponent clean in half. A strange, very tall man had spoken to him from a shadow one night when Quil'ton was staggering back to the hutch, more than a little in his cups.

The man whispered to him in a deep rumble, the time would come when his ward would need a sword suitable to the greatness of his name. The deep rumbling voice gave the half-sauced man directions to a certain cave wherein the lad could find such a weapon.

Quil'ton had tossed off the memory the next morning, attributing it more to fermented grape than truth. When the time came, however, to release his son to his destiny, the words of the shadowy figure came back to him, and he repeated them to the lad.

So, the legends about the ability of the blade to cut through anything were true. Interesting.

He had very little time after that to find anything interesting. The Gutians had overcompensated for Tul'ran's legend by producing numbers far greater than reasonable. Quil'ton was older than Tul'ran, it was true, but he still trained every day. His body may have been stiffer than his younger self had enjoyed, but he was a honed veteran of warfare. So the Gutians discovered, to their chagrin.

The first wave of barbarians came at Erianne and Tul'ran, screeching their war cries, but they turned quickly into screams of pain. Tul'ran met the first thrust toward him with Bloodwing, sheering his opponent's blade with a backstroke and cutting the man in half with the return stroke. A second man came in too fast, too recklessly, and Tul'ran cleaved his skull in twain. A third man ran in, swinging his scimitar wildly, as quickly as he could. Tul'ran parried the blows, then cut the man's left leg off at the knee. When the man fell, Tul'ran swung the Blade up, opening the man's torso from waist to shoulder and spilling his guts to the ground.

Erianne met her first attacker with a parry of her sword, and drove her dagger into the man's chest, ending his battle and his life. A second man dove in, swinging his sword at her ankles. She blocked the thrust deftly, trapping the man's sword against the ground long enough for her dagger to drive into his throat. Another man rushed in, hesitated too long to consider how he should attack the tall woman before him, and died with her sword embedded in his heart.

And so it went. The enemy came at them, and the enemy died. It was hard, hot work, and it wore their energy to the bone. It didn't help that days of travel with little sleep had exhausted them. Several times, Erianne missed the mark with a parry, and a sword slammed into her ribs. The protective fibers in her clothing didn't allow the blade to draw blood, but the blows brought with them pain and tears to her eyes. One such blow caused her to double over, her breath taken away, and she panicked, struggling to straighten herself. She felt rather than heard Bloodwing sweep the air above her head and watched as her enemy's head fell to her feet. She caught her breath just in time to block, cut, and send another barbarian to his death.

Tul'ran fought two men at once, blocking their slashes and thrusts until he could exert enough force with his blade to shear their weapons and then their heads. Sweat menaced his vision. Blood and gore threatened his footing. He was so tired. No sooner had he dispatched one Gutian to death when another rose to attack him from the very stone whereupon the dead lay.

Even he, the Sword Himself, couldn't defend against every strike, every thrust of the sword.

His left biceps burned as a sword found its mark before Tul'ran drove Bloodwing through the Gutian's eyes and out the back of his head. A knife thrust clipped his thigh, and dark spots danced in Tul'ran's eyes from the pain. The blood from the wound would make his footing slippery. Not enough to create an advantage for the barbarian with the knife. Tul'ran threw El Shaddai's Knife into the man's chest and recovered it after killing two more Gutians.

On and on it went.

They were winning. The barbarians came at them in droves. The bodies littering the ground and the confined space hampered the Gutians. Erianne felt

Tul'ran at her shoulder and then at her back and at her shoulder again. Enemies pressed against their defenses and died at their feet. Her furtive, quick glances in Quil'ton's direction showed Tul'ran's adopted father gleefully killing any barbarian who dared to come within range of his blade.

Tul'ran felt like they fought for hours. He was aware of the slender woman at his back, and he was desperate for her safety. The only way to keep her free of harm was to kill their attackers, and kill them he did. The enemy just kept coming, swinging weapon after weapon, and dying in agony at his feet.

Then, of a sudden, silence.

Erianne wiped blood from her cheek where a blade skipped past her guard and cut her while she gutted her foe. It stung, and it bled like a pig, but it wasn't deep and wouldn't even scar.

She frantically scanned Tul'ran. He had cut a clean piece of his tunic away and was wrapping the cloth around his left biceps where a sword had cut the skin but not the muscle. Tul'ran was also bleeding from a leg wound, but her skillful eye noted the injury to be superficial. He looked tired and angry, and his eyes, before he caught her looking at him, showed pain, but he lived, and it was enough.

He suddenly looked around.

"Where's Quil'ton?"

Erianne pivoted toward the canyon's entrance. She noted the horses and the donkey were still there, watching, ears flickering constantly. The two warriors scanned over the dead, dreading the thought of finding familiar leathers in the bunches of blood and cloth. Not seeing Quil'ton in the mess, they began frantically searching through the pile of bodies. Then they heard a whistling sound coming towards them from the entrance to the canyon. Quil'ton limped around the horses, a crooked grin on his face and a severed head in his hands, which he contemptuously threw onto the pile of corpses.

"This one tried to run away, no doubt composing in his head the newest stanzas to the immensely impressive Ballad of Tul'ran the Sword."

They laughed, more from relief and gratitude than anything else. Erianne couldn't believe the number of carcasses scattered on the ground within the canyon's walls. A quick count showed forty men dead at their feet, and there was blood and gore everywhere. Tul'ran's force had sustained a few minor injuries. Quil'ton received the fewest of all.

"They mainly focused on the two of you," he explained. "The Gutians attacked me almost as an afterthought. Whatever grudge they had against Tul'ran az Nostrom and Lady Erianne of Kabolon, they were vicious in their desire for its fulfillment."

"I guess we will never know," Tul'ran said in a murmur, "for it is certain none of these will confess."

He swung around to face Erianne.

"What now, milady, for this is your campaign."

Both were too tired to appreciate they had given something away to Quil'ton, but if he recognized it, he gave no sign.

"This way," Erianne said, and turned to the rear of the canyon. She had given up all hope of finding her team there. The Gutians had either killed them, or they had escaped to the future. The scene would tell the tale, and she fervently hoped it was the latter.

She had seen enough cadavers for one day. She furtively cast aside the MetaMaterials camouflage and led the men and horses into another narrow corridor, making it look as if they had disappeared.

Hidden in the rocks, a Gutian in his teens watched them go, silently retching while clasping a hand over his mouth. He was there to create a ballad of the Gutians' glorious victory over Tul'ran the Terror, but would sing one day instead of the Massacre at the Gap, adding stanzas of horror to Tul'ran's Ballad.

The victors wound their way through the canyon until they arrived at a large, round opening in the rock. The area was pristine, with not even a loose pebble lying on the rocky floor. Only one thing stood out of place: a metallic object lodged in the rock's base, off to one side. It was the length of a sword and narrowed from a bulbous top to a skinny base. The crown was a large, red jewel. It was ornate and out of place, but not entirely alien.

Erianne ran to the Temporal Scepter and examined it carefully. She was immensely relieved to find the crystal intact and the device functional. There was only one problem: a major one. As hard as she looked, she couldn't find her Navigation Coin. Her heart fell. Without the Coin, she was going nowhere.

"Is something amiss?" a concerned Quil'ton asked, noting her dismay.

She nodded. "This stick belonged to my father, and he left it here in hopes I would find my way home, but something is missing from it. I fear it may be useless to me if I do not find the missing part."

Quil'ton bent down and retrieved something

from the dirt.

"Is this what you seek, milady?"

Her heart leaped into her mouth and then receded again. The aged warrior held not a quasi-crystal, quasi-metallic coin, but a flat piece of metal resembling an old-fashioned credit card. It was a message, but coded in the shorthand of the Time Historian. The message said her fellow travelers had not left, but had fled deeper into the canyon when they heard the Gutians coming. They had her Coin with them; she read with relief, and they were eager to reunite with her. She had but to press on into the canyon and she would find them waiting for her there.

All this she explained to the two men, not caring if they were curious about how she could read the information from the small bronze square in her hand.

"The two of you must go," Quil'ton said, "Erianne to her people and Tul'ran at her back in protection. I will stay here and guard the horses. If others arrive, I will yell loudly and back my way in your direction, horses in tow."

"But," he finished, critically eyeing them up and down, "you cannot go like this. The sight of you will be enough to scare your company to the ends of their lives."

Tul'ran and Erianne looked at each other and saw what lay in Quil'ton's gaze. Blood and guts covered them. It matted their hair, spattered their faces, and drenched their clothing. They looked like demons sent out to gather souls. Tul'ran gestured toward Darkshadow.

"I have water and some cloth, though it will be less than ideal. Unless you know of a pool nearby, the lack of water limits our means of becoming clean. I am loath to leave this canyon and return to the desert; clearly our path is forward."

Erianne stood quietly and chewed at her lip, casting a furtive glance at Quil'ton. There was a cleaning station nearby, concealed by MetaMaterials. She could reveal it, but it meant one more person in this timeline becoming exposed to her secret. It wouldn't do.

"Milord Tul'ran, let us manage as best we can to cleanse each other with your resources. Perhaps our presence will elate my companions too much to see us dressed in the trappings of death."

Tul'ran jogged to Darkshadow, happy the horse had sustained no injuries in the frantic battle. He removed a water bladder from the warhorse's back. The only cloth he had for cleaning was Katja's wedding dress.

He walked back to Erianne and Quil'ton, bladder and cloth in hand. Erianne crinkled her forehead slightly at the material he carried.

"Milord Tul'ran, I hate the thought of adding the blood and gore of our enemies to your hallowed cloth."

"I sympathize with your heart, milady Erianne, but we have no other choice."

Tul'ran and Erianne did the best they could to bathe the detritus of war from each other. They couldn't do much for their chitons in the absence of soap and a goodly amount of water with which to scrub. When they finished, they looked reasonably human once more.

Tul'ran restored the bladder and cloth to his horse and turned to Quil'ton.

"Father, if something should transpire ahead and the enemy takes my sword from me, I urge Darkshadow into your care. He is more than a horse to me. He is a brother and a friend. Care for him, I pray, as you would your son."

The words rocked Quil'ton's head back, and he slapped Tul'ran gently on the shoulder.

"Give your head a toss, boy. There is no enemy ahead of you. If one exists, it cannot withstand your might. Speak your name, alone, and they shall flee before you like rats from a flood. You are Tul'ran the Sword, and from what I have seen this day, you have earned every stanza of your Ballad. Go with the peace of this knowledge: you will return to your horse. On this foretelling, I would wager my life."

Tul'ran grinned, a taste of savagery in the showing of the teeth. He drew his blade and nodded to Erianne, who drew hers as well. She bowed her gratitude to Quil'ton for his service and turned to follow Tul'ran onto the narrow, winding path ahead.

Quil'ton az Peregos waited for a good long while, listening carefully as their voices receded into the distance. He regarded them fondly and rejoiced in the warmth he saw in their eyes for one another.

There wasn't much time left for him.

He knew Tul'ran would be sad to lose his adopted father forever, and the thought grieved him. Loss, however, was a part of life. At least he had conveyed to his son how much the young warrior claimed a part of Quil'ton's heart. For many years, Quil'ton had believed he wasn't worthy of anyone's affection and shunned it for fear of the tremors it would cause to his soul were love taken away.

He waited a little longer to make sure Tul'ran and Erianne were not returning before he made his move. It was time. He walked over to his horse and his donkey and stripped from them all he had strapped to their backs. He removed halters and harnesses, turned them to the path leading them out of the canyon, and slapped them on their rumps. They were desert-experienced and knew where to find sustenance and water. They would be fine. Their master was no longer in need of their services.

Darkshadow and Destiny's Edge he left alone, for they were the concern of his son and his son's Lady, and not his with which to tamper.

Quil'ton reached into the pack carried upon the donkey's back and removed some clothing. These items of apparel were old, but he had preserved them carefully for this day. It took a lot of work as he aged to stay in the same body shape as he had been in when he got these items twenty years earlier. They shouldn't be with him now. Quil'ton had purchased them from the Temple and smuggled them here. It wasn't lawful for him to possess these arraignments. He knew this when he gained these items. Even then, he had the inkling of the Plan, which made this clothing a necessity. Bundled within the clothing were other items expressly forbidden to him. He had smuggled them in with his clothing; a minor miracle. After he dressed, he concealed the forbidden things on his body within the garments. He was ready.

Quil'ton walked back to the Temporal Scepter

and considered it somberly. By all rights, he should destroy it, for its use could bring nothing but pain. He couldn't do so, however, for its destruction wasn't part of the Plan, and the Plan claimed primacy.

Cautiously, he pulled from a hidden pocket the small, quasi-metallic disk he had, the day before, withdrawn from the Temporal Scepter. It wasn't his desire to deprive the Lady of her treasure, but he answered a higher calling. He fervently hoped she would forgive him.

Quil'ton az Peregos, the Instructor to the Sword Himself, inserted the Navigation Coin into the base of the Temporal Scepter and watched as the jewel lit to a vibrant red, before transmuting into an emerald green.

It had taken him years to learn how to use the Scepter and how to play with its settings to send him where he wanted to go. He coded the Coin to its new time and location before entering the instruction to activate the device, praying his mathematics were correct. The bulb pulsated, and the air took on a distinct shimmer, which confused the eye about what was and wasn't there. He took one last, longing look down the path trod upon by Tul'ran az Nostrom and Lady Erianne of Kabolon.

"Goodbye, son," whispered Lamek Davis as he disappeared.

CHAPTER THE FOURTEENTH:
THE END AND THE BEGINNING

The end of a Legend is always a curse,
Because great ballads would no longer be sung,
Warrior and Beauty would fade from our memory
For their Ballad did end where all legends begun.

As with most of written history, the beginning looks like the end, the end is forsaken by the beginning, and neither is cemented in the purity of absolute Truth.

This would never be so apparent as the scene awaiting Erianne and Tul'ran at the end of their path.

They trudged for a long while through the winding canyon. The path rose and descended in a shallow grade. The walls of the canyon pressed around them, but not so close as to make them uncomfortable.

"Your people have hidden themselves well,"

Tul'ran said lightly, though his heart was far from light. They were walking to her tribe, and every step spelled a moment closer to her departure from this time.

He didn't want her to leave. Fate thrust them into each other's company. She was more than just a companion. Erianne was intelligent, and he loved talking with her. She often laced her observations with a sly joke, making him laugh. She was tall, which Tul'ran didn't find intimidating. He had a deep sense of certainty in himself. He could not deny she was beautiful and desirable.

All he wanted was another taste of her lips, with danger past and almost forgotten. He wondered, as he followed her through the canyon, trying to match the fast pace of her long legs, if she was thinking the same way about him.

"What holds you so deep in contemplation, Erianne, if I may be so bold to ask?"

"All I can think about is finding my Team. I want to know if they are alive and well. Their extended and dangerous stay is my responsibility. It burdens my heart. If they are well, all the terror I have experienced in the last number of days will have been worth it."

They rounded a corner and came upon the last thing either of them expected.

Someone carved an archway into the canyon wall. It swept around a large opening in the cliff face. Through the opening, they could see beyond into a beautiful, clear blue sky and lush vegetation. The air from the opening smelled rich. What distracted them from the sights and smells were two stone statues flanking either side of the archway

The two figures were colossal and intimidating. Someone formed them like a man, but each statue had four faces and four wings. The four faces were that of an ox, lion, man, and eagle. Each of the four hands held a large, flaming sword. The way the flames danced and moved gave the impression the swords were spinning.

Whatever purpose the flaming swords had; they were not blocking access to the entrance of the archway.

"Erianne, do we go through?"

"I do not know, Tul'ran. Nothing in my briefing talked about this. When the First Team came through, they scouted the area around Insertion Point very well and provided a detailed report of the surroundings. Their first duty was to ensure safety for the Teams and no surprises. It is hard to fathom how they would have missed this."

"Yet your people came this way, for there was no other branch or turn in our path. We have not yet encountered them; they must be inside."

She couldn't fault his logic. She looked at the gigantic statues again. Recognition was tugging at the back of her mind, telling her she should know what these were, but the memory wouldn't come.

She turned to him.

"Do you think we face danger through the doorway?"

"I sense it not. I feel an unusual peace within me; it is a peace unwarranted by recent events. It is safe to proceed if it is your desire. I suggest we put up our weapons and move forward."

She nodded her assent, and the two of them put their swords back in the scabbards. They stepped forward and walked through the archway into the most incredible garden either of them had ever seen. The entire garden was lit in a soft, white light, though neither of them could see the source.

Erianne marveled at the colors. Never had she seen grass so green, leaves so iridescent emerald, and the colors of flowers so vibrant. It was as if everything she had ever observed in her life was a mere shadow of the magnificence laid before them.

They found their feet on a path, and by unspoken agreement, walked forward. They both exclaimed in surprise as they saw the side of the mountain curve up and inwards in a semi-circle. A cascade of diamond-bright water poured over the edge of the cliff and into the garden.

As they walked, they saw many berries, fruit trees, and vegetables growing here and there. The fruit looked large and luscious, healthy and vibrant, and delicious.

"Are they good to eat?" Erianne asked, wonderment gilding her words.

"Of course," said the Voice, behind them. Both spun, frightened, hands going to swords.

A man was standing there, taller than Tul'ran but shorter than Erianne. He had long, mahogany brown hair and a matching short-cropped beard. The skin of his face was olive-colored and handsome. It was hard to detect the color of his eyes because they were luminous and almost appeared to be lit from within. He was wearing sandals and a simple, long, white robe tied at the waist with a cord.

He smiled at their astonished scrutiny.

"Greetings, Tul'ran and Erianne. Welcome to the Garden of Eden."

A smile lit Tul'ran's face like a searchlight. He knew the Voice!

"El Shaddai?"

El Shaddai's smile widened.

"Indeed, My son, it is I whom you have known by voice and now by sight."

"My Lord," Tul'ran confessed, perplexed, "I am uncertain what I should do. My mind flits from thoughts of kneeling in worship and supplication to a fervent desire to hug you."

El Shaddai grinned and spread His arms wide as the Deliverer of Death launched into them like a child running into the arms of his father.

As they hugged, Erianne stood in place, rigid, her eyes wide and her mind in a conflicting maelstrom of evidence of reality and stubborn disbelief. After the men disengaged their embrace, He turned to look at her.

"Um, sir?"

"Yes, Erianne?"

"I am looking for a group of people who said they would wait for me at the end of this path. Are they here?"

"They are not. Within days of your capture, they traveled back to your future, fearing for their lives. They left the Temporal Scepter behind with the hope you would return to the Insertion Point and make your way home."

His answer might have well been a slap in her face. The words lanced into her heart. These were people she trained with! People she knew! They had made vows to one another to defend each other to the death. What happened to all that?! How could they just... just... leave? The survival kit they left wasn't in aid because they lost her. It was to aid her because they tossed her! How could they just abandon her? She looked up at El Shaddai, protests welling up on her lips.

"But the Coin, it was missing, and the message board, written in my language, said they would be here, at the end of this path..."

A look of concern and sympathy crossed El Shaddai's face. He stepped forward to meet her eyes, welling as they were with tears.

"It was I who left the message board as an invitation for you to come here. As for the Navigation Coin, I am distressed to say someone has deceived you. The man you know as Quil'ton az Peregos had on his person the Navigation Coin when last you met, and he is no longer present in this era."

Both of their mouths hung open in shock. Tul'ran shook his head, his body stiff.

"My father would not do such a thing. How would an old warrior from a small village have any knowledge of the use of the thing, even if I were to admit he was a thief?"

"He is not a thief, son," said El Shaddai, "nor is he a man from a small village in Mesopotamia. His name is Lamek Davis, and he is from Erianne's time."

Tul'ran's eyes widened. The statement staggered him. He turned a piercing gaze onto Erianne's shocked face.

"Did you know?"

"No! I am as distressed as you are. I know the name Lamek Davis. He was on the First Team sent to this era. My people deployed Davis and his Team to Ur to set up the Insertion Point. They established a place to stay for the Historians who would later come to study the city and its inhabitants."

"I was not on the First Team. I learned through whispers on the day before their return, Davis disappeared. No one knew where he had vanished, and no one knew where to find him. The First Team returned to the future and my Team came back here twenty years later, Antiquity Time, to look for him. I did not know Davis was Quil'ton. To be honest, I had a theory Lamek Davis was one Tul'ran az Nostrom."

Her admission left Tul'ran staring at her in disbelief. She turned to El Shaddai.

"Where did he go? Did he go home?"

"I will never lie to you, Erianne, but sometimes I will choose to not tell all the truth. This is one such time. Lamek Davis is on a journey, and it is not for you to know where it goes or how it ends."

"What of the Gutians?" Tul'ran asked. "If more come, they will follow the path which will lead them here."

El Shaddai smiled.

"While it is true your enemies still pursue you, Tul'ran, they cannot come into this Garden. My cherubim guard the entrance to this place, night and day, and they will not permit it."

"You mean those stone statues in front of the

doorway?" Erianne asked. Her voice held a little belligerence born of fear. "What are they going to do?"

"Those stone statues are among the most powerful of my angels, and they are as animated as you and I. They only gave the appearance of immobility so as not to frighten you away. They knew you came here by My invitation and so allowed you passage. No one else will come into this Garden while you are here."

Erianne felt pain lance through her temples, from one side to the other. She was confused, frightened, and disoriented. Erianne had worked hard for years to prepare for any exigencies of traveling through the quantum realm. She knew the pitfalls of landing in a country made foreign by centuries passing each other like horses on a track. None of her training prepared her to stand in an ancient mythological garden and speak to a god who wasn't supposed to exist.

"Daughter?"

"I am not your daughter! My father is dead."

"Indeed, you are mistaken. Both Luke and Priya held onto their belief in Me to the very end of their physical existence on Earth. My Father and I live in the Kingdom of Heaven with them. They abide in young, healthy bodies. We have opened their brilliant minds to the fullness of Our knowledge and understanding. They serve Us now, but in capacities bringing them joy, wonder, and fulfillment. While they are no longer husband and wife, they live in the same mansion, for their friendship has endured into eternity."

It was too much. Erianne sank to her knees, and tears flooded out of her eyes from grief? Confusion? Loneliness? Pain? El Shaddai kneeled beside her and put an arm around her shoulders, drawing her into His chest.

"Be at peace, Erianne, and feel from Me their joy."

And she did. Happiness flooded her heart in a tidal wave of comfort in which she could almost hear her mother's giggle and her father's voice. Could it be real? Did God and Heaven exist? Did it mean she could one day hold her parents again and tell them how much she loved and missed them? This was so overwhelming; she didn't know what to believe.

"I need..." she whispered. "I need some time to absorb this, to think."

"Of course," said El Shaddai, rising and gesturing into the Garden behind them. "Take all the time you need. Everything in this Garden is yours. The water is pure. You may use it for bathing and drinking. Every fruit is edible and will replenish and nourish your body. The Light cannot burn your skin. Shed your armor and wear as little as you please. Should you desire modesty, I have left robes for you beneath the base of the majestic tree under the waterfall."

"I caution you both of only one thing. In the center of the Garden, you will find two massive trees laden with fruit. The first tree is the Tree of the Knowledge of Good and Evil. The second is the Tree of Life. You may eat of the fruit of any other shrub and tree in the Garden, but you shall not eat of those two trees. Should you do so, you shall die."

"Don't worry," Erianne promised fervently. "I

remember full well what happened to the last humans who ate the forbidden fruit."

Tul'ran looked at her, puzzled.

"What happened to the last humans who ate the forbidden fruit?"

He looked a little offended when both El Shaddai and Erianne laughed. El Shaddai took his elbow.

"Come, my son, walk with me in the coolness of the trees, and let us give Erianne some time. I will answer your every question. You have My word. And, if you will allow Me to say it, you could use a bath."

Erianne watched as the two men, talking like old friends just reunited after a long absence, took a path to a grove of trees laden with oranges.

Her mind was a torrent of confusion. Her team wasn't here. Enemies, future and present, who pursued her death without pause, had chased her for four days. The character of everyone she thought she knew wasn't what they turned out to be. Her mind was overloaded and overblown.

She turned to take a path through the Garden to where she heard water flowing. A bath. What she needed was a bath.

Her path curved around, and she found where the waterfall met the ground. Sure enough, at the base of a large tree was a pile of cloth. She walked up to it and felt the robe. It was, well, luxurious. The texture was smooth, silken, and light. Just as she was about to remove her leathers, a slight motion drew her eyes to the right. Steam was rising from a pool. She bent to trail her fingertips along its surface. It was as warm as a bath from the time in which she lived and just as inviting.

She slipped off her leathers and chiton. Her body ached everywhere. Every time a sword had run past her guard and touched her body, the blow left a mark. The ancient blades didn't cut through the advanced protective fibers of what appeared to be cloth and leather, but the force of the blows hurt. She winced as she removed the leather leggings, seeing several hematomas.

They tattooed her body with marks, which would soon be bruises. She sank into the hot water, gratitude flooding her heart.

Erianne de mi Corazon leaned back and let the Garden take her. She closed her eyes and listened to the melody of songbirds in the distance, luxuriating in the feel of hot water massaging her body and seeping into the ache in her bones. The light all around her was soothing, comforting. She let her mind drift, refusing to think of where she lay and how impossible it was to be here. She asked for a moment of peace, and peace granted her a moment.

Erianne didn't know how long she lay in the pool. She had no sense of time. Finally, feeling cleansed, she arose from the pool and walked over to her clothes. A large, white terrycloth towel lay next to the white robe. Emblazoned on one corner of the towel, in large gold script, were the initials "EdmC." The odd personal touch warmed her heart. She towel dried her hair and body, feeling refreshed for the first time since she left the future.

It took her several minutes to realize not only did she feel refreshed, but she was also pain free. Even the bruises were gone. The realization caused her breath to catch and a momentary panic to seize her. Her mind, cultured in an advanced age, couldn't fathom a miraculous cure. It defied science and logic. It made her afraid.

Afraid in a place in which a man who might be God assured her she was safe. It took her several minutes with a breathing exercise to calm her heart rate and breathing. She shook her head and thought she was going to have to get used to the miraculous oddities in this place.

Disdaining her leathers for the moment, she put on the silken gown, almost crying out in joy as it slid over her body, caressing its contours.

Time to explore. She left her leathers where they lay, suspecting they would be available to her when she wanted to put them on again. All she took with her was the dagger, which she slipped into the rope belt knotted around her slim waist. Even though she was told she would experience no danger here, she couldn't feel comfortable without a weapon.

As she wandered, the beauty surrounding her mesmerized her. It seemed as if something new presented itself for her inspection wherever her gaze fell. She saw fruits she loved as a child, though fruits were rare and difficult to come by in her era, even for the rich. She plucked a peach, marveling at its size. When she bit into it, the juice flowed out over her hand, and the sweet taste of the pulp was beyond anything she remembered. She hadn't realized just how hungry she had become. She devoured the peach and then found a pear tree not far away. The pear, too, was delicious and amazed her senses with delight.

A banana followed, then a small pineapple, a handful of strawberries and a piece of fruit she couldn't recognize, but smelled and tasted delicious. Satiated, she dipped her hand into a nearby brook and took a long drink of the icy water. If this were only the Garden of Eden, she couldn't imagine how much more wonderful Heaven must be.

As Erianne turned away from the brook, an animal stepped into her path, and she froze. It was a deer; a doe, if her memory of history served her correctly. Deer were extinct in her world. Her only interactions with them were through holograms. This one was alive and quite real.

She watched in wonder as the deer walked up to her, unafraid. The doe stretched her neck forward and sniffed at Erianne. Tentatively, Erianne reached down with one hand to stroke the doe's head, reaching back to pull at one long, soft ear. Not only did the doe not seem to mind the touch, but she appeared to enjoy it. The doe stood without moving for several minutes as Erianne ran her hands along her face and neck. When the attention satisfied the doe, she moved on.

It took Erianne a moment to absorb the experience. There was happiness to be had in this place of peace and tranquility. More joy than she had ever experienced in her entire life, in fact. She continued to follow the winding path, overwhelmed by the variation of foliage and colors presenting themselves as she walked. Eventually, the path took a sharp turn to her left, and she found herself in the center of the Garden.

Before her were two immense trees. The tree on

the left bore the most exotic, enticing, pungent, and colorful fruit she had ever seen. Its leaves rustled invitation and the smells coming from the tree delighted the senses. Every color known to humankind, and some she doubted existed in her world, painted the fruit and the leaves. It was mesmerizing, inviting, enchanting... tempting. Something in her mind said, though it wasn't a voice she heard, "Beware! The Tree of the Knowledge of Good and Evil."

To the right of the first tree was another, larger one. This tree had fruit, bark, and leaves only in shades of brilliant silver and gold. This tree didn't offer pleasure to the senses or satisfaction of desire. It offered wealth and the abundance of eternity. She knew this was the Tree of Life. Eating its fruit would grant immortality.

Erianne shuddered. The allure of these two trees was overwhelming. For the first time since her father recounted the story of the Garden of Eden and Adam and Eve's fall from grace, she felt sorry for Eve. She now experienced how the trees spoke to her heart and her desires. How much more powerful would it be on an innocent, newly minted human being? Especially one tempted by a deceitful angel.

Movement again caught her eye, and a large lizard crawled onto a rock within feet of her, almost making her jump out of her skin. Then there was no discernible thought, just action. With the speed which had impressed Tul'ran several times over, she whipped the dagger out of her belt and held the tip against the lizard's throat.

"No! Not one word! If I hear so much as a croak

come out of your mouth, I'll cut your throat!"

The lizard looked at her with its fixed gaze and flicked its tongue in her direction. She heard a chuckle behind her and turned to see El Shaddai standing there, grinning.

"I am impressed, Erianne, with your defense of My edicts, but you can put away your dagger. Satan and his minions no longer have access to this place. I have denied it to them since the day My angels escorted Adam and Eve into the world. No evil can come here, for I have commanded against it and all evil is subject to My command."

"Master, may I ask you a question?"

"Ask, and I shall answer. We will withhold nothing from you, child."

She took a breath, trying to phrase her query in a way not insulting or aggressive.

"We looked for You, Master, after my parents discovered time travel. We looked and looked and looked. Every time we tried a different angle, a new set of coordinates, the Lens simply refused to transport us to any point in Antiquity in which you lived. Why was Your history denied to us?"

He gestured towards her heart.

"You already know the answer, child, for you and My son discussed it on the way to the mountain."

"So Tul'ran and my parents were right. You denied us access to the events of the Bible because you didn't want us to prove your existence scientifically."

"I would not have you prove what you *wanted* to prove, scientifically," He corrected. "Would you have played to the worldwide audience My miraculous conception, or the words given by Our angels to Mary and Joseph? Could you say they would have played every single second of My life, from beginning to end? Would you have displayed My Words and deeds completely in context or shortened them to ten second sound bites? Does the world have enough attention span to walk with me for thirty-three years, taking part in every moment?"

"Do you see how easy it would have been to distil My life and My message into a sixty-minute documentary containing very little of the essence of both?"

He made sense. She was aware of how her world manipulated, warped, trimmed, and spun messages. How long would it have taken for many people in the world to discard the truth because it took too long to watch or reject it because the words were too hard to hear? His Story would have become history. Interesting, perhaps, but ineffective for sure.

"The Scriptures. Were they all true?"

"Every word in the Holy Bible is God-breathed and inspired by the Holy Spirit. We gave the world as much information as they needed to come to faith in Us."

"But millions of people lost faith in you because the Time Historians couldn't prove the truth of Scripture."

"It was not for them to prove anything. Those who lost their faith were the rocky ground upon which the seed of faith fell, but did not take root. My Father and I do not force faith. We ask for it, We reward it, and We rejoice in it. But We will not force it by proving beyond all doubt We are who We say

We are."

Erianne took a deep breath.

"Are You who they say You are?"

His eyes softened but grew brighter with the Light from within.

"I am the Alpha and the Omega, the Beginning and the End, the First and the Last. All things made, were made through Me. We are Elohim, the Transcendent God of Creation. El Shaddai, the Majestic God of Protection; God Almighty. El Elyon, God Transcendent. The Father and I are one. No one comes to the Father except through Me."

The words were a power flowing through her like a tidal wave and battering her senses.

"Yes, but are you Jesus, the One they called the Christ?"

"I am Jesus of Nazareth, the Christ, the Living Son of the Living God. I am the Messiah who came into this world and will come again in glory to judge the living and the dead. Remember what my servant, John, wrote: 'For God so loved the world, He gave His only begotten Son, that whosoever believeth in Him should not perish, but have everlasting life.' I am the Son."

He stepped out of his sandals and held out His open palms. She saw terrible, horrible scars on His wrists just below the base of His palms and similar scars on His feet.

"Behold, the wounds I bore for your sins and the sins of the world when My beloved children nailed Me to the cross."

The evidence He presented with His words and His body flattened her last cynical objections. She became overwhelmed with the comprehension of her sin in the presence of the One who died to cover it.

Erianne sank to her knees, tears flowing from her eyes as she heard His words and beheld His wounds. It was as if she were there, at Calvary, watching herself drive the nails into the hands that had healed many and raised some from the dead. She heard herself cursing Him as she drove the nails into His feet. It was her sin placing Him on the cross, and it was her sin keeping Him there until He breathed His last.

She moaned and pushed her face into the grass, tears bathing the emerald stems.

"Lord, I'm so sorry! Please have mercy on me!"

His hand was touching her shoulder.

"Daughter, do you now believe in Me? Do you believe I am the only Son of God, begotten from the Father before all ages? Do you accept in your heart I came down from Heaven, became incarnate by the Holy Spirit and the virgin Mary, and was made man? Do you believe they crucified Me for you under Pontius Pilate? I suffered, died, and they buried me in a tomb sealed by a massive stone? Does your heart accept on the third day I rose again, according to the Scriptures and ascended into Heaven, where I sit at the right hand of My Father?"

"Yes, Lord. I believe all of what You have said to the very core of my being."

"Then I forgive you your sins, cast away all your trespasses as far away from Us as the east is to the west, and clothe you in My righteousness. Stand, Erianne de mi Corazon, child of My heart, for you are now a Daughter of God."

She stood, helped up by His firm grip, and felt the warmth of the Holy Spirit flood into her veins. She tottered for a moment, but His grip remained strong and reassuring.

El Shaddai was smiling at her still, waiting for her to gain her equilibrium.

"Are you well, Erianne?"

Breath exploded from her in a rush.

"I am more well, my Lord, than ever have I been."

"Good! Then let us find what has become of My son."

As they walked, Erianne felt as if her feet were not even touching the ground. Her entire core flared as if the Lord had flooded it in a white flame which soothed and caressed, instead of burned. A troubled thought edged its way into her mind.

"Lord, why did you choose Tul'ran as your servant to do Your will on Earth? He is a violent man and kills seemingly without thinking. Are You not afraid if someone learned his account entire, it would cast an unfavorable shade upon You?"

"Have I not used many sinful men and women to do My will and represent Me on Earth? Tul'ran is a violent man because evil broke him as a child. No one gave him a chance to heal. What he endured before and after he was twelve years old, I would have none of My children suffer. He lives in a brutal time, where men pursue their lusts without restraint and evil is rampant in their hearts. I chose him to be My Judge in his era, and to bring to justice the vilest of men. He has done so faithfully and well. Has he overstepped his bounds and sinned from time to time? Of course. Have you?" He asked pointedly.

She blushed, wondering if there were any of the Ten Commandments she hadn't violated at least once.

"Right. Judge not, lest ye be judged. Got it."

"May I ask you a question, Erianne?"

"Of course, Lord! Anything!"

"Why did you activate the recording devices in your body after I froze Time for you and Tul'ran in the desert?"

Erianne's mahogany skin wouldn't permit her to turn red, but she felt as if it had.

"I was afraid. Nothing like it had happened before. Tul'ran became a stranger to me the instant Time froze, and I found myself in the middle of the stoppage. Everything I thought I knew about him disappeared, and questions replaced understanding. I didn't believe him when he told me about You. I thought he was mentally ill."

"You thought he was a time traveler suffering from displacement psychosis who invented a way to stop Time. When you returned, you would have had recorded proof of his ability to do so, regardless of whether he followed you. Advancement, accolades, and a Nobel Prize would follow."

Erianne hung her head.

"It sounds awful when you say it."

"There is a reason We made pride a sin, Erianne. Pride draws into its shadow greed, lust for power, and overweening ambition. It is true you were afraid. I know your heart as if it were My own. Beneath the fear, however, you desired fame. The recordings were your ticket to celebrity."

"I'm terribly sorry, Lord. Does Tul'ran know I have a recording of everything taking place after the eight members of the Order of Purity tried to ambush us in the desert?"

A shadow of a smile crossed El Shaddai's face.

"Erianne, you know I could never tell a lie."

Her face was stricken.

"So he knows?"

"How could he? The recording does not exist."

She looked up at Him, eyes hopeful.

"It doesn't? How does it not exist? I can't turn it off. Only TTI techs can access it."

"Before you turned the last corner to behold the entrance to the Garden of Eden and My cherubim, I removed all the nano robots and the computer from your body. You no longer have bots attached to your optic and auditory nerves. Your molar is only bone and tissue again. The TIRAD does not exist near your heart."

A grateful sigh escaped her lips.

"You did this to save me from Tul'ran's pain and rage when he found out?"

"It was a secondary reason. I could not have you keep a record of Me, this Garden, and our conversations. I deemed it wise to remove the recording and the potential for making another. Are you distressed I did so?"

"No! I'm pleased! It's good there's no recording of this place, for all people must accept its existence by faith, as You have said. I also don't want to hurt the man who saved my life many times over. He doesn't deserve the pain of knowing how I might have betrayed him. Where is he, by the way?"

They found him soon enough. Tul'ran az Nostrom, the Sword Himself, Prince of Death, Master of Bloodwing the Blade, Sword of Judgment, Deliverer of Death, was lying beneath a fruit tree with low-hanging branches. The tree presented small, ripe, round plums within feet of his body. It was clear from the wetness of his hair and the healing of his body that he, too, had bathed in the Garden's miraculous waters. He clothed himself only in a fresh loincloth, his head resting on his leathers.

'He certainly enjoys getting naked,' Erianne thought, a delighted grin curling her lips.

Tul'ran was poking at the branch above him with Bloodwing. When the sword loosened a small plum, he strove mightily to catch it with his mouth. Several lay near his head as evidence of his failure.

She noticed, for the first time, a scar running horizontally along his left shoulder muscle and then vertically down the outside of his arm. If one didn't know any better, one would think it a jagged cross. She gave El Shaddai a side glance. He nodded at her unspoken query.

"My son received the scar from his first major battle. He would have died, but for Our intervention. We allowed him to keep the scar as a reminder the core of service is obedience, and, sometimes, sacrifice."

Tul'ran saw them coming and sprang to his feet with a vigor confirming his full recovery from the battle.

"El Shaddai! Erianne! How fare you?"

Erianne's eyes were lit with joy, and her face glowed. She ascribed a half bow.

"I am well. I see you are enjoying our respite."

He nodded and looked slyly at El Shaddai.

"The respite is welcome and well appreciated, but I sense our Lord is about to tack purpose and vocation onto the back of it."

El Shaddai looked upon His bright child and nodded.

"Dress, children, and come with Me."

Erianne and Tul'ran exchanged glances, saying, 'Oh well, this couldn't last forever,' and moved to change back into their fighting gear. She returned to the pool where she had left her gear and discovered herself to be alone. The gear was remarkably, wonderfully cleaned and repaired. So much so they didn't even bear the scars of past conflict. They even smelled nice, having lost the lingering scent of combat sweat. She returned to where they had found Tul'ran, who was also admiring his cleaned and repaired leathers.

They greeted each other as battle comrades will, clapping a hand to shoulder and gently bumping their foreheads together. Turning, they walked until they found El Shaddai standing in the center of the Garden before the Tree of Life and the Tree of the Knowledge of Good and Evil.

Tul'ran's eyes widened as he beheld the splendor of the two trees and absorbed the enticements they offered. Speechless, he stood there for several seconds, consumed with awe. Succulence and pleasure rolled at him in waves, offering promises of satisfied desire far beyond what he had experienced. There was delight to be had, were he but to reach out a hand...

Erianne dug an elbow into his ribs, startling him out of his bewilderment.

"Don't get any ideas," she said in a soft but dangerous tone.

He jumped at her words, and then nodded seriously, recalling El Shaddai's admonition.

"Understood." He glanced back at the trees and marked them as he would a dangerous enemy.

El Shaddai looked up at the sky above the trees, and the day turned to night, revealing the universe in all its glory. There were billions upon billions of stars. He let Erianne and Tul'ran stare at the display for a long time, absorbing its beauty into memory, before He spoke again.

"Behold, Our creation."

"It is so beautiful, Lord," said Erianne. The vista so captivated Tul'ran, he couldn't speak.

"In Our creation, We made many stars and around those stars many planets. For centuries, humans have questioned whether there could be life on other planets and what such life would look like. You are the first of your kind to receive the answer directly from the lips of the Creator: Yes, there is life on other planets. They look like you."

"They are human?" Erianne blurted out.

"We made them in Our image, just as We made Adam and Eve in Our image. Every populated planet in the cosmos has a Garden of Eden. In every Garden of Eden, We created people, male and female. We put a great distance between each planet so Our children could not discover each other and affect each other's development."

"We made humans to experience four dimensions

and be aware of a fifth. Three dimensions allow you to experience the space in which you live. The fourth dimension allows you to experience time. The fifth dimension is the spirit world, where even now your father and mother dwell, Erianne. Tul'ran, I sent your mother and sisters to you in spirit to sit at your side when you lay wounded. They, too, dwell with Us in the Kingdom of Heaven."

Tears rolled down Tul'ran's cheeks. His mother and sisters were alive and lived with El Shaddai! He would see them again and give them the tale of his life. He would cherish them in eternity as he cherished them when their hearts beat and they drew breath. Tul'ran noticed El Shaddai omitted the mention of his sire, which suited the warrior well. Men such as his father did not deserve the luxury of Heaven and the nurturing of a merciful God.

"Each Garden of Eden exists in the first three dimensions and in the fifth, but not the fourth. Those who are in the Garden do not experience time. It is for this reason humans never discovered the Garden of Eden on any of the worlds on which it exists, unless Our children still live within them."

"This Garden of Eden, on the planet you call Earth, was the first created. Every other Garden of Eden in the universe connects to this one, and each one to the other. From any Garden of Eden, you can travel to any other populated planet in the universe instantaneously. Your heart only needs to express its desire."

Erianne's brain was hurting again. Tul'ran looked like he was struggling with too many advanced concepts at once. It creased his forehead with lines she had not seen before.

There were human beings on other planets! Was there even a Nobel category for this?

El Shaddai smiled at her.

"Though I love you with all My heart, Erianne, I will not let you have proof of the existence of human beings on other planets to enable you to capture the Nobel Prize."

She blushed. Right, pride. She sighed. She was going to have to work on her overweening ambition. The Lord continued speaking.

"I tell you this for one purpose: when Luke and Priya discovered time travel, they did more than prepare the way for travel in time on your Earth. They paved the way for travel to other planets through the quantum realm."

There was silence for a moment as He allowed this information to settle in their overburdened minds.

"Someone in your world has gained this information and has accessed the quantum realm for this purpose. He has sent his agents out to establish a beachhead on other planets to escape his judgment."

El Shaddai paused for effect.

"Of course, it will not happen. There is no place he can go in this, or any other universe, which will allow him to escape Our wrath. What he and his acolytes can do, however, is cause immeasurable damage to other people in other worlds. We cannot allow this. I have brought you here to present you with these options."

"First, I can send each of you back to your own

times. You cannot go together into Erianne's time, but you can return together to Tul'ran's era. Erianne, if you go back to the year from which you traveled, you will face a trial for the breach of your covenants. You may be acquitted, imprisoned, or sentenced to death. If the two of you stay in Tul'ran's age, then the Order of the Purity and the Protectors of the Time Travel Initiative will continue to hunt you."

Tul'ran uttered his second set of words since they arrived at the Garden's center.

"Those prospects do not bode well."

"Indeed," said El Shaddai, "they are bleak. However, I offer a third alternative."

He had their full attention now.

"If you are willing, We will send you and your horses out into the universe. I will conduct you to planets on which other humans live. We will task you with ferreting out the agents of evil and repairing Our relationships with Our people. It is a colossal task and an even bigger ask, but We will be with you in the cosmos as We were with you here."

There was another silence, this one longer.

"Forgive me for the abruptness of my speech, Lord," said Erianne. "I mean no offense by it. What's the catch?"

"The catch is this: you must leave today. You will go from this planet to the next."

"If Erianne, you choose to go home, you will never see Tul'ran again. I say this with certainty, so you will know. I have seen the heart of My servant, the Sword Himself, and he will go for Us into the cosmos, unless you choose to remain with him in his Age."

"Erianne, El Shaddai speaks the truth. I have decided. I will stay in this Age with you or go it alone with El Shaddai. Those are the only two courses open to me now. The universe is too resplendent to ignore such an opportunity."

"Erianne, your blades."

She looked startled but handed over to El Shaddai her dagger and her sword. He looked at her sword first and frowned. Holding the hilt in His left hand, He passed His right hand over the blade twice. As He did so, the blade developed a silver sheen, with a bright ribbon of gold winding its way down the center of the shaft. Near the hilt, the letters 'EdmC' appeared in sharp golden relief. He then took up her dagger and spat on the blade, wiping the spittle free with the edge of His robe. He handed her weapons back.

"Be careful of these, for I have made them as sharp as the edges of angelic swords. They will cut through any material, and nothing can break them. You will never need to sharpen them. You must name your sword, for it lives in the sense it contains a remnant of My spirit. However, if you choose to return to your future, these blades will not accompany you. They are for Tul'ran's Age or for another world."

Erianne put them into their respective scabbards and noticed they, too, were now different. Of course, they had to be, or the blades would simply cut right through them.

"Erianne and Tul'ran, if you choose to travel into the universe, you are bound only by this condition: you must never spill blood within any of my

Gardens, wherever you find them in the cosmos. The ground on which you walk is holy. It was upon this ground We walked with Adam and Eve. So it is in every Garden."

Tul'ran nodded instant acceptance. It didn't differ from the oases in which El Shaddai granted him respite time and time again.

Erianne looked at the ground. Her thoughts were not on the Gardens scattered throughout the universe. She focused them on her own conflicting desires.

Staying in the past or traveling into the cosmos meant never seeing her friends again. She would never breathe Earth air, nor know the joy of family and children; provided she survived her trial. Erianne was being asked to give up wealth, fame, and prospects of family to gallivant around the universe, taking on evil.

The universe above their heads blinked out, and a sky colored in the gentle blue of a robin's egg replaced it.

El Shaddai raised His hand, garnering their attention.

"Join your hands together."

At once, Tul'ran and Erianne complied. He spoke again.

"Close your eyes."

They did as He bade them to do and felt the most subtle of shifts in their bodies.

"Open."

They opened their eyes and were astonished to find themselves at Insertion Point. Tul'ran was happy to see Darkshadow and Destiny's Edge standing there safely. A sharp pang dashed through his heart when he noticed the pile of gear from the backs of Quil'ton's horse and donkey. A good man cared for the welfare of his animals, no matter what else or who else he might have been. Tul'ran thought him to be a good man still, for he would always be his father in his heart.

El Shaddai gestured to the rock face behind them, and they gaped at a live picture glowing from the rock. It was a portrayal of the Garden of Eden, but not the one they had just left. The colors of the vegetation were of subtly different hues under a uniformly pink sky.

"There is the way to the first world crying for the attention of Our champions, if you cast your choice to go for Us."

He gestured to Erianne's left, and she turned to look at the Temporal Scepter embedded in the canyon's rock floor. When she looked back at El Shaddai, He handed her a Navigation Coin.

"My daughter, there lies the device to send you forward to return to your time. It will only work for you, for, as I have said, My son cannot go with you, nor can Destiny's Edge. Both belong in this Age or whence I would send them into the cosmos."

"Should you choose to return to your time, I comfort you with this thought. You are Our child, now. Nothing on Earth can take away your salvation, which you have received because of your faith in Us alone. Even if you should lose your corporal life on Earth, you shall still have eternal life with Us in the Kingdom of Heaven."

"If you choose to go with Tul'ran, the Temporal

Scepter will remind behind. So it may not fall into the hands of evil, you must crush the Navigation Coin beneath your heel and destroy it ere you pass through the Gate."

"My son, here lies the divide in your path. You can return to your life in this Age, and I will re-write history to tell of your story, up to your death as an old man. Or you may step into the Garden I have set before you on a world inconceivably far away. In both circumstances, you will remain Our Chosen Judge. You will forever have My promises and My Voice will be with you wherever you go."

He then addressed them as a couple.

"You may go your separate ways, you may both go back to the desert, or you may both step into the Garden on the distant planet of Pulchra. I leave you now to choose."

El Shaddai walked over to Darkshadow, who put his head into the Lord's chest. El Shaddai placed His palms on either side of the horse's muzzle and whispered in a voice too low for the ears of the two humans.

"Darkshadow, I breathed fire into your heart when you were a colt to make you fierce and give you the courage to stand with My son, Tul'ran. You have acquitted yourself well. For so long as My son lives, you, too, shall live and remain strong."

El Shaddai kissed Darkshadow on the forehead. He turned to Destiny's Edge, who walked over to Him, put her head in His chest, and whickered. He held her head and whispered to her as well.

"Destiny's Edge, I have selected you to carry and protect My new daughter. Should she choose to walk with Tul'ran in this world or the next, you shall be with her. To acquit yourself in this task, I give you the heart of Darkshadow, the fierceness of a lion and the speed of a gazelle. In you, Erianne shall find a companion and a friend, should she elect to stay with you."

He kissed the mare's forehead, stroking His hand alongside her right cheek. Horses were among the best of His creation, and He cherished them.

El Shaddai turned, smiled at the two warriors, and then... was gone.

They were alone. They avoided each other's eyes, torn by the agony of indecision. A brief silence ensued, which Erianne broke by clearing her throat.

"Tul'ran."

He looked up at her. His mournful look almost broker her heart.

"I hate to leave you, but I cannot stay with you out of fear for my future. I have family and friends I wish to see again. If I stay here with you, in this era, the Order of the Purity and the Time Travel Initiative shall hunt us to the end of our days. I may be the reason you die a premature death."

He shook his head.

"And who, pray tell, offered me a long life? I am engaged in a profession for which there is no certainty of long days or restful nights, with no injury. Besides which, El Shaddai was right. I will only stay here if you choose to stay in this Age. Otherwise, I am for the stars."

Her eyes shone with unshed tears as the thought of him dying, somewhere, anywhere, alone, haunted her heart. She told him so.

"Then come with me," he said, smiling into her doubt. "In my right, I am a force with which to be reckoned. With you at my side, the gods of this world shudder and hide their eyes to not give us insult."

She giggled. He pressed on.

"Are we not now on a road bringing our hearts closer? Do you not think us capable of progressing further on this journey?"

His statement stopped her cold. How did she feel about this man? They had spent only four days together. Could anyone fall in love in only four days? But it was more than four days, wasn't it? When she first discovered Tul'ran, he was an anomaly in a database, a rendition of numbers nudging curiosity.

With every morsel of data she gleaned from history, she discovered his deeds and gained some insight into his character. True, she had learned several things, some of which had been amazing since she met him. All of it had only honed her admiration for him. What she felt now wasn't impossible, was it?

All they had faced together was danger and death. All they might face if she stayed with him, whether in his time or in the next world, was danger and death. Then again, was there anyone else with whom she would rather face danger and death?

And how did he feel about her?

His face gave her no answers. He put on a blank face, as stoic and calm as one would expect from a warrior of his age and experience. He would protect her and give his life for her, no doubt. His Code and sense of honor could do no less. She sensed his attraction to her. Maybe, perhaps, he was even falling in love with her. Was maybe enough? No, she decided, 'maybe' and 'perhaps' were not enough to go with him to the stars.

"Erianne, urgency tugs at my heart. I mistrust calmness and silence outside the Garden. We must decide on our next destination, and quickly. The wolves from your future will not be content with our survival. Even now, they may amass to come into this place and attack us again."

"El Shaddai brought us here, giving me reason to believe He will not permit us another retreat into the Garden. You must go or you must stay. If we stay here, in this era, together, we must hurry to abandon this canyon. Without Quil'ton's aid, which was far greater than he pretended to believe, we could not survive another onslaught. I have chosen my path. You must choose yours and forthwith."

"Indeed."

Indeed. What a silly word to sit on to decide between life and death. Life and death. If she returned to her time, Earth meant a certainty of an untimely death; she had no substantial evidence to reduce her sentence. The TTI Judiciary would convict her of transgressing the most serious of Time Laws.

If she stayed with Tul'ran in antiquity, she worried her enemies would use increasingly sophisticated means to hunt them down and, at some point, kill them. The alien Garden in front of them offered a chance at life.

Logic spoke sense, but something deep inside her wanted more. She looked down at him, into his eyes, and spoke her heart.

"Tul'ran, I am challenged to forego my life and all I know for a chance at peace. But before I can commit myself to your right hand, I must know you are with me for more than the fact that I am your covenant-mistress, bound by oath. How do you see me, milord?"

She held her breath.

He looked up into her beautiful green eyes, shining with unshed tears.

"Erianne, with wonder, I see you: a brave, intelligent woman who can be tender in one moment and a fierce warrior in the next. A woman unlike any I had met in this Age, and whom I might never see again. The thought of never seeing you again is painfully unacceptable."

He sank before her to one knee.

"Erianne de mi Corazon, I see you with the love you have embedded deeply within my heart. I thought I would never love again any woman in this Age, and I was right. I was waiting for a woman from four thousand years into my future. If you will have me, I will be your husband. I will go with you wherever you go, and your people shall be my people. Your enemies shall be my enemies, and I will defend you against them until death."

Erianne tackled him and knocked him to the ground, just as she had seen him do to Quil'ton az Peregos or Lamek Davis or whoever he was. She laughed into his shocked face.

"I love you, too, you great ox. I will marry you as quickly as you can get me to a priest," whereupon she planted on his lips a rich and prolonged kiss.

They untangled themselves eventually and stood.

Tul'ran smiled at her, his head a little dizzy from the mad rush of emotion and his ribs a little tender from where the hilt of her dagger had dug into his chest while they kissed.

"We do not need a priest, my lady love."

He took the puzzled woman's hand and led her to Darkshadow's side. Tul'ran dug around in the leather bag on the horse's back and came out with a piece of folded green material. He let it unfurl, and she saw it was a sheer scarf in the color of her eyes.

"I found this," he said, "in the city market when I was buying food, as we were taking our leave of Ur. I purchased it so you would have a means of tying back your hair, but had no opportunity to give it to you until now."

His look was intense; his face serious.

"Erianne de mi Corazon, I cannot promise you a long life, for if we ride together, we ride in danger of our deaths. I covenant my love and my every effort to fill your life with peace and gladness, such as I can in all circumstances. Will you have me as your husband for the duration of our lives together?"

A smile lit up her face and gave her eyes a warm, soft glow.

"Tul'ran az Nostrom, I have traveled four thousand years to find my heart's desire. I will have you as my husband until death do us part. I will journey to the stars with you as your wife. Know I do so with exultation."

Tul'ran blinked through the sudden mist in his eyes and swallowed the lump in his throat. He placed the green scarf over her head, covering her face and shoulders. He looked around and smiled. There were only two witnesses available to them for the declaration.

"Darkshadow, Destiny's Edge, attend me."

Both horses lifted their heads, responsive to the command in his tone. Tul'ran took Erianne's hand and turned her to the horses.

"She is my wife."

The horses flickered their ears back and forth in puzzlement, and they laughed, their elation sent echoing into the canyon. Tul'ran raised the veil from Erianne's face, and she bent her head down to accept another long kiss.

She stared into the love shining in his dark eyes and smiled.

"Is our marriage real?"

"We are married within the customs of my time. Our marriage holds as fast as any other."

"Yes," she persisted, "but are we married in the eyes of God?"

The Voice was in both of their minds then, a velvety kiss of tenderness.

"You are My children. It was I who brought you together in the hope you would find in each other love and contentment. As you have joined your hands and hearts by the customs of your kind, so, too, have I bound your hands and hearts in the Kingdom of Heaven. You are married in the Sight of God, and We celebrate with you."

It was Erianne's first experience with the Voice inside her mind, and it left her shaken. She looked at her husband with awe, realizing the truth of his relationship with El Shaddai in all its weavings.

He smiled sympathetically.

"It takes a while to get used to, but it never grows old."

She allowed the thrill of him to wrap around her heart as she slipped her fingers through his.

"I guess we have made up our minds where we travel next," she said, lifting her chin to the other world sitting patiently nearby.

"Indeed," he said, chuckling at the mimicry of her dry utterance moments earlier. "Let us step into this next world and see what mayhem awaits us. I sense we have much to learn, my beautiful and dangerous wife."

He made a gesture with his chin, and their lips met again in a luxurious kiss. When they parted, a mischievous twinkle was dancing in Erianne's eyes.

"Milord, the night is long and our journey is far..."

They burst out laughing and turned to where Darkshadow and Destiny's Edge stood, patiently waiting for the clowning to end.

The two warriors took up the reins of their horses and walked, fingers linked, to the edge of where the Garden from another world touched the rock of the planet upon which they were born. They faced forward, took deep breaths, and girded their courage to step through the portal into a world light years away.

Almost as an afterthought, Erianne dropped the Navigation Coin to crush it beneath her heel, as El Shaddai had asked.

It never made it to the ground.

Time froze.

ABOUT THE AUTHOR

Dale lives with his beautiful wife, Anika, their dogs, Pacey and Smudge, and their three cats, Molecule Dawa, Jack Sparrow, and Hobbes, in the city of Cochrane, Alberta, Canada. He is a self-proclaimed geek who has treasured the stories found in comics and science fiction books since his age numbered in the single digits.

The Ballad of Tul'ran the Sword is the first book in the Tul'ran series. There are seven subsequent books in the series, which are now published and available through Amazon in hardcover, paperback, and e-book. The titles are listed at the beginning of this novel.

Dale authored this book when he was 62 years old, which many would consider being later in life, but which he would suggest proves one thing:

Nothing is impossible with El Shaddai.